D0961477

THE WITCH, THE SWORD, AND THE CURSED KNIGHTS

ALEXANDRIA ROGERS*

ILLUSTRATIONS BY MANUEL ŠUMBERAC

LITTLE, BROWN AND COMPANY

New York Boston

---

* She may be the author, but it is I, the one and only
Madame Mystérieuse, who shall tell the tale.

This book is a work of fiction. Names, characters, places, and incidents are the product of the author's imagination or are used fictitiously. Any resemblance to actual events, locales, or persons, living or dead, is coincidental.

Text copyright © 2022 by Alexandria Rogers
Illustrations copyright © 2022 by Manuel Šumberac

Cover art copyright © 2022 by Manuel Šumberac. Winged horse vector art on case copyright © by elmm/Shutterstock.com. Title lettering by David Coulson. Cover design by Jenny Kimura. Cover copyright © 2022 by Hachette Book Group, Inc.

Hachette Book Group supports the right to free expression and the value of copyright. The purpose of copyright is to encourage writers and artists to produce the creative works that enrich our culture.

The scanning, uploading, and distribution of this book without permission is a theft of the author's intellectual property. If you would like permission to use material from the book (other than for review purposes), please contact permissions@hbgusa.com. Thank you for your support of the author's rights.

Little, Brown and Company
Hachette Book Group
1290 Avenue of the Americas, New York, NY 10104
Visit us at LBYR.com

First Edition: February 2022

Little, Brown and Company is a division of Hachette Book Group, Inc. The Little, Brown name and logo are trademarks of Hachette Book Group, Inc.

The publisher is not responsible for websites (or their content) that are not owned by the publisher.

Library of Congress Cataloging-in-Publication Data
Names: Rogers, Alexandria, author.
Title: The witch, the sword, and the cursed knights / Alexandria Rogers.
Description: First edition. | New York ; Boston : Little, Brown and Company, 2022. | Audience: Ages 8–12. | Summary: Much to their initial dismay, a twelve-year-old boy and girl discover they are destined to become knights of King Arthur's legendary Round Table, but first they must find and reforge Excalibur and break a curse that has weakened the magic of the Twenty-Five and a Half Realms.
Identifiers: LCCN 2021010568 | ISBN 9780759554580 (hardcover) | ISBN 9780759554573 (ebook)
Subjects: CYAC: Blessing and cursing—Fiction. | Knights and knighthood—Fiction. | Magic—Fiction. | Swords—Fiction. | Witchcraft—Fiction.
Classification: LCC PZ7.1.R644 Wi 2022 | DDC [Fic]—dc23
LC record available at https://lccn.loc.gov/2021010568

ISBNs: 978-0-7595-5458-0 (hardcover), 978-0-7595-5457-3 (ebook)

Printed in the United States of America

LSC-C

Printing 2, 2022

To my parents, the most supportive in
all twenty-five and a half realms

THE TWENTY-FIVE AND A HALF REALMS

FOUNDED BY THE FAIRY GODMOTHER IN THE AFTERMATH OF THE FALL OF CAMELOT

REALMS MOST RELEVANT TO THE TALE

Arthurian: encompassing Camelot, Iselkia, and the Montagne des Chevaliers

Aurelia: Ellie's home realm

Glentess: home to the Rubissia Forest

Lac des Reines: seat of the DeJoies' power and home to the Evermore trees

Midsummer: home to the Fairy Godmother Academy

Mistoria: famed for its palaces and fashion

New World: nonmagical realm spanning most of the world, including Boulder Falls, Wisconsin

Tragevelia: home to Roses and Needles Finishing School

REMAINING REALMS

Aristi

Avalon

Cherrault

Croakenville

Dragon

Emerald

Enevizia

Hobgobble

Lendian

Lira

Manyloch

Merelle

Nymareath

Regali

Rue Charmante (the Half Realm)

Selkieswamp

Underground

Unseen

MADAME MYSTÉRIEUSE

Dearest Reader,

It is for you that I write, though my tears blot the words and my aging heart trembles and quakes.

Too long have I lived with these secrets. Too long have I shouldered the lies.

The truth, hidden at night,

Must now come to the light.

You see, dear reader, when the world was young and I was old, magic did abound. Kingdoms and castles of dappled sun—houses and cities in clouds and seas.

Until one day, that fateful day, it all disappeared from your stories.

Pages were wiped.

Minds forgot.

And the world continued on.

Wars were fought, machines were made, memory of magic a ghost.

But not for us all. No, not at all.

I beg your forgiveness, dear reader. I should have told you much sooner.

And now I fear, oh yes, I fear, we shall all pay a terrible price.

But let's begin in the middle, where all stories start and stop. 'Twas an autumn day, worlds away, with a boy and girl yet to fly.

Once upon a time...

ONE

ELLIE

A COPPER TANG STUNG ELLIE'S NOSE.

Fairies above, was that... *blood*? Bianca, Ellie's fluffy white cat with mismatched blue and black eyes, twitched her tail once.

Twice.

Thrice.

Three tail twitches. Spiders skittered down Ellie's spine. Bianca smelled blood, too.

Ellie was unharmed, her bedchamber unmussed, her overdue library books still cluttering her desk, fire still crackling in the hearth. Nothing was out of place. Yet the smell remained, its source invisible. Haunting.

Ellie peeked up her chimney, where gremlins were prone to hiding after snatching secrets and tucking them into their pockets.

Nothing. No sign of blood.

Ellie shivered, glancing at the mysterious letter on her bedside table—and the reason she was still awake at thirty minutes to midnight despite her Fairy Godmother Academy entrance exam in the morning.

Sir—she double-checked the name on her letter—Sir *Masten* had to explain himself soon. Ellie had never heard of him. Yet the letter was there, all the same, addressed to her, down to the last detail:

Dear Ellie Bettlebump, neglected stepsister to the gracious, beautiful to-be Princess Bella, frizzy hair in both rain and sun, excruciatingly average:

The last word snagged Ellie's focus. *Average.* Slumping into her cushions, she looked down at her body, still adorned in her drab school skirt and cardigan, her wild mess of dark curls covering half of it.

Mother would be most displeased to hear she was, in fact, excruciatingly average.

Ellie shook her head and continued reading.

At midnight on the eleventh of October, you will receive vital information. You have been dutifully informed by Sir Masten, Knight of the Twenty-Five and a Half Realms.

(4)

Ellie's eyes darted to the ticking grandfather clock for approximately the 836th time that day. 11:36 PM.

She groaned.

Would some stranger burst into her little bedroom? She'd tidied just in case. Her Castle Tending professor would be so proud. She'd fluffed her cushions, swept the floors, and crammed her dirty clothes into the wardrobe she'd accidentally enchanted to screech when it didn't like Ellie's outfits, which was most days.

In a school with over a thousand rooms, Ellie's bedchamber was the only space she loved. She had to show it off. With its sloping ceiling and tapestry of unicorns adorning the stone wall, it was a happy place, with just Ellie and her thoughts.

Her toads loved her.

Her cat loved her.

No one could hurt her here.

Tilly burped in her face for the sixth time that night. Ellie scrunched her nose and nudged the spotted toad off her quilt, toward Tilly's toad friends near the flickering fire.

Ellie had no real human friends to speak of, but toads? Oh, she had toads. Despite attending Roses and Needles Finishing School since she was five for her ever-so-important "socialization," Ellie had yet to meet anyone who could stomach her rather prominent toad collection, much to her mother's dismay.

(5)

It wasn't Ellie's fault. She couldn't help that she was, you know, a *witch*.[*] And as we all know, toads adore witches. Find their toes quite sugary.

That's not to say Ellie *liked* the toads. How could she when they were solely responsible for her eternal banishment from any high-society event forevermore? Including her own stepsister's wedding. Mother's words still burned in her ears: *How am I meant to trust you at such a grand occasion? You're sure to make a fool of yourself. Why, just this Solstice past, Headmistress Olga informed me one of your toads hopped onto Her Majesty's wig at teatime!*

A minor mishap.

Ellie's skin prickled, the way it always did when she focused too deeply on Mother, for somewhere in her heart, she knew: Her banishment wasn't about the toads.

No matter how many times Ellie promised never to accept her witch magic, as long as it remained, Mother would never approve.

She waited for a glimmer of grief, a speckle of tears. Nothing came. She'd already cried. Tears wouldn't help her now.

Bianca twitched her tail three times again—but there was still no blood in sight.

With nothing else to do, Ellie paced. If only she had her own fairy godmother, like Bella and Bella's great-great-great-

---

[*] But please don't tell; she's highly sensitive about it.

(6)

great-great-grandmother Cinderella before her. She could help Ellie attend the wedding.

11:42.

Ellie scratched her palms. This night needed to end.

She hopped to her window and peered at the school entrance, bordered by the renowned Glitter Lakes. How would Sir Masten find her? Could he even get past the boarding-school guards?

Unlikely. The guards were enchanted stone lions with a ferocious appetite for bones. It took all Headmistress Olga's efforts to keep them from eating students, let alone intruders.

Would a new letter fly through her window? Ellie had kept it wide open.

As the International Fairy Postal Service wasn't required to abide by societal rules, it sent letters zooming through the sky with reckless abandon. Mother revealed it caused quite a stir at court.

11:44 and thirty seconds.

This was impossible. How was Ellie supposed to wait another—she counted on her fingers—fifteen minutes and thirty seconds?

Groaning, she lifted her gaze to the star-stippled ceiling enchanted to catch her daydreams. A great city with steel buildings that spiked through clouds glimmered across the stars and stones. She didn't know the name. Mew Fork? New Cork? She'd only heard it once. It was forbidden, people said. They wouldn't understand us, others said. The twenty-four

(7)

and a half magical realms must keep to themselves, hidden across the earth behind impenetrable walls of magic. It was the first rule Ellie remembered ever learning, enrapt as she was with the notion of adventure.

Once, there were no walls, no separation, millions united under the Pendragon Empire. That was Before. Before the Fall of Camelot. Before the Deep. Before three quarters of the world lost all memory of magic, sending those who knew the truth into hiding.

Needless to say, the response to Ellie's desire for adventure had been a resounding no. But maybe the councillors and queens and Mother and everyone else she'd ever met were wrong, and nonmagical people would be more accepting of her witchiness than her own people were.

She stretched her fingers as if to catch the image of the unnamed city in her palm, and it vanished into wispy smoke.

Perhaps not.

No matter; as soon as the Fairy Godmother Academy accepted her, she need never worry about her witchiness again.

Everyone revered fairies—*they* weren't the ones responsible for the Fall of Camelot.

Witches, though…

This was the second rule Ellie remembered learning: Never reveal she was a witch, for witches' contaminated, malevolent magic brought down the greatest empire the world had ever known.

Far better to be a fairy, and at the academy, she would study under the Fairy Godmother herself. Surely that would grant her an invitation to Bella's wedding. When Mother saw Ellie in her brand-new tulip gown, she'd exclaim, "Oh, how lovely you look! How fortunate I am to call you my daughter!" Stepsister Bella would coo over Ellie's blossoming fairy magic. For once, no one would mind the toads....

The letter burned out of the corner of her eye.

Unless this *Sir Masten* got in the way.

She paced. And paced. And paced. Until at last, as the clock struck midnight and Ellie nearly burst from her skin, Bianca hissed at Sir Masten's letter—which now dripped scarlet blood.

Ellie's heart pattered so quickly, she could hear it through her thick gray sweater. As the ringing clock reverberated in her bones, Ellie snatched Sir Masten's letter off her dresser.

Where blank space had been before, an invitation was now scrawled in blood.

Dear Ellie Bettlebump, average:

Well, at least they'd left out *excruciatingly*.

You have been drafted to serve as a Knight of the Round Table, Protector of the Twenty-Five and a Half Realms.

(9)

Ellie's heart no longer worked. She read the letter again and again, yet no matter how many times her eyes scanned the horrible contents, they remained unchanged.

Drafted.

She'd been drafted. And according to the letter, she had only until October 31 before the knights stole her away.

She'd always known there was a chance, but with only twenty-five new twelve-year-old recruits from the whole world every year, the chances were slimmer than slim. They were almost nonexistent.

Ellie hugged her pillow, willing her fingers to stop shaking. This couldn't be happening. She had her Fairy Godmother Academy exam in the morning. Bianca stalked into her lap, tail still twitching back and forth, pausing every three beats.

Yes, she knew there was blood. It was all over her fingers now.

She squeezed her eyes shut, her future mysterious and foggy.

No one knew exactly what the Knights of the Round Table did, other than protect the realms. Shrouded in secrecy since the Fall of Camelot, they supposedly guarded King Arthur's long-gone broken sword. But how they did that? And where? And *why*?

No one knew.

Only that it was a requirement—sealed by the deceased Merlin's powerful, ancient magic—that there must always be twenty-five new recruits, lest the world tumble into darkness once more.

And that once drafted, people served for life.

This was a death sentence for everything Ellie had ever known. Everything she'd hoped for.

She balled her fingers into fists.

Ellie would not go quietly.

She would take her exam in the morning. She would pass. She'd be granted a special fairy godmother bedroom in the flowering towers of Treelala Castle. No knight could reach her there.

She still had time.

Ellie counted on her fingers. Twenty days to be exact.

"Forsooth, thou must depart my weary sight; be gone into the lost Forgetting Place," she whispered, clutching her fairy scepter.

She couldn't remember when she'd first heard the fairy spell, nor the moment she'd discovered she was part fairy. She hadn't inherited the wings, pointy ears, or penchant for eating daisies. She certainly wasn't granted a scepter at birth by the great Fairy Godmother herself, as is customary. But fairy magic listened to her, and this spell had lingered in her mind as long as she'd known life, as true to her as her name. She didn't know where that place of lost things was, only that it had accumulated its share of Ellie's possessions and horrible memories, bottled so she didn't have to remember.

Best for some memories to remain lost, and things to remain forgotten.

(11)

The letter whisked into the night, but not before droplets of blood sprinkled her duvet. Ellie's heart seized as she took in the form they left behind—a sleeping dragon, for King Arthur's fallen Pendragon Empire.

She hurled the duvet to the ground, though later, as she attempted to sleep, shivering beneath her thin sheet, she couldn't help but think: Some fates, not even she could escape.

TWO
CAEDMON

CAEDMON LIKED TO WANDER.

Those looking for wanderers never found them. It had to happen by accident. Caedmon didn't mind meeting people that way. It was his parents he wanted to avoid. Fortunately, parents only ever found footsteps, which were easily concealed.

This particular wander brought Caedmon to a great tree with drooping leaves cascading into a bubbling brook, near the edge of the forest of Boulder Falls, Wisconsin.

He didn't know how many minutes passed as he dropped

---

* Which happens to be the same as 715 YATRDOC, for those of you who have not taken my Lessons for Children on the Importance of Timelines in the Twenty-Five and a Half Realms; How Realm Thirteen, the Dragon Realm, Severely Miscalculated the Length of Its Existence, Sending All Realms into Chaos for a Hundred Years; and How We Shall Not Forgive Them No Matter the Price, Particularly Stanley.

sticks and stones into the water, watching them float and sink, float and sink, again and again.

Maybe his friend Jimmy would like to join.

Maybe his ghost would come spend time with him.

Or, more likely, tease him for moping.

Caedmon stretched out in the grass, the sweet smell tickling his nose. Ghosts weren't real. He knew that. And neither was Jimmy.

Not anymore.

Mom said she understood. Dad said Caedmon would get through it, though as far as Caedmon could tell, there was nothing to *get through*. There wasn't one side and another, like the tunnels he and Jimmy used to race through, listening to distant trains screech.

There was only empty space where his best friend should be. Only the sound of plunking stones in water. Plunk, plunk, plunk, buzz and chirp and a whistling wind.

Caedmon preferred it to people speaking.

Mr. Barnsworth had warned Caedmon he couldn't miss another class, and that next time, he really would tell the principal. Words like "expelled" and "failed" had floated through his ears.

Caedmon couldn't bring himself to care.

He ran a hand through his floppy brown hair, scrunching his pale forehead. School had always been his *thing*, even to the point of letting Jimmy copy his homework.

But what was the point if your best friend could die, your life could change, and there was nothing you could do to stop it? No amount of learning could help him. Nothing helped him.

He flipped to his back and lay utterly still, despite the faint tickling of a worm inching across his ankle and the warmth against his cheeks warning him to wear sunscreen. Maybe, if he were still enough, he could stop time. Stop his mind from replaying those final days in the hospital.

No one knew how Jimmy got so sick, so quickly. No one knew why he died. Only that one day he was fine, and the next his heart stopped working.

And he was gone.

Sometimes he thought he saw Jimmy out of the corner of his eye. Laughing, as usual, his hair sticking up in all directions. Jimmy would've hated the funeral. If ghosts were real, Jimmy would've pulled pranks on everyone there. When Jimmy's little sister slipped on a banana peel at the wake, Caedmon could've sworn he'd heard his friend cackle.

But it'd only been Jimmy's mom screaming, afraid a second child of hers was about to die. Another sound Caedmon would have to banish from his embarrassing, terrified thoughts at night.

A faint rustling stirred the grass.

Probably a squirrel.

Though that didn't explain the hairs rising on Caedmon's neck.

(15)

The rustling grew louder.

Caedmon peeked through nearly closed lids. If his mom or dad had found him, would he run? Trudge home and sneak out again later? Groaning, Caedmon propped himself up on his elbows. "Sorry, Mom."

Silence.

No one was there.

Even the brook seemed to have stopped bubbling. The cicadas didn't stir; the grass stood still.

Something crinkled, like pieces of paper, as a red droplet appeared on Caedmon's foot.

Red like…blood.

Caedmon lurched upright, though his ankle felt healthy enough, free from scrapes or bites. Something wet and warm dripped onto Caedmon's neck—there, a letter, tied to a branch.

That explained the crinkling.

The paper was blank but for the dripping of blood from the corner. Like it hurt to reveal what it needed to say. The weeping willow creaked, listening. Waiting for him.

In majestic, looping handwriting, words began to scratch the page. Every fiber in Caedmon's body wanted to bolt, but his feet refused to move.

Because his own name stared back at him.

Dear Caedmon Tuggle, depressed friend of deceased Jimmy Bensen, despicable grades for

(16)

someone of above-average intelligence, crush on Mellie Melowski, modest upper-body strength, still believes in Santa Claus:

Caedmon's cheeks flamed. Okay, it's not that he *believed* in Santa Claus; he just thought it was stupid to rule it out completely just because nobody had met him. There was a difference. And he'd never told *anyone* about Mellie, not even Jimmy. He shook his head and continued reading, only to be reprimanded for ignoring a previous letter telling him he'd receive *this* letter. Come to think of it, his mom had mentioned something a couple of days ago—but he cared so little about anything these days, he'd promptly forgotten.

You have been drafted to serve as a Knight of the Round Table, Protector of the Twenty-Five and a Half Realms. Your escort will arrive at 9:00 PM sharp on the thirty-first of October, 2019 AD / 715 YATRDOC. Please bring the following required materials:
- Your finest fighting sword
- Your best example of craftsmanship in any art form
- One Familiar (Two can be requested upon application. Three is poor luck and worse manners. Must not exceed 1,000 pounds

(17)

each. As of 710 YATRDOC, portapoofs are strictly prohibited.)

- *Sir Artemis the Great's Lessons Learned Throughout the Realms* by Sir Unken Fendlefiemmer (Available in most local bookstores, though an order form for the Fairy Godmother Shop of All Things has been included should you not find it or live in the nonmagical realm.)
- Three common poisons of your choosing (Rogle root, pixie's breath, and gargoyle toe are all appropriate options.)

Poisons? Knights? And what on earth was a rogle root? Was pixie's breath a flower? Caedmon turned the paper over, his mind catching up to his fear. That couldn't actually be blood. There had to be a trick to it. But no matter how many ways he turned the paper and squinted at it, he couldn't find the trick.

Unless…ghosts really were real and Jimmy was playing one of his darker pranks. Goose bumps rippled up his arms.

He dropped the letter in the dirt and ambled toward home. Pranks or no, Jimmy was dead.

And it was unfair to remind Caedmon that all Jimmy could ever do again was play pranks from the grave.

THREE
CAEDMON

CAEDMON NEARLY FORGOT IT WAS HALLOWEEN UNTIL trick-or-treaters showed up on his doorstep wearing costumes. Of course, it wasn't actually Halloween; Boulder Falls's superstition banned trick-or-treaters from asking for candy on Halloween because the last time they did, the mayor fell into a beehive. So instead, kids dressed up a week earlier. Tonight, a goblin, a princess, and a ghost held out plastic orange jack-o'-lanterns.

The smallest—the ghost—grabbed Caedmon's hand, her fingers sticky. "Do you have lollipops?"

For a moment, Caedmon only stared at her. He hadn't thought of Jimmy's ghost note in days, banishing it to the back of his mind along with everything else, so all that existed in his head was a pleasant buzz. A complete absence of anything.

But the girl's oversize white sheet reminded him of Jimmy's ghost sending him letters. He didn't like being reminded. Caedmon glowered. "No." He slammed the door and stalked back inside, ignoring the little girl's wails of protest.

From the living room, the TV flicked off. "Were those trick-or-treaters?" his dad called. Though Robert Tuggle looked like a ferocious bear with his wild beard and broad frame, he was one of the gentlest people Caedmon knew and probably wouldn't approve of his behavior.

"No," Caedmon lied. Lying felt good. It was the only thing that did these days.

"I made apple pie, bud," his dad continued. "Your mom and I were about to have some. Come join us?"

"No," Caedmon repeated, jumping the stairs two at a time so he could escape to his room.

Once inside, he leaned against the door. His blue walls were the same. The orange bedspread was the same. The comic books on the floor, the abandoned Xbox in the corner he hadn't wanted to play since Jimmy died.

All the same.

And all…empty.

Caedmon didn't even reach the bed before collapsing in exhaustion, sprawled on the floor. He squeezed his eyes shut as hot tears prickled. Crying was stupid. It wouldn't change anything.

"That's an odd place to spend your time," murmured a strange voice.

Caedmon's eyes flared open. He screamed.

Upside down from his spot on the floor, a woman with a sparkling blue dress, tiara, and violet spiky hair swung her legs

(20)

from his windowsill. She pouted. "Wait, why are you screaming? I put my face on and everything!"

"You…you put your face…?" Caedmon shook his head. "Who are you and why are you in my room?"

Rather than answer him, she hopped off his windowsill and started picking random items off his bookshelf and flicking through them. "Peculiar taste in books, too." She pulled out his school textbook on ancient civilizations and squinted at it, turning it upside down, her strange silver eyes roving over the pages. Eyes that didn't look…human. "What's this Rome place?"

"That…that's for school!" Caedmon protested, flipping upright and inching toward the door. "Rome is…it's a city in Italy and…the ancient Romans were really powerful…."

He grabbed the doorknob. It didn't budge.

The woman threw her head back and laughed, the sound too large for someone so small. "Oh, I forget how delightful it is to talk to New World recruits. You have nothing inside your skull, little knight, and it pleases me."

Caedmon took some offense to that. If nothing else, he was good at school. Maybe not these days, but still.

"Who are you and what are you doing here?" Caedmon tried again.

"Roxie, Roxie, I go by sweet Roxie," she chanted. "And trust me: This is the worst part of the job. But you know, it pays the bills, and I like my rum collection." She pulled out a bottle of rum from her poofy dress. "Rum?"

(21)

"I'm twelve," Caedmon stammered.

Roxie shrugged. "Legal age is fourteen in the Dragon Realm. Though that might be because they're terrible mathematicians and miscalculated...well, everything."

"The Dragon Realm? What?"

Roxie grinned, revealing pointed, glittery teeth. Caedmon flattened himself against the door. He was embarrassed to admit it, but for the first time in weeks, he wished for his parents.

All they'd done since Jimmy's death was rush upstairs to coddle him, and *now* was the time they chose to leave him alone?

"It's a realm far from here."

"Like...a parallel universe or something?"

Roxie cackled. "Oh, you delightful fool. Not that far. All this universe, all this world. *Realm* is the ancient word for kingdom, and our kingdoms are ancient, honored things. The magical realms are simply unknown." Her eyes sparkled. *"Secret."*

"That's impossible," Caedmon whispered.

"Nothing is impossible with a healthy dose of magic, dear one. There are twenty-four and a half magical realms hidden around the world, with walls of fire and ice and brittle bone to keep out sneaky, pesky, prying things."

Caedmon cleared his throat. "Sure. Okay." He had a feeling if there were walls of bones around the world keeping

(22)

them from magical kingdoms, *someone* would have put it on social media by now.

Her eyes narrowed, as if reading his mind. "You would never see the walls from this side. All you would see is barren nothingness that stretches into the rest of time. It fills human hearts with such sadness, such unending grief, their souls unable to understand why they cannot touch and taste our magic, that they ignore. They do not see. So, what is empty to your eyes remains magical to ours."

Caedmon blinked. Her description stirred something in him. Some long-forgotten emotion. Like…want. Curiosity. He buried it back down. "I don't believe you."

"Little knight thinks he's cleverer than Miss Roxie! Little knight, little fool. The Dragon Realm is"—Roxie twirled his globe and pointed somewhere in the middle of the Mediterranean Sea—"there. Surrounded by flames as glorious as the sun. But don't worry: Actual dragons have been dead for centuries. If they ever existed at all." She winked. "'With arrows in their wings and ice on their tongues, they plunged to the sea, one by one. The curse of Camelot had wrought its worst, its screaming people all dispersed. The children cried when the dragons died, now their memory remains mere legend-spun.'" Roxie sighed. "Sometimes I wish I could fly back to the time of the curse and understand what we lost that day. And see if the dragons really did exist, once upon a time."

"They didn't," Caedmon said flatly. She sounded *really* confused.

(23)

Her eyes twinkled. "You have so much to learn, young knight."

"Knight? I…"

Jimmy's ghost letter. Blood pounded in Caedmon's eardrums. "I'm not a knight," he managed to whisper. "I…I've never used a weapon." He took archery class at camp one summer, but he was pretty sure that didn't count.

"Not yet. But you're going to become one of the twenty-five. Would you rather stay here, Boy Who Reads Books About False Histories? Whose best friend died, leaving him alone? Or would you rather come with me and learn about every secret the world's been hiding from you? Would you rather become someone special, guarding ancient, terrible secrets that could send cities tumbling to dust if left with the wrong person?"

This was too much.

Everything this woman said was ridiculous.

And yet…there was nothing for Caedmon here. He was nothing here. Just emptiness. Suddenly, the past few months of darkness, of living in his own shell, threatened to engulf him. What Roxie promised meant escaping, and escaping sounded good. Escaping sounded like it could make him whole.

And it was that flicker of hope that made him hesitate. "I…can't," he protested, then shook his head. He knew better than to believe in the impossible. "You're lying."

"Naught but facts, naught but truth, naught but reasons, little knight. Reasons you seek, answers you must know, of a

(24)

death that should have never been." Her strange eyes watered. "Of lost life you still mourn."

Breathing became difficult, his lungs frozen, everything frozen. "What reasons? What are you talking about? How... No one knows how he died." His voice broke on the last word.

He hadn't mentioned Jimmy by name, but Roxie's eyes whirled, like she knew. Like she saw.

"The world changes, little knight, and my bones like it not. Because you're a nonmagical recruit, you have more time to prepare. Be ready in a week, Caedmon Tuggle. The Knights of the Round Table are waiting for you."

With that, she hopped onto his windowsill and fell head-first to the earth. Caedmon yelped, lunging for her—but she was gone.

FOUR
ELLIE

ELLIE WOULD NOT WAIT FOR KNIGHTS TO DECIDE HER fate. As October 31 loomed and the Fairy Godmother Academy had yet to deem her worthy, she hired one of the school carriages.

The *Daily Fairy* had mentioned her stepsister would choose her wedding dress at the Mistoria Palace that afternoon, which meant the Fairy Godmother would surely be there.

And Ellie would arrive to impress.

She clutched her satchel of handmade veils, each spun with the finest fairy magic she could muster. What was more impressive than a veil woven from frothing sea spray? Or another with flowers that never wilted? Or her favorite, spun with glittering stars? The Fairy Godmother might just grant Ellie admittance to the academy on the spot! And come July, Ellie would attend Bella's wedding celebration. Mother would coo in delight; Olivia DeJoie, the meanest girl alive, would cringe in jealousy; and Ellie would be the belle of every ball forevermore.

She peeked at her starlight veil to make sure it was still there, still perfect. Ellie was unusually gifted with starlight magic—bottled, woven, sparkling in soups.* Most people damaged the starlight somehow, so it eventually lost its splendor, or worse, its pure light and hope-giving magic.

Never so for Ellie. It would dance in her palms, sparking and wild and beautiful. She even kept a tiny fragment of starlight in her pocket for luck. The essence of starlight was rather common, but figments of stars themselves? Ellie considered herself blessed by every saint to have found such a treasure.

The carriage jerked, jostling Ellie out of her daydreams.

"Stay sharp, mademoiselle," the driver said. "Looks like trouble on the border."

Ellie nearly toppled out of the carriage to glimpse the commotion.

The *Daily Fairy* often reported tales of teenagers trying to break the walls with shattered glass or young children turning left when they ought to turn right, staring at the walls for hours upon hours as if waiting for the walls to slip or yank them through and imbue their hearts with untold magic.

---

* Such soups are known to spontaneously combust. Please stay clear unless you are a highly powerful witch or have plans to travel to the Fae Courts of Nighever, in which case, bring the soup and give it to Stanley.

Ellie understood. The walls were magnetic. Hypnotic. Forged with some of the most powerful magic of the realms.

And all were heavily guarded.

This one was pale, translucent, and swirling with brightly colored mists.

Soldiers surrounded the fleeing culprit with pointed swords, a glowing golden light gathering in a maelstrom around their weapons.

A middle-aged woman screamed, fingers scrabbling for the wall, hair burning in the light.

"Look away, mademoiselle," the driver instructed.

The woman shot a bolt of silver light toward the sky. Something in Ellie quivered, like it was listening, watching. It yearned to help.

A second bolt of light speared the walls. They shuddered and quaked, the vibrations rippling into the earth and the curling cobbled path beneath their carriage. Ellie's blood went cold as she slammed against the gleaming wooden door. Her grip on her satchel tightened. This was not a mischief-seeker or a wandering lonesome child. This was a witch. She'd heard rumors of witches trying to sneak into the New World to hide, hoping, as Ellie did, they would find kinder souls, but she'd never seen an attempt herself.

"Curtains, shield!" the driver commanded. With a reluctant twitch, the curtains wriggled shut. Ellie tried tugging them open, but they wouldn't budge.

(28)

The woman's screams filled her ears—claws raked down her heart. What was happening? What had they done to her?

The driver gasped. "What in the name of Saint Guinevere?"

Ellie clutched her fingers to still their trembling. "Is it not always like this?"

His face colored, as though he hadn't meant to speak aloud. "Ahh, *no*. The Knights of the Round Table are generally at the border to prevent fighting between fleeing citizens and the—ahh—*temperamental* DeJoie soldiers guarding the walls."

He frowned. "The Knights of the Round Table are meant to protect us, but there have been reports of their failures as of late. And by the saints, if they fall, we all fall." He glanced at her, face pinched. "Oh, please don't worry, mademoiselle," he assured her with an unconvincing wobbly voice. "Whether or not I always agree with the DeJoies' methods, they keep us safe from the evilness of witches." He smiled, calmer now. "She won't hurt you," he added, mistaking Ellie's fear for the witch as fear *of* the witch. "I hear the greatest sorcerers in the realms make the DeJoie weapons. Not even a witch could best them."

Something curdled inside her. Something like jealousy. Her finishing school mistresses would have a fit. Jealousy was highly unladylike. It was highly unfairylike for that matter. But still, her heart twisted. Witchcraft, girls' magic, was considered wicked; sorcery was merely dangerous. No one seemed to care they were the same.

"She was going to the New World," Ellie whispered.

(29)

"To inflict pain upon those innocent, frail people, who won't even have magic with which to defend themselves, no doubt." He shivered. "Nothing more terrifying than a witch. The power to destroy…create…make something out of nothing? Never know what they'll do. It's unnatural. Gives me a fright, I tell you."

Ellie nodded numbly, for that was right and that was good. Ellie had decided to live the life of a fairy, not a witch. If she had any hopes of impressing her mother and attending Bella's wedding, of finally being *accepted*, she had no business thinking about witchcraft. No business feeling that bolt of light pierce the clouds and wishing to hurl one in response, just to let the witch know she was not alone.

But as the carriage rumbled forth and the curtains trapped her in musty velvet, all Ellie could hear was the witch's screams.

And her own buried witchcraft—rumbling, furious, and silenced.

~

"No, no, no, we must use ivory. The pure white is far too harsh. Just think how lovely ivory will look beneath the candlelight!"

"This is a royal function, not a clandestine soirée. Ivory sends an inappropriate message!"

Ellie raised her fairy scepter for courage, heels clicking on echoed stone as she wended through swathes of tulle and silk, dresses billowing and bustling in her wake. The grand

(30)

ballroom of the Mistoria Palace was one of the greatest in all the magical realms, gilded and glittering, thousands of fairy crystals swooping across the ceiling like frosted garlands of ivy.

Fairy Godmother Apprentices, demure as swans, swished from tablecloth crises to flower-arrangement debacles. Ellie's heart raced, the horror on the road nearly forgotten as she beamed at the fairy magic on display.

These were her future peers. One day, she would wear the silky blue robes and carry the Fairy Godmother Apprentice scepter.

"Hello?" she ventured. "Is Bella here? I'm her stepsister."

"Who let that girl in here?" one of the apprentices muttered. "She looks like she needs a bath."

Ellie flushed. She'd nervously sweat through her dress throughout the carriage ride, unable to banish the screaming witch from her thoughts.

Her grip on her scepter tightened. It was chipped, was missing most of its gemstones, and always pointed east when she asked it to point north. But it was hers, and wings or no—witch or no—Ellie was still a fairy.

She still belonged here.

"I'm Bella's stepsister," she repeated, loudly this time. Where was the Fairy Godmother? "I'm here to help."

At last, one of the apprentices turned around. She might have been pretty if not for her scrunched expression, like she lived in perpetual disgust. "You're Ellie Bettlebump?"

"Yes! That is I…er, me. Erm. Hello." She waved awkwardly.

"You traveled in from Tragevelia, right?"

"Yes, I—"

"So you must have seen the fight near the border?"

"Some of it."

Her friend wrinkled her pert nose. "To think—a witch on the loose, so nearby."

Ellie leveled them a look. That was three hours away by fairy coach—hardly "so nearby."

"Our Princess Bella deserves better." The first girl smiled, but it didn't reach her eyes, so her face only turned scrunchier and meaner. "I'm Nina. And I heard the witch was smuggling the blood of forbidden creatures across the border to the troll courts. And then she tried to murder all those soldiers."

Her friend shuddered. "Trolls and witches belong together. The fairies should have kept the witches out when they made their walls."

"Perhaps it's time to change the law."

Ellie's heart raced. She knew witches were hated, but she never considered her world would ban them entirely.

"Did you see it?" An all-too-familiar cold, clear voice turned Ellie's skin to ice. Mother, impeccable as usual, in her pearled jacket, glided toward them, dark hair arranged in an elegant chignon. Ellie winced. Mother deplored when Ellie left finishing school. But she also deplored traveling;

(32)

Ellie never anticipated she'd bother venturing this far from home.

None of the apprentices spoke. Whatever they thought of her, they'd never dare say before Lady Eleanor.

Mother's eyes flashed. "Back to your work."

The fairies scuttled off, leaving Ellie all-too-aware of her unbrushed hair and sweat-dampened dress.

"What are you doing here?" Mother's voice was quiet, lethal, pleasant in tone if you didn't know her.

But Ellie knew her. "I brought veils," she squeaked, inwardly scrambling for the excitement she felt in the carriage.

"Hmm," was all Mother said, guiding her toward a private alcove. Ellie followed, wishing her feet could turn to stone and keep her safe in the bustle of the crowd.

Mother's words always reminded her of needles, poking again and again, just to make her bleed.

"I made them and they're beautiful and the Fairy Godmother will love them and I'll be a good fairy," she explained in a rush, fingers shaking as she unfastened her satchel and displayed her best, her favorite, her perfect veil of starlight.

Just holding it sent waves of calming energy from her fingers to her toes.

Mother clasped Ellie's wrist. She blinked up at her in surprise. "Mother?"

"What *is* that?" she hissed, glancing around them, as if Ellie had just exposed a poisonous snake.

(33)

"It's starlight magic. Isn't it beautiful?"

The apprentice closest to them gasped. "Oh, how pretty! Did you make this yourself?"

Ellie beamed, a glimmer of courage returning. "I did! With starlight."

"I've never seen starlight woven so beautifully before. Oh, this is just *perfect* for the wedding. The light and hope it will give!"

Ellie was bouncing now. "Exactly!"

The apprentice appraised her. "Have you ever thought of applying to the Fairy Godmother Academy? You know, if you do, we'd love your help preparing for the wedding. We could really use you."

Ellie mashed her lips to keep from squealing in delight. They *wanted* her. She would, at last, be part of something. It was all she'd ever wished for.

"Back to your work," Mother demanded, pulling Ellie outside the great hall, into an enclosed garden, empty but for dancing statues and a gusting, biting wind.

"Mother?"

"Starlight is *witches'* magic."

Ellie blinked. "But...I...I've never heard anything of the sort."

Mother looked around, eyes wide and darting. Ellie retreated. Mother never lost decorum. "It is not commonly spoken of."

"But fairies use starlight, too." Even nonmagical people could use bottled starlight in potions—if they were very, *very* careful and didn't mind losing a finger or two.*

"Not like this. Only witches are powerful enough to touch pure starlight. They call it a witch's hope."

Ellie's throat tightened. She was always taught witchcraft was magic of the night. A shadowed thing, wherein wreaths of black smoke wended around fingers. Not gleams of glittering stars. She let the veil cascade through her hands, the stars' pinpricks of pale light, bright against her skin.

"But…it's beautiful," was all Ellie could think to say. And yet it was a lie, her lie, witchcraft concealed by threads of fairy magic. Her two selves, hiding behind each other.

Mother tore the veil from her fingers and ripped it into pieces. "It is *evil*."

"*No!*" Ellie screamed, voice cracking, heart breaking.

"I'd hoped finishing school would help you, but…"

"It has! I'm all finished!" Hot tears prickled her eyes.

"But you are not fit for society. Go, Ellie. Before you make a scene."

Ellie jutted her chin, so Mother would not see and would never know, how her words speared. "I shall become a fairy

---

* As I describe in my masterpiece, *Protecting Oneself Against Everything That Might Ever Kill You*, elvish gloves will protect your fingers from the use of bottled starlight, though you must proceed with caution, as it will likely still spear into your mind and mix up your Thursdays and Tuesdays forevermore. 'Tis an insufferable way to live, dear reader. Trust Madame Mystérieuse.

(35)

godmother of the realms and renounce all witchcraft. I swear it."

"Did you master your secret charm yet?"

Ellie flushed. It was one piece of fairy magic she'd always struggled with. And Mother knew. Although a relatively simple charm meant to conceal small objects, it backfired whenever Ellie attempted it, detecting Ellie's hidden identity as a witch.

But it was only one charm. She performed other charms splendidly. "I would be a good fairy godmother. Nobody would ever know I'm a witch."

"There can be no hiding what you are. Go."

Ellie would never recall leaving the palace grounds, trudging over the hills to her carriage on the side of the road, replenished with fairy fuel. Her driver didn't ask questions, and she didn't provide answers as he whisked her away from Mistoria, past the border wall, into the network of tunnels connecting the magical realms of the world.

The moon hung low, a crescent jewel curled around ancient spires, by the time Ellie traipsed into her bedchamber. Her heart was somehow both shriveled and bloated, weighing heavily, yet too crumpled to find any light.

She didn't notice the letter until she sat on it, parchment crunching beneath her skirts. Ellie gasped, shooting to her feet. Another note from the Knights of the Round Table?

No…Ellie's shriveled heart ballooned, fairy lights casting a

(36)

golden glow upon the gilded crest. Bianca meowed, pouncing on the letter—a letter from the Fairy Godmother Academy. Saints, she was saved! Nudging a reluctant Bianca aside, Ellie tore open the envelope.

Dear Ellie Bettlebump,
We regret to inform you that while your application was admirable, we do not have space for you in the Fairy Godmother Academy. Best wishes in life, Ms. Bettlebump. May you forever sparkle.

Tears welled in Ellie's eyes. This wasn't real. This wasn't happening. Before she could fall to the floor and cry, a horrifying *pop* cracked the silence, cracked through Ellie's world. A woman in a sparkling blue dress and glittering tiara appeared on her windowsill.

No, not a woman.

A skeleton.

Ellie stifled a scream, scrambling for the door, but the skeleton was inhumanly quick. She gripped Ellie's wrist with lethal strength and flashed pointed teeth. "No time for dawdling, fairy girl. You're going to become a Knight of the Round Table. *Now.*"

(37)

FIVE

CAEDMON

ROXIE HADN'T COME LIKE SHE'D PROMISED.

Caedmon stared at the moon from his bedroom, eating leftover casserole he'd snuck upstairs so he wouldn't have to listen to his little sister Carly ramble on about pigtails or dolls or whatever she talked about these days. Like clockwork, in about five minutes his parents would come upstairs and ask if he wanted to talk, he'd say no, they'd leave and whisper in the hall, and Caedmon would put his headphones in and forget about it all until tomorrow.

But tonight…

He sat on the edge of his bed to make sure he had a full view of the street, just in case Roxie got the wrong address.

Tonight, he'd hoped Roxie would show.

He knew it didn't make sense but…what if she wasn't lying? What if there really was a secret fallen empire, castles of knights, and lost dragons? And—he squeezed his eyes shut, hardly daring to believe it—what if Roxie really did know what doctors couldn't understand? What if she knew why Jimmy died?

Shivers crawled down his spine—like someone was watching him.

He opened his eyes.

But no one was there.

Nothing but darkness curling around the moon.

"Caedmon?" his mom called from outside his door.

"Can we come in?" his dad joined.

Before waiting for a response, the door clicked open. Carly lurked behind them, her chocolate hair swinging from her signature pigtails, tied with perfect pink bows.

"What do you want?"

Carly pouted. "Why won't you play?"

"Mom, make her go away."

"Carly, sweetie, why don't you go brush your teeth?" his mom prodded.

Carly nodded, but when his parents turned back around, she stayed behind them, hugging her stuffed bear to her chest, eavesdropping.

Caedmon flopped back on his comforter and closed his eyes. He couldn't deal with this tonight. "What do you want?" he repeated.

Though he couldn't see them, he could clearly picture his parents: His mom would be wringing her hands, dark hair slipping out of its messy bun, while his dad wrapped a burly

(39)

arm around her bony shoulders to calm her down. They'd exchange some sort of our-son-has-problems look and leave. He started counting backward in German to pass the time—a trick some bizarre old lady at Jimmy's funeral taught him.* It kept his mind busy.

"I know you said you don't want to talk," his mom hedged. "But I think it's time we all sit down. This has gone on too long."

His dad cleared his throat. "What's going on in your head, Cad? We're here. We want to know."

Stop it, he wanted to scream. *Shut up, shut up, shut up.* But the words wouldn't come. His tongue was a useless slab of concrete inside his mouth, refusing to move. He refocused his thoughts on his German numbers. Where was he? Forty-three? Thirty-four?

"Please, Caedmon." The bed creaked as his mom sat near his feet. She just didn't get it. He didn't want to talk. He'd told her a million times, and she still didn't listen. Nobody did.

Blood pounded in his ears, his cheeks warming, heart thumping. He felt close to exploding.

"You can't keep missing school. Your dad and I have been thinking, and we've decided we'd like you to speak to a therapist."

---

* I find this immeasurably insulting. I shall never attend funerals to teach German again. Ungrateful cretin.

(40)

Talking to more people was the last thing in the world Caedmon needed. What he needed was to be left alone. "No."

"Cad—"

Caedmon sat up, fire igniting in his veins. "I'm not going."

His mom placed a hand on his knee. "I know you're upset, Caedmon. I really do. But talking to us like that isn't kind or acceptable. This has to stop."

"Shut up."

"Caedmon," his dad warned.

But his mom just kept trying, infuriatingly, relentlessly *nice*, no matter how awful he was. Caedmon couldn't take it. Something inside him cracked, emotions flooding past a broken dam, and before he could take the words back, he said, "I wish you'd died instead of him."

His mom recoiled as if he'd slapped her.

Carly sulked from the doorway. "Caedmon, that's not nice."

"I wish you'd died, too. Not even instead of Jimmy. Just because I hate you. I wish a truck would run you over."

Time itself stopped as the weight of his words settled in the room, shoving aside furniture and happy memories to make space for their sickly, oozing presence.

Dad was the first to speak. Glowering, cheeks reddening: "Caedmon Tuggle, you apologize to your mother and sister immediately."

He kept speaking, but Caedmon couldn't focus. His gaze

(41)

was glued to his mom, whose composure slipped as tears welled in her sea-blue eyes.

He'd never fought with his parents this badly.

And he'd never made Mom cry. She was stalwart, facing challenges with a lion's gaze. But not tonight. Tonight, she trembled, tears drying on her jaw. Caedmon's gaze slid to Carly, who hugged her stuffed bear, tears leaking from her wide, earnest eyes.

His stomach sank to his toes. They'd never forgive him—and they shouldn't.

He wasn't worth it.

Suddenly, all he wanted was sleep. He'd give anything in this world to be as far from his family as possible. He'd give anything to be someone else, someone better, someone who didn't make his family hate him.

He shoved past them, sprinted down the stairs, slammed his feet into his shoes, and ran into the night.

No one ran after him.

SIX

CAEDMON

CAEDMON SPRINTED TO HIS FAVORITE SPOT BY THE water's edge, where the strange letter first appeared. People seldom bothered him here.

Except he wasn't alone.

A familiar sparkling gown glittered beneath the moon.

"Roxie?"

Roxie turned, and it took all Caedmon's willpower not to flinch. It was definitely her—she had those same glowing eyes that peered into him like she could see every cruel thought and misdeed—but her face was gone. She was pure skeleton.

She must have noted his stunned expression, for she patted her cheeks and sighed. "I thought I felt a bit lighter today. Apologies, I keep doing that. We don't wear our faces back where I'm from. I only do it to make humans feel more comfortable, which grows wearisome."

Caedmon ignored his thumping heart and sat beside her so their feet dangled over the riverside.

"You're not…human?" He didn't mean it in a rude way, but he was dying to know, questions he should have asked last time brimming to the surface. He'd officially seen a skeleton talk, which meant that at least some of what she'd told him *had* to be real.

Roxie clicked her heels together. "I'm one of the Urokshi. Or what's left of us."

He started to ask about Jimmy—demand answers—but he couldn't form the words.

"We live on the island where King Arthur built one of his castles," she said, oblivious to his inner turmoil. "There were three, you see." She smiled wistfully. "Three great isles in a lost sea where King Arthur held court—Camelot, Iselkia, and the Montagne des Chevaliers. The first two have been cloaked in darkness since the Fall, but the third remains. *That* is what you should have learned about instead of *Rome*." She rolled her eyes. "The Urokshi's island washed away long before the Fall of Camelot." Her lips twisted as if her words tasted sour.

Ask about Jimmy. Get it over with. The words were garbled, stuck, sharp. "How did Camelot fall?" he asked instead.

"That, little knight, is the question of the age." Her tone was light, though a band of red lined her snowy eyes.

"Are you…all right?" Then, remembering her absence, he added, "Why didn't you come to my house?" Caedmon's heart flipped. Had it all been a mistake? He shouldn't have cared so

(44)

much, but now, tonight, the idea of escaping was more appealing than ever.

Roxie wiped silver slime from her skeletal face. Tears, maybe? "I was debating whether I would tell the Knights of the Round Table you died so you didn't have to go."

"Wh-why would you do that?"

"But then I heard the message," she continued as though he hadn't spoken. "Words that should never be said. Quests that should never be made. The message will make you want to go, but it's too dangerous to do so, and I could not decide what was right. So I sit here awaiting deliverance."

Caedmon's head spun. "There was a message for me? From who?"

"My bones whisper to me in my dreams, Caedmon Tuggle, and they tell me no lies." She crept closer, eyes wide, those whispering bones trembling. "They hear his voice. They see his spells. His magic...it wakes."

"Who? Whose spells?"

"*Merlin.*" The name seemed to cast a spell on the air—winds blew and the river rippled, and the hairs on Caedmon's neck rose.

"Merlin...is *alive*?" Caedmon leaned against the tree. This might have crossed into information overload territory.

"May he rest in the sweetness of night, he has been gone for many moons. Many stars. Long dead, long silent. But

(45)

magic…heart…these things remain. His magic has spoken to *you*, Caedmon Tuggle."

Caedmon's mind buzzed. This couldn't be real.

"Shall I tell it?" Roxie whispered.

"Huh?"

"The message, Caedmon Tuggle! The message!"

"Uh, I guess?"

"Oh, if only you had a brain!" Roxie wailed.

"That's the message?"

"No, merely my deathly wish. If you had a brain, you would leave this spot and never think of this again." She sighed. "His message was this…" And as she spoke and as she told, the rippling river and blowing winds stopped. Listened. "'Your kin will only be safe if you become a knight and find the sword. The Knights of the Round Table will only be safe if you become a knight and find the sword. You will never be safe again if you become a knight and find the sword. Find the sword.'"

"My kin…Does that mean…?"

Roxie nodded, gripping her bone fingers. "Your family. Your closest. Your loves. Unless you become a knight and find the sword, I fear…oh, Caedmon, I fear the worst."

"It…I…" It took Caedmon a moment to remember how to breathe. Thoughts wouldn't connect. It was all too much. He snorted a false laugh. "This is ridiculous."

"Madness, yes, but madness can be truth. The Urokshi

(46)

hear secrets in songs, lies and truths in winds. We worship language. I know what I heard is coming."

"I don't believe you." His voice came out strangled and high-pitched. "Merlin wouldn't have a message for me. Merlin doesn't exist. And the sword. He doesn't mean. He can't mean…"

Roxie nodded through tears. "Excalibur. The shattered blade, lost to time. It must be found. It must be *made*. 'Tis a terrible fate for one so young, and while it has been so very long since I've been so very young, my bones weep for you."

"If I have to go, why were you going to tell the Knights of the Round Table I'd died?"

Her voice deepened, ominous and foreboding. "Because then you shall meet the person whose curse has weakened us all."

Caedmon's neck hairs stood on end. "Curse?"

Roxie nodded, glowing eyes peering at him through splayed fingers.

"Who's cursed, Roxie? Is…" He took a deep breath, forcing the jagged words out. "Was my friend Jimmy cursed? Is that what you meant before about there being reasons for his death?"

"To that I say nay, but also yay, little knight. Jimmy was not cursed, but as the curse grows, as it sinks teeth into the earth, wicked magic everywhere arises." Her snowy gaze met his. "It was a malevotum that killed this Jimmy of yore, a remnant of

(47)

magic so potent and vile, it once felled a city. They say it is lost. But it spreads. It, too, *wakes*."

Caedmon swallowed bile. He was going to be sick. What she claimed was impossible, but somehow, he wasn't shocked. When doctors explored every option and still didn't understand, what was left but magic? "What *is* a malevotum?"

"A dreadful creature born from a rotten, blood-soaked wish. It has eyes of teeth and prowls the night, looking for a heart to curdle with broken dreams. It preys upon the innocent and rots their hearts. But it is never satiated for long. There will be more blood ere the end."

Caedmon nodded, going numb. He thought knowing would make it better.

But Jimmy was still gone.

Caedmon swallowed multiple times before he could trust his voice. "Do you know who cast this curse?"

Roxie looked to the stars, like they might whisper secrets. "Alas, they do not say. But it hangs and it thickens and it threatens and you, child knight. You, fleshy human…" The silver mists in her eyes swirled. "I feel your bones calling to this curse caster. Your heart is there and your blood will rebuild and all could be lost." She shook her head. "All could be lost."

"I…really don't think my bones call to someone casting a curse, Roxie."

She gripped her head and winced, like there were voices

(48)

beating against her way-too-visible skull. Caedmon glanced around the clearing for something, anything to help—sticks? Grass? Would grass help the undead hearing curses on the wind?

"Your lives, they weave, they twine. Unless you *stay*." She gripped his shirt. "Here, you will be safe. Here, you might never meet this curse caster."

Caedmon gently removed his shirt from her grasp, trying to ignore the sinking in his heart. "But Merlin's magic told me my family will die if I don't go."

Roxie nodded dismally.

"Why me?" His voice cracked. "Why has he sent a message...to me?"

Roxie tutted. "I listened to his magic; we didn't have a lengthy chat over tea." Her gaze turned forlorn. "Much as I wish that." She cleared her throat. "Merlin was one of the most powerful sorcerers to ever live, little knight. He saw woven, united threads of fates that might pass, others that never shall. Perhaps his message is for you because by your hearing, others will do, or by your doing, others will hear. Merlin was an architect of fates, and all had roles to play in his plans."

"I still don't believe you," Caedmon protested half-heartedly. He was, after all, speaking to a skeleton. "I'm just...I'm from Boulder Falls, Wisconsin. I'm...not really anybody."

"That may be true. And yet here you are, at the turning of

(49)

the tide, and you must choose, Caedmon Tuggle." She lowered her hands from her face, fixing Caedmon with her eerie silver stare. "You must choose."

Before Caedmon could reply, an ambulance whirred past, jarring his senses.

Roxie's eyes widened. "No. No, upon sweet Death, it cannot be!"

Caedmon's insides turned…cold. Hollow. "What is it?" His voice came out a rasp. What could scare the dead?

"It…it has begun." She crouched, animalistic. Predatory. "Do you not smell its rot? The malevotum…it has returned."

Caedmon's breathing echoed in his ears for a single second.

Blood rushed to his head.

The river whooshed past.

Crickets chirped.

The ambulance's siren blared.

He heard everything in this single second that haunted him so deeply, it tore through his bones and shred him to pieces.

"Little knight—"

Caedmon wasn't listening. He *bolted*. His legs slammed against the pavement. *Faster. Faster.*

The ambulance's red lights gleamed at the end of the street.

Please turn right. Go right. Into town, away from his quiet street. Away from home.

(50)

It veered left.

Sweat beaded down his forehead. His heart rammed against his rib cage. *Don't go home. Please. Please.*

The ambulance swerved into his driveway, where Dad was waiting, gorilla arms limp at his sides, uncharacteristically nervous—small.

"Dad!" Caedmon yelled—but the run had knocked the wind from his voice. His dad didn't hear him, practically pulling the woman from the driver's seat. The paramedics grabbed a stretcher from the back of the ambulance and followed his dad into their house.

They emerged seconds later—with Carly on their stretcher.

Silent.

Still.

Deathly.

Caedmon stumbled to a stop across the street, his lungs squeezing.

Carly's stuffed bear slipped from her fingers, thumping the pavement. Their mom picked it up, brought it to her face, crumpled to the ground.

And wailed.

Caedmon sunk to the earth directly across from her, the shadowed road between them. *I wish you'd died, too. I wish a truck would run you over.*

"I didn't mean it," he whispered, shaking his head, cold

mud seeping into his jeans. "I didn't mean it." It was all he could think to say, his mind empty. Dark.

Carly might annoy him in a little-sibling way—but she was his *sister*. It always felt okay to be annoyed because...he knew, even if he wouldn't say it, that he loved her. That if anyone at school ever bullied her, he would always protect her.

No matter what.

Roxie joined his side, wiping slime from her face. "The malevotum has gone. For now." She followed his gaze. "There is nothing more you can do for her here."

Caedmon forced himself to breathe. "Is she...Did she...?" His voice was strangled. *Not again. Not again.*

"She's still alive."

He swallowed, but his throat was filled with glass. "Will she live?"

Roxie began to shake her head, when her gaze caught on Carly's disappearing frame. Her limp pigtails. Her little bare feet. Her macaroni friendship bracelet, a twin to the one she'd made for Caedmon. Caedmon rubbed his bare wrist. He'd left his on his bedside table.

"She may yet, little knight. She may. The malevotum's magic is powerful. But so, too, are children's hearts. The younger the child, the more likely they'll survive." Her face broke into a smile. "I daresay, I already hear her heart beating with renewed life." She placed a hand on Caedmon's shoulder. "There is hope."

(52)

Caedmon's dad helped his mom to her feet as they followed Carly into the ambulance and drove away.

Carly might be okay. She might be just fine.

Caedmon's mind flashed to Jimmy's funeral.

Might wasn't enough.

"What about Excalibur? Will it help her?"

"The sword's secrets are yet unknown. All that is certain is Excalibur was made to protect." She stared at his quiet, dark house. "And people shall need protection."

"Mom." Caedmon's voice cracked. "Dad. They're not safe here."

"No. Their hearts would never survive the malevotum's magic."

Caedmon stumbled away from the familiar white shutters, the driveway with Carly's bear abandoned on the pavement, where he'd played basketball with Jimmy a hundred times, Carly taking turns on their shoulders.

He shivered so violently, he nearly lost his dinner. *A broken dream, a blood-soaked wish.* What was Carly feeling right now? Was she in pain?

His heart clenched. And what about his parents?

He dug his hands into his coat to ward off the chill, his fingers finding something soft and mushy. He pulled out a bag of his mom's chocolate chip cookies. Tears burned his eyes. He shoved the cookies back in his pocket and squeezed his fists.

Roxie told him this was a choice, that he must choose, but

(53)

she was wrong. This wasn't a choice. Not for him. Death had already claimed his best friend.

Maybe even his little sister.

It wouldn't claim his parents, too.

Caedmon had been a terrible brother. A terrible son. He knew that. But he could be better. He *would* be better.

Caedmon would become the greatest knight the world would ever know. And it began tonight.

SEVEN

Ellie

THE WINTRY WORLD WAS POWDERED IN SNOW. NEE-
dles of glittering ice cascaded toward the horizon, where the
roaring sea crashed against starlit glaciers.

Ellie was alone. The skeleton named Roxie had abandoned
her with nary a farewell—merely an instruction to board a
boat.

Or perish in the wilderness.

But the boat surely led to knights, so Ellie could not—
would not go.

She wrapped her arms around herself, wishing, for the
first time in her life, that her toads had accompanied her. Only
the moonlight, a flimsy trickle through puffed clouds, stood by
Ellie's side.

An indignant meow erupted from the snow piles. Gasping, Ellie dropped to her knees. "Bianca?"

Meow.

Ellie searched the snow, freezing ice melting away to soft

white fur. Her peals of relieved laughter echoed in the vastness as Bianca shook the remaining snow from her body and leapt into Ellie's arms, shivering against her chest. Beside Bianca lay her chipped fairy scepter. Ellie nuzzled the cat and cradled her scepter, her heart lifting. Maybe not so alone after all.

Though what were a cat and a girl to do, lost in a frozen world?

As soon as the question formed, a tiny boat, seemingly carved from ice, caught in Ellie's peripheral vision. She inhaled sharply. *The knights' boat.* She could have sworn it wasn't there before.

All the magical places in the world were mapped out (the nonmagical territories infuriatingly kept blank), and none, as far as Ellie knew, were far north or south enough for moonlit glaciers to rise from the water like ghostly wardens of winter.

So the boat couldn't have magically appeared.

Right?

It seemed to shimmer in response.

Every ounce of Ellie knew to be afraid, to run, to scream and hide. Knighthood was not her future. This boat was not part of her plan.

And yet...her heart *leapt*. How many other magical wonders lay beyond the confines of the world she knew?

She reached for it—and stopped herself. What was she doing? She was a fairy, rejected application or no, and her first order of business was finding a way back to the magical realms without freezing to death.

(56)

Holding her scepter tightly, she murmured a spell, conjuring a flicker of warmth, but fairy magic wasn't strong enough to ward off a chill so deep.

There was always her Evermore dust, though! She plunged her hands into her pockets, searching for the leather pouch of magic dust gifted to all humans of the magical realms every year to perform small tasks, such as conjure harmless flames for the hearth. Since the contamination of magic during the Fall of Camelot, the royal DeJoie family had regulated the Evermore trees, whose leaves created their revered golden dust. Ellie had to ration her portion carefully so as not to run out.

But it was not to be—she'd left her pouch at school.

She glared at her chipped fairy scepter. If she'd been accepted to the Fairy Godmother Academy, she wouldn't be in this mess. "*One* secret charm. I just needed you to perform *one* secret charm."

She gave everything she had to her application. Her magic, her brain, her heart.

And it hadn't been enough.

Tears welled to the surface and froze on her cheeks, sobs she'd been holding back coming out in quick, hiccupped gasps.

Ellie wasn't enough.

Maybe she had only fooled herself into thinking she had a chance.

She was so lost in her thoughts, she hardly noticed the

(57)

gradual shift in the air. The smell of fresh snow souring. A smoky haze over a steaming heap of rot.

Ellie blinked through stinging eyes, still damp with tears, her grip on her scepter tightening. Though she couldn't explain why, something deep within her recoiled in fear.

Something like...magic.

Ellie's hand flew to her heart. Her witchcraft. That was her *witchcraft* sensing danger. Feeling for magic with tentacles it shouldn't have. Listening when it ought to stay silenced.

Ellie swallowed, like she could bury the magic, bury the truth.

Barely daring to move, Ellie tread a small circle in place, scanning the horizon—a strip of pale silk. The snow at her feet. The glaciers, her own footprints. All was still. Uncannily, deathly still.

Except—

She blinked.

A distant shadow of a figure glided forth, an apparition born from winter. It set her heart thumping so quickly, Ellie feared it would bleed out. The shape was too vague to be certain the creature was even human.

Another blink—

Ellie gasped, the smoke taking the form of something humanlike but too long, too thin, wreathing smoke replacing flesh, its face covered in...

(58)

In daggered teeth. Instead of eyes, a nose, cheeks—nothing but teeth.

Without thinking, Ellie held Bianca close—and *ran*. If she could just get to the boat, if she could run a little faster—

The creature gained on her.

"Bring me your heart, little one," it crooned.

"Let me feed.

"Let me feast.

"Let me make...

"A blood-soaked dream."

Ellie whimpered, slipping on ice, feeling—*knowing*—the exact moment her heart no longer belonged to her. An invisible fishhook dug into her heart. And *yanked*. The magic in her soul bucked under its weight, but it couldn't stave off the enchantment.

Ellie screamed—couldn't stop screaming—and couldn't stop running.

The boat glimmered again.

Almost there.

Nearly there.

Breathing was too difficult, her heartbeats slowing, magic draining. Bianca's cries echoed in her pounding ears. Her mind turned silent.

Empty.

Dark.

As if her feet belonged to someone else, they slowed. Paused. Waited for the snarling creature. "Please," she begged her scepter, unable to think of a spell. "Help me."

Her witchcraft awoke inside her, waiting to be needed, waiting to save her life—but no, she couldn't use it. Wouldn't be evil. Wouldn't prove her mother right. Wouldn't be like the witch at the border, imprisoned for existing.

Another scream—but it was not hers.

The monster—smoke and shadows swirling around blanched bone—shrieked at a glowing beam in the night. Her *scepter*. That was her scepter casting a brilliant white light behind her, deflecting the swarm of clattering darkness, though Ellie hadn't uttered a spell.

Her heart swelled, grateful, for once, that her scepter was defective, prone to casting its own charms on occasion. It spurred her forward.

In a final sprint, Ellie leapt into the boat, knees landing on hard ice. At once, it thrummed to life and swept her into the frothing icy sea.

The creature burst into smoke at the shoreline, as if it didn't dare cross.

As if Ellie had perched on the tip of danger's claw and Merlin's ancient magic had snatched her up and placed her out of reach.

Because Ellie belonged to the Knights of the Round Table now.

The monster's hold on her heart vanished—though an ache lingered. She rubbed it, shocked tears streaming down her face, as the last trace of darkness disappeared, leaving behind nothing but freshly powdered snow. She clutched a mewling Bianca for assurance as they trembled against each other.

"You will not take me," she whispered, though she couldn't say if she spoke to the monster or the knights.

The boat navigated glaciers with expert deftness. The wintry sea, the salt, and the snow washed away the remaining stench of rot—though nothing could banish from Ellie's mind the shadow of a figure cloaked in death.

She knew deep in her marrow—in her *magic*—that something was horribly, terribly wrong.

It wasn't until the lost island of ice became nothing but a distant white glimmer that she realized such an attack should never have happened. That's what the Knights of the Round Table were for. To protect, to serve, to fight.

To keep malevolent magic at bay and give people peace.

The words of Ellie's carriage driver grew fangs and claws and gripped her mind with a force that sent her teeth chattering.

The Knights of the Round Table are meant to protect us, but there have been reports of their failures as of late. And by the saints, if they fall, we all fall.

She shivered. If the knights were struggling, surely the world would need another fairy godmother.

(61)

She trailed her fingers over her chipped scepter. It had saved her from certain death. If anything proved she was meant to be a fairy of the realms, rejected application or no, it was this. She closed her fingers around it. Ellie *would* be a fairy godmother. She would prove to the Fairy Godmother she was the most deserving applicant of all time by performing the most admirable of all fairy tasks: saving a lost cause by granting their greatest wish.

And what greater place to find a lost cause than a castle full of drafted knights, just like her?

Her heart flamed with resolve as she leaned forward on her boat, and adventure called her forth.

EIGHT

CAEDMON

FIND THE SWORD. BECOME A KNIGHT. FIND THE SWORD. become a knight. It was Caedmon's mantra, sustaining him through a bitter night of sloshing water, frigid air, and a haunting wind that whispered, "Welcome, Caedmon Tuggle, to the Valley of Knights," as his boat careened down a pathway lined with stone knights erupting from the sea.

If he did as Merlin asked, his parents would be safe.

As for Carly…His mind stopped functioning when he let himself think about her.

So he couldn't.

He repeated Roxie's reassuring words over and over—that she was young, that she might survive—until they almost felt real. Until he could almost lock them away.

And focus.

Dawn finally gilded the water, revealing glimmers of scales and long, webbed fingers. Caedmon gasped and nearly fell out of his boat, his legs buckling from sitting all night. Were those *mermaids*?

The water turned clear and turquoise, husks of sunken ships silent purveyors of the living, mermaids slithering in and out of their rotten crevices. His hands grew clammy as he drifted closer to what must have been the grandest building the world had ever known.

With a deep breath, he looked up. And up. And up. Green vines peppered with magenta flowers looped around bright white walls, while at least a thousand glass turrets speared the clouds and glinted in the sun. Caedmon lost count of the waterfalls clinging to outer walls, falling off the edge of the world.

And it was floating.

A rocky mountain supported the structure, like both castle and land had once dwelled at the bottom of the sea and someone had raised them to the sky.

With a jolt, he remembered magic existed, and that maybe, someone had done just that.

Caedmon blinked like the mirage might vanish, but it only stared back at him. It had more towers than one human would ever have a chance to explore.

An enormous blue flag flapped in the wind, a coat of arms with twenty-five swords forming a sun. Swooping beneath the symbol were across it emblazoned the words *Château des Chevaliers*. Castle of Knights? That made sense. For once, he was

(64)

glad his mom forced him to learn French, though they both thought he'd use it to study abroad, not understand writings on flags hidden from the world.

The other boats of draftees drifted closer and closer, until they were all in a circle.

Except…

He rapidly counted.

There weren't twenty-five like Roxie said. There were fifty. If possible, his stomach grew even queasier.

One boat rammed into his. "Hi! Hello! Greetings!"

Who had the nerve to be this perky right now? The speaker was a girl about his age with olive skin, kind hazel eyes, an enormous toothy smile, and tumbling dark hair peeking out from a velvet hood. Her fluffy, white cat peered at him from the crook of her arm.

"I've been on this boat for *hours*. Are you a new knight, too? Where are you from? I attended Roses and Needles Finishing School in Tragevelia. Have *you* heard anything about what we'll be doing? I haven't. Other than the legends, of course. Do you think this is really for life? Do you think we'll ever see our families again? And you are?"

Caedmon gaped at her. He didn't think any one person could speak so much at once. "Did—" he began, but he wasn't quick enough.

"You wear odd clothing. From which realm do you hail? The

(65)

Unseen, perhaps? I find that when they traipse into neighboring realms and see themselves, they're quite surprised by their garments. I once met a mysterious old woman who wore capes covered in olives and I found it very—" *

"Hold on." He raised his hands. "Go back to never seeing our families again. What did you mean?" He hadn't realized this was so...permanent.

"I can't be certain, but that is what legend foretells. What's your name?"

Caedmon gritted his teeth. This was what his sacrifice truly meant. He would never apologize to his family for the terrible things he said; he'd never go to another football game with Dad or go fishing with his grandpa.

But they would be safe. And that was enough. For a flash, he felt it all—the searing anger, the blood pumping in his veins, the unending sadness. In a second flash, it vanished, replaced by the numbness he'd come to know.

Ever since Jimmy died, it was like Caedmon had, too. His mind had turned to mist, and all he could see for miles were distorted images and spikes of metal protruding from the earth. It wasn't a nice place. He often got lost there.

The girl was somehow still talking. He tuned back in to what she was saying—and immediately understood why he had tuned out.

* ...Do go on.

(66)

"Ri-tarle errinde?" She tilted her head as if it were a question. *"Tor ork ten kenchaki?"*

"Uh, I'm Caedmon Tuggle," he said to get her to stop.

She screwed up her face. "Well, then why didn't you answer the first time? I'm Ellie Bettlebump, and don't worry: There aren't any toads hiding in my cloak. I triple-checked." She beamed again, revealing a gap between her two front teeth.

Caedmon blinked at her. "That's...that's great."

The other recruits eyed Ellie strangely. Her voice did carry. Ellie's head lowered. She'd gone curiously quiet, fiddling with her old-timey cloak.

Caedmon was tempted to leave it, that quiet nothingness drawing him back into the place in his mind where he could sleep in the mists, when tears slid down her cheeks.

His mom's face popped into his head. He swallowed, doing his best to bury it. Even before their fight, he hadn't known what to do when people cried. Dad told him crying was normal and human, which he understood, he just didn't know what to *do.* He barely knew what to do when *he* cried, let alone some random girl he'd just met.

Still, he couldn't just sit there. A tug of some emotion beyond nothingness or anger found him. He wanted to help. "Do you want a cookie?" Caedmon pulled the plastic bag out of his pocket. They were crumbled and squished, but Ellie's face brightened, like he'd offered her a cake covered in golden

(67)

frosting. She reached for it, then snatched her hand back, forehead scrunching suspiciously.

"You're giving me a cookie? Why?"

"Uh...because...you seem sad? And...um..." He really wasn't good at this. "Just take the cookie." He felt so uncomfortable, he accidentally threw it, smacking her in the face.

Still, she smiled through her tears and nibbled on it. "Thank you. No one's ever given me a cookie before. Well, unless I've purchased it with coin."

Purchased it with coin? "Where did you say you were from again?"

"Well, I'm *from* Aurelia, where Cinderella's great-great-great-great-great-granddaughter is getting married soon. She's my stepsister."

Had she just said Cinderella? Like with the pumpkin?

She must have noticed his blank expression as she pulled out the strangest map of the world he'd ever seen. The country shapes were mostly the same, though they bulged in places, and everything he'd ever known was left blank—sprawling masses of land labeled NEW WORLD REALM. She pointed at a spot in France near the Pyrenees labeled AURELIA REALM.

"Here! But I've attended Roses and Needles Finishing School for most of my life, which is in the Tragevelia Realm." She pointed at what he thought was Luxembourg. She puffed up her chest. "Aurelia was the third realm created after the Fall of Camelot, and a lovely one at that. The history museums are simply divine!"

(68)

Caedmon stared stupidly at her, his mouth hanging open. When Roxie described the realms, he thought they were in the middle of oceans or places like the Amazon. But was this girl telling him there was a secret kingdom in France? Could that even be possible?

"No affiliation with Trolleaux, though," she added with a shudder.

"Trolleaux?" Caedmon asked weakly.

"The troll court just beyond the Aurelian border." Ellie reached into Caedmon's bag of treats and began scarfing down another one of his mom's cookies. "King Mathieu is simply horrendous, isn't he?"

"King...what?"

"Not that we've been properly acquainted, naturally. Trolleaux is beyond our magical realms, so I've obviously never been able to visit. But the stories! Oh..." Her eyes narrowed. "If I were to meet him, I would *scold* him," she threatened as if this was the worst imaginable fate.

"Oh my gosh!" She squealed and fluffed her hair, getting crumbs mixed in with her curls. "It's Lorelei DeJoie!"

Caedmon blinked, his head turning to mush as he tried to process everything. "Do I even want to know who that is?"

Ellie gave him an incredulous look. "Only the heiress to the entire DeJoie family fortune, the last descendants of Godfred the Good, and one of the most important people in all twenty-five and a half realms! Though she's also related to

(69)

Olivia DeJoie, who's the meanest girl alive—we went to finishing school together—but I think they're only third cousins or something. Lorelei is a *princess*."

"Okay, what's with this twenty-five and a half thing? Is anyone ever going to explain this to me?"

Ellie tilted her head and squinted. "I don't know what needs explaining."

"How is there half a realm?"

"How wouldn't there be?"

"That…that's not…that's not an answer."

"Oh!" She nearly leapt into his boat, sending her cat meowing. "You're from the New World! The one and only nonmagical realm! The tales you must share with me, the stories I've yet to hear! Tell me everything! Literally everything ever! Immediately!" She coughed, settling back down. "If you please."

Before Caedmon could respond, a thunderous boom sounded from the clouds, rendering them silent. The castle glittered innocently above, the source of the noise invisible—as, Caedmon noticed, were stairs or any way to reach the castle.

Caedmon tugged on his shirt collar. Roxie had mentioned trials when she dropped him off in his boat. Was one of them getting into the castle? Were the boats going to fly? Was he supposed to know how to fly? Sweat trickled down his forehead. He hadn't thought any of this through when he decided to leave home.

More thunderclaps resounded, a starry cloud gathering around the castle's turrets, lightning streaking across glass walls.

(70)

No…those weren't just lightning streaks.

From the cloud emerged a beast with the body and head of an eagle and tail of a serpent slicing through the air, morphing into a lightning bolt in flashes. It soared toward them, carrying a rider.

As they approached, Caedmon couldn't help but gape. The creature was enormous, eyes lined with fire, scaled wings black in the gathering storm. Lightning flashed again, filling Caedmon's nose with smoke.

The rider, an imposing man with a bushy beard and enormous shoulders, brandished his sword, which shone red in the light as the storm cloud dissipated. "Future Knights of the Round Table," he boomed, voice echoing across the sea. "Welcome. To the Château des Chevaliers."

Caedmon shivered. The knight bore no armor, which somehow made him look more intimidating. Like not even steel could hurt him.

"I am Sir Masten, First of His Name, Leader of Knights, Keeper of the Peace, Protector of the Realms." He smiled, softening his demeanor.

With a flap of the beast's wings, they circled the future knights, looking each of them in the eye. "Under my command, you will learn to resist the grips of poison and fell your most fearsome foes."

Eagle and rider flew closer, the creature leaving trails of thick smoke in its wake. "You will learn how to master your

(71)

fear." Sir Masten locked eyes with Caedmon. "And how to survive against all odds."

Sweat pooled beneath Caedmon's arms, Merlin's message clanging in his mind. *You will never be safe again.*

Sir Masten returned to the center of the circle. "Most importantly, you will learn how to live with honor, die with honor, and how to be brave—no matter the cost. But first, twenty-five of you must fail."

"*Pardonnez-moi?*" Ellie exclaimed.

Caedmon's stomach dropped.

"Last night was your first trial," Sir Masten continued. "Measuring the courage of those of you willing to embark into the unknown." His grin widened. "For the first time in ten years, all fifty of you passed." His eyes twinkled. "I see there will be some tough competition this year. Your tasks will grow in difficulty as the months wear on. Being a knight requires a multitude of skills. We will test your physical strength, yes, but your mental resilience is just as vital. We will test your willingness to learn, your courage, honor, kindness, respect, cleverness, speed, strength, magical ability, and wit."

Couldn't they just test his French and be done with it?* Couldn't he be a knight interpreter or something? He wasn't super strong, but he wasn't weak, either, so he could probably perform decently in the strength tests. He refused to be

---

* A reasonable question.

a coward. And he supposed some could call him clever. But mental resilience? He wasn't sure about that one lately. Not since Jimmy's death. And kindness…

His insides squirmed.

He was pretty sure his mom and sister would have something to say about that. The real challenge, though, would be the magical ability. How on earth was someone from the New World Realm going to perform magic? Ugh. He was already calling it the New World Realm. What was happening to his life?

"Throughout the trials, those who do not meet our standards will be escorted home, your memories of this place forever vanished to protect the sanctity of our work. The twenty-five of you who excel will begin training in earnest in five months' time."

Caedmon was going to be sick. He couldn't afford to lose his memories. What about Merlin's message?

"Your next trial is about to begin."

Fifty slinky white ropes cascaded through the sky, tethered to the castle, landing in the boats, along with fifty tiny bags of golden dust. "When lightning strikes the ocean, you will race to the top of the castle. You may use Evermore magic in any way you see fit to aid in your climb in this test of strength and magic. Those of you who fail will plunge into the sea, where the mermaids will take you. Whether you drown will be beyond my control. So do not fail."

Caedmon gulped. What ever happened to getting a bad

(73)

report card your parents had to sign? And were mermaids bad or something?*

Ellie was doing something weird with her face, scrunching and unscrunching it, opening her mouth wide, and blowing out puffs of air, all while wielding a deathly looking scepter.

"*Ummm*...you all right?" It was a ridiculous question. They were probably about to fall to their deaths, but this seemed like particularly bizarre behavior.

Ellie's eyes popped open. "What? Oh, yes. Just seeing if I can summon gloves to protect my fingers." As if that were the most normal thing ever.

"Oh. Right."

"It's not working, though. There must be some strange magic around this place, blocking my fairy magic."

Strange didn't begin to cover it.

Sir Masten grinned, his cheeks ruddy. "I will see the conquerors in the Great Hall for supper." With another great flap of scaled wings, the eagle flew toward the clouds.

A glint of something thin and silver deep in the sands below snagged Caedmon's attention. His heart skipped. Before he could investigate further, lightning struck the ocean. Their next trial had begun.

---

* Oh, you sweet, ignorant fool.

NINE

ELLIE

CAEDMON. THE BOY WITH THE COOKIES AND SAD BLUE eyes, frowned at the sea as Ellie sprinkled Evermore dust on her fingers, murmuring a spell to protect them—not as foolproof as fairy gloves, but it would have to do.

She placed Bianca around her neck, climbed a foot—and slid right back down.

Oh, sweet fairies, however was she meant to do this?

A glint of scales flashed below. Ellie swallowed a yelp, hastily jumping out of the way. A mermaid's tail slapped the water, fangs dripping with blood and fish bones.

Swift and snakelike, the mermaid lunged for Ellie's feet. Whimpering, she clung to her rope. Eyes squeezed shut, pulse too quick, breaths ragged—saints above, she could die here, alone, hovering above the frothing waves.

The clouds darkened, mist thickening the air.

A second mermaid joined the first, circling her boat like

a shark. With an enormous tug, Ellie inched higher. A little higher. The next time a mermaid swiped, Ellie was safely out of reach. She'd be the last to win the race. But she would not perish at the bottom of the sea.

Not this day.

She chanced a glance below—as Caedmon dove straight into the water.

"No!" Ellie screamed. "Caedmon, stop! The mermaids will kill you!" She froze, scanning the waves for signs of him.

He broke the surface, gasping for air. Ellie slid down the rope—offered her hand. "Here!"

"El—" His garbled yell was cut short. Six yellow talons dug into his neck. And dragged him down.

Ellie's heart stopped. The water darkened with blood.

"Stay in the boat," Ellie ordered Bianca, before diving into the water. A thousand freezing needles stabbed her skin, salt stinging her eyes.

The magic that resisted her call before bubbled inside her, momentarily blotting out all else.

It wasn't her calm, peaceful fairy magic—the kind that smelled of flower petals in the day and roasted vegetables at night.

It was her witch magic. The pools of power she'd never learned to control. She swallowed it back down, like bile in her throat.

Instead, she punched the nearest mermaid, wrenching a snarl

(76)

from the dreadful creature. It was rather unfairy godmother–like. But drastic times, no?*

The mermaid twisted. Reached for Ellie's throat instead. She kicked with all her strength, wrenching free. Caedmon punched another mermaid, but the blow was feeble.

His eyes turned glassy, more blood eddying around them. Saints, he was losing air!

Ellie bit and scratched, fighting her way toward the surface. Fighting her fears. Her own squeezing lungs. Grabbing Caedmon's wrist, she swam—gasped when she broke above the sea and gulped delicious salty winds. Caedmon heaved beside her, clinging to the edge of her boat.

"Wait!" He hacked up water and wiped his eyes. "The sword. I thought I saw…"

A mermaid's talons swiped at Caedmon's throat.

"Quickly," Ellie rasped. "Get in."

Ellie pushed Caedmon, trying to shovel him into his boat.

His eyes bulged. His yell cut short as he slipped under again, just as knifelike talons found Ellie and yanked her down. She thrashed, her skin punctured and stinging.

The water held her, filled her, overtook her.

This would *not* be how it ended.

Sensing the panic in Ellie's heart, the perilous situation of her lungs, her witchcraft rose to the surface.

---

* Hear! Hear! My dear!

Too strong to conceal, too powerful to tame, stronger than she'd ever felt it.

It would burst forth and kill them all. It would make her evil. It would make Mother hate her. She couldn't—

An arrow made of pure flame pierced the mermaid's tail. It shrieked, and before Ellie could think, a hand yanked her shoulder and pulled her out of the water, into a boat. A moment later, Caedmon slumped beside her, gasping for air. Ellie flipped onto her back. Was it over? Were they gone? She took in her surroundings: the great mast, the sleek planks, the black flag bearing a white skull.

Her nerves returned in full force.

This was not her tiny boat.

This was a pirate ship.

TEN

CAEDMON

EVERY LIMB ACHED. CAEDMON'S EYES STUNG. HIS lungs felt like flimsy threads, barely working.

But he forced himself to rise and immediately wished he was still fighting mermaids. A skull and crossbones on a black flag couldn't be good, no matter the realm.

Heavy footsteps stalked behind him. He whirled around, fists raised, ready to defend himself—and nearly toppled right back off the boat in shock.

The dreaded pirate was a boy about his height with tousled sandy-blond hair, bright-green eyes, and a broad smile. "Ahoy! Thanks for that; we've been trying to catch the serpentelles for months."

"We?"

A barefoot girl with dark skin and smiling amber eyes glided into view. Ellie's cat trotted at her heels, sopping wet and scowling. "Princess Isadora of the Mermaids." A golden trident in her hands glinted and her voice resonated with authority, though she couldn't have been much older than them.

Caedmon settled somewhere between a goofy smile and half bow. She was a mermaid? Where was her tail?

She was also, he couldn't help but notice, incredibly pretty.

Unfortunately, Princess Isadora turned her attention to Ellie. Remembering his manners, Caedmon helped the girl to her feet. Both of their arms were slashed with claw marks.

"Thanks," he murmured. She'd almost died because of him. And he hadn't even found the sword.

He'd been so sure he'd seen it, blade sharp and broken, peeking out of shifting sands. He had no idea if it was Excalibur, but he had to try. But when he dove for it, he'd met only sand. Well, sand and murderous fish women.

The mistake had cost him.

Grimacing, he forced himself to look at the ropes tethered to the floating castle. Most of the other draftees had nearly reached the summit. Two had disappeared. Had they fallen? He hadn't noticed anyone else in the water. They must have just reached the top first. Caedmon and Ellie would certainly be last—which meant he'd failed the trial. Maybe they could still try—

A horn blasted, lightning struck the water, and the ropes disintegrated. One draftee still on his rope screamed as it vanished, and he fell through the sky. Just before hitting the water, he disappeared entirely.

(80)

A shudder rippled down Caedmon's spine.

"He'll be okay." Princess Isadora cut through the buzzing in Caedmon's brain. "Sir Masten speaks grandly, but failed draftees rarely truly die. More often they're simply punished and eventually sent home without their memories."

That didn't sound much better. Either way, Caedmon couldn't afford to lose another trial.

"Failing once doesn't necessarily spell doom. What is your name?" The princess touched his shoulder, her seashell bracelets clinking. She was warm, like sunlight, and her voice reminded Caedmon of velvet and honey.

Wow, no, it didn't—what a weird thought. Caedmon shook his head. Had he bumped it or something? He was focused. He was a knight. Well, going to be. He didn't have time to think about good-looking princesses who might secretly have tails.

"Ellie Bettlebump," Ellie wheezed.

"The to-be Princess Bella's stepsister? You must be so excited for the wedding."

Ellie blushed. "Well…sort of. That's the goal, at least. I'm not exactly invited."

Princess Isadora offered Ellie an enormous smile that sent Caedmon's stomach into a series of flip-flops. "Well, Ellie Bettle-bump, perhaps I can change that. You have freed my sister, for which I owe you a great debt."

"I…what?"

(81)

"The serpentelles do not believe in what the Knights of the Round Table stand for, so only an act of great courage here, in these waters—which you performed when you jumped into the ocean to save this young boy—could have freed my sister from a curse they laid upon her."

Caedmon bristled, straightening to look taller. Young boy? Okay, maybe she looked a *year* older than him, but that was stretching it.

"I...Anyone would have done it," Ellie said, breathless.

"Nope," the pirate chimed in. "I live on this boat and see a lot of people around the world. Most wouldn't help."

The princess tutted. "Well, I don't know about *most* people. *You* just associate with heathens."

The boy's grin widened. "Very true. I'm Mickey by the way. Mickey Murphy."

"Caedmon Tuggle."

"You two new knights?"

"Yeah. Well...trying to be."

Mickey bumped Caedmon's shoulder. "Don't feel too bad. I failed last year." His arms spread wide. "But I get to be a pirate and do whatever I want now, so I can't complain, really."

It did look appealing. Still, Caedmon couldn't help but wonder: Where were Mickey's parents? And if their memories were wiped, how come Mickey remembered failing?

The pirate opened an enormous treasure trunk and heaved—nothing.

"Invisible magic stairs. Really useful. You just put a stair beneath where you want to go and a staircase forms. Thought I'd give you a lift to the castle."

"Isn't that cheating?" Ellie frowned.

Mickey shrugged. "So? Beats climbing those dumb ropes." He rolled his eyes. "I hated that trial. Blisters for weeks."

"What were some of the other ones?" Caedmon asked.

Mickey shrugged again. "Dunno, I left after the second trial. Never looked back. Been sailing the world ever since."

Caedmon's heart thundered. If anyone was likely to find a lost piece of Excalibur, it was someone who traveled the world. "You must have seen a lot then."

"I suppose, yeah. There were some pirates talking about the dragons waking up last month. Something about fires seen at the bottom of the sea."

"Really?" Ellie asked.

The princess pursed her lips. "Don't listen to him. Dragons are myths."

This was a bit strange coming from a mermaid, but Caedmon didn't comment. He took a deep breath. Believing Excalibur existed already stretched his comfort zone. Asking a total stranger if he'd come across a famous sword that was meant to be completely imaginary? Caedmon might feel more comfortable battling serpentelles again. "You haven't, um, you haven't *seen* Excalibur around have you?"

Princess Isadora didn't laugh, but she did smile like he was

(83)

a boy playing make-believe. "No one has seen Excalibur for centuries."

Mickey nodded. "What she said. Not worth the time, mate."

Ellie scooped up her cat, who leveled them a look of extreme reproach. "You don't believe it can be found."

Mickey shrugged. "Well, it's been lost since the Fall of Camelot, hasn't it? It would have shown up by now."

Caedmon's meager hope shriveled until—"Well, *that's* no way to find a lost sword." Ellie scoffed. "Have they looked in *every* gremlin hovel? Gremlins are known for hiding shiny things in their hovels." She turned to Caedmon. "Do you want to be the one to find it?"

"More than anything. I…" He faltered. *Merlin told me to* sounded ridiculous. "I have to."

They all blinked at him.

"Something about a curse?"

He'd expected them to freak out when he mentioned Excalibur but at this, they all squawked, squealed, and balked.

"A curse?"

"What curse?"

"Whose curse?"

"A curse upon me is a curse upon thee!" Ellie shook her head and blushed. "Sorry, it's an old saying."

"What curse?" Princess Isadora pressed. "Who spoke of it?"

Caedmon flushed. "Roxie...I don't think she has a last name. She's..." What had she called herself? He imagined she'd be offended by *talking skeleton who wears too many sparkles.* "Oh! Urokshi! She's a Urokshi. She said it's hanging over the world."

Mickey frowned. "Maybe talk to Sir Masten. If Roxie knows about the curse, he probably does, too. And..."

"What is it?" Ellie prodded.

Mickey shrugged. "I just think he has secrets. If you can get him to talk, you might find what you're looking for."

"Do you think he has something to do with the curse?" Caedmon asked.

"Doubt it. I mean, he did threaten to obliterate my memory forever but that just comes with the scary knight territory. He didn't seem like a bad guy. Just...someone who hides things. Also, when I snuck into his office to steal these invisible stairs, I overheard him talking to another knight about keeping something secret, so there's that. I'll see what I can find out, though."

Princess Isadora nodded. "As will I." She slammed her trident against the boat deck. With a flash of light, a scroll bearing Caedmon's and Ellie's names fluttered to the floor. "We have an agreement with the Château. This is a royal pardon from our kind to protect you from being accused of cheating in this trial. If you're questioned, give it to Sir Masten."

"I'll catch you when I catch you," Mickey called as the

(85)

princess waved and dove into the sea. A green tail glimmered, her trident flashed, and she was gone.

Caedmon's heart sank. He hadn't even asked how to contact her again. Though he doubted phones worked in underwater palaces.

"Mermaids get a bad reputation," Mickey explained, steering the boat toward where he wanted to place the invisible staircase. "They're mostly human, though. The serpentelles are the ones to look out for. They keep trying to invade the mermaid palaces around here. Their hearts are more snakelike than anything. They just look the same, except serpentelles have spiky tails."

Elle crossed her arms, which, thankfully, had stopped bleeding. "I've never heard that before."

"Most people haven't. Mermaids like their reputation. It keeps the DeJoies out of their business."

"How'd you two meet?" Caedmon asked.

Mickey squinted as a flaming sunset painted the boat rose and gold. "Sailing accident."

He didn't offer more information than that, so Caedmon didn't ask. Besides, his eyes suddenly wanted nothing more than to shut. After months of ignoring the world, this much talking and thinking and doing had utterly exhausted him. Yes, he needed to save his family and find Excalibur and *remake* Excalibur and become a knight and somehow not die from malevotums or a mysterious evil curse hanging in the air. But first, he really needed sleep.

Mickey plunked the invisible stair down on his boat, grinning at them. "Stairway to the sky! And hey, if you ever get tired of following the rules and need a pirate around, come find me. I anchor in the lagoon."

Caedmon and Ellie promised they would, and as Caedmon glanced at the pirate one last time, envying his carefree life, he couldn't help but think the boy looked lonely, dwarfed by his imposing boat in the silent sea.

Climbing the invisible staircase was the second most terrifying experience of Caedmon's life, right after battling serpentelles and nearly drowning.

One step in front of the next, he kept reminding himself, though there was nothing but the gaping maw of the awaiting sea below.

That, and Ellie's shrieking cat. Its hair stood on end, its meowing somehow shriller with every step, which didn't exactly help Caedmon's concentration.

He clung to the railing as if his life depended on it.

Because, he remembered, it did.

He wasn't in class anymore or safe in Boulder Falls.

If he missed a step, he'd plummet to the ocean, and this time, Ellie, Mickey, and the mermaid princess wouldn't be there to save him.

His cheeks still burned thinking about the incident. His first real trial and he'd failed—miserably. Ellie panted from the climb, her curly hair sticking out in different directions as it dried in the wild wind.

She'd saved him. She could have died, too, but she'd saved him. They barely knew each other, and, he supposed, were competitors. Princess Isadora and Mickey's conversation rewound in his head. They were right. Not everyone would have done what she did.

She slipped a bit on the stairs, and Caedmon pressed a hand to her back.

"Thanks," she wheezed, sending him a tired smile.

"No problem."

For a moment, they paused, halfway up the world, to catch the dying sun as it sank beneath the ocean, sending a riot of stars cascading through the sky. Above, the glass turrets, set aflame with light an hour ago, melted into a softer indigo sheen.

Twenty-five swords of the imposing flag bore down on Caedmon. Twenty-five swords for twenty-five knights. Knights, not failures. The sight strengthened his resolve. He would be better. He must be. "This is our life now, isn't it?"

Ellie's brow furrowed. Up close, a smattering of freckles dusted her skin. "Not forever, Caedmon Tuggle. Not for me."

ELEVEN
ELLIE

BY THE TIME ELLIE AND CAEDMON FINISHED CLIMB-
ing the staircase, the moon had risen, and Ellie could view the
castle in its full glory.

Waterfalls cascaded over pale stone, into the faraway sea
where iridescent serpentelles glittered. They were far lovelier
when not trying to strangle her.

It'd been impossible to see from down below, but ruby
paths decorated with intricate whorls twisted through breezy
turrets, while looping glass bridges and ponds filled with
multicolored fish decorated the grounds.

For being among the clouds, the island was temperate, as
though magic settled about the world, soothing the elements.
It resembled a summer palace more than the dungeonesque
castle she was expecting.

The only indication this place trained knights was a grand
courtyard where a great, round table inlaid with twenty-five
swords stood beneath the moon.

The strangest part of Ellie ached, knowing she'd leave.

She'd had so few adventures in life, sequestered behind the walls of Roses and Needles Finishing School, spending her days sewing and practicing her penmanship. She shook herself.

This wasn't Ellie's forever place.

This was about Bella's wedding and becoming the greatest fairy godmother the world would ever see. She tightened her grip on her fairy scepter.

Nothing could distract her.

Caedmon cleared his throat, sending a jolt of electricity through her knees. She'd completely forgotten he stood beside her. "*This* is where they train knights?"

Ellie beamed. "It's so pretty."

In Ellie's admittedly limited experience, boys didn't normally agree when she called things pretty. But perhaps because no one else was around, or they'd just survived drowning and serpentelles and climbing to the top of the world together, Caedmon smiled at her. "It is."

"Caedmon Tuggle? Ellie Bettlebump?"

Ellie did everything she could to swallow her scream. Caedmon was not so fortunate and let out a high-pitched yelp before mashing his lips together.

Another Urokshi—polished bone dressed in a dapper ruby velvet cloak and oversize beaded spectacles—inclined her head. "Dame Yora, Poison Resistance instructor. Princess Isadora already sent word. Your scroll?"

(90)

Caedmon fished it out of his pocket and handed it to the skeleton, who tapped it. A puff of salty green dust emanated from it before the scroll turned to water, spraying their feet.

"Perfect. You missed supper, so I shall escort you to your lodgings."

Without further ado, she turned and floated toward the vast doorway, which whooshed open at her approach.*

Ellie and Caedmon exchanged looks, then rushed after her, Bianca skirting their feet. The entry hall dazzled, starry constellations shifting across pale walls, morphing to scenes of blazing deserts and ashen jungles.

"What are those?" Caedmon asked.

"Stories," Dame Yora replied. "From a great land far away, that may need our help some distant day."

Ellie craned to catch a glimpse of winged beasts tearing through a night of three moons before the vision blackened.

Her heart skipped a beat, leaning into the call of adventure.

She ignored it.

Purpose. Her quest. The wedding.

"Come," Dame Yora instructed. "Caedmon, your bedchamber is near the Sword Garden."

They wound across arching crystal bridges festooned with pixie-laden flowerpots, finally arriving at Caedmon's room. It

---

* That is not a typo, dear reader. I assure you, she floated. The Urokshi are known to do so now and again. You may learn more in the *Encyclopedia of The Dead and Undead*. 'Tis a masterpiece. I wrote it.

was on the ground floor beside an explosive magical garden of spiky plants, swords, cabbages, long-stemmed waltzing flowers, and shrubs waddling to and fro, conversing in Shruberese.

Ellie was fluent in multiple languages, but she had yet to master that one. Too many different grunts, though she did recall that *oomph* translated to "feed me," and *ooomph* meant "I shall strangle you in your sleep." She inched away from Caedmon's bedroom window. Saints above, please let her bedroom be far away from murderous plants.

"Well, friend, I bid you good night." Ellie froze, her words catching up to her brain, heat flooding her cheeks.

Did nearly drowning together qualify as friendship? What would her Etiquette professor think? Caedmon Tuggle was a strange boy she just met.

He was not a friend.

Caedmon half smiled. He never actually smiled. Not with teeth. There was something sad about him, like a lost puppy. Ellie wanted to give him a hug, but of course, such friendship acts were out of the question. Besides, Ellie was leaving soon. Making friends—or at least half friends with people who didn't actively dislike her—would be a waste of time.

So instead, Ellie offered a formal handshake. Caedmon eyed it like she had grown a third hand.

"What are you doing?"

"It's a handshake."

"I know *what* it is. Why do you want to shake my hand?"

(92)

Dame Yora clicked her fingers. "Quickly now. Bert needs to be fed, and if he doesn't receive his midnight toast, he will wail until the rooster crows." She cocked her head. "Likely eat the library again, too. We still haven't rebuilt it, leaving everything floating in the amphitheater. Blasted overgrown worm."

"Who's Bert?" Ellie asked.

Dame Yora shuddered.

Ellie bit her lip, then spat out, "Bye, then. I wish you luck finding the sword."

"Thanks…"

Something in his gaze was so shuttered, so haunted, Ellie paused. "I do believe it's possible. Difficult…but possible."

"It has to be," he murmured almost more to himself than her.

"Erm…if you don't mind me asking…Why does it matter so much to you?"

Caedmon opened and closed his mouth three times, like he formed three answers and regretted them. Glancing at Dame Yora, he lowered his voice so only Ellie could hear. "The curse I mentioned? It's making evil magic wake up. I know one is called a malevotum, but Roxie said that's just the start. She said…she said Merlin sent me a message that if I don't find the sword and become a knight, wicked magic might kill my family."

A chill swept through Ellie's bones, the ache in her heart visceral, as if the creature of smoke and fangs hovered in the hallway, hooking its magic into her blood.

(93)

He shook his head. "I don't fully understand it, but I think the sword must be able to stop more of this magic from escaping into the New World." When he met her eyes again, dark circles visible, face drawn, something deep within Ellie cracked. Like she would do anything in the world to make his sadness go away. "I have to stop it."

Twenty minutes later, safe in her new bedroom, Ellie was still reeling. The curse explained why such an awful creature attacked her on her journey, though she still didn't understand why the Knights of the Round Table hadn't helped.

And if that wicked magic was only growing…if not even Caedmon's nonmagical family was safe…who was?

She dropped her cloak to the floor of her tiny turret, cradled by glass, overlooking the sea. Even with all the glass, it was cozy, vines curling up the ceiling, a squishy bed with a heap of pillows awaiting her tired head, and a plush rug adorned with swooping dragons beneath her feet.

Before collapsing, Ellie yanked off her clothes, crusted with blood and seawater, and dumped them on the floor. Thank the saints, a fuzzy white nightgown had been provided. She could shower later, when her muscles and bones didn't resent her so.

Bianca, who might never look at Ellie again, curled at the foot of the bed, her butt to Ellie's face. Honestly, she couldn't blame the cat. They'd been through a lot.

Snuggling into bed, she rested her head against the glass wall and gazed at the sea. She was on the opposite side of the castle she saw when arriving, giving her a view of what looked like an ancient amphitheater filled with floating bookshelves, orchards speckled with mouth-watering laplie fruits, and, most impressively, an enormous stone dragon erupting from the water, guarding the castle.

A stone dragon for the lost Pendragon king.

The children cried when the dragons died, now their memory remains mere legend-spun.

Without bones or blood or any trace at all, scholars argued the dragons were mere myths—a powerful symbol King Arthur took as his emblem to frighten enemies.

And yet...curled here, high above the world, she could almost see their shadows swooping through a flaming sky. How could such a story persist if they *hadn't* been real?

There were even fewer stories of malevotums, reserved for the wickedest roles in fairy tales.

And yet, yet, yet, yet, yet.

Ellie's heart beat too quickly, as if making up for beats lost to the malevotum. What other monsters lurked throughout the world? Ellie wrapped her arms around herself. Would finding Excalibur truly make a difference? And could Caedmon Tuggle do it?

Not alone, a voice whispered in her heart. Ellie knew nothing about swords other than she should definitely never be trusted with one, but she knew a lost cause when she saw one.

(95)

When she'd vowed to save a lost cause and grant a wish, she'd expected something simple, like an unrequited crush.

But simple or not, she knew—in that certain, heart-stopping way she knew how to weave stars—that this was her task.

If Caedmon needed to become a knight and find Excalibur, Ellie would see it through. And when they succeeded, the Fairy Godmother would welcome Ellie with open arms.

TWELVE
CAEDMON

AS CAEDMON SEARCHED THE CHÂTEAU FOR SIR MASten's office the next morning, he kept pinching himself, expecting the dream or nightmare to end.

It wasn't working.

When he went to sleep last night, he thought he'd wake up in Boulder Falls, his parents standing over him, telling him he'd smashed his head. He wouldn't have said those horrible things to them. Maybe even Jimmy would be there, the past few months an imagined horror. And none of them would be in danger.

But a sweet, grassy, ocean breeze had roused Caedmon from sleep instead, his circular window overlooking a summer garden fit for knights, where shards of metal sprouted from the earth among tropical, spiky plants and fat shrubs—which he could have sworn had moved in the night.

Having already scoured the west and northern wings, Caedmon moved east, heart skipping every few beats. What if

Sir Masten left on important knight business? If Caedmon did find him, how was he supposed to persuade the head knight to share his secrets? At the very least, he'd let Caedmon contact his family…right?

He was so distracted, he ran headlong into another Urokshi, bones draped with jeweled necklaces, bracelets, and crowns, like he'd burst forth from a treasure chest. "Ahh! You there. Small human. What do you think of my outfit? Too garish? Or daring and exciting? I feel as though the gold timepiece in my abdomen adds a certain panache."

"It's…um…great." Caedmon cleared his throat. "Sir, where's Sir Masten's office?"

"Why, the tippity top, of course."

Caedmon craned his neck; the tallest tower was shrouded in clouds.

"But he will be leaving for the Great Hall shortly." The Urokshi's snowy eyes whirred. "As you well should be."

Caedmon could have hugged him.

After following a complicated set of instructions that involved indecisive pathways, compliment-demanding doorways, and a set of screeching feathered wings hovering indecorously outside the boys' bathroom, smacking people in the face if they got too close, Caedmon skidded to a halt, momentarily stunned.

The Great Hall was as great and vast as its named suggested. The arched windows were glassless, permitting a fresh,

(98)

salty breeze belying their height above the world, and the ceiling…

Caedmon sucked in a breath.

He'd never been one for art, but even he had to admire this. It was an enormous painting stretching from one end of the hall to the other, filled with golden figures against a deep blue sky, with crimson flame clawing the edges.

It was a story, he realized, one panel leading to the next. Likely to do with the Pendragons. Before he could make out the details, Ellie tackled him in greeting, frizzy curls smacking his face.

"Caedmon! Cad, hi! Hello there! Greetings! Bonjour!"

Some of the other students eyed them warily, bringing a blush to Caedmon's cheeks. At least he blended in more today. There'd been an assortment of capes, boots, pants, and tunics in his wardrobe all suspiciously in his size, and thankfully, everyone else wore similar outfits.

"Come, sit," Ellie demanded, linking elbows and guiding him toward one of the circular wooden tables around the hall, already laden with tropical fruit, eggs, potatoes, scones, crepes, and all sorts of foods that made Caedmon's stomach grumble. How long had it been since he'd eaten?

He twisted as he walked, scanning the unfamiliar faces for Sir Masten's imposing frame, but the head knight was nowhere to be seen.

"…And that's why I'm going to grant you any wish you desire," Ellie concluded, plopping him in a chair. "Which I'm

(99)

assuming is the whole find-the-sword, protect-your-family thing, but you just let me know."

That seemed weird. It probably didn't help he hadn't been listening. "Oh, right. Thanks, Ellie."

Her eyes welled with tears. Oh no, not again.

"I thought…" She smoothed her lace dress beneath her cape, avoiding his gaze. "I thought you'd be…Never mind."

That wave of exhaustion he kept at bay lashed out without warning, as it liked to do these days. It threatened to overtake him, everyone's voices morphing into an endless hum that wouldn't cease.

He should have stayed in bed.

Ellie stared at him with those wide, bright eyes of hers. *Say something. She's just staring at you; you have to say something.* Words wouldn't come. Sometimes even breathing hurt.

Fortunately, he was spared a chance to explain when the enormous double doors opened to Sir Masten's commanding frame, flanked by hounds. At once, everyone stood.

Caedmon tensed. He wasn't normally impulsive, but suddenly, he felt himself lurch forward, open his mouth—Ellie held his wrist. He blinked. The hall was silent, immobile. She surreptitiously shook her head, bringing Caedmon back to reason just as the head knight strode through the hall and took his seat around the largest circular table. No one spoke, apparently waiting for some cue. Sir Masten clapped his hands. "Knights of the Round Table. Protectors of the Realms. What is lost, we shall find."

"What is found, we shall protect," the knights responded as the dogs barked.

At once, hundreds of chairs scraped against stone, chatter resumed, and everyone sat.

Everyone but Caedmon.

Now was his chance.

"Whoa, what's the new kid doing?" A girl at his table with high cheekbones and a sleek black ponytail shoved his shoulders, forcing him back into his seat as Ellie tugged on his wrist again. "I saw you looking at the Head Table." Her eyes narrowed. "*No one* visits the Head Table during meals."

"But I have to speak to Sir Masten."

She snorted. "Good luck. I've been here for ages and have never been allowed a private audience with him. And I'm lucky for it. Someone in my year was expelled for accidentally interrupting his chess game once, and *he* had an appointment." She passed him a pot of steaming, rich coffee. Caedmon sat up straighter. His parents never let him drink coffee. "I'm Rosalind, by the way. Rosalind Ramna. Eat. Drink. And try a little harder not to get in trouble on your first day. Draftees have enough problems without making your own."

Caedmon took the coffee pot wordlessly, tongue sticking to the roof of his mouth. How was he supposed to persuade

(101)

Sir Masten to help him if he wasn't even allowed to speak with him?

One of the knights at the Head Table—a squat woman with flashing eyes and a wild mop of white curls—extracted a flask from beneath her cape and poured a heaping portion of its contents into her coffee. Catching Caedmon's eye, she raised her mug and winked.

"That's Dame Ethyl Botts," piped in Ellie's cheery voice. "I woke up at sunrise for my stretches and some reading. Did you see there are already textbooks in our bedrooms? One of mine detailed information about each of the knights here. Dame Ethyl Botts teaches people about enchanted and cursed objects. She's highly gifted with Evermore dust. That's magic powder everyone's allowed a yearly supply of."

On Caedmon's other side, a tall boy with an easy smile and dark hair flopping over his eyes passed a jug of orange juice. "Want some? You're new, right?"

Ellie leaned across Caedmon and smiled. "Hello! Hi! Yes, we are brand new. The newest. What's your name? Where are you from? Oh, I'm Ellie. This is Caedmon. I'm part fairy. He's from the New World."

"I've been here a couple of years. We don't get a lot of recruits from the New World. What's it like?"

"Um…" Caedmon's cheeks heated as everyone at the table looked at him. "I just live in a small town in Wisconsin."

Blank stares.

(102)

"Is that in the United States of America?" asked a burly knight with thick eyebrows and a crooked nose.

Caedmon nodded. "The Midwest. Which isn't really the middle of the west. It's kinda more east. But not, you know, *east* east. It's north. South of Canada." His cheeks were so hot, he was sure they'd ignite any moment.

The eyebrow boy frowned. "Wait, so is it north, south, east, or west? Or in the middle?"

"Stop it, Jorro," Rosalind admonished. "Jorro here is always mean to the new recruits."

"But it made no sense."

Ellie piled heaps of pancakes onto her plate. "Sure it did. East of the middle, west of the east, south of Canada, north of most of America."

Everyone shifted to stare at her.

Oblivious, she pulled an oversize pink basket Caedmon hadn't noticed toward her.

Some of the heat in Caedmon's cheeks simmered down. He couldn't say Ellie was…normal.

But she was a good friend.

The boy next to him cocked his head and smiled. "I'm Omari Evelant."

The basket slipped from Ellie's fingers. "Ellie. Oh, wait, I told you that."

Jorro sneered. "Omari Evelant. From the esteemed Evelant family."

(103)

Omari flashed a movie star grin. "If you want to put it that way, sure."

Ellie extracted a steaming jug of a lumpy, brown liquid from her basket and beamed. "Anyone want fungleberry juice? I brought it to share. Some of my favorite items arrived in my room this morning. Such excellent service! Anywho, it's a fairy drink. I made it myself last week."

Nearly everyone recoiled. It smelled like feet. Caedmon forced himself to smile. It was the least he could do for someone who'd saved his life. "I'll have some."

"Same." Omari offered his glass. The orange-haired girl next to him, who introduced herself as new recruit Mackenzie Mayberry, gagged.

"Perfect! *Parfait!*" Ellie said in lilting French, then shook her head, as if to wonder why she'd just done that. She hastily poured the juice, dragging the cuffs of her sleeves through maple syrup.

The drink was, surprisingly, tasty. It was like fruit punch on a hot summer day, cooling, soothing, and refreshing all at once.

Magical.

He smiled.

Omari grinned into his drink. "Wow, you really are part fairy! My nanny was as well. She used to make us poppyseed bread that always gave us nice dreams. Did you ever think about going to the Fairy Godmother Academy?"

(104)

"There's an academy?" Caedmon asked.

Jorro laughed. "I always forget how stupid the New World people are."

Rosalind rolled her eyes. "Spare me, Jorro. Omari, Grace wanted me to tell you she'll meet you in the library for your study date before Dame Yora poisons us all." She made kissing noises at him.

Omari grabbed a pastry. "Oh, thanks, Rosalind. Grace likes raspberry, right?"

Rosalind shrugged. "As I said, we're all getting poisoned soon, so who cares?"

"I think she likes raspberry," Omari muttered to himself. "I'll see you all later. Nice meeting you, Caedmon. Ellie. And thanks for the juice! I hope you guys do well in the trials." He smiled again.

Ellie made a weird, strangled sound as he jogged off, waving to other friends in the Great Hall before disappearing.

Rosalind Ramna, Caedmon learned, was in her second year of training, and apparently excellent at Serpent's Tail, some brutal game played in the ocean that involved a lot of trying not to die. Cora Larson, her best friend, joined them later, sporting the same sleek ponytail and sharp tongue, though they were utterly opposite in looks: dark to golden hair, brown to goose-feather pale skin. And Jorro Tarkx, in his third year, was dutifully mean to everyone else who walked through the dining hall.

(105)

There were others: a boy in Caedmon's year named Killian Rye, who threatened starting a food fight when Jorro teased him for a set of magical braces that popped off of his teeth and shrieked at him when he tried eating popcorn; Nadia Farhi, a girl he recognized from the trial with a slight lisp and intricate braids woven around her head in a crown; Lucy LuBelle, who insisted people address her pet ferret as Your Majesty.

He would never remember them all.

A sickly feeling settled in his stomach; he wouldn't need to. Half of them would be sent home.

By the time the breakfast platters emptied, Caedmon's stomach was in knots. Any minute now, Sir Masten would stand, breakfast would officially be over, and Caedmon could speak to him about Carly, the curse, and finding Excalibur...and hopefully not get thrown out of the castle in the process.

Sir Masten clapped his hands. At once, the room silenced. "Knights in training, your lessons and tribulations await. Draftees, you will remain."

The older, taller knights passed in a flurry of bright capes, Rosalind mouthing the words "good luck" to Caedmon and Ellie before Cora ushered her away.

Soon, only the draftees remained. Caedmon's palms grew sweaty as he counted. There were forty-eight of them. Two must have already been sent home.

Sir Masten lifted his hands. "Rise."

Caedmon obeyed. The tables and chairs disappeared,

(106)

leaving those too slow to stand falling to the ground. Sir Masten continued, though one of the knights behind him—a hardened, wizened man in a simple black cape—scribbled in his notebook. Caedmon straightened his posture. If they were judging them outside the trials, he wouldn't give them any reason to kick him out.

"Welcome to our Great Hall." Sir Masten gestured to the ceiling. "To the site where twenty-five knights guarded their honored king's castle as Camelot fell and the empire crumbled, preserving Merlin's magic here—" His voice caught, his shoulders rounding. "Forevermore. This is the site of the Treatise of First Men. The palace where the great sorcerer Merlin taught a young boy named Arthur how to be a king. Where years later, King Arthur courted the beautiful Guinevere. In this very hall, Sir Utred the Great stabbed the giant Percesoles, and Dame Joanna the Undying took flight upon the last dragon of this earth, saving the realms of life from peril. You are standing amid greatness. And you will honor that greatness."

Caedmon took in the imposing knights, the stories carved in whirls of wood and painted in brushes of ruby and gold, and something inside his heart pinched. How could the world have forgotten?

"Here is where we will gather. Where twenty-five of you will be declared Knights of the Round Table, Protectors of the Realms. But first"—a wolfish grin—"you will compete. And we shall see who among you is worthy."

Bedlam broke as the knights dispersed, Dame Yora started passing out schedules, and Sir Masten strode out of the room. Caedmon fought through the crowd, heart seizing. "Sir Masten!"

The head knight glanced his way—but did not break his stride. Caedmon tripped over a stray chair, banging his knee. "Sir Masten! Wait! My sister—" The oak doors slammed shut behind the knight's retreating back, his hounds staying behind, growling at the draftees.

"Caedmon Tuggle," Dame Yora scolded, "if you have any intention of becoming a knight, you will come here and retrieve your schedule."

Caedmon barely listened. He leaned against the wall, giving in to the pounding in his head, the fogginess threatening to bring him back down, down, to darkness and cold. "This is hopeless," he muttered. Merlin had picked the wrong person. How was Caedmon meant to find the sword when he couldn't even get the head knight to listen to him? He might as well give up. He'd already lost Jimmy.

Maybe even Carly…

No, a small voice in his mind whispered. *Roxie said there was hope.*

Something periwinkle and jeweled tapped his nose. He started. Ellie smiled at him, scepter raised above his head. "Uh, what are you—"

"Be gone with thee, unwanted gloom. Go 'way; farewell and let us live a healthy day."

Warmth spread from his toes to his nose, a shimmering light sparkling around Ellie's face. She smiled through the glow. "Better? You looked unwell."

"Yeah." His voice broke. He cleared his throat. "Better, thanks. What was that?"

"Just a little fairy healing spell. I think the reason my fairy magic didn't work last night was because I was trying to use it for the trial, but it seems fine otherwise. Have you thought more about your wish?"

Before he could reply, Dame Yora shoved schedules in their faces. "Good knights pay attention!"

The wizened knight scowled and scribbled in his notebook again. Caedmon hastily obeyed, scanning his class list: Poison Resistance, Star Speaking, Archery, Swordsmanship, Outsmarting Dangerous Beasts, Curses and Spells, Strength Training, and History.

Caedmon's first lesson was History, which didn't sound as exciting as Swordsmanship, but was probably for the best considering apparently everything he'd ever known about history was wrong.

Ellie lingered as everyone else scrambled out of the Great Hall, her enormous pink basket draped over her shoulder. "So…what is it?"

"What's what?" Caedmon squinted at his schedule. How was history class in the southern-northern wing of the château?

Ellie stomped her foot. "Your wish."

"What wish?"

"*Your* wish!"

He finally looked at her, befuddled. "I didn't make a wish!"

She placed her hands on her hips. "Everyone has a wish. What happened to finding Excalibur and being a knight?"

A giggle sounded from behind them. A girl with large blue eyes and perfectly curled blond hair, shining beneath an even shinier tiara, smirked. At least he didn't have to dress *that* fancily.

Ellie's mouth hung open. "You're Lorelei DeJoie!"

The girl from the boat. She did look familiar, though most everything from last night blurred together.

Lorelei swept her hair over her shoulder. "Obviously. And I heard about you," she said to Caedmon. "You're from the New World, aren't you? You don't know anything about our world or our magic. New World recruits never survive the trials. You weren't meant to be a knight. If anything, you were drafted to fail."

She glided away, each delicate footstep a stomp on Caedmon's heart. There went that hope. It was foolish to believe in something like fate. He knew that. But with Merlin and magic and curses and castles that floated above an untamed sea, anything was beginning to seem possible.

Even him being destined to be a knight.

Your kin will only be safe if you become a knight and find the sword.

Find the sword.

The hairs on Caedmon's neck stood up. Whether he was wanted here or not, whether this was some accident of fate or undiscovered destiny, a mysterious curse hung above the world. His parents' lives were at stake. They needed him.

He turned to Ellie. It couldn't hurt to have her on his side. Beyond being part fairy, which had to count for something, she was a friend. She saved him. She defended him against a guy twice her size without blinking. Maybe she was a better friend than he deserved.

He ignored the squirming feeling in his stomach he got whenever he asked for help. "What do you mean you can grant a wish?" Hadn't she mentioned something about this earlier? He needed to learn how to pay attention again—how to exist beyond the nothing place his mind liked best. Tomorrow, he promised. Tomorrow, he would be a better listener, a better friend.

Ellie gave him a wide grin, making the gap in her teeth more pronounced. "I want to become a certified fairy godmother at the Fairy Godmother Academy. To do so, I'm going

(111)

to grant you your heart's greatest desire if it's the last thing I do."

"How? Do you just wave your scepter or something?" He couldn't keep the desperation out of his voice.

Her face fell. "It's a bit more complicated than that."

"Caedmon, Ellie," Dame Yora barked. "Off to your training."

The white-haired instructor—Dame Ethyl Botts—chuckled and winked again. "You better go. Dame Titania 'does not abide by tardiness,'" she mimicked in a prim, crisp voice.

Caedmon liked her. Still, he had too much to lose and couldn't afford to get in trouble on his first day. Not after yesterday's trial. Even if they hadn't been punished, he couldn't imagine cheating had done him any favors. "Later," he whispered to Ellie. "In the Sword Garden. Meet you during lunch?"

Ellie agreed, and the two of them sprinted out of the room, Sir Masten's hounds chasing after them.

THIRTEEN
ELLIE

IF ONLY SAVING REALMS AND FINDING SHATTERED swords was a simple matter of waving her fairy scepter. Ellie ruminated over Caedmon's question the entirety of her Poison Resistance class—a shocking mistake, as she was so distracted, she accidentally spilled poison over her hands. Her fingers were so green and swollen, she had to visit the healing ward when she was meant to meet Caedmon for lunch.

Neither could Ellie meet her lost cause during dinner or even their evening study break because of her three-hour Star Speaking class, held once a week, taught by Sir Remy, a Urokshi dressed in jewels and scarves. He spent the entire time critiquing the Knights of the Round Table's fashion sense—"All those brightly colored capes! Whatever happened to subtlety? The death of pastels is upon us!"—while Ellie bottled the essence of stars in magically sealed containers and listened for their wisdom. But after three hours, all Ellie heard was a low rumbling that was likely her stomach.

To top the day off, a *toad* had found her. That's right. A toad. Lumpy and warty, it snuck up on Ellie without her consent and wouldn't leave her alone.

Only after midnight, when the moon hung high and the lone loons sang, could Ellie sneak away to help Caedmon's cause, the toad (since dubbed Mr. Petalbloom) hopping happily behind. It was too late to meet him, but Ellie could start conducting research. A lightning storm flashed too brightly in the east for Ellie to sleep anyway.

She encountered no one in the tightly spiraled staircase leading from her bedroom to the crystal corridor, where moonlight stalked the arched halls like a languid lion.

No one still, down the staircase leading to the Great Hall.

No one anywhere.

No one at all.

As she peeked around a corner, she thought she heard noises emanating from a gilded mirror with glass churning like pools of liquid silver.

Snarled whispers from across the world. A hollow wind across a desert as vast as seas. Something scaled and shadowed crawling up algae-coated stone.

And then, a voice.

"Secure…château!"

"Beast!"

"…mischief."

"I'll hold it off!"

(114)

"...far from their chambers."

Ellie stopped, heart skipping beats, listening for the disembodied voice in the night. Though garbled, the voice almost sounded like Sir Masten...but the liquid pools were mercurial and swift, undulating into tunnels of bones and crowns of golden leaves.

The voice was gone, likely imagined. Ellie paused, ears alert—but no sounds of terror sounded from outside the château.

She trailed a finger down the edge of the mirror. The thumbnail of starlight she kept in her pocket for luck hummed happily. She started, squeezing it, then remembered—starlight was a witch's hope. And the mirror was surely the work of witchcraft or sorcery. The whole château brimmed with magic forbidden in all other realms. Yet here, somehow, it flowed freely. She had never known such a place.

Her witchcraft bloomed in her heart, yearning to join it.

Mr. Petalbloom croaked, startling her, and hopped down the hall, so Ellie continued on, alone in the starry night.

When she reached the library, shivers swept through her. Shelves floated in the great amphitheater filled with stone pillars reaching for the heavens. How many stories it must hold! How many facts and clues and secret truths!

After finding a book on knighthood, she moseyed to one of the long stone tables in the center of the amphitheater, around which stacks of books curved into monstrous spires. A

(115)

net of garlands and pink flowers cascaded overhead, protecting her from a light pattering of rain—the perfect sound to accompany her reading.

Though it did encourage more toads. A second one waddled to her feet, belching happily. Resigned, she picked up her two toads and plopped them on the table. "I suppose I'll let you be friends." She adopted her sternest voice. "But know I am greatly displeased."

She settled back in with her book.

> The Knights of the Round Table have
> existed since King Arthur's court.

She scanned the contents. Honor, valor, yes, yes. Standard. Growing bored, she nearly turned it in for another book when a passage caught her attention.

> The sword of Excalibur, famed for its
> appearance amid King Arthur's reclaiming
> of his great-grandfather's legacy during the
> Dragon Wars, shattered into three pieces the
> day Camelot fell. According to legend, Excalibur
> could grant the user near invincibility and serve
> as a conduit for powerful magic. Superstition
> states that the sword must be reforged around
> walls of stone, where light cannot penetrate.

(116)

Many thieves over the centuries have assembled metals and jewels believed to be that of Excalibur. Their lives always end in perilous deaths.

Ellie decided the last part about perilous deaths was a touch dramatic. But near invincibility? She'd never heard of such a gift. No wonder Caedmon wanted to find it.

A chuckle interrupted her concentration. A second muffled laugh followed.

She abandoned her book, following the noise to a tree with great waxy, glittering leaves the size of her torso, where Omari Evelant, the most attractive boy she'd ever seen in this realm or another, sat with a girl.

Sharing apple pie.

The girl noticed her first. She poked Omari, who jumped and scrambled to his feet before recognizing her. "Oh! Ellie. It's just you."

Her heart sank. Yes. Just Ellie.

He brushed his luscious black locks away from his perfect golden forehead and looked at her with those lovely amber eyes. "We're celebrating Bert not monitoring the château tonight. I think a few others have snuck out, too."

The girl, who must have been the mysterious Grace that Omari mentioned earlier, smiled and offered her a plate. Her rich, auburn hair cascaded in the prettiest waves down her

(117)

back, and her bright slate eyes twinkled the way eyes do when they're always ready to laugh. "Want some apple pie?"

Ellie's shoulders slumped. Sweet saints, how did they know kindness was her biggest weakness? Followed directly by delicious sweets? She was powerless to resist them, and plopped beside Omari and his girlfriend, accepting the apple pie, though a scheming, jealous part of her heart was satisfied she'd interrupted their date.

"*Who* is Bert? And what?"

Grace paled. "He's the one who makes sure we don't leave our bedrooms past curfew."

"He's been known to lock students in the dungeon beneath the sea," Omari added. Ellie stole as many glances at him as she could, trying to emulate the casual grace with which he leaned against the tree, as if nothing could ruffle him. She, on the other hand, was as ruffled as a peacock squawking in a tornado.

"But he's sick tonight, so a lot of us decided to..." Grace bit her lip. "I really don't normally break the rules."

"What's Bert look like?"

Omari grinned. "He has a lot of legs. You can't miss him."

"Is he...human?"

Omari and Grace shared a look, making a part of Ellie's soul shrivel. People with crushes on each other got to share looks. Whenever she tried to share looks with boys, she was always told she looked like a bug.

"Not exactly," Omari hedged.

"Just be glad he's not here. He likes to bury people alive."

"And eat them."

"Hi."

Ellie nearly jumped out of her slippers, terrified this mysterious Bert had decided to come visit, but it was only Caedmon, wearing blue pajamas with the Pendragon crest, brown hair stuck up in funny directions. "I couldn't sleep."

"It's fine. It's a good night for it. Apparently if we'd done this tomorrow, we would have been eaten alive. Or buried alive."

"Or flayed alive," Grace added.

"Yes, flayed. So, welcome!"

"Thanks?"

"Since we're both here, do you want to get to work?"

"What are you working on?" Omari asked. "Is it for the trials? We could give you a few pointers if you want."

Caedmon shifted his feet. "Actually, there is something I could use your help with. I really need to talk to my parents. My sister..." He faltered. "I just...have to talk to them. Is there an academy phone or...?"

Ellie tilted her head. Phones? Oh, the New World delights he had yet to share! "We have Fairy Letters, if that's what you mean."

Omari shook his head. "Sir Masten restricts access for draftees. Thinks it makes it harder to succeed when you're still

(119)

connected to your families." He smiled. "He's secretly a softy though. Sometimes he'll let you read letters your families send, so maybe you'll hear from them first. Don't worry about them not knowing the address; fairy magic always finds us."

Caedmon's head hung. "Oh…thanks."

Ellie's heart twinged. She didn't know much about the New World Realm, but…maybe Caedmon's parents wouldn't think to send a letter without an address on it.*

Cora, blond ponytail swinging furiously, strode into view, two swords strapped to her jeweled belt. "Wow, everyone's out tonight. I just caught Jorro, Kacie, and Thor sneaking cakes from the kitchens." She rolled her eyes. "Sir Masten will make them run laps tomorrow but whatever, not my problem. Hooray for Bert being sick!" She cringed. "That wasn't very chivalrous of me, was it?"

Omari laughed. "Well, Cora, we all know that's not why you're here anyways."

She tapped a finger against her lips. "True. Very true."

"Why were you made a knight?" Caedmon asked.

Good, Ellie thought. She appreciated a boy who did his research.

Sparks shone in Cora's eyes. "My excellent swordsmanship. Grace, I need your help. Immediately."

* That's the most preposterous thing I have ever heard. What is wrong with these people?

(120)

"Is everything okay?"

"No. I have a shoe disaster."

Omari's eyebrows lifted. "A shoe disaster?"

"Judge me and die. Grace?"

Grace glanced at Omari, shrugging. "I guess I should…"

"Go. I'll find you tomorrow."

Grace smiled and ran off.

Omari watched her go for a moment before shaking his head, as if remembering Ellie and Caedmon were still there. "Right! Yeah, can I help? Do you have questions about the trials?"

Caedmon nodded. "I *have* to become a knight. I can't be sent home no matter what."

Omari's smile was kind. "I wanted it that badly, too. You'll be fine. Just stay calm and know the trials can happen at any time."

Caedmon shook his head. "It's not that," he said, explaining the message he'd described to Ellie. He was blushing by the end. "Have *you* heard of Merlin sending people magical messages?"

"No, but I've been here long enough to believe anything can happen. And the Urokshi value integrity. If Roxie said Merlin sent you a message, I'd believe her. But malevotums…" He blew out a puff of air. "You're sure she said *malevotums*?"

"They're meant to be myths," Ellie told Caedmon. "But they're not." She absentmindedly rubbed her heart. "They're definitely not."

(121)

Omari's eyes were wide with horror. "Okay. Hold on a second. So, there's a curse hanging over the world, no one knows who cast it, and it's somehow making *other* wicked magical things wake up, including malevotums?"

Caedmon's face was grim. "Yep. And the more the evil spreads, the more likely everyone is at risk. Including my family. There were already two attacks in my hometown."

"And on my journey here," Ellie found herself saying, "I met a malevotum."

Caedmon paled. "Wait, *what*? Are you okay? Why didn't you say something? What happened?"

Omari looked just as worried. "Did it hurt you? Do you want me to take you to the healing ward?"

Ellie blinked at them, momentarily confused. They... cared. She'd never had anyone care before. "I'm okay," she remembered to say. "My fairy scepter saved me. But Caedmon's right: Something terrible brews. I can feel it." Even now, her witchcraft sensed it. Danger sizzled in the air. "I read that Excalibur can make you nearly invincible. That must be why Merlin wants Caedmon to find it." She frowned. "That doesn't explain why he would want you to become a knight, though."

"Merlin could read futures," Omari mused. "There must be a reason his magic picked you." Some boys would be jealous; he just sounded concerned, and it turned Ellie's heart into melting, lovesick goo.

After thirty minutes, Omari, Caedmon, and Ellie sat in a

(122)

circle, books on Excalibur, knighthood, and curses scattered around them.

Omari tossed aside a tome entitled *The Allure of a Witch's Toes and a Sorcerer's Nose: What to Do When Toads and Ferrets Come A-flocking* by Madame Mystérieuse.

Ellie discretely tucked the discarded book into her bag. The title sounded weird, and Ellie found it a little pretentious to call oneself mysterious,* but maybe it could help with her toad affliction.

A stroke of lightning like the one that had woken Ellie flashed on the far eastern side of the mountain.

A third stroke.

Her magic hissed, alarmed. Urgent. She sat up straighter, mind churning, the voice from the magic mirror suddenly loud in her head. What had she heard exactly? Something about securing the château, holding off a beast, mischief, and…"Far from their chambers," she murmured. Far from where they were all getting up to mischief, staying out of bed, stealing cakes and pies from the kitchens…

Maybe the voice she'd heard in the mirror *was* Sir Masten. And if it was him…and he was fighting some beast…they could be in serious danger.

Ellie's blood went cold. "Omari, is it *normal* for Bert to get sick? To not have curfew like this?"

---

* I beg your pardon?

(123)

"Not as far as I know. Have to enjoy it while it lasts."

Her heart thumped louder, faster. Saints above. "I think… something might be happening at the château."

A fourth stroke.

Omari looked to the sky and frowned. "That almost looks like Aurelius. The skyvor Sir Masten flies," he said in response to Caedmon's questioning look.

"Sir Masten?" Ellie squeaked, adrenaline pulsing, ideas brewing. "I heard him. In the mirrors. I thought I imagined it but…" Her magic flared again, as it had with the malevotum and the serpentelles, reaching out to protect her. Sensing she wasn't safe. "Something feels wrong."

Omari and Caedmon stood, their gazes eastward, as the whole sky turned veined and white.

"Sometimes the skyvor flies at night," Omari said slowly, as though even he wasn't convinced.

"What if Sir Masten's in trouble?" Caedmon countered. "And we're the only ones who know?"

The sky turned black. In the distance, someone screamed.

"We should go over there," Caedmon urged.

Omari nodded. "Quickest way to that side of the mountain is through the Witches' Wood."

They sprinted through the amphitheater, toward lithe, clawed trees. Ellie held her fairy scepter aloft, ignoring the swirl of witchcraft in her blood.

The chaos called to it.

(124)

Her fairy magic was too soft for this. Fungleberry juice and healing spells weren't enough for lightning bolts in untamed seas or nefarious creatures prowling the skies. She took a deep breath, trying to focus on pretty breezes, the sweetness of petals, the magic of the seasons. Good, pure fairy magic.

She could almost taste the roasted vegetables, almost see the pink and gold sparkles of her magic—

"We're...here," Omari panted, skidding to a halt before a bone-bleached gate seemingly carved from magic itself, for how it frothed and shifted in the moonlight. "The Witches' Wood." He hesitated. "It's normally off-limits to students."

The trees were elder and yew, birch and oak, and rarer species—dragon's claw and crooked finger, known for their magic, known for their hunger, known to speak to a witch's soul.

With shaking hands, Ellie opened the gate and guided them forth.

The tingle of her fairy magic died.

Immediately, shadows swirled around her arms, her witchcraft leaking from her soul, begging, needing to be seen. *No! Fairy magic! I need good fairy magic!*

But the moon hung low and shadows shifted through the trees. It was a reckoning for a witch, and her magic screamed to be released from its cage.

Ahead, lightning flashed, the air electric and burning.

Their race slowed to a crawl, stepping around shadows as if they were inky pools of poison intent to swallow and drown.

(125)

"Some of the most powerful spells and curses are cast at midnight," Ellie said to steady herself. "Did you know?"

She wrapped her arms around her stomach, willing the shadows to still. She couldn't let Omari see, for then he would know, and the reviling would begin. Then her life would be in danger. Caedmon's, too, for what would he do without a fairy godmother to help him?

Please, don't let them see. She wanted Omari's gaze on her, wanted his attention, but not right now, as her magic was spilling, threatening to reveal itself. *Let it be safe, let it be hidden.*

Fortunately, the night was dark, and Omari's and Caedmon's focus remained on the charred horizon. "Yes." Omari's throat bobbed. "Witches are the most powerful at night, aren't they?"

Ellie nodded. She had never practiced her witchcraft. Not once. But oh, the things she read in the dark. All her life, she had longed and feared to know this piece of her soul that itched to break free, so she studied, and she listened, and she learned all she could, as covertly as she could.

Perhaps this, she thought dismally, was why her Fairy Godmother application was rejected. Perhaps the Fairy Godmother knew Ellie hadn't truly renounced her witchcraft, much as she tried.

"And sorcerers' magic is the most powerful at midday," Ellie said, breathless with effort to keep herself contained, to

(126)

keep her magic small. The Witches' Wood called, beckoned. *Ignore, ignore, ignore.*

She nearly slumped in relief when the path of ash, lavender, and brittle golden leaves abruptly ended at the edge of the cliff—then she remembered why they marched, and what they stood to lose.

The cliffs were dark, alit only by a shrouded moon and faraway stars.

On instinct, Ellie clutched the starlight in her pocket, letting her fairy scepter fall limply at her side. As soon as she did, the clouds broke. The full moon shone bright and red.

But no skyvor, no creature of fang and scale. And no knight.

"Where's the skyvor?" Caedmon whispered.

A growl cut through the night. Claws scratched stone. Ellie clamped a hand over her mouth to rein in her scream. Perhaps she'd been hasty bringing her brand-new friends to cliffs of death.

"I don't know." Omari unsheathed a dagger at his waistband. "Have you taken a swordsmanship or magic lesson yet?"

"No?"

He gave them an anxious smile. "Okay...that's okay. Just, erm, try not to die."

"I'm beginning to think that should be the school motto," Caedmon grumbled, raising his fists as a loathsome creature heaved itself from the cliffside to the mountaintop.

Its black, spiked tail thrashed against the earth.

Bloodstained claws gouged the stone.

It scuttled toward them on eight legs—valiant skyvor and knight nowhere to be seen.

"Three against one, right?" Ellie squeaked.

Caedmon shot her an incredulous look. "Are you always so optimistic?"

"I've always found it's better—" She shrieked, sprinting from a spot in the ground the creature's tail thumped. "To look on the bright side!" Ellie rolled in the dirt, spitting out leaves, and squinted at the flashing sky.

The flashing sky!

Sir Masten's roar was loud enough to wake the mountain as he leapt from the skyvor. One sword in each hand, he landed on his feet atop the horrible creature's scaled, thorned back.

"Stay away!" He sprinted up the creature's hide.

Steel slashed scales.

It shrieked, limping backward.

Ellie grew dizzy—the monster gurgled blood.

At some point, Omari and Caedmon reached Ellie's side and dragged her to her feet. She thrust her fairy scepter to the sky. "Protect from harm and shield us from this foe!" A sparkling bubble of protective magic formed around Caedmon, Ellie, and Omari. She shouted the fairy charm again, and a second wrapped around Sir Masten.

But fairy magic wasn't made to battle monsters. The

(128)

creature spit acid and venom—it was breaking through Sir Masten's bubble. It would kill him. They would all die here, tonight.

"No!" Caedmon shouted as the creature's tongue split through Sir Masten's bubble and wrapped around his torso.

Ellie couldn't stop shaking.

Sir Masten would be devoured. He'd be gone. He—swung his sword and pierced the monster's eye.

The creature shrieked, whimpered, and, at last, slumped.

Dead.

The head knight strode toward them, bathed in red moonlight, two swords aloft, like he was the most powerful being on this earth, and not even creatures from darkened, evil places could hurt him.

And he was *furious*.

"What," he panted, "in the name of King Arthur, are you *doing here*?"

Caedmon stepped forward. "You said you were testing us on courage. So…we're…here to…" He glanced at the dead monster. "Help."

Sir Masten sheathed his swords and marched past them, leaves and twigs crunching under his boots. "A knight does not seek danger. Omari, I expected better of you. All three of you are henceforth disqualified from the Knights of the Round Table. Your memories shall be wiped, and you shall depart these lands at dawn."

(129)

FOURTEEN

CAEDMON

DISQUALIFIED? CAEDMON COULDN'T BE DISQUALIFIED! He'd just begun. He'd barely had a chance to prove himself. His mind buzzed, unable to focus, as Omari protested on their behalf.

Ellie's eyes burned. "Sir Masten, I *refuse* to accept your declaration. Caedmon will be a knight. It is his wish, and I shall stay until it is granted."

"You shall go because it is my command."

"Not this day, Sir Masten!"

He assessed them, expression shadowed in the night. "Go," he finally grunted, head hung low as he turned to the dead monster strewn across the leaves. "I have matters to attend to."

Caedmon's breath stilled. He stared and stared, as if through plated glass, unhearing, floating above his body.

The malevotum...it has returned.

All could be lost.

You will never be safe, never be safe, never be safe, never be safe.

"You told us to be brave!" Caedmon found himself shouting, as though a stranger had invaded his body. "You told us to be honorable! To do what is right no matter the cost. We are *here*, doing what is right, because of *you*."

"It was foolhardy." Sir Masten's voice was quiet. Resigned.

Caedmon grabbed him by the arm to turn him around. The knight was nothing but corded muscle, arms thick enough to squish him. His inner fire spluttered—but then Ellie joined his left, Omari his right—and somehow, he felt braver. "I don't know how to do magic. I don't know how to fight. And I don't know why I was chosen but I was. I came here to be a knight, and I'm not going home. Roxie said Merlin sent me a message. I have to think it was for a reason."

If Caedmon thought mentioning the legendary sorcerer would sway the knight, he was mistaken.

Sir Masten unstoppered a glass vial and spread dark liquid that smelled like licorice over the beast, which began to dissolve in smoke. "Come," he finally said. "Bert and the other knights will take care of the rest. I want to show you something."

"Where *are* the other knights?" Omari asked.

Sir Masten's gaze cut to the west. "They are protecting you. Or meant to be. How did you enter the Witches' Wood? It is enchanted so only sorcerers, witches, and their companions may enter."

Ellie squeaked.

"But, Sir, you're not a sorcerer," Omari pointed out.

(131)

"No, but all knights' lives are tied to Merlin's magic once anointed. Enough of his sorcery lives in our blood to bring us through the woods safely." He cricked his neck, marching back the way they'd come, the skyvor trotting alongside him. "Always gives me a migraine. Too much magic in here."

Ellie twitched all through the Witches' Wood, her arms locked around her chest. Caedmon couldn't blame her. The place made him queasy. Even he could feel the magic in the air. It was heavy. Thick. Like the air turned to syrup. And it seemed to...know. Want. Think. It lurched through his memories, rifling through thoughts kept buried and deep. He breathed freely when the shimmering gate creaked shut behind him. Omari shuddered, but none were as affected as Ellie, who slumped to the ground, whimpering.

Sir Masten passed her a small vial of amber liquid. "Here. Helps calm the nerves."

Ellie nodded wordlessly, sipping the drink.

Omari frowned. "Ellie, maybe you should go back inside. You look sick."

"I'm fine," she insisted, though her voice was hoarse.

Sir Masten helped her to her feet. "If you feel faint, lean on Aurelius. No warrior falls under the skyvor's watch." Aurelius raised a bloodstained talon and licked it.

Caedmon could think of many things he'd rather do than lean on the skyvor but Ellie obeyed, silently sipping her potion again. She looked up at Sir Masten, expression softening. "Thank you," she murmured.

Sir Masten nodded and guided them away from the magical woods, past the orchards, to the statue of a dragon clawing its way from the sea depths.

A red sun rose over its charcoal wing, lines of algae alighting so they almost looked like veins. Otherwise, there was nothing remarkable about the cliff. Soft grass, the same salty breeze that permeated the rest of the floating isle, and enormous birds singing to the brightening sea.

"This is where they stood." Sir Masten was quiet. In the light, he looked weathered, dark eyes bloodshot and tired. "There were others, of course, in the castle, around the grounds, but the true heroes...they were here, guarding the last of Arthur's strongholds the day Camelot fell." He unsheathed his sword and drew a circle around them. The ground shuddered, and from the earth rose a white stone tomb, dirt and moss and bramble falling away. The tomb was bare—but for six letters.

MERLIN

Caedmon felt momentarily dizzy. Merlin's tomb. His actual, real tomb. Even Omari gasped, and as Sir Masten knelt beside the stone and pledged his fealty, Caedmon had a suspicion this was not something most knights in training ever saw.

Still on bended knee, Sir Masten placed his hand on the tomb. "Merlin was among the knights, and together they stopped the worst of the foul magic from seeping into the mountain. This is where they say Merlin cast a spell to ensure there would always be knights to guard the realms. Even in his death. A tomb was created in his honor, though all those warriors burned that day."

Distant whales sang to the slip of moon, still visible in the brightening sunrise. "His magic fades. And the knights' power with it."

Omari reeled toward him. "What do you mean it fades?"

Sir Masten sighed. "Years ago, beasts like the one you saw—they never would have dared attack this mountain."

"But they dare now," Ellie said.

"They dare now. It is not the first, nor the last. In truth, the magic has been fading for centuries, but in the past few years, the situation has become dire. There's a curse that hangs above this land, of which I am sure Roxie informed you." He rolled his eyes, the most relatable gesture Caedmon had seen him make. "It is a leech upon our power. I fear the Knights of the Round Table will not survive for very long if the curse does not lift."

"Who cast the curse? *What* is the curse?" Omari asked.

"We know infuriatingly little. Only that the Knights of the Round Table are given sacred magic that has always allowed us to guard ancient gates that keep monsters from invading. We are Protectors of the Realms," he said softly. "But as this curse gains in strength, our ability to guard the gates weakens.

(134)

Creatures...monsters...are waking after centuries of sleep. And they're slipping through." Sir Masten shook his head. "Many years ago, a talented young man heard a message from Merlin's magic."

Caedmon's heart thundered against his rib cage.

"He believed that the only way for the knights to regain their complete power was to find and reforge Excalibur. It is true that finding it would be a mighty gift of magic to combat this curse." His face was grim. "But the knight died in the quest."

"You know about my message," Caedmon said quietly.

"I know what happens on this mountain." Sir Masten looked to the bloodstained sky. "You are not the first knight Merlin has spoken to, Caedmon Tuggle. Nor are you the first to seek Excalibur. Merlin believed in woven, united threads of fate, but his plans were never as clear as they seemed."

"Am I the first he has *told* to seek Excalibur?"

"No."

The word was a shard of glass in Caedmon's hope. For a moment, he'd almost felt special. Worthy.

"None before you have found it. Most drive themselves to ruin. Death. A lifetime of searching with no recompense." Shadows haunted his eyes. "I would not bestow such a fate on any man, let alone a boy barely strong enough to lift a sword."

Caedmon stood straighter. "I am strong."

Sir Masten eyed him, then threw his sword on the ground, clinking against the empty tomb. "Then lift my sword."

(135)

Caedmon's soul shriveled. He wasn't *that* strong. But he refused to seem intimidated, so he grabbed the hilt—and barely managed to heave it upright with one arm.

Sir Masten took it, his fingers calloused and rough, and placed it in its scabbard. "You are not strong enough to search for a weapon that, in the wrong hands, could kill us all."

Caedmon blinked back sudden, furious tears. From exhaustion. Humiliation. Desperation. Sir Masten was right: What was Caedmon doing looking for a sword he wouldn't even be able to lift?

Sir Masten's hand clapped his shoulder. "*Someday*, Caedmon, you may be strong. If you practice. If you work hard. As you grow. But not today. You still have time to be a boy."

"I *don't* have time. My family is in danger. My sister was already attacked."

Ellie whipped toward him, deathly still. "You didn't say the attack in your hometown was on your sister."

"Is she okay?" Omari asked.

Caedmon's cheeks heated, the same pressure he felt when Mom tried to talk to him about Jimmy building, boiling. He buried it all back down.

So he could function. So he could breathe.

Sir Masten appraised him, scratching his beard. "You were right," he said abruptly. "In the Witches' Wood. You acted bravely tonight. Foolishly. But bravely. I hereby revoke your expulsion. Ellie and Caedmon, you have a fair chance at becoming knights, just like the other draftees. You shall remain as well, Omari."

"That's not enough," Omari protested. "Merlin's magic said Caedmon's family will die if he doesn't find the sword."

"Can you at least tell us where not to look for it?" Caedmon pleaded. "How have other people failed before? Please, Sir Masten."

"This is not your fight."

"Someone disagrees." Ellie, still slumped over Aurelius, pointed at Merlin's tomb. At first, Caedmon didn't understand why, like she could see into a world none of them could. But slowly, a maelstrom of color and wind stirred above the silent stone. No messages, no hand reaching out to grab Caedmon's and guide him toward the sword. Only sunlight and whispers and—

"Magic," Ellie said. "That's Merlin's magic, isn't it?"

Omari circled it, eyes wide in awe. "What does it mean?"

Sir Masten did not answer them. He merely bowed his head over his sword, the brightening day gilding his chestnut hair, as though crowned. "Come," he said at last. "You all have class soon." His harrowed gaze settled upon Caedmon. "May the saints be with you in your trials ahead."

Though he must have meant the knights' trials, Caedmon couldn't help but think Sir Masten foresaw far more dangerous tests in his road ahead, and for his entire lonesome walk back through the château halls, he was left with a nagging feeling that he'd missed something.

(137)

FIFTEEN

ELLIE

AN HOUR AFTER EXPOSURE TO THE WITCHES' WOOD, Ellie still shivered, even tucked under her fluffy duvet. Sir Masten thought it was from overexposure to magic. If only he knew her secret.

Her body was exhausted, her heart heavy. Never in her life had she been so tested. Never had her witchcraft felt so at home, so alive, untamed, untempered.

But it was the walk back…after her fairy magic had failed to protect Sir Masten, would have failed to protect Caedmon and Omari, when she nearly lost control.

She was a fairy, not a witch, and she had to prove it.

Ellie couldn't stop crying as she raised her scepter over her head and cast her secret charm again. And again. And again. Gasping and sobbing through the magic. "Alas, I'm gone, concealed from very sight; not banned, but hidden, much to my delight." Her scepter shuddered. Her hand ached from gripping it so hard. No matter how many times she tried, the toothbrush she was attempting to hide refused to tuck itself into a secret spot behind her mirror.

She poured her curls into her hands and cried until her eyes itched. Weary, she finally took a deep breath and splashed her face with cold water.

Perhaps Mother was right. Perhaps Ellie wasn't good enough for the Fairy Godmother Academy.

Perhaps she should just accept her witchcraft and be done with it.

Of course...if she fully accepted her witchcraft, she might have a better chance at protecting Caedmon, granting his wish, and receiving entry into the Fairy Godmother Academy. There was a spell to accept one's magic, one she never dared utter, in a book she never dared admit to reading. Once cast, a witch would have full access to her powers and could never keep her magic secret again, for a silver moon mark would curl around her hand like a tattoo. Ellie still hadn't checked to see if the book had arrived in her bedchamber with her other belongings.

Perhaps she could just check...just see...

"Ellie?"

Ellie jumped at Caedmon's voice. She still couldn't believe he hadn't told her about his sister.

"Are you coming to our Curses and Spells class?"

Ellie groaned into her pillow. This mighty headache would surely be her doom.

(139)

"I...I brought you a muffin."

Slowly, Ellie rose. No one had ever brought her a muffin before. She stole one last glance at her wardrobe, where her spellbook may or may not be hidden beneath her clothes, and joined Caedmon for class.

Ellie's thighs burned by the time they finished climbing the glass turret where Dame Ethyl Botts greeted them with a toothy smile, easing some of Ellie's lingering heartache.

Blooming vines cascaded across glass, figments of emeralds dazzling in the light, while the oddest objects hovered in midair, some spinning, some growling—one spouting what smelled like chamomile tea.

Dame Ethyl clapped her hands. "Welcome! Pick a desk, any desk. I am sure many of you are unfamiliar with witchcraft and sorcery, so we will begin the knightly way: with gusto! Diving right in. Please note: Any derogatory language toward witches will result in immediate expulsion. You will be sent home without your memories, and, most likely, shoes. Got it?"

Everyone nodded. Ellie looked around in surprise, heart lifting a fraction.

"Good! Now then. One of the key skills you must acquire as a knight is the detection of curses. It could make the

(140)

difference between saving a life and dying pantsless in a blizzard. It is difficult in a classroom, presented before you neatly."

She muttered an incantation, and the window darkened, shifting to snarling panthers and swaying trees. "It is far more so with distractions."

Lucy LuBelle gasped and whispered to Nadia Farhi as Killian Rye whistled.

But of all people, it was Lorelei DeJoie who smiled at Dame Ethyl in what almost looked like respect. "You're a Registered witch."

"Nope! But I'm the best with Evermore dust you'll see in this castle," Dame Ethyl corrected. "You all need to knock my socks off with your Evermore skills if you have any hope of surviving with all your organs."

Caedmon scooted his desk closer to Ellie's and whispered, "What did she mean by a Registered witch?"

"Witches and sorcerers are all required to Register with the Realms' Magical Registry, led by the DeJoie family," Ellie whispered back. "Their powers are clamped when they're young to keep from developing."

Caedmon's brow puckered. "How does that even work? Is it like…like an amputation…? Does it hurt?"

Ellie lifted her arms. "I wouldn't know. But the side effects can be awful. Some witches and sorcerers who've been clamped can never use Evermore dust, and some lose other abilities,

(141)

like their sight or hearing." She glanced at Lorelei, lowering her voice even more. "The DeJoies don't like people to know. It doesn't happen to everyone, so they get away with it. Most go on to train with their limited abilities, which are still so much more powerful than Evermore dust, that people forget about them."

"Why though?" Caedmon pressed. "Why is it so bad for someone to have all their magic?"

"It's to make sure magic doesn't become contaminated again, creating more evil."

"What do you mean magic became contaminated?"

"That's what happened during the Fall of Camelot. Magic became too abundant, grew contaminated, and then the medieval plague broke out and most people lost all memory of magic. The towers of Camelot fell, King Arthur died, and Excalibur shattered. For a long time, they only clamped witches' powers. Not sorcerers. Now *no one* gets to live unclamped."

Ellie tilted her head from side to side, trying to picture those fateful days. Were people afraid? Did every witch's magic turn evil, or did it only happen to some? What about the younger witches, barely old enough to speak? Surely they weren't blamed…right? How did they feel having their magic clamped after the Fall?

"But not fairies?"

Ellie absentmindedly doodled, banishing the memory of her own horrifying near clamping. "Fairies aren't human, so

(142)

they don't have to follow the same rules. Not that the DeJoies don't try."

"But why—"

Dame Ethyl cleared her throat, shooting Ellie and Caedmon a warning look.

Ellie understood that clamping magic was for the safety of society and that she was a leper for not having done so. But it was a judgment she was willing to live with, for if clamping meant losing her ability to use magic entirely, or even to see or hear, she would gladly take exile.

It was, perhaps, the only thing she and Mother ever agreed on. Mother always insisted she remain unclamped at the risk of the DeJoies' wrath. That didn't mean Ellie could accept her witch magic—she couldn't recite the incantation to ignite it fully—but Mother didn't approve of others stopping its development, either. "Barbaric and shortsighted," she'd chide.

Ellie could still smell the antiseptic from the scheduled day of her almost-clamping. Still see the stark white walls, the polished steel wands curved into hooks like a pirate's.

"It will be painless," the doctor assured her, wielding the terrifying pirate wand.

Mother, donned in fur, her elegant dark hair swept into her signature chignon, peered down her nose at the small, mustached man. "Do I receive a guarantee?"

"Pardon, madame?

(143)

"You've claimed it will be painless; you must administer a guarantee, so that if Ellie has the slightest inkling of pain, you can be properly punished for your inept practice."

"Inept? Madame—"

Her mother held up a lone, gloved finger, demanding silence.

She sniffed.

Sneered.

And took Ellie's hand.

They rarely held hands anymore—not at the mature age of six, when Ellie was meant to be through with such childlike dealings—but that day, she took her hand. They were on the same team. Her mother would protect her. "Come near this girl again and I will see to it that you spend your remaining days in a dungeon." They marched out of the office and never looked back, the doctor too terrified of Mother's standing at court to report them.

Ellie didn't know where her magic came from. Mother wasn't a witch. She claimed Father wasn't a sorcerer either, though Ellie had never met him. He died when she was just a baby. According to textbooks, witchcraft was a recessive gene. Like a family illness.

But for all her coldness, Mother made sure Ellie was never parted from this core piece of herself. She'd protected her ever since, placing her in Roses and Needles Finishing School, entrusting her lifetime friend, Headmistress Olga, to protect Ellie's secret.

(144)

A tap on Ellie's knee jolted her out of her thoughts. "Ellie?" Caedmon prodded.

Ellie snapped back to attention. "S-sorry. I got lost."

Caedmon peered at her in a funny way. Like he understood. Because he sometimes got lost, too.

"Caedmon…about your sister…"

He pressed his lips together, face turning white. "She's fine. She…she'll be fine."

Because she had to be, Ellie realized. Because he couldn't face anything else. She nodded and gave him her brightest smile. "Okay."

"Unfortunately," Dame Ethyl was saying, "as we are not witches or sorcerers, we're not able to detect the full nature of the curses around us, but you *can* develop ways to sense magic set to ensnare you and learn how to manipulate Evermore dust to protect you."

Ellie's heart thundered. If she meant…

If Ellie truly understood…

"It starts with your sense of smell. A good knight follows their nose. Depending on the severity, curses can smell metallic. Sometimes they're unusually sweet, to mask the vile magic beneath."

Ellie shot her hand into the air. "Dame Ethyl, were you saying that in order to fully understand a witch's curse…you need a witch?"

"Yes," Lorelei interrupted. "Obviously. I've already been taught that. Because I'm a princess."

(145)

"Are you sure you don't just need a really talented fairy? Or a gremlin? What about an elf?"

Lorelei eyed her strangely. "*No*, only witches can read another witch's magic."

Ellie was in freefall. If there truly was a curse about these lands...only another witch could understand it.

She barely paid attention the entirety of the class, head too heavy and full. From a faraway world, Caedmon mentioned meeting her for lunch as the other draftees left the glass turret.

"Ellie?" Dame Ethyl sat on the edge of the desk beside her. "Are you all right?"

"You know there's a curse," Ellie whispered, as if saying the words made them all too true. "You must know."

Dame Ethyl started. "How did you—"

"Can you hear it?" Ellie asked desperately. "Do you know what it means?"

"I know it's there. We all know it's there. But no." Dame Ethyl laughed ruefully. "Irony of worlds. Evil has come, like we all feared, and now we need a witch."

"Well, then get someone!"

"We tried."

"And?"

"This is advanced stuff, kid. Far beyond your level." Ellie didn't budge. Dame Ethyl sighed. "When people are clamped, they lose the ability to read magic beyond their own power." Dame Ethyl wandered to the glass wall, overlooking the

(146)

turbulent sea. "This curse…is beyond any Registered witch's or sorcerer's reach."

Ellie's heart sank, realization dawning. "Which means… whoever cast it is Unregistered."

"Yes. It would take a witch or sorcerer with equally unclamped power to understand it."

Equally unclamped. Someone like Ellie. Dazed, she grabbed her bag and trudged toward the tower steps. Doing this would break the Fairy Godmother rules. *No intentional practicing of witchcraft.* She'd skirted by for years, as all her witchiness was entirely unintended. But this, to listen for a curse on the wind, would be a leaning in, when she ought to be leaning far, far away. "Is there *anyone* who can help?" Ellie asked.

"The only known, respected witch the DeJoies have allowed to remain Unregistered is Loreena Royenale, because of her extraordinary gifts. But she's a recluse. We've reached out. Haven't heard a peep."

"What will happen?" Ellie asked on the threshold of the tower. "If you don't understand the curse?"

"We don't know. That's the problem. We know it hangs all around us. And we have no idea why. We don't know who cast it or where to look for danger. So I suppose…anything could happen."

Although not as irredeemable as spell casting, listening for magic could still hurt Ellie's chances at getting into the Fairy

Godmother Academy. And yet…how could she grant Caedmon's wish if she didn't?

And the deeper question: What was right?

What was good?

What would make her feel whole?

Ellie cradled herself as she realized what her answers meant. Tonight, she must return to the Witches' Wood. Tonight, she would discover what curse hung above this isle.

Tonight, she must be brave. No matter the cost.

SIXTEEN

CAEDMON

CAEDMON WASN'T INTENDING TO BREAK CURFEW TWO nights in a row. He'd barely managed to survive expulsion his first night; he couldn't risk a second.

But with the château's twists and turns, Caedmon was completely lost. He couldn't even tell if he was in the right wing of the building. Didn't his bedchamber face west? As he retraced his steps through an airy, arched hallway, lit only by a waning moon, there was no sign of the Sword Garden. Only the salty breeze and rolling grass, rippling into the rocky cliffside.

At the end of the hallway, he turned right, planning to loop back around, when a glimmer of firelight caught his eye through a cracked door. Slowly, he pushed it open.

Rows upon rows of swords lined the walls, some curved and elegant, others small but lethal, like a dagger for a heart. An iron candelabra, ivory wax molded to its sides, swung in the evening breeze, illuminating concentric ruby and gold circles, lackluster under a thick sheen of cobwebs and dirt.

It was a training arena. It looked as though it hadn't been used in years. Decades. Caedmon placed his palm against the walls, frescoes of a thousand warriors riding into battle blurred beneath a film of dust.

Lift my sword.

Sir Masten's challenge still burned his memory. He'd barely been able to do it. He'd failed. He hadn't been able to detect any curses in Dame Ethyl's class either, and his Outsmarting Dangerous Beasts lesson went horribly from the moment he admitted he'd never had afternoon tea with a centaur. Sure, he squeezed it in between homework and soccer practice, just like most seventh graders.

You should just go home, a small voice whispered to his heart. Complete and utter exhaustion gnashed out with blackened teeth. It wanted to drown him. To keep him in a dark place where monsters dwelled. He took a deep breath, steadying himself against the wall.

What was Caedmon even doing here? Jimmy had been the risk-taker, the adventurous one. Once, he managed to persuade Caedmon to skip school and take the train down to Chicago. They spent all their savings on a football game, and Jimmy fabricated an amazing excuse that involved a hospital visit, a llama set loose in their middle school, and a fake broken arm—cast included. Jimmy would have probably already found Excalibur. But Caedmon wasn't made for this.

"I have news of your sister."

(150)

Caedmon jerked toward the gruff voice as Sir Masten strode into the training arena, candlelight flickering across his ruddy face.

He looked less haunted than when they last spoke, the creases in his forehead smoother. He smiled, eyes crinkling. "She lives, Caedmon."

Caedmon took a deep breath, like he'd been holding it for days. Alive. Carly was alive. Safe. Not with Jimmy. Not gone.

He gave a shaky nod, not trusting his voice for several seconds. "Thank you," he finally rasped. "Will...is...," he struggled.

"I sent scouts to your hometown after we spoke; she seems to have made a full recovery."

His heart leapt. "Are the malevotums gone?" Could he be so lucky?

Shadows returned to Sir Masten's gaze. "No. Not yet. In fact, they attacked again. A teenage girl by the name of Katie Williams."

Caedmon nodded wordlessly, ice flooding his bones. Katie Williams's younger brother Peter was on Jimmy's baseball team. They all used to hang out together before...before the death. Before Caedmon stopped seeing anyone.

Poor Peter...

And Caedmon's parents were still in danger. Merlin's message still rang true.

But Carly is okay, that same hopeful voice from before whispered.

(151)

Ellie's voice, he realized.

Right now, for a second, he could let himself breathe.

He'd spent so long feeling numb that he couldn't laugh or cheer. But something within him cracked open, light shining through. He met the head knight's gaze and smiled. "Thanks, Sir Masten," he said again, stronger this time.

Sir Masten clapped his shoulder and strode around the arena. "I'm surprised I found you here. This room hasn't been used in centuries."

Goose bumps rippled down Caedmon's spine. *Centuries.* "Why not?"

The knight's eyes glittered. "No one has looked. The château has many secrets, Caedmon. I don't pretend to know them all. It doesn't reveal every room to every person. Just like a person doesn't reveal all their secrets to everyone they meet."

"I wasn't looking. I just got lost."

"Aye," he grumbled, rubbing his beard. "Maybe that's the bloody point."

"Sorry?"

Sir Masten was silent as he appraised him. "That friend of yours is sharp. Ellie?"

Caedmon nodded, throat dry.

"She was right. Saints help us, but she was right. Merlin's magic spoke as I refused to help you. I'm a soldier, Caedmon. I'm not a sorcerer. I don't know why magic speaks to one and not another. I don't know why the other knights he's spoken

(152)

to have died. I know how to protect. Defend. I don't believe you will find Excalibur, and I highly suggest you abandon all hope of ever doing so." Sir Masten shook his head, as if this was against his better judgment, and tossed Caedmon a small wooden sword. "But if you do find it, you have to be able to pick it up."

Caedmon frowned at the toy sword. "Even if I can use it, I'm not sure I can fight with something that heavy."

Sir Masten pressed his lips together in thought. "I don't like to send boys into battle, so perhaps I was...hasty in my judgment. You should know that Arthur was a warrior who would be a king. But once, he was just a boy. Excalibur was not made for a warrior king. It was made for a boy with indomitable courage." The knight gave him a wolfish grin. "And some skill with a blade. Pick that up, and do not stop. To stop is to die, to tire is to die, and you will not die by sword, Caedmon Tuggle. Not if you train with me."

Caedmon nodded, and, meeting his gaze, he believed him.

"Pick up that sword and hold it above your head."

Caedmon blinked. "That's it? *That's* the training? This thing is light."

"It won't be after an hour."

"An *hour*?"

"You want to train? You want to be a knight? You were not drafted to sit at a desk and recite what we tell you. To be a knight, a *true* knight, takes work. It takes heroism. It takes

(153)

more than you will have ever poured into anything in your life. Do you understand? Do you want to be a guardian? A protector? A knight of the realms whom the rest of the world relies upon?"

Caedmon sucked in a breath. "Yes." And he meant it. Not just for his family, he realized. But for all of it.

"Then lift. Your. Sword."

Caedmon obeyed, holding it high above his head as Sir Masten circled him.

"This is a matter for knights, not draftees, so I will say only this, and then we will not speak of the curse or Excalibur again: We've looked for Excalibur everywhere we can. We've never looked where we can't."

Caedmon's heart skipped. "Where can't you go?"

The knight's eyes twinkled. "Beyond the realms of knights."

"But I thought the knights presided over all the realms."

"Yes, well, if this were easy, someone would have reforged the sword by now."

Caedmon stayed in that position until his muscles ached, and sweat dampened his shirt, and in that hour, Sir Masten spoke of Camelot—of horselike creatures of the night called chevolants who guarded the once all-powerful witches, of the legendary dragons that swooped over golden spires. Gone, but not forgotten.

For in their knighthood, the Knights of the Round Table

fought against the forgetting. The forgetting of valiance, of Merlin, of magic, of all they once stood for: the faith that Protectors of the Realms would never abate. That they would fight for what was right and what was good. No matter the cost.

So, Caedmon held the piece of wood above his head until his arms felt like they'd break. He would not tire. He would not stop. Even through the pain, even as that monstrous exhaustion nipped at his mind and tried to drag him down, he smiled, Ellie's voice drifting through his head: *not this day.*

SEVENTEEN
ELLIE

"ELLIE, I DON'T UNDERSTAND WHAT WE'RE DOING." Caedmon fumbled to clasp his cape.

He'd mentioned something about Jell-O arms—about holding a piece of wood above his head—something about exhaustion. She couldn't be sure. She was awake, she was insistent, and nothing would slow her down.

For she had to do this. She had to listen to the curse, and Caedmon deserved to be there.

For the first time in her life, she would reveal her secret. And pray to the saints she would not come to rue the day.

"Just come with me."

He grumbled something incoherent, stumbling through the stone archway after her.

A slithering across strewn leaves outside the open corridor quickened Ellie's heart. Bert? Holding her breath, Ellie flattened herself against the wall until it passed.

"Just tell me what we're doing."

Ellie's breath hitched, every limb sparking alive in fear.

And...hope.

Ellie had never had true friends before. The kind who brought her blueberry muffins when she wasn't well or asked about her toads without mocking her. Even Bianca liked him, and she was the pickiest cat alive.

He will revile you.

He will tell the DeJoies. They will lock you away.

She squashed the voices down into their crevices and marched to the Witches' Wood. Her head was high, her boots were laced and black, her knightly cape a weave of midnight in the wind. She was meant to be a fairy. She was meant to leave this château and find her true life elsewhere.

And yet she marched all the same.

At the edge of the creaking bone gate, Ellie paused, casting one last look over her shoulder. The knights' glass towers glittered in the moonlight, enormous, emerald birds swooping forth. She should go back inside. She should return to her room, to her fairy spells, to learning how to cast the secret charm without her witch magic intruding.

"Ellie?"

She gritted her teeth, steeling herself against the shadows and whispers of the dark. Witches weren't meant to be afraid of the night. It was when they were powerful. But Ellie was afraid. Perhaps years of denying her witchcraft had lessened it somehow. Perhaps she couldn't do this. And the fear that haunted, keeping her away from dreams…perhaps she would never be a very good fairy or a very good witch. She was both, yet neither.

Ellie took a shuddering breath as she opened the creaking gate and led Caedmon to the heart of the wood. For it had to be here. She didn't trust her voice to speak, so she would show.

"Sit," she commanded.

Caedmon stared at her. With a reluctant grunt, he plopped to the dirt. "Ellie, I—"

"The curse was cast by someone who's Unregistered," she blurted.

Caedmon blew out a puff of air, like he was resigning himself to having this very confusing conversation. "Okay…but didn't you say everyone has to Register?"

"They do. It's illegal not to. And really rare."

"But…that would mean that the curse caster is more powerful than any of the Registered witches or sorcerers, right?"

"Yes."

He tried scrambling to his feet but Ellie held him down. "I'm not finished. If the person who cast the curse is a witch, another Unregistered witch will be able to hear it."

"But you just said that's really rare."

"I…" For the first time, Ellie's voice snagged. *Lock her away, keep our families safe. Lock her away for the hope of better days.*

Ellie squeezed her eyes shut. Now. She had to do this now. Or she never would. Or...she would never know how it felt to be free. To not have to hide from someone.

Her fingers brushed against her star.

A witch's hope, her mother had called it. She clutched it, hoping, wishing, and with a whimper, she released the grip she had on her magic, like loosening a breath held underwater too long. Her magic unfurled, gasping for air—and then settled about her, wreathing shadows around her arms.

Such darkness, such wickedness, such—

A woodland wind blew, cinnamon and cloves, seaspray and fire, and with it, starlight and moonlight and all the secret colors of the night came to life in a maelstrom of magic around her. Glimmers of light refracted off her cape—whirls of magenta, pops of emerald, sapphire, and ruby, swirling like multicolored stars, dancing through her curls, billowing her cape in a night-kissed wind, flapping around her black boots as silver crescents looped around her wrists like bracelets of moon.

Tears leaked from Ellie's eyes. It was...beautiful. Just as her starlit veil for Bella had been. And, in the smallest corner of her heart, she felt like she'd come home.

Slowly, Caedmon stood. Just as slowly, Ellie met his gaze. He looked at her with awe. Wonder. But no hatred. No fear. "You're an Unregistered witch."

"No one can ever know," she whispered.

(159)

His gaze drifted to the magic swirling around her like fireflies. "Maybe they should…"

Ellie's heart was relentless. It pounded and it rattled and it was so afraid. "But…witches are evil. They brought down Camelot."

He laughed. "You're the least evil person ever."

Ellie let her arms drop, the magic subsiding. Now that she wasn't holding the witchcraft back, it didn't hurt to be surrounded by its intensity anymore.

He nudged her shoulder. "Do witches really ride brooms? Are you going to start wearing all black now?"

She laughed with him, her heart lighter than it had ever felt. "No. But the black does help block out other people's magic."

"Will you turn someone into a toad if I don't like them?"

"I don't think the Fairy Godmother would approve."

He grinned. "We'd change them back. Come on, it'll be fun!"

She giggled. "You seem…different."

He shrugged. "Sir Masten told me tonight my sister is alive, so…I'm feeling better than normal, I guess."

Ellie blinked, staring at him. *And you're only telling me this now?!*

His grin turned sheepish. "I don't like…talking about stuff. But yeah. The malevotums are still pretty dangerous."

That smile dimmed. "And my parents might get attacked. But…Carly's okay for now."

Ellie bounced on her toes. "Ooh, I'm so pleased!"

Caedmon's smile fell as he watched the slivers of moon dance around them. "So…the curse was cast by an Unregistered witch like you."

Ellie shook her head. "I don't know yet. It could have been a sorcerer. I…I have to listen. I've never practiced witchcraft before so I don't know if I'll even hear anything." How Ellie was meant to hear a curse, she had no idea. But she had to try. For the knights, for herself…and for Caedmon, her first friend, she would lean in to her magic.

Caedmon nodded, giving her space as Ellie sat in the hollow of a dragon claw tree, its one golden eye knotted and simmering, gnarled branches cocooning her from the wind-tossed magic that sizzled in the air. She dug her fingernails in the soil. Listen. She was meant to listen.

Ellie took a deep breath. *This isn't spell casting*, she reminded herself. With all the magic in these woods, the Fairy Godmother might never know. She might never see.

Owls hooted. Crinkled leaves rustled like parchment, Caedmon cleared his throat, and the sea crashed against the frothing stone dragon, mermaids slapping tails in the turbulent waters below.

She scowled. This wasn't working.

(161)

Listen more, a small voice in her heart whispered. *Listen to the in-between spaces.*

In between the crashing sea, in between the waves, the rocks, the crinkling leaves and Caedmon's breathing…there was magic. It pulsed, and it lived, and it breathed, and it—

Ellie gasped. It sickened.

She instinctively grabbed her starlight for good luck—and then she heard it. A curse foul enough to stoke fear in the hearts of knights. Foul enough to turn islands to rubble and bones to memories.

"It's another witch," Ellie rasped, eyes flaring open. "It—" Her head pounded as magic poured in. The words were garbled, twisted. She felt as though she'd missed something. But at least it was more than they knew yesterday. "'This knight of new for realms of old, is one. My curse is cast beneath this midnight sun. Bring me to the crescent moon. Let this magic unspool the knightly doom. Let it call upon the lost. The magic is mine.'"

Ellie took a deep breath. "*Let it call upon the lost….*That must be why lost evil magic is waking up." Dread spooled in her gut. She sat on her hands to hide their shaking. "The knight of new for realms of old…that has to be *you*, Caedmon. You're the only draftee this year from the New World Realm."

Caedmon's eyes widened. "Roxie said that she thought my bones called to the curse caster. But what could she want with me?"

(162)

"Maybe…maybe she has fortune-telling magic like Merlin did. And…maybe like Merlin, she knew you might become a knight and find the sword. And for some reason, she doesn't want you to?"

"Because if I find Excalibur," Caedmon said slowly, "I'll be able to give the knights their strength back, which would stop the evil magic she's unleashing, so she wants to stop me?"

"I guess?"

Caedmon pressed his palms to his eyes. "We have to talk to Roxie. She was the one who told me about the curse and Merlin's message. Sir Masten won't help more than he already has."

"But the Urokshi famously keep their whereabouts hidden. I read that not even the knights who've lived here for decades have been able to find out where they live."

"Then we'll have to try harder," Caedmon said. "Because if anyone can help, it's Roxie. We're going to find her."

EIGHTEEN

CAEDMON

ELLIE'S SEARCH FOR ROXIE WAS RELENTLESS.

Unfortunately, their tactics weren't working. Whenever they asked the Urokshi about Roxie or where they lived, all of them glided away, clicking their fingers and whispering in a rhythmic language that reminded Caedmon of bones and stones smacking together.

They told Omari of their discovery, omitting the whole Ellie-is-secretly-an-illegal-witch part, but even he didn't know where the Urokshi lived.

A week later, they still didn't have answers, so Ellie focused solely on the curse. She swore it sounded strange, and consumed so many books trying to understand why, she'd taken to walk-reading, which meant Caedmon spent half his time preventing her from wall-crashing.

When he wasn't in class or with Ellie, Caedmon poured his energy into swordsmanship training—which didn't amount to much. He'd progressed from holding a tiny wooden sword to a slightly less tiny wooden sword. But he obeyed Sir Masten's orders, meeting him at dusk for his extra training every night in preparation for the impending trials.

With each passing day, Caedmon grew more nervous. Was his family safe? Were the attacks on Carly and Jimmy random? What did the witch want with him? Would he be able to beat the other draftees in the trials?

He trained in strength, in courage, in knowledge.

The next trial tested his magic.

Dame Ethyl Botts welcomed draftees into an empty classroom, frowning at Killian Rye. He was trying to shake a tiny, mossy, fancy-coat wearing creature off his elbow, knocking into people in what looked like an awkward dance. "I—hate—gremlins!"

"Aha, caught your secrets!" the gremlin shrieked, before slamming into the wall.

Dame Ethyl sighed. "Poor Gernie. Happens every year." She took a swig from her flask and leaned back in a wing-tipped chair. "*Buongiorno!* Welcome to your third trial." She hiccupped. "Everyone find a desk. Come, come, ignore the gremlins. That's right. You too, Killian." Once everyone was seated, she waved her jeweled hand at the desks of cauldrons, bottles filled with gold dust, and an assortment of ingredients. "Evermore dust! Simple enough, right? Don't mess up too badly and you should keep your organs."

Caedmon's heart pounded as he took his place behind one of the desks. He really needed his organs. Was he supposed to drink the bottle, like in Poison Resistance class? Or maybe use the magic to turn it into a gremlin?

He peeked at Ellie, whose forehead scrunched, freckles bright, fists clenched, in what he'd coined her Determined Pose.

"Your task this trial, if you choose to accept it, and not be sent home with your memories wiped, etcetera, etcetera, is to create your own spell. The scenario is this: You have been sent to rescue a lost child, only to arrive and discover poison-breathing boars roam the lands. You have five minutes and the following ingredients in your arsenal, and no weapons. What do you do?"

Run? Really, really fast?

Dame Ethyl Botts clapped her hands. "Impress me with your creativity and magic. And..." She flipped a sand hourglass upside down. "Begin!"

Lorelei DeJoie's hand shot in the air as everyone else dove for the empty vials and bottles filled with ingredients like "pumpkin rind chewed on by borker bat" and "fairy daisy jam."

"Dame Ethyl?"

"Ms. DeJoie?"

"This is strictly forbidden. The DeJoie family will not stand for such insubordination. My grandmother will be greatly displeased."

(166)

Dame Ethyl took another sip from her flask. "You tell your grandmother that if she has an issue with how I run my trials, she's welcome to come speak to me." Her grin turned devilish. "Tell her I remember Tahiti."

Lorelei pursed her lips. "What's Tahiti?"

"*Where* is Tahiti," Dame Ethyl corrected. "Now make me a spell."

Lorelei blushed, but unstoppered her bottles and quieted.

Caedmon's brain was a fuzzy, empty mess. Ellie was doing something strange with her arms, swinging them like a windmill in opposite directions every three seconds, Lucy LuBelle sang to hers, while Killian blew on his concoction—though probably because it had caught fire.

Lorelei finished before Caedmon even examined the full ingredient list. With a huff, she placed a bottle, now the color of turtle shells, on Dame Ethyl's table, and turned on her heel.

"Your spell?" Dame Ethyl called after her.

"You won't need one." The smallest smirk played on her face. "The magic is potent enough to work on its own. Drink it, and you'll heal from any poison for a year."

The room quieted. Lucy stopped singing. "You incorporated healing magic?" she asked.

"She didn't," Killian protested. "That's way too advanced. I don't believe it."

Lorelei flipped her golden hair over her shoulder. "May I be excused now? My tiaras require polishing."

(167)

Dame Ethyl's eyes sparkled. "Class, please clap for Miss DeJoie."

The response was unenthusiastic at best. People either ignored her or openly scowled.

Lorelei's smirk slipped.

Despite being a princess, she wasn't liked by a single person here. Caedmon couldn't blame them, but it didn't stop his insides from squirming with guilt as her bottom lip trembled, tears rolled down her cheeks, and she sprinted from the classroom.

Dame Ethyl Botts cleared her throat. "You have four minutes remaining."

Caedmon didn't have space in his brain to spare Lorelei a second thought. He had to come up with something—now.

"Remember: You must *feel* the magic."

Caedmon was growing desperate; his mind was blank, and his nerves too jangled to start combining random ingredients. What if they exploded? He raked his hands through his hair.

"Think of what you want to exist," Dame Ethyl prompted.

What Caedmon *wanted* was to find Excalibur, save his family from joining Jimmy, and not need to do this trial. He eyed the ingredients again. He had a feeling that if a simple spell could attain those things, there wouldn't be centuries of dead knights on the trail of a lost sword. He picked up the pumpkin rind. What had Dame Ethyl just said? You feel it? He scowled. All he could feel was leftover pumpkin slime.

(168)

"Two minutes."

Sweat beaded down his neck. Five of the ingredient labels weren't even in English. One was German, which, thankfully, he could read,* but a few were written in markings from a different alphabet.

"Thirty seconds."

Without a second thought, Caedmon dumped the contents of every ingredient and the entire bottle of magic into his cauldron. He cringed, waiting for it to explode in his face—but... nothing. His cauldron bubbled with murky, bumpy slop, reeking of sewage. Somehow, this was worse.

"Your time is up."

Caedmon stared into his cauldron like it could drown him. He'd completely, utterly failed. Only a pigtailed girl two seats away from him, sniffling before her untouched ingredients, seemed worse off. In a flurry of tears, she sped out of the class.

She'd be gone by morning.

Caedmon's heart raced. If he wasn't careful, he'd join her.

"Caedmon?" Ellie's voice was soft. Pitying.

He turned away, keeping his head down. "I'll be there in a minute."

She lingered, like she'd say something else, before leaving.

He took a deep breath. He couldn't get enough air into his

---

* You are ever so welcome.

lungs. What was he *doing* here? The dark exhaustion lashed out. Pulled him down.

Sleep.

He needed to sleep.

"You're a logical one, aren't you?"

Caedmon jerked. He thought he was alone, but Dame Ethyl Botts strode toward him, frizzy curls bouncing. She peered into his cauldron and chuckled. "Logical minds help the world go 'round. But they're not always great on their feet. They get stuck in their heads, thinking when they should be *doing*."

Caedmon nodded, trying to focus, trying to listen, to be better.

But he really needed sleep.

"Sometimes, you'll have all the instructions. But other times, you'll need to think on the fly. This trial was testing your ability to improvise as much as your skill with Evermore magic." She let out a friendly cackle. "I watched you. You didn't improvise. You froze, and then poured everything into the pot!"

"I don't understand..." His voice cracked. He cleared his throat. "I don't understand how I'm supposed to improvise if I don't know what the ingredients do."

She squinted. "Are you calling my trial unfair?"

"No!"

She cackled again. "Well, you should! It wasn't fair. You know little about magic. But you also froze. You panicked. A trial in a classroom, surrounded by knights who would lay

(170)

down their lives to protect you, is not a crisis. Someday, you might experience true danger."

The image of Sir Masten battling an invading monster burned his mind. Maybe sooner than Dame Ethyl realized.

"Think: What could you have done differently?"

Caedmon blinked. He had no idea. If he'd studied the ingredients more, sure, but…

Jimmy's face flashed in his mind. What would he have done?

He would have made it fun, he realized. And he would have tried something. Anything. He would have gone for it—fearlessly.

"Stop worrying," Jimmy assured him as he dipped his paintbrush into the vat of white. "Our moms will love it."

Caedmon wasn't so sure—but Jimmy had already started painting the grass vibrant white.

That morning, their moms had complained that it wasn't going to snow for Christmas, so, never to be outdone by nature, Jimmy had found a bucket of white paint in his garage and insisted they painted their front lawns. Next stop: their third-grade teacher's house.

"That way, they'll look out the window and it'll be just like snow!" he claimed.

Caedmon plopped beside him in the cold dirt. "What if they don't like it?"

(171)

Jimmy stopped to paint his face. "Better fake snow than no snow, right? They'll love it. It's our Christmas present. Here!" Jimmy dumped a box of tinsel on the wet paint and grinned. "See? Now it's Christmassy!" He handed Caedmon a paintbrush and red ornament. "You try."

Still nervous, Caedmon splashed white paint against a barren tree and hung the ornament from its branch.

He smiled. Jimmy was right. Much more Christmassy. But he still thought Mom might get mad.

Jimmy beamed. "See? Everything's fine."

"But…how do you always know things are fine? What if they're not?"

Jimmy shrugged, sunlight brightening his freckles. "Because that's not as much fun. Sometimes you just have to do what's fun, you know? Oh!" His face lit up. "Let's go get pillows! Feathers will help make it look even snowier!"

People were still finding traces of tinsel, paint, and feathers in Boulder Falls by Saint Patrick's Day.

Their moms had not liked it.

At first.

But over the years, it became their favorite story, until no one could tell it without laughing.

"I could have…had fun with it?" Caedmon answered. "And…tried it, even if I didn't know if it'd work?"

Dame Ethyl smiled kindly. "That's it, kid. You could have

(172)

focused on what you wanted to create. It's *magic*, Caedmon! Sure, yeah, it's a science, but it's also an art. It's..." She looked around and smiled, spreading her arms wide. "Part of everything. You might have botched it, but a lot of those draftees botched it—do you really think a small ball of fire will save a child from poison?" She laughed, referring to Killian's magic. "No! But there was *intention* there. Focus, and the magic will follow." She winked. "And maybe study a few key magical ingredients while you're at it."

Caedmon nodded silently.

"Hey, kid, you're not outta the game yet." Her eyes sparkled. "C'mere. Let me show you something." With a click of her fingers, a scroll appeared in her palm. She handed it to Caedmon. At first, he didn't understand, when...

CAEDMON TUGGLE

BOULDER FALLS,

WISCONSIN, NEW WORLD REALM

BORN MARCH 6, 2007—FOUND OCTOBER 31, 2014

Caedmon's heart leapt. It was one thing to be drafted. It was another to have proof. They *found* him. They wanted him here.

"Caedmon Tuggle, your name has been on the draft for five years. Merlin's magic wouldn't have drafted you if you weren't capable of being a knight." Her eyes twinkled. "So go *be* a knight."

(173)

NINETEEN
ELLIE

TODAY WAS A GLORIOUS DAY.

Today, Ellie got to teach Caedmon about *magic*.

His alarming near failure in their last trial aside, Caedmon had great potential if he could simply quiet his mind and focus on his *feelings*. Oh, what fun this would be.

They agreed to meet in the southern sitting room after dinner. The perfect ambience. Gold trees snaked up teal walls, curling into a latticework of crowns over their heads. She set up shop by the fire, creating rows of ingredients and cauldrons in various sizes and shapes on the plush rug.

Thankfully, other students polishing daggers and practicing spells gave her a respectably wide berth, and in the spare moments before Caedmon arrived, she worked on her fairy secret charm.

An hour later, her hair had reached ultimate frizz level, she could barely hold back tears, and Bianca had started a war with Mr. Petalbloom over the latest pebble she was trying to hide.

"Okay, little pebble, just hide under the chair. Please hide under the chair? Please?" Clutching her fairy scepter, Ellie recited the charm, but instead of zooming into the hiding space, the pebble disappeared.

"No! Bad pebble! You come back here right now!"

"...Hi."

Ellie shoved her curls out of her face and looked up at Caedmon, who eyed her like she'd sprouted extra ears. She belatedly realized how strange she must look, surrounded by piles of rocks.

"You okay?"

"No, Caedmon Tuggle, I am not okay. My fairy charm isn't working and I will never get into the Fairy Godmother Academy until it works and oh, I am just *furious*."

He plopped on the floor beside her. "Oh."

She shot him a glare. Emotions? Hello?

"That sounds...bad," he said with the shocking eloquence of a door. "Why isn't the fairy charm working?"

She slumped, casting the stones and her discarded fairy scepter withering stares every few seconds. "Because I'm—" She glanced around, but everyone studied as far away from her as possible. "A witch," she whispered. "The charm is meant to keep things secret, so when I cast it, it's supposed to hide something, like these stones I'm using to practice, but because I have this enormous secret I'm keeping from the world, the charm never works." She pouted. "The stones just disappear completely."

(175)

Caedmon's eyes widened. "That sounds way cooler."

"But it's witch magic," she hissed. "Fairy magic can't create pockets of space out of thin air. It can't create anything. Or destroy anything, actually. That's all witchcraft. Fairy magic just changes or moves what already exists."

"Ahh, that explains the pumpkin!"

Ellie crossed her arms. "We're speaking of stones, Caedmon Tuggle, not pumpkins."

He shook his head. "No, like in Cinderella. I always wondered why the Fairy Godmother needed a pumpkin for Cinderella's carriage. Why not just *make* a carriage? But you're saying she couldn't, right? She'd need to be a witch."

Ellie nodded, groaning. "Oh, woe befalls me!"

Caedmon patted her back. "Maybe your scepter just isn't working. Can fairy scepters malfunction? Maybe you should buy a new one."

"No, the problem is *me*. Besides, fairy scepters must be given, not bought. It is the fairy way of things. I was lucky to get mine at all."

"What do you mean?"

Ellie dropped her gaze. "Most fairies are gifted scepters when they're born, but…not me." She took a deep breath. "I wished for mine on the seventh fae temple."

Caedmon blinked, nonplussed.

"Fairies are descendants of fae," she explained. "They're all gone, but some of their temples remain."

(176)

"What do you mean they're gone? Did they all die?"

"I don't know. They're just…gone. Our greatest scholars are meant to hold those kinds of secrets, but they have yet to tell me."

Caedmon grinned. "But you've definitely written them asking about it."

She smiled back. "As any responsible fairy should. Anyways, the fae believed in the magic of numbers. Seven was the magic of fates, and there's an old temple dedicated to their seventh goddess on my mother's estate." She toyed with the laces of her boots. "It's where I used to hide from my mother and wish my scepter would come. And then one day, poof! It was there. It's a silly superstition, but I always thought it was a sign I was fated to be a fairy godmother." Her hope dimmed as she examined the discarded pebbles. "I must have been wrong."

"Well, you've told *me* you're a fairy godmother. A lot. Like, every day. So maybe you don't need an academy."

His words were like starlight. She beamed. "Well, that's very true. Still, I wish I could get this charm to work." She sighed, then made a strangling sound as Omari entered the sitting room, hand in hand with Grace.

Lorelei, polishing her tiaras alone at a nearby table, pranced over to Omari. "What are you doing spending time with Lady Eleanor's daughter?" she asked loudly enough for Ellie to hear.

Oh saints—of all people, did she have to ask Omari?

Lucy LuBelle, reading alone on a chaise lounge with her back to Ellie, silvery hair fanning around her, glanced up from her book. "Do you mean Ellie?"

Ellie curled her shoulders, trying to be as small as possible. With all her fairy spells, why didn't she know one that would help her disappear?

"She's in some of my classes and she's *so* nice."

Ellie's heart nearly burst. She didn't know Lucy very well, but in that moment, she could have kissed her.

Lorelei's nose wrinkled. "Well, my cousin Olivia said she's *foul*. They were in boarding school together for years."

"Icicles and Sleigh Bells?" Grace asked. "My sisters and I went there."

"The DeJoies only go to Roses and Needles, Grace *Otania*." Lorelei pronounced the girl's last name as if it were a swear word.

Omari placed his arm around Grace's shoulders. "My aunt went to Icicles and Sleigh Bells Boarding School, and now she's one of the most respected researchers on pixie magic in all the realms."

Ellie took a shuddering breath, willing her jumbled emotions to fizzle out. *Breathe in, two, three, out, two, three.*

"You okay?" Caedmon asked in a low voice.

"Mm-hmm."

(178)

But he was no longer looking at her. His focus was on Lorelei, whose cheeks flushed. The princess clutched her tiaras to her chest and stalked to her lonesome table, where she merely sat, staring at her jewels, tears welling in her sapphire eyes.

Caedmon squirmed. He wanted to talk to her, Ellie realized. She frowned, trying to decide how she felt about it, when Omari made his way toward them, ignoring the strange looks his friends gave him for bothering with the weird draftees on the floor. "Hey! Ellie said she was helping you with magic so I thought I'd stop by and..." He frowned at Caedmon's bag of ingredients. "Are you making soup?"

"Huh?"

He pointed at the chicken stock Caedmon had borrowed.

"No, it's for potions. I grabbed everything I could find in Dame Ethyl's cabinet."

"Ahh. Well...lesson one: Sometimes chicken stock is just chicken stock." His smile was genuine, his teeth were so perfectly white, his hair perfectly trimmed, his clothes perfectly neat, his—

"What are you doing here?" Caedmon blurted.

Ellie elbowed him. "Cad, shh."

"Why are you helping us? You have friends. Lots of friends. You have a life. We're not even in your grade."

"First of all, it's year, not grade. If you're going to be a knight here, you have to learn to talk like one."

(179)

"Fine. Year. Whatever. Why are you helping?"

Omari's gaze flitted to her. Her cheeks turned hot. She lowered her head. Oh saints, was that jam on her shirt? She surreptitiously tried wiping it off as Omari said, "Would you rather me not help?"

"No! I just...don't get it."

"I guess I..." He cleared his throat. "Last year, my sister died."

Ellie's head shot up, Omari's words clattering stones in the silence.

"The troll courts are at war, and she was in the wrong place at the wrong time. And my parents..." He barked a humorless laugh. "Well, I don't know if they'll ever be the same. I offered to help you out with the trials because I was just being nice. But I'm still here because I know what it's like to worry about your family. Plus, you remind me a bit of my sister," he added to Ellie.

Ellie balked. "I remind you of your *sister*?"

"Yeah. She was maybe a year younger than you, but you have the same sense of humor."

"I'm not funny."

"You are," he insisted. "It's cute. Like how you talk to yourself."

"I talk to myself?"

"Yeah, it's like a constant muttering," Caedmon said. "You didn't know?"

(180)

Ellie groaned, mumbling, "Oh, this is such a dreadful revelation. I'm sorry about your sister, though. Truly."

"Thanks." Omari pressed his hands together. "Right! So where do you want to start?"

"I was just about to tell Caedmon that when using Evermore dust, one must be polite, intentional, with only good will in mind. Otherwise, it won't work. Magic is very sensitive."

"Oh..." Caedmon's face fell.

They worked all night, and no matter how nicely Caedmon requested the Evermore magic to turn his cup of chocoswirl into *hot* chocoswirl, it wouldn't listen.

"You're too stressed out," Omari insisted. "Try to relax."

"And *feel* the magic."

He squeezed his eyes shut, looking very much like his head might explode.

"Look." Ellie grabbed the mug and sprinkled it with Evermore dust. "From ice to flame, from moon to sun and blaze, undo this cold, release me from this pain. Please and thank you."

Steam puffed from the cup, magic swirling through his drink.

"Why can't you just say, 'Make my drink hot?'"

"Ooh! I have the answer for that!" Ellie pulled an enormous tome toward her. "I've been reading about the wording of curses. All spells have the same rhythm. It's just something we know when we're raised not to be oblivious to the world

(181)

and all its secrets, such as yourself. I never knew why before. But look here: All spells are written in iambic pentameter. So, ten syllables with alternating stresses on each syllable."

"Wasn't that what Shakespeare wrote in?" Caedmon asked. "Mrs. Harlow made us read *Romeo and Juliet*, and it was pretty annoying. Was Shakespeare a sorcerer?"

"Oh saints, no. But he caused a craze, and for about a century, everyone spoke in iambic pentameter."

Omari nodded eagerly. "Dame Ethyl taught us this! It was a mess from the sounds of it. Nothing got done. And when things did get done, people misunderstood the directions."

Ellie cleared her throat and read:

The New World Europe had a Renaissance.
The other twenty-four and a half realms had a
highly confusing century. Wrong people were
executed. Realms declared war on the wrong
rulers. Many scholars attribute this bloody
confusion to the gremlin riots of 348 YATRDOC,
as it was eventually determined their protests
were sparked by a troubadour lamenting his
inability to eat sheep's cheese,* but due to his
inadequate rhyming, inadvertently implied

---

* My dear friend Francoise was highly distressed over this traumatic occurrence and does not appreciate your judgment.

gremlins' rights to free speech had been revoked.

"As all our spells were rewritten after the Fall of Camelot, they ended up in iambic pentameter," Ellie continued. "Only in the past few decades have people dared writing new spells again; they've been so afraid of causing another plague, they haven't tried. The new spells tend to be simple. No élan! No artistic flourish! No..." Passages from her books wavered in her mind. Cobwebs swept away, leaving her with startling clarity. "No rhyme..."

Caedmon glanced at Omari, who shrugged.

"This was all very helpful," Ellie suddenly squeaked, ushering Omari away. "We should all sleep. Late. Very late. And I'm battling wild boars in Sir Nyroni's class tomorrow, so..."

Omari yawned. "You're right. Good luck, you two. Let me know if you find out anything else?"

"Yes, yes, bye-bye!" As soon as Omari left, Ellie whirled on Caedmon, her mind spinning. "It's in partial rhyme," she hissed. "The curse is bleh!"

"The curse that could destroy the Knights of the Round Table forever is *bleh*?"

"Incredibly so." She paced, gesticulating wildly. "And given that curses can be difficult to get right, isn't it strange that a curse this powerful doesn't sound grander? And isn't it also strange that it's in partial rhyme? I *knew* it sounded wrong!"

(183)

"So…you figured out it's not in iambic pentameter?" Caedmon clarified.

"No, I knew that a while ago. I assumed it was a New Age curse, but it's too complex. Too powerful. But reading about the Renaissance, it all just clicked. Caedmon, I think the witch used a curse that existed *before the Fall of Camelot*. I think what I heard was a translation of magic in the wind."

"Which means…?"

Ellie bounced on her toes. She felt light enough to float up like a balloon. "In one of my books, I read there are multiple old tongues spells were written in. They're far more powerful than the Renaissance or New Age spells." The words of her textbook swam before her eyes, making her dizzy. Saints, this could really work. "So powerful that they cause *traceable ripples of magic*."

Caedmon frowned. "Okay…so, we just see if there's a…a wave of magic in the air or something?"

Ellie grabbed her textbook and flipped to the section on old tongues. "Not exactly. But there *is* a potion I can make. See here? It says that different old tongues have different magical properties: 'An old Avalonian curse will create a different ripple than an old Arthurian curse,'" she read. "'To track a witch or sorcerer casting in an old tongue, you must know the language said witch or sorcerer has spoken in, so you can create the corresponding tracking potion. This is simpler than it sounds, as witches' and sorcerers' strongest magic always comes through their native tongues.'

"Caedmon, do you realize what this means?" She grabbed his hands. "If we can figure out which language the curse is in, *I can find the witch.*"

TWENTY
CAEDMON

CAEDMON KNEW HE SHOULD BE RELIEVED ELLIE might be able to find the witch—but it only reminded him of his current failure to find Excalibur.

His family wouldn't be safe without it. The *world* might not be safe without it. And he had nothing to go off of other than Sir Masten's vague comment that the knights had never looked where they couldn't. He planned to persuade Sir Masten to talk again, but the head knight left for some mysterious expedition and was gone all week.

At Caedmon's request, Ellie joined him in the library to comb through a book outlining the knights' rights to journey into different realms. "Well, it says here they cannot simply march into your private bedchamber," she recited from *An Ode to My Plethora of Chivalric Deeds.*

"But Roxie magically appeared on my windowsill."

---

* One of my greatest masterpieces.

Ellie's brow puckered. "Hmm. Mine too. Ahh, yes, see?" She pointed at a miniscule line of text. "The legal term here is *march*. Well, that just seems like cheating."

Caedmon nodded absentmindedly, replaying his lessons with Sir Masten, hunting for clues in his memories.

He found none.

Only a looming sense of racing time.

Caedmon spent so many hours reading about the knights' rights to travel through different realms, he had a headache during his next Poison Resistance class.

Ellie sat beside him, as usual, but the seat next to her was empty.

"Where's Lucy LuBelle?" Caedmon whispered, the sweet, pale girl and her signature pet ferret noticeably absent.

Ellie shrugged. "Maybe she's sick."

Nadia Farhi sniffled behind them. "Nadia?" Ellie prodded. Some of the other draftees twisted to stare at them.

Nadia wiped tears from her cheeks, bracelets clattering on her dark wrists. "Lucy's gone. Sh-sh-she was sent home. Without her memories!" Nadia poured her head into her hands and cried.

Caedmon caught Ellie's eye as she patted Nadia's shoulder. This was getting more dangerous by the day.

Dame Yora bustled into class, took one look at Nadia,

and pointed at the door. "Crying knights must leave. Crying knights have no business being knights."

"That's not fair," Ellie protested. "She's upset."

Caedmon kicked her shoe. The last thing he needed was Ellie sent home, too.

The Urokshi's expression was hard to read as her snowy eyes swirled. "You all knew twenty-five of you would be sent home. It is ill-advised to make attachments until then." She sighed, softening. "Being a knight will require more. The very most. Sometimes danger will stare you in the face and demand to be dealt with, no matter how you feel. We have emotional healers at the château to speak to, for crying is important and good. But not when faced with death. So today, now, act as though I am that Death, for if you do not learn now, you shall either leave or, someday, perish."

Nadia slowly quieted, nodding. Everyone else went deathly still.

Dame Yora nodded. "Good." She passed out vials of nine vapors, ranging from sparkling pink to smoky black, along with the most bizarre periodic table Caedmon had ever seen.

"You are all familiar with nitrogen, hydrogen, and oxygen, but there are also nine *cursed* gases—those that were once natural but were permanently altered by evil magic. They lurk in bedrock and, frequently, goblin caves."

Caedmon recoiled in his seat at the fumes, head pounding.

(188)

Two were cloyingly sweet, one reminded him of bad eggs, but the clear one was the worst. Hospital beds. Beeping monitors. White roses and an old, musty funeral home.

The invisible vapor smelled like Jimmy's death.

"Many believe malemento vapor is the most dangerous." Dame Yora indicated to the clear gas. "For it conjures one's worst memories. It can be debilitating. If ever faced with it, you must find hope."

After Dame Yora's speech, everyone seemed to be trying harder than normal to impress their instructor, but the poison was too strong. Ellie was the only one still in her chair, glaring at her vial, as though determined to stare it into submission. To not let it break her.

Caedmon found his gaze drawn to Lorelei, whose attention was homed in on Ellie, eyes bright and observant—far more so than people gave her credit for.

Ellie placed the malemento vapor beside her, like it was nothing but air, and pulled a book out of her pink basket.

"The second most lethal is the algozar gas," Dame Yora continued. "Pain unlike you've ever known." She proceeded to describe the remaining gases and how to combat each one, but Caedmon barely took it in, still wandering the hospital halls. He placed his hand over the jar of malemento vapor to stop from passing out.

"If you survive your remaining trials, you will likely

(189)

encounter all nine poisons in your tenure as knights. So I suggest—" Dame Yora faltered, jaw clenching as a lumbering figure strode past the windows.

Sir Masten? Caedmon's heart leapt to his throat. He was back from his expedition early. And he was limping.

"Class, I…I'll be back in a moment. Work on neutralizing the poisons." Dame Yora's fingers shook as she adjusted her glittering beaded spectacles and fled the classroom.

Caedmon nudged Ellie. "Hey, what do you think Sir Masten is doing back early?"

Ellie tracked his gaze, but both knights had disappeared down a corridor. "We could follow them," she suggested, eyes glinting.

Before Caedmon could stop her, Ellie hopped out of her chair and slunk out of the classroom. Relieved to get some distance from the malemento vapor, Caedmon followed, Lorelei DeJoie's gaze stalking his movements. Even after he left the classroom, he couldn't help but feel he was being watched.

Sir Masten had a hurried conversation with a few of the professors in an empty room before striding down the halls.

"You follow Sir Masten," Ellie whispered from their hiding spot behind a door. "I'm going to see if I can get Sir Remy to tell me anything. I'm basically his favorite student."

"Aren't you failing his class?"

Her cheeks flushed. "I have a loud stomach! How am I supposed to hear *whispering stars* at my midnight snack hour?" She brushed her curls out of her face. "I let him dress Bianca in the most adorable cat sweaters though, so he likes me. Go," she ushered, giving Caedmon a shove. "Before you lose him!"

Caedmon crept down the quiet, vaulted halls, treading a familiar path—straight to their training arena.

Sir Masten lifted an enormous broadsword off the wall. It was blunt, Caedmon realized. Ornate.

…Ceremonial.

"Sir Masten?"

If Caedmon thought he was being stealthy, he forgot who he was dealing with. Sir Masten didn't even register Caedmon's question, entirely unphased by his appearance.

"Sir, what is the sword for? Why—"

A low, echoing, monk-like chant cut him off. It resounded through the castle, as if emanating from the walls. Sir Masten bowed his head and joined, his voice surprisingly soothing, though the song haunted. Caedmon didn't understand the words, but the eerie notes wrapped around his bones, freezing him from the inside out.

His neck hairs stood on end. It was just a song.

Musty funeral homes. Hospital bleach.

Just a song.

Through the window, a procession of knights dressed in black marched toward—

(191)

Something in Caedmon went dark. Quiet.

A pyre. They were circling a pyre.

Caedmon dragged his focus back to Sir Masten, whose cheeks were blotchy, gaze distant. Like he wasn't really there. Caedmon knew that expression. Had worn it in the months since Jimmy's death. Blood rushed in Caedmon's ears, his family's faces flashing through his mind.

At last, the chanting subsided, leaving Caedmon chilled and shivering. "Who died?" he rasped. Maybe he was wrong. Maybe everything was fine. Maybe it was just a song. Maybe—

"One of our active-duty knights." Sir Masten rubbed his jaw. "He was a good knight."

Caedmon took a deep breath. Warmth trickled back through his limbs. Not his family. It wasn't his family. Instantly, he hated the selfish thought. "I'm really sorry, Sir Masten." And he meant it. "Was it a malevotum?"

"It was something worse."

Caedmon opened his mouth to ask what could be worse—but Sir Masten's expression was so grim, so final, he stopped. His stomach clenched. He didn't need to know.

Sir Masten gazed out the stained-glass window, toward the flaming pyre. "The curse is growing in strength. It's picking us off one by one."

His words scooped something out of Caedmon's heart, leaving him empty. Lost. "I'm sorry," he repeated, though he knew those words did nothing. Not for Sir Masten, and not for him. What if this creature went to Boulder Falls like the malevotum had? What if it came *here*, to the castle?

How long did he even have?

After several quiet minutes, he started to back out of the training room to give the head knight space, footsteps echoing in the quiet.

"Caedmon..." Sir Masten's gaze remained fixed on the pyre.

"Yes, Sir?"

"They say..." His jaw clenched. "Saints, I will regret this," he grumbled. "They say it was kept, it was given, and it was frozen."

Caedmon blinked, momentarily stunned. "Excalibur. *You're giving me a clue to find Excalibur.* Wh-where was it kept? Who kept it?"

Sir Masten met his gaze, piercing and brutal. "All who seek Excalibur die, Caedmon. Every single one. Again and again."

"But...it's the only way to keep everyone safe. A malevotum killed my best friend and tried to kill my sister because—" Caedmon faltered. Reminding Sir Masten of his failure was too cruel. Not tonight.

"Because we weren't there to protect them." His voice was gruff, resigned.

"It will kill my parents, too," Caedmon continued. "And maybe all of us unless the knights get their strength back. You told me Excalibur would help. *So help me look for it.*"

(193)

Sir Masten gazed at the pyre for so long, Caedmon didn't think he'd answer when he said, "The sword was forged by more than steel. It was carved from the depths of magic. It will not simply be found because you find it. It has to want to be found. It wants to feel earned." He paused, contemplating. "It has to feel...understood. So you see, I cannot help you, because then you wouldn't have earned it. You wouldn't have understood."

A curl of orange flame and black smoke wreathed around the pyre, snaking into the room and filling Caedmon's nose and lungs. "You should go, lest they accuse me of playing favorites." Sir Masten's face was grim, but at that, his eyes twinkled, and something in Caedmon felt solid. Sure. Planted here, at the academy even as death hung in the air, even as the smoke made him want to gag, even as his family remained unsafe. He...belonged here.

"Sir Masten? What will happen to you if we don't find Excalibur?"

Shadows obscured the knight's expression. "I have been heading toward the same fate for a long time, Caedmon. Whether Excalibur is found or not...I shall meet it."

It was kept, it was given, it was frozen. Kept, given, frozen. Kept, given, frozen.

Kept.

(194)

Caedmon was too shaken to relay what he'd seen—to give death any thought at all. Instead, he searched.

If the sword was kept, who better to keep it than the Knights of the Round Table? Sir Masten said Caedmon was the first knight in centuries to find the training room in the western wing. Maybe the castle wanted to help him. Maybe he'd get lucky twice. He spent all afternoon scouring empty armories, dusty storage rooms, training arenas filled with live fires and growling lions—but there was no sign of a broken sword.

He became so consumed by the hunt, he didn't notice the empty halls, the flickering torches, until it must have been nearly curfew, and his feet were blistered and sore.

Resigned, he trudged through the windowless hallways, smoke wafting through archways, barely aware of where he was going until he found himself in the candlelit sitting room— didn't realize who he was looking for until he found her.

Ellie was easy to spot. White powder erupted from her cauldron, turning her shocked expression ten shades paler than normal, her dark curls snow-like.

Caedmon joined her, allowing Mr. Petalbloom and Bianca to crawl into his lap. "Nice job." His voice was hoarse from lack of use.

She frowned. "I was trying to make soup. I swear, my scepter is getting worse. Did you find out what that horrible chanting was?" She shivered. "It made me feel so...cold."

(195)

Caedmon explained everything in a rush, eager to get the words out, to be done with the thoughts of writhing smoke and burning pyres and solemn, chanting knights, looking upon their fate.

His fate.

Ellie's fate.

His family's.

Everyone's, if they didn't find Excalibur.

Ellie was enrapt, fingers already scrabbling for a textbook before Caedmon could finish. "Kept, given, and frozen. There must be something..." She flicked through a dusty tome at random. "Somewhere..."

"I think if it was in a book, someone would have figured it out by now." This was beginning to feel impossible.

"But there have to be clues," Ellie insisted.

Caedmon nodded slowly. "I think the Knights of the Round Table kept a piece. But I don't know where or why Sir Masten won't tell me."

Ellie hesitated. "If they kept one though, don't you think there'd be a record of it? That one of the knights would have seen it before?"

Caedmon pressed his palms to his eyes. "Yeah," he groaned. "But..." But he couldn't banish the image of a shard in the water, glittering out of sight as soon as he swam too close. Of Sir Masten's warning that he must understand. He must earn it.

He felt certain a piece belonged to the knights, somewhere in the world, but he didn't know if he would ever understand in time. And if he didn't, another person would end up like Jimmy or this fallen knight, family and friends left behind, dead too soon.

TWENTY-ONE
ELLIE

ELLIE HAD EVERY INTENTION OF ABANDONING HER classes, shirking her responsibilities, and devoting her entire self to Caedmon's cause. Truly.

But the next morning, all thoughts of the Fairy Godmother Academy, the trials, Excalibur, and curses abandoned her.

For Mother had sent a spoken letter.

Incredibly expensive and rare, spoken letters required fairy magic and could only be sent through the International Fairy Postal Service, excused from traditional human rules of magic. The letter writer could speak to the person of their choosing, regardless of where they were in the world. It was, in Ellie's humble opinion, the most brilliant magic to grace the realms since the invention of flying thrones.

Though this particular day, she wished for nothing more than to be far from her mother's discerning gaze.

"I still don't understand how you even knew where to send

this," Ellie admitted as Mother sipped her tea from the watery image on the crumpled parchment.

She was seated at the pretty bistro set beside the golden elvish fountains on her family estate, while Ellie roamed the cliffs beyond the laplie orchards, squinting at the background scene for more details. Was Bella visiting? Perhaps Ellie could make an ardent case convincing her sister that she must attend the wedding.

Mother tutted, wiping a speck of dust off her silk shawl. "*I* didn't know. Despicable fairies never tell the courts anything, no matter how esteemed the family. The Fairy Godmother's magic was able to send the letter, though I doubt even magic told *her* where it was going. And now you're trapped there, far from your family. Your home."

Ellie pursed her lips. She'd been away from her family and home since she was a child.

"When I heard news of your recruitment, I nearly fainted! The DeJoies were so proud of their young Lorelei. But you..." She set down her teacup. "That is no place for people like you."

"People like me?"

Her thin brows knitted, hazel eyes going cold. "Witches."

That was what troubled Mother? Oh, sweet saints. Well then, did she have good news! "That's not true! My friend Caedmon fully supports it. He—"

Mother raised her gloved hands, and the very parchment steamed, tendrils of smoke puffing from the curled corners. "You told a boy? You told him you're a witch?"

(199)

"Don't worry. He won't tell the DeJoies. I'm safe. But he accepts me! We're friends! Mother, it's *marvelous* to have friends." She beamed, then pressed her lips together as her mother's gaze darted to the gap in her teeth. Mother hated when Ellie's smile revealed her teeth.

Her mother grabbed the parchment, so her features distorted as it crumpled. "This is why you've spent your life in Roses and Needles Finishing School. You can't be trusted with anything. No matter how much I persuaded Olga to deter other children from spending time with you, here you've gone and ruined your entire life. You stupid, foolish child." Her pale cheeks flushed as her left eyebrow twitched.

Ellie couldn't remember the last time she'd seen Mother so furious. She opened her mouth to comfort her, but then her words took form. "I...What do you mean?"

"I mean that no one can know you're a witch. It will ruin you!"

"No...the part about Headmistress Olga and the other children. Are...Did *you* make sure I never had any friends?" The truth was too abominable to grasp. All these years, Ellie thought that she, the freak, the toad girl, scared people away. But had Headmistress Olga been secretly telling people not to go near her on her own mother's command? Was this why she was so alone? Why she spent so many days and nights listening to her own thoughts, for no one else would speak to her?

"Of course I wanted you to have friends, Ellie. Once your

(200)

fairy magic took over and we learned to control the witch-magic outbursts."

"I can't always control it!"

"Which is why you cannot have friends. Not until you are cured. Not until there's no trace left, and no one can guess who you are."

"What are you afraid of, Mother?!" The explosion startled a nearby nest of birds, who fluttered to a distant tree. "Do you truly believe I'll become evil if I accept my witch magic?"

"I'm afraid of that temper, little girl."

Ellie bit her lip. Sometimes her emotions had nowhere to *go*. They just squatted inside her, festering, until they burst.

"You do not know how to control yourself. You do not know what is right. Being a *witch* will be your downfall."

"What about Loreena Royenale?" Though she'd never met the glorious witch, she'd read every book about her she could find since Dame Ethyl mentioned her. Ms. Royenale was her last great hope that Ellie, too, could be appreciated some-day. That she'd be seen as a benevolent witch, not a monster.

"*Ms.* Royenale is an outcast." Ms., not Lady or Dame. The truest insult in Mother's eyes. "Is that what you want, Ellie?"

Tears rolled down Ellie's cheeks, dampening her favorite lace dress. "Why didn't you just let me be clamped? Why pro-tect me only to hate that I'm a witch my whole life? Being a fairy isn't worth this."

Ellie swallowed more tears. This wasn't true. Being a fairy

(201)

was worth everything. But sometimes, facing Mother's scorn, her thoughts jumbled, the wrong words slipped from her lips, and her world tilted. Sometimes she couldn't see up from down, sideways from backward, and would do anything to claw herself back to feeling normal and loved. She'd say whatever she needed to regain her balance.

"And have the whole court know I raised a witch? Better to be Unregistered and squash it, darling, than Registered and vilified."

After a few breaths, Mother smiled, returned her parchment to its perch, and smoothed a nonexistent flyaway in her perfectly smooth chignon. "Ellie, everything I've done has been to protect you. Because I love you. This boy never will. He cannot accept you. If you promise never to associate with him again, perhaps I can speak to the Fairy Godmother. See if she can persuade the knights to send you home. Maybe even reconsider your *failed* application."

Heat rose to Ellie's cheeks. Ellie wanted to deny she'd failed—but what if Mother really could compel the Fairy Godmother to change her mind? Could such a thing be so? Ellie's heart leaned in to the offer. Oh, how she longed to train beneath the fairies of the realms, to be one of the most adored people in society.

Caedmon's face swam in her head.

Even if Mother was successful and the Fairy Godmother

accepted her before Ellie mastered her secret charm and saved a lost cause, she couldn't leave now. She'd made a promise.

Ellie closed her eyes, unable to watch her mother's reaction. "I can't yet. I have something I need to do."

"With this boy who knows your secret?"

"He won't tell anyone."

"Perhaps not. But he will hate you for it. He will see you as a terror. Remember, darling. I'm the only one who can ever love you."

Ellie shuddered, more tears splashing down her cheeks, the sun warming her closed lids, like she could be asleep, and this could be a terrible dream—one she was half tempted to whisk away to the Forgetting Place so she needn't remember it. "May I see you at Bella's wedding when I finish my task?" Her voice was so meek, so small, and she hated it.

The parchment ripped, sending a jolt through Ellie's heart. Her eyes popped open. Mother's face was slashed.

Another tear, another rip.

Mother tore and crumpled the spoken letter until her image vanished completely, as if it had never been there at all.

No answer to her question, no wish of good luck, no farewell.

Only silence, leaving Ellie crying, alone on the cliffs, with no one to hear her but the sea.

TWENTY-TWO
CAEDMON

CAEDMON'S EYES DROOPED. HIS BODY WAS HEAVY. Words from his textbook mushed together, sleep calling.

A sharp tapping jolted him. He hopped out of bed, abandoning his book on the Urokshi, to find Ellie at his window, tears streaming down her face.

"Are—" She hiccupped and wiped snot from her nose with her sleeve. "Are you available for a leisurely walk through the castle grounds?"

An owl hooted. It must have been close to midnight.

Ellie wrapped her arms around herself and sobbed.

Caedmon reached for his cloak and clambered out the window. "What happened? Are you all right?"

She nodded, though more tears splashed down her face. "I just…fancied a walk…," she wailed.

Caedmon awkwardly patted her shoulder. "It's all right. Everything's okay. Sure, let's walk." He was exhausted, his body and brain utterly finished with the day, yearning for the numbness of sleep, but he forced himself to smile and led Ellie toward the orchards.

She offered no reason for her tears, so he didn't inquire further, but the more they walked in silence, the more she quieted, until the only sounds were their soft footsteps in the grass and the twittering of birds.

Unlike before, they encountered no one—no Omari and Grace sneaking out for a date, no Rosalind or Jorro or Killian or any of the professors.

It was as if the world slept but for them, and it hit Caedmon, all over again, how enormous this secret truly was: There were magic and hidden kingdoms and all sorts of wonderful things concealed from the rest of the world.

He nearly said as much when a faint scuttling met his ears.

Ellie stopped, eyes growing wide. "What was that?"

"Snakes?"

The scuttling grew louder, closer, until the most disgusting, horrible sight came into view: An enormous centipede the size of Caedmon's house prowled the grounds, tiny feet crunching the grass.

Bert.

Caedmon flattened himself against the orchard vines, laplie fruit sticking into his back, smelling faintly of peaches and strawberries. He stood completely still.

The blubbery creature was vile, slime dripping from his body, antennae poking the vines for prey.

Caedmon's pulse rocketed—he couldn't die like this. He couldn't be giant centipede food. How had he not insisted he keep a sword with him at all times?

After a few minutes, Bert scuttled away, to the other side of the castle.

Caedmon's legs nearly gave out beneath him. "That was close," he breathed, but Ellie was nowhere to be seen. "Ellie?" Had Bert somehow snatched her without him noticing?

"Up here," Ellie called from a majestic tree with enormous branches reaching for snippets of sky.

He climbed up the bark to sit beside her on a sturdy branch with a perfect view of the full moon. They sat in silence for at least an hour, until Caedmon's heartbeat finally normalized, and he no longer wanted to scratch his arms for feeling like bugs crawled on him.

Ellie's tears had long since dried, her expression growing more contemplative. "I'm not sure my mother will ever accept me," she finally croaked. "At least…it doesn't seem that way. I thought being invited to Bella's wedding as a fairy of the realms would help but…" She shook her head. "I don't know if anything ever will. And I'm so horribly, terribly sad."

Caedmon didn't know what to say to that. He did have a mother who accepted him. Who loved him. And he'd been selfish enough to throw that in her face and hurt her.

"Maybe, someday, I'll be okay. But I'm not okay today."

This, Caedmon understood. But if anyone could be okay

(206)

again, it was the girl sitting beside him, with the enormous smile and determination that should frighten every knight here. "Not today," he repeated. "But someday. Definitely, not maybe."

She smiled weakly. "Someday. Definitely, not maybe. Caedmon...Do you think fully accepting my witch magic would make me evil?"

"What? That's ridiculous. Is that why you haven't?"

She nodded. "Mother believes it will ruin me. The whispers are one thing. People suspect, but it is far different to know. And far more dangerous. There's a spell for it," she explained in a rush. "And I've never dared utter it, but there have been times when I've wanted to. And I've never told Mother, because she already believes me wicked and knowing I'd willingly dabble in my evil heritage will surely confirm her worst suspicions! But it...it *calls* to me. The magic wants me. And...sometimes..." She took a deep breath. "Sometimes I want it, too. Sometimes I feel as though people think me strange and revolting anyways, so perhaps I should be what they believe me to be. Perhaps I should accept myself. My full witch self. But if I do, I can't be a fairy godmother. And I'm beginning to wonder which matters more.

"But will it make me evil? Will the magic become contaminated and twisted? Will it bring down cities and kings? And what if Mother never lets me come home again?"

Caedmon chewed on his tongue, choosing his words

carefully. "I'm not from the magical realms. So I don't know if magic really can become contaminated and bring down cities and kings. But...I don't believe you'll suddenly be evil. And..." He rubbed his forehead. He wasn't great at the advice stuff. It made his head ache. But Ellie's large eyes were fixed on him, imploring, waiting.

His own advice was no good. But his mom's voice filled his head, and though he wouldn't admit it, her words could always soothe any hurt. So he let her speak for him. "You said you're a witch, even if you don't cast the spell. And...well, my mom says accepting who you truly are is one of the bravest things a person can do. So maybe, casting that spell won't make you evil. Maybe it will make you brave."

"It's who I truly am," Ellie repeated, frowning at the sea, as if it might spit out a different answer for her. "I'm a witch."

"And that's not a bad thing! What about Loreena Royenale? I looked up Unregistered witches after you told me your secret, and she's not evil. I think you'd be like her."

Ellie's face broke into a true smile, which was a relief. Only one of them could be miserable all the time.

Owls hooted and loons sang, and for minutes or hours, they sat, watching Bert nibble on a bag of cookies near the amphitheater and waves crash against the starlight.

"Caedmon?" Ellie at last interrupted the silence. "Why are you lost?"

"I'm not lost."

(208)

"In your head. You get lost there. Will you tell me why? Is it because of your family?"

Caedmon untied and retied his shoelaces to give his fingers something to do. "I was mean to my mom and sister before I left."

"Sometimes we're not nice to our families. You're working hard to help protect them—you're still a good brother. And I'm sure your mom isn't upset anymore."

Unexpected tears sprang in Caedmon's eyes. Luckily, it was dark, and Ellie didn't seem to notice. He blinked them away before they fell. "Thanks." His voice was hoarse, and maybe because the jar holding his thoughts and feelings in place had been knocked over, contents spilling out like oozing honey, he said, "There's something else. My best friend, Jimmy. He died a few months ago. From a malevotum."

Ellie sucked in a breath. "Oh, Caedmon. And then with your sister…No wonder you're so worried."

"He told me something was wrong," he whispered. He'd never told anyone this. Never revealed that he was there that night, watching his friend sprint from some horror in the trees. And now that he said it, the words tumbled out.

"There's an old graveyard in the middle of the woods some of the high school kids visited at night to prove they could. They dared Jimmy to go, and Jimmy wasn't someone who could say no to a dare.

"I waited for him in a park nearby. But…he ran out of

there like someone was trying to kill him." Caedmon shook his head, wondering, for the hundredth time, why he hadn't just gone into those woods with him. If they'd both still be alive. Or if they'd both be dead.

"He told me his chest felt funny. That he saw something in the woods. I could tell he was freaked out, but I thought it was just from the graveyard. The next day, he said it still hurt but that he'd be fine, so I...I didn't say anything. Then suddenly, he was dead." His voice broke, the dam barring him from his sadness breaking along with it, but Ellie didn't make fun of him. So he stopped holding back and cried for the first time since Jimmy's death—tears he hadn't let himself show at the funeral spilling, and still, Ellie didn't judge or laugh. She just sat there with him, listening.

Caedmon shook his head. "I should have told someone. Should have made him go see a doctor. *Something*. But I didn't. And now he's dead."

"You couldn't have known," Ellie said softly. "I don't even know if there's a cure once the heart is infected."

"You're still okay, though."

"Not because of a healer. It just didn't have a chance to fully infect me. It's not your fault." She placed a hand on his shoulder. "But that doesn't make it less sad. I've never had friends before you. And now that I have one, I think my heart would break were I to lose a friend. I'm sorry, Caedmon."

Caedmon nodded. Rather than feel worse, as he'd feared,

(210)

talking made him feel better, like a pressure that had been building around his lungs lessened, and he could breathe a bit easier. He remembered what his parents said in what felt like another lifetime: that they wanted him to see a therapist and that it'd be good for him to talk to someone.

Sitting there beside Ellie, he realized maybe they were right. Telling Ellie felt good.

He didn't have answers for her, and she none for him, but it was okay. Because they weren't alone. Things wouldn't be better tonight or tomorrow, but someday—definitely, not maybe—they would be.

TWENTY-THREE
CAEDMON

THE NIGHT IN THE ORCHARDS CHANGED SOMETHING in Caedmon. For the first time in months, he felt truly hopeful again and began to understand how lucky he was to have Ellie on his team.

He could never do it all on his own.

With his studies, Ellie's magic lessons, Swordsmanship, and preparing for the next trial—which Caedmon suspected involved the ocean, as his Strength Training professor Sir Tochure had insisted they swim laps with blood-sucking fish every class—Caedmon could barely keep his eyes open. He slouched over his history textbook in what was becoming his usual spot in the Sword Garden.

> In 3500 YBTRDOC (Years Before the
> Regretful Demise of Camelot),* explorers

---

* And 3,570 years before Stanley sent the Dragon Realm into a clockwork frenzy, causing a riot, and forever ruining a perfectly good birthday party. But was it actually 3,570 years? Who knows? I don't, because of Stanley.

discovered an island home to the ancient

civilization of the Urokshi, protectors of gréueur

leaves, famed for their properties in reviving the

dead.

Caedmon read the passage over and over, trying to force his brain to absorb the information.

"What are you doing in my spot?" A high-pitched voice interrupted his reverie. Ink spilled over his textbook as he jerked, a pair of very sparkly shoes coming into view. Princess Lorelei stood over him, tiara glittering in the sun.

The garden was otherwise empty, with plenty of other spots to sit. "I've never seen you here."

Lorelei flipped her golden hair and sat beside him. "So? I want your spot. It has the perfect balance between shade and sunshine, and it's by the prettiest sword. What are you reading?" She took his textbook from his hands. "Oh, the Urokshi? I love them! They always make me blueberry tarts when I visit."

"Wh—you know where they live?"

"Sure. They're quite welcoming. Well, when they like you. And they like me. I mean, who wouldn't?" Her smile was dazzling, exuding confidence, though her voice snagged. Up close, her eyes were red and puffy, like she'd been crying again.

Did anyone ever check up on her to make sure she was all right?

He doubted it.

Caedmon didn't like the idea of asking her for help—not after she'd made fun of Ellie and bullied him. But they were running out of options, and if she could help, he'd take it. Besides, there was clearly more to her than she let on. "Will you tell me where they live? I need to find it."

She tilted her head, blue eyes assessing him. "You've been sneaking around with Omari and that Ellie girl a lot."

"We're not *sneaking*—"

"Yes, you are. I know sneaking when I see it, and I do not appreciate being excluded." The princess lifted her chin. "It's rude to exclude people."

"You're rude to everyone."

"That's not the point. I, Princess Lorelei DeJoie, heiress to the DeJoie family fortune, hereby decree that you take me with you. To do...whatever it is you're doing." She nodded, like that was final. "I will show you where the Urokshi live, Caedmon Tuggle. I have come to you in your hour of need—"

"I wouldn't exactly say that—"

"And I shall fulfill my princess duties by helping you, ignorant peasant. 'Tis decided."

(214)

TWENTY-FOUR
ELLIE

THE MOON, ORANGE AND DIPPED IN HONEY, FLOATED low in the sky by the time Caedmon, Ellie, Omari, and Lorelei slipped out of the castle.

Ellie had protested Lorelei's addition to the group, but seeing as Lorelei knew how to find the Urokshi's ancestral home, Ellie was outvoted.

Besides, it's not as if she couldn't use more friends. Especially princess friends Ellie wanted to impress—that'd be sure to make Mother proud and hopefully forget their horrible argument—but she had to keep her secret from Lorelei. Caedmon was one thing. Lorelei DeJoie was entirely different.

The night they planned to find Roxie, Ellie tucked Mr. Petalbloom, Horrace, Figgleswap, and their friends into their favorite blanket by the fireplace, next to a sleeping Bianca, and prayed they'd remain there until her return.*

---

* They did not. It was bedlam. War was struck. Alliances were made. Betrayal. Grief. Vengeance. Bianca is now queen of all toads forevermore, and you owe her your respect.

Princess Lorelei, bundled in the loveliest glowing fur coat Ellie ever did see, strode to the edge of the mountainside in sleek boots, hands on her hips. "To find the Urokshi, we have to get down the mountain."

Omari glanced at the orchards, where a snarl sent birds shooting into the sky. "That will be Bert. We should be quick. Lorelei, there aren't any ropes. How do you plan to get down the mountain?"

Caedmon rolled up his sleeves. "We just do it. Come on, guys." He marched to the edge of the cliffs and began climbing.

"As...*lovely* as that looks..." Lorelei strode to another part of the cliffside. "This way, underlings. I shall show you the secret staircase. This is why you're grateful I found you."

Ellie frowned. Caedmon was *her* lost cause, not Lorelei's.

Lorelei stopped before draping ivy covered in poisonous red thorns, barring them from the cliff edge. The princess whispered to the leaves, brushing her fingers over their night-blooming petals, and stepped back. "Have you not ever wondered why the DeJoies regulate the Evermore trees? We're gifted tree whisperers. They listen to us. Which helped me find..."

The vines parted, revealing a crumbling, half-complete set of stone steps curling down the mountainside, hanging off the edge of the world. "The secret staircase."

That was being generous. The stairs were crumbling, old, untrustworthy things. Ellie daren't step on them.

(216)

Omari whistled. "Wow. That's incredible. I can't believe I've never found this!"

This was one of the worst ideas she'd ever had. Ellie didn't really *need* to be a fairy godmother, did she? But she couldn't turn back now. Not after her promises to Caedmon. Whether she was ready to be a fairy godmother or not—whether she was prepared to make the sacrifices she needed to make, her one and only friend in the world depended on her. The Knights of the Round Table depended on her.

Without allowing herself to question her life choices again, she followed Princess Lorelei and Omari down the stairs, the girl's glowing coat a guide in the wind-whipped night.

Partway down the climb, clouds spooled and raveled. Moments later, pelting rains poured from the sky. Ellie's boot slipped on a rain-slick step. Her heart jumped to her throat; the world tilted beneath her—

A hand grabbed her arm. She looked at Caedmon behind her, hair plastered to his pale forehead. "You all right?" he shouted over the storm.

"Splendid!"

Thunder rumbled, lightning crackled, and the mermaid palaces below glittered, the ocean gleaming white and bright.

"How much longer?" Caedmon roared.

"We're almost there!" Lorelei screamed back.

Trials were nothing in comparison to this, the quest to find Roxie—and not die in the process.

(217)

Ellie steeled herself. One foot in front of the next. They were almost there.

Another bolt of lightning gnashed the mountain, sending rocks tumbling into the water.

At last, Lorelei halted before a door carved from bones. Despite the hazardous climb, her tiara was perfectly secured in her luscious hair, which Ellie bet dried beautifully—frizz-free. Oh, the envy.

With a single knock, the door swung open. A bone arm snatched Lorelei's dress, and pulled her inside, her pink tulle and fur coat disappearing in a whoosh.

Ellie lurched backward, bumping into Caedmon. "What in the saints?"

"Remind me to never trust her again," he muttered.

Omari plastered a fake smile on his adorable face. "Erm... this looks like...fun! Like a...a great *adventure*."

Ellie and Caedmon exchanged dubious looks.

"Erm, I'll go next," he offered, the picture of chivalry. A bone arm shot out and stole him away.

Caedmon held out his fist. "Rock paper scissors?"

Ellie snorted, easing some of her tension. "I'll go."

Caedmon shook his head, spraying her with icy water from his flopping hair. "Ugh, now I have to go. If they try to steal my bones, I'll scream to warn you."

Ellie stuck her tongue out at his smiling face as a bone grabbed him, too.

At last, a bone flung out of the hole in the mountain, awaiting Ellie's hand. She carefully stepped onto the remaining stair, reaching for its fingers.

Rock crumbled beneath her.

She gasped, teetering—and slipped on moss.

Her foot felt the earth change before her mind understood.

With a single misstep, the world whooshed out from beneath her.

Her arms flailed, scrabbling for a rock to cling to as the Urokshi bone hand clutched her cloak, attempting to pull her inside. The cloak wrenched free from her body.

And Ellie tumbled from the mountain.

It couldn't have lasted more than a few seconds.

But time split eternity apart. For a lifetime, all she knew was the racing of her heart, the sharp wind cutting her cheeks, the looming dark abyss of the ocean. Waves that would kill her. Waves that would be her end.

Ellie's mind cast out to every fairy spell she knew, to no avail: That magic was too small and sweet for life and death.

The waves came closer, closer. She squeezed her eyes shut. Her mind landed on a witch's spell she'd learned as a young girl, and promised to never cast, for she'd been warned crows would flock to the dead and sleeping beasts would wake if she dared.

Another second, another breath, closer to death.

Mother would never forgive her for this—she would never accept her.

(219)

People everywhere would revile her.

She could become the same evil that brought down Camelot.

I'm good, though, her heart whispered. *I could never be evil.*

Caedmon's voice rang in her mind. *Accepting who you truly are is one of the bravest things a person can do.*

Whether she liked it or not, Ellie was a witch.

Another breath closer to leaving life unfulfilled, destiny incomplete, lost cause unsaved, wishes never granted.

She refused to have such an end.

So, she dared, and cast the first witch's spell of her life. *"If there be aid, then let it come to me; this witch requires magic's boon and beasts!"*

The incantation burst from her lips, magic pouring from her heart.

And all went black.

TWENTY-FIVE

CAEDMON

IN THE HEART OF THE MOUNTAIN, CAEDMON EXPECTED stone. Perhaps even a stone city, hidden beneath the Château des Chevaliers.

Instead, he was in a forested world, paths of pine needles twisting through palm trees and spruces, oaks and birch trees, bright tropical flowers cascading into fields of heather and thistle.

Some trees were bare, frost crawling up trunks, red berries a pop of color against tufts of snow. Others bore flaking orange and yellow leaves. Still, others had just begun to flower, while some were bright and wilting, at summer's end.

It was as if all the climates and seasons in the world converged in the mountain.

But most spectacular were the gemstone trees. Made of glittering emerald and silver bark, they towered above the rest, silver silky leaves drifting around him, warm to the touch.

Staircases looped around trunks, with wooden platforms

built between branches to create a city. Birds tweeted above, flying in and out of tiny holes throughout the mountainside, where the torrential downpour outside trickled into a soft rainfall.

And there weren't just Urokshi. The bone people shared their city with creatures the shape and proportions of humans, though with enormous animal heads. A frog-man strode over to them, polishing his eyeglass on his waistcoat. "Ahh, splendid. The lovely Lorelei and her guests. Guests, I am Sir Blainsey the Ever-Green. Miss Evaline mentioned you'd be arriving soon."

Lovely Lorelei? Did they know a different princess?

Lorelei beamed. "Hi, Sir Blainsey! Unfortunately, I'm here on a business matter." She nudged Caedmon forward. "He has something to talk to you about."

"I see! Well, all discussions are preferable over tea, are they not?"

Caedmon had to disagree. Tea was gross. "Shouldn't we wait for Ellie?"

Sir Blainsey waved a webbed, green arm and gestured for them all to sit. "Miss Evaline will bring her in." He clicked his fingers, and a feast sprang to life over a mossy stone table.

Caedmon was momentarily stunned. Silver platters overflowed with hundreds of different sandwiches. Gilded plates held chocolate cakes and fruit tarts, while ice creams of every flavor sat in delicate crystal glasses. A steaming teapot floated above the table, pouring smoldering amber liquid into whistling cups.

(222)

Part of Caedmon wondered if he should even eat it. That much magic couldn't be good for him, right?*

Tiny sparkling winged creatures popped out behind a set of acorns, gawking at him. Or potentially at Lorelei, who somehow managed to look elegant despite being sopping wet.

A Urokshi in a purple cape and flowery rain boots floated to Caedmon's mossy chair. "You have not been here, little knight."

"No, I haven't."

"You do not know our ways." He gestured skyward. "This is what our home used to look like. Before."

"Before the Fall of Camelot?"

He shook his head, looking to the glittering stars in the mountain rock. "No. Just…before."

"Could you tell me more about it?" Omari asked in that polite, crisp accent of his.

"But of course! I do love it when you small humans care to know about Death." He shuddered. "Unlike the creatures of evil who stalk these halls."

Caedmon was staring at the entrance, waiting for Ellie when the Urokshi's words took hold. "Creatures of evil?"

He nodded, gesturing toward a corner of the hall, where

---

* On the contrary, the fact that he has not read my *Ode to Delicacies: How to Determine Which Magical Sweets Shall Be Your New Favorite Treats or Untimely Demise* is unforgivably insulting!

the rock was charred, the stars dim, branches blackened. "Come."

Caedmon and Omari followed him to where notches etched the stone, like the pencil markings Caedmon's mom made on their wall as Carly and he grew taller.

A smoky red substance encroached just past the most recent notch—as though it were spreading.

"This is the vile magic creatures of evil want to pour over our world to watch us melt and scream. As the gates weaken, their poison unfurls ever higher every day. We have already evacuated our lowermost caves."

"But that would mean—" Omari's eyes widened. "The knights' castle will fall."

"Eventually." Slime covered his face, like tears. "If nothing changes, and the knights cannot hold the gates, we will all fall."

Caedmon shivered.

They were running out of time.

He turned back to the tea table to tell Ellie—but she still wasn't there.

"Ellie?" he called to the forested city. He paused, waiting for her breathless, giddy laugh.

Silence greeted him.

Omari grew quiet, eyes narrowing at the empty doorway. Even Lorelei stopped, setting her cup of tea on its saucer.

Omari's gaze darted to hers. "Where is she?"

Her sapphire eyes grew wide. "I have no idea! I swear it. She was right behind us."

The Urokshi who'd pulled them in glided toward them, head bowed.

Without any sign of Ellie.

Breathing grew difficult. Caedmon couldn't swallow. Where was she? He began to sweat despite his cold, damp clothes. He hadn't come all this way to save his family, only for his first friend since Jimmy to die.

If something had happened to her, it'd be all his fault. He was the one who'd requested such a dangerous wish. Why couldn't he have asked her for something simple, like a new video game?

"She's taking too long." Caedmon raced for the doorway. "We have to find her."

Omari rushed after him, Lorelei and Sir Blainsey following. Caedmon pushed against the stone entrance—it wouldn't budge.

"Let me try." Omari shoved with his shoulder, but it remained stuck.

Thunder boomed beyond the mountain.

Lorelei readjusted her tiara and lifted her chin. "Sir Blainsey, Ellie Bettlebump is still out in the storm. This must be fixed at once."

Sir Blainsey polished his glasses. "How curious. One

moment." He extracted a silver wand from his waistcoat pocket and twirled it in midair like a baton.

"Hmm. Must be malfunctioning. I wonder if—"

"Wait." Omari cut him off, stepping past him to retrieve a wadded lump of fabric on the floor.

Caedmon's heart sunk. Ellie's cloak.

A hiss of bones and branches swept through the cavernous hall, and one by one, the candles winked out. Though he couldn't see her, Caedmon felt Lorelei tense beside him. "This wasn't part of my plan," she squeaked.

"What *was* part of your plan, *Your Highness*?" Caedmon snapped.

"I don't know! I just..." Her voice was thin, so Caedmon had to strain to listen over the growling storm. "I just wanted people to like me."

Before he could respond, a cackling laugh echoed off the trees and rocky walls—one he knew all too well. "Hello, little knight."

"Roxie! Roxie, I need your help."

One lone candle illuminated the woman's face, her violet spiky hair unmistakable. Even with skin, her bones seemed to peek out, and all Caedmon could think was, *I've seen your skull*. He shook his head. "Roxie! You have to help us. My friend didn't make it inside."

Roxie clapped her hands. "*Oooh*, how delightful! You've made friends!"

(226)

Panic clawed Caedmon's throat. He didn't have time for this. He shoved his fist against the door, though all it earned him was a throbbing arm. "Let us go, Roxie!"

Roxie cocked her head. "Go? Why should you go? You were looking for me, were you not? Oh yes, the Urokshi talk. They speak of young knights looking for Miss Roxie. You wanted to find me. You have found me, young knight. Share your secrets. Spill your thoughts."

Lorelei stomped her foot. "If you don't let us go, Madame DeJoie—"

"The DeJoies have no power beneath the mountain," Roxie hissed, her teeth growing pointed. Caedmon blanched. Was that blood dripping from them? "We enjoy seeing you, Miss Lorelei. Do not mistake our welcome to you, little girl, pretty knight, fearsome thing, as respect for your family." She caressed Lorelei's cheek. "You can be better than them." Her gaze hardened. "Or you can fall." She stood back. "You are at the mercy of the Urokshi now. You never should have come."

"Please," Caedmon rasped. What was happening? Roxie had seemed so helpful when they met. "My friend—"

"Oh, young knight, how foolish you remain." Roxie clicked her tongue. "If your friend is meant to be a knight, she will survive. If she's not, she won't. 'Tis as simple as that. Now. Why did you want to see me? Be quick, young knight. Be forthright and true. Or I fear I must set Balorai on you."

Balorai? What was with everyone here giving monsters

(227)

names? Caedmon swallowed, fighting a wave of nausea. "It doesn't matter why I'm here; I have to make sure Ellie is okay."

Roxie wagged her finger, skin disappearing, slowly becoming a creature of bone once more. "Tsk, tsk, little knight. The sooner you ask me your questions, the sooner I will let you leave."

"The curse on the knights," he spat out. "It has to do with me, doesn't it?"

"Hmm, how insightful you are; how clever you must be. Yes, indeed, a curse for thee."

"Is it in another language? I want to know everything you know about it."

"Is that truly what you'd like to know? Or would you like to know how to save your friend outside these walls?" Roxie smiled. "She's dying, you know."

Caedmon began to speak, but Roxie cut him off.

"Tread carefully, little knight. You can help save your friend or learn your fate. What is your wish?"

Sir Blainsey scowled but remained silent.

Omari cursed. Lorelei glanced Caedmon's way, her curls drooping. This was up to him. And he had no idea what to do.

He couldn't abandon his family to the curse—but Roxie said Ellie was dying. He couldn't leave her, either.

No. He refused to accept his choices. He wouldn't save one person, only to let another die. He would find a third option. He'd create one himself. Roxie once said the Urokshi

(228)

worshiped languages, didn't she? So, what if he used language to trick her?

"You promise you'll help me if I decide and give you my command?" Caedmon clarified.

Roxie bowed. "I swear on my bones."

He shifted, as if debating—but he knew his answer. "Will…" He took a deep breath, making the experience look painful, and picked his following words carefully: "Will you take me to Ellie?"

"As you wish, young knight." The candles flared back to life, followed by the click of a lock.

Roxie, silver eyes churning, glided to another door set into one of the emerald trees. "Follow me."

TWENTY-SIX
ELLIE

IF THIS WAS DEATH, IT WAS A LOVELY PLACE.

Glowing flutterflies and pixies frolicked by Ellie's feet, a glittering crystal cave at the base of the mountain sheltering her from the steady storm.

And beside her…

She gulped, shaking fingers hesitantly reaching to pet it.

The incantation she'd cried to the night was meant to call for a magical creature's aid, for she'd once read such beings could hear a witch's call from across the world. She never thought magic would ever deem her worthy enough to save her, particularly as she still hadn't even accepted her full witch magic.

Except it *had* saved her.

The chevolant saved her.

Ellie still couldn't believe it.

Long ago, before the rise of the Pendragon kings, chevolants soared across skies. Over the centuries, their numbers dwindled, until there were no more.

With body and mane as black as raven feathers, and hooves the color of stardust, the flying horse was a sight to behold. Its entire body sparkled, like it belonged to the night sky.

How lonely it must feel without any of its kind left in the world.

The winged horse stomped its hooves, nuzzling Ellie's neck.

"Thank you," Ellie whispered, bringing her hand to its head. "What shall I call you?"

It threw its head back and neighed, blue eyes glinting.

"Are you a girl?"

A sharp neigh.

"A boy?"

It nuzzled her again. Ellie took this as confirmation. "A boy, then. I shall call you…Dee?"

He glared at her.

"Henry?"

A snort.

"Okay, hold on." She ran her fingers down his silky mane, over his star-dusted back. "Galahad, for your gallantry."

The chevolant neighed softly, and Ellie beamed, her heart full to bursting. Ellie had cast her first witch's spell, and the earth hadn't swallowed her whole; beasts hadn't clawed their way through skies or torn apart cities. No pestilence or famine or even a sunlight-eating borker bat. Not even a toad to lick her toes.

She felt free enough to fly.

"Will you take me to the Urokshi home?" Caedmon,

(231)

Omari, and Lorelei had to be worried about her. Well, at least she hoped they were worried.

Not excessively so—she couldn't wish ill thoughts upon her friends—but mild concern would be nice.

Galahad nodded and guided her toward the center of the cave, where not even the flutterflies and pixies dared venture.

A gentle dripping clanged in Ellie's ears, so unending was the silence.

She shivered. Her cloak had vanished, though she doubted it would have helped much if it were as sopping wet as the rest of her clothes.

Ellie stumbled through the labyrinth of caves, one hand on Galahad's sparkly back, the other in front of her face. As her eyes adjusted, she first caught only shadows and shapes: the outline of a table, a cloaked figure. She blinked, and they vanished, sending prickles up her arms. Where was the chevolant taking her? Who lurked here, so far beneath the castle?

The faint glow of Galahad's coat cast the softest light on a small temple before them, four pillars surrounding a stone statue poised on a dais. Her cape of scales billowed in a non-existent breeze, and she bent her head in reverence, as if bowing to a second statue Ellie hadn't noticed before: a crown of cresting waves arching into stars. Who was this immortalized figure? Why was she buried here, so far beneath any signs of life?

Ellie shivered. She needed light. Warmth. She raised her

(232)

fairy scepter, the spell on the tip of her tongue, ready to turn dripping water into fire. And stopped. Her breath caught.

She didn't want to cast a fairy spell. To turn one thing into another.

She wanted to create a flame from nothing. Witchcraft.

She already broke the law once tonight. What was one more time? Other than perhaps her entire future? "Fairy God-mother, please forgive me," she whispered, lowering her scep-ter, then chanting: "A flame from whence the nightly shadows grow; a witch's flame too powerful to tame."

A wisp of witchy shadows swirled around her—but the spell conjured no heat, no light, no flicker of warmth. It made sense, she thought miserably. She should have insisted she train, illegal or no. Should have forced herself to practice in secret. Though how could a magical-creature summoning spell work, while a simple heat-conjuring spell didn't?

Galahad nuzzled her, whinnying. Perhaps...he was look-ing for someone to save. So he wouldn't feel alone.

Grumbling, Ellie raised her scepter and muttered a fairy spell. At once, a cheery glowing fairy light appeared at her feet. She brought the glowing orb to her face and squinted at the statue again, catching an engraving she missed the first time.

IN HONOR OF PRINCESS DIANNA OF THE LOST ISELKIANS, WHO PERISHED DURING THE FALL OF CAMELOT. MAY THIS ANCIENT FAE GODDESS OF UNITY WATCH OVER HER SOUL.

Ellie's heart clenched. The Iselkians. Princess Dianna.

(233)

Everyone grew up learning about their tragic past. Iselkia was the nearest isle to Camelot, and when witches' magic grew too contaminated, Camelot was the first to fall, followed swiftly by Iselkia. Malevolent magic coalesced above the island, and the Iselkian princess, their last hope for survival, died before she could help them.

Then came the Deep, when the earth opened and swallowed Iselkia's inhabitants whole.

No one knew why.

All they knew was Iselkia was a cursed place, the island lost to history, its relics destroyed, but that it took with it the witches' contaminated magic that brought down the Pendragon Empire.

If not for the Deep, the Fall of Camelot would have caused more than the medieval plague and three quarters of the world to lose their memory of magic; it would have destroyed all life.

The story was too large for Ellie to fully understand. She'd never lost a city. Never lost a home. Never truly had one to call her own to begin with.

Still, she could understand that the pain meant something to someone. And whether she ever attended the academy or not, her job as a fairy godmother was to understand. To feel for people beyond herself. To bring light to their darkness.

The compulsion to help gripped Ellie, as real as if hands reached out and clasped hers. She had nothing to give other than her own fairy light. The light in their darkness.

(234)

For Princess Dianna, for her doomed people.

Ellie placed the orb in the ground. "For your sacrifice," she whispered.

A strange wind blew through the corridor, sending the light dancing.

Tink.

Clink.

Scrape.

Ellie paused, heartbeat rocketing to an unbearable speed. *Someone is down there.* Rather than flee, a wild impulse tugged at her heart. *Follow the noise. See where it leads.*

She glanced at Galahad, who trotted after the sound, as if he could read Ellie's mind. This wasn't safe. This was reckless.

But curiosity was stronger than caution. Gathering courage, she embarked down the hallway. At the end of the next corridor, a door stood ajar, a bright light glowing red from within, jewels scattered in the sand.

Someone coughed. The chevolant sniffed, treading forward.

"Watch where you're going!"

Ellie whipped around. Lorelei? Voices filtered in from the left, away from the glowing room.

The stone door slammed shut, and the light from the orb Ellie gave to the lost Iselkians winked out. Ellie blinked in the shocking darkness, voices growing louder.

"Ouch, that was my *foot,* Caedmon."

(235)

"That was *my* foot."

Rattling bones.

"What about my feet? No one seems to be treading carefully near my feet."

"You're dead."

"That doesn't mean my bones don't bruise! I'm as delicate as a peach."

"You didn't seem very delicate when you locked us in your city."

"Well, it comes and goes."

Ellie's heart calmed. She knew those voices. "Caedmon?" she whispered. "Lorelei? Omari?"

The voices stopped. "Ellie?!" boomed Caedmon.

Ellie winced. If the mysterious stranger came and attacked them now, she knew who to blame.

Caedmon catapulted into view, sweat streaking down his face. He beamed, revealing dimples. It was the first time she'd seen him truly smile. Even the princess smiled at the sight of her, though she didn't crush Ellie in a smelly hug like Caedmon did.

Ellie's heart twinged, wishing Omari had been the one to hug her instead.

"You're not dead!" Caedmon exclaimed.

"No, apparently, I'm the only dead one here," Roxie muttered, "as you all love to remind me."

"There's someone down here," Ellie whispered. "Through that door."

(236)

Roxie glided ahead of them, hair thrown back—unnervingly clinging to her otherwise skeletal frame. "Let's see, shall we?"

"Wait!" Ellie warned, but the word died on her lips as Roxie thrust the door open, revealing an empty, abandoned cavernous room. No noise or burning red light.

Had it all been a dream?

She turned to Galahad for reassurance—but the chevolant, too, had vanished.

TWENTY-SEVEN

CAEDMON

"THANK YOU." OMARI GRIPPED ROXIE'S FINGERS.

Roxie cocked her head, not answering, taking Ellie in. "What have you given, girl?"

"Hmm?" Ellie peered around the corridor like she was looking for something.

Roxie sniffed. "Magic given is never lost. It is never forgotten." Her silver eyes darkened. "For evil or not, I cannot say."

Caedmon resisted crying in relief. "What happened to you? How did you get down here? One minute you were behind me, the next you were just gone. And then the Urokshi said they've evacuated some of their city because of the evil magic the curse unleashed and I thought you'd…"

No, she hadn't died. She was just fine, though she did still look distracted. Had she hit her head?

"Oh, I…" Ellie focused as each of them turned to stare at her. "I fell but…a wind. It…it knocked me into a cave, and I was okay. I've been trying to find my way back." She scraped her foot against the earth, though she didn't break eye contact with him, like she was determined to make him believe her lie.

Because she was definitely lying.

Jimmy used to get the same look in his eye when he was trying to convince Caedmon that what he'd planned wasn't as reckless as it was.

Like the time he thought it'd be fun to race their bikes across a frozen lake. The ice had cracked beneath Caedmon's tires, and Jimmy pulled him out of the freezing water. Though Caedmon always went along with Jimmy's plans, they were always *Jimmy's* plans. Nothing was too dangerous. Too risky. And Caedmon was beginning to think Ellie might be similar.

Roxie stepped before Caedmon, sparkling dress flapping around her. Caedmon's heart lurched. Now was the time to reveal he'd tricked her—that he'd never given her a true command and that she'd vowed to help him when he did.

Roxie clapped her hands. "You passed the test! That was some clever trickery, as well. Oh, I do love a twist of words, a feat of language. How sinfully amusing!"

"I—what?"

Roxie smiled, revealing her jagged teeth. He wished she'd stop doing that. It creeped him out.

"You chose to save both Ellie and learn your fate, because it was right, because it was brave, and because it was clever. Never clever enough to best Miss Roxie, but your attempt delights me. Oh, I'm so relieved."

(239)

"You mean…?"

Roxie bowed. "The Urokshi may not help little knightsies unless they prove their worth. A shared creed on our shared mountain." She beamed. "But you passed, so I will help you. What is it you'd like to know about the curse? What is it you'd like to see?"

Caedmon could scarcely hear her over the roaring in his ears. "Everything," he croaked. "Tell me everything."

Roxie's eyes shimmered. "Only the familiar can call to its brethren. I am not a witch. I cannot know all there is to know."

Lorelei's eyes narrowed. "Who—"

"The Knights of the Round Table found a witch to listen for it," Caedmon interrupted. It wasn't exactly a lie. He repeated what Ellie told him in the woods.

"But the witch said she might have heard a translation," Ellie concluded. "From an old tongue."

"Can you hear anything in it?" Caedmon asked. Something—anything, he silently pleaded. With whatever secret magic she possessed.

Roxie clicked her bone fingers, cocked her head, and pressed her ears to the stone. "What a life, this stone has seen, what a world this mountain has known. Many secrets and lies have passed through these halls. Stories untold yet come to pass. Curses can be a tricky business…difficult to get right." Her eyes widened, a whispering wind stirring rivulets of sand. "I smell its poison. Hear its treachery."

(240)

"How?" Omari asked. "How can you hear magic?"

She shifted toward him, swift and snakelike. "Young Evelant boy. That is your name. Omari, yes? Hmm…" She tapped her fingers where her lips should have been. "I have yet to make up my mind about you." She whirled back to the stone, raking it with her fingers, as if she could claw the secrets it contained. "I can smell and hear and *taste* magic because it leaves an imprint. Because I am Dead and time is something different to me."

Roxie tilted her head. "Magic rustled in the winds that night. The sniff and the strangeness and the oh-so-very sweet." She clicked her bone fingers together. "It caught my attention, for it was different. Its cadence…strange. Unheard, unknown. And so very ominous. It resonated in my bones."

Caedmon nodded—then realized she probably meant that literally.

She held up a single finger, threatening them to be quiet.

Nothing stirred, but Roxie must have heard what he couldn't, for her gaze roved the walls, and she gasped, then clutched her skull and caved into herself. Caedmon went to help her, but how do you help someone who's already dead? "Oh, my soul, my wretched soul, how it loathes your words! How it loathes this place!" She sank to the ground, digging her fingers in the sand. "The curse caster was here," she rasped. "On our sacred mountain. In our sacred pools!"

Caedmon's heart thundered. "She was *here*?"

(241)

"Yes, *thieving* our sacred leaves! I hear her," she whispered, scraping the stone wall. "I hear your magic, wicked one. I hear the remains of your curse, and I shall punish you, yes. You shall suffer the wrath of the Urokshi."

Lorelei stumbled back, tiara, for once, askew. Omari placed a protective hand on her shoulder.

Ellie knelt beside Roxie, eyes glistening. "I'm sorry, Roxie. So sorry." Her voice was steady, convincingly brave, though her hands shook.

"Give me no apologies, fairy girl." Roxie bared her teeth in a feral grin. "Give me vengeance. The curse caster never should have crossed the Dead."

"I still don't understand why you won't just put your face back on." Lorelei pursed her lips at Roxie, who bent her skull to listen to a whispering book.

Roxie shot her a glare, glowing eyes and violet hair the only remainder of her living form. "Because I like to watch you squirm."

Caedmon rolled his eyes. He was too tired for this. They'd climbed an inner staircase of the mountain on what apparently was the Urokshi's daily route in and out of the castle, leading to the top of the star-speaking tower. Though exhausting, it was far better than the climb of doom they'd taken earlier that night. Roxie had scoffed when she'd heard of their travels.

(242)

"Far too dangerous. Tell me: Do you generally suffer from bouts of foolery? For if you do, I must know; it quite affects our partnership."

"Other brave Urokshi showed me that route," Lorelei protested, head held high.

"The Urokshi like you and our tea parties, princess," she'd said to Lorelei, "but not enough to show you our true entrance."

Lorelei had been sour ever since, complaining that she didn't need to help them and that they should all thank her on bended knee. And yet, she stayed.

She didn't actually *help*.

But she stayed.

Caedmon was tempted to tell her to go away during her fifth retelling of the time she learned she was the most talented person in her family,* but he couldn't get her tears off his mind, or words out of his head. *I just wanted people to like me.*

"Your skull is distracting me," Lorelei grumbled.

"Oh, is it?"

"Yes. Could you please remove it and bury it? I'd welcome the silence."

It'd been three hours, dawn loomed, and still, they were no closer to understanding who the curse caster was. Caedmon, Ellie, Roxie, Lorelei, and Omari sat huddled around the stone tables of the library, poring over books, some written in

---

* A fair assessment.

(243)

languages designed to be heard, not read, so the books sang mournful tunes, which echoed in the amphitheater, bouncing off the broken pillars that reminded Caedmon of ancient Rome.

They'd also had another encounter with Bert.

Caedmon shuddered, though it'd been an hour since Bert had appeared, gnashing his pointed teeth, threatening to make them his breakfast.

Roxie, being a Urokshi who occasionally worked for the school, and thus, an authority figure, managed to shoo him away, but not before he stole the snacks Roxie had retrieved from the kitchens.

Roxie chucked the book she'd been listening to into a gurgling fountain. "That one's no good. Another!" With a click of her bone fingers, another book sailed toward her.

Caedmon groaned. They were getting nowhere.

Lorelei had taken to painting her nails.

Caedmon placed his head in his hands, forcing his brain to think. "So, we know it's a curse. And we know whoever cast the curse lives in the castle."

"Not lives," Omari corrected. "They were just here to cast the curse. And steal from the Urokshi."

"Who steals leaves?" Ellie asked.

"People who are desperate," Lorelei answered, surprising everyone. She glanced up from her nails. "I know things. Which you all would realize if you accepted that I saved you all from peril and deserve your unending devotion and friendship, but that's fine."

"Your plan nearly got Ellie killed," Omari reminded her.

"*Nearly*, Omari. *Nearly*. Not *actually*. Ungrateful peasants."

A foggy memory unfurled in Caedmon's mind. "Wait, what were you saying about the leaves? I think I remember reading about that. They help raise the dead, don't they?"

Roxie snarled. "At a cost. They're an essential ingredient for such things, but only combined with malevolent magic, too unwieldy to control—magic not even a witch as powerful as Loreena Royenale could harness. It would have to come from somewhere—or something—else. The Urokshi use our leaves to help the living pass to the Dead in peace. They're meant for our kind alone." She clicked her bone fingers. "La da de, la da do."

"Is that a spell?" Caedmon whispered.

Roxie shot him a look. "I'm singing, nitwit. Singing helps me think."

Ellie pouted, placing another book in her reject pile. "Another one on how curses are evil. Did you know that if you're caught using the bird-beak curse, you have to live as a bird for a whole year? A whole year eating worms!"

"What's the bird-beak curse?" Caedmon asked.

"Haven't *you* ever wanted to see what you would look like with a beak?" Lorelei challenged.

"...No?"

(245)

"Well, *I* have. Not that I can cast it, but it is a curious thought. I'm so beautiful; I wonder what it would take to mar my perfect complexion."

"Can I throw my skull at her?" Roxie whispered in Caedmon's ear.

"What? No!"

"Just once."

He scowled. "Have you heard anything else in the curse?"

Roxie pranced around him, hair dancing wildly. "There are blocks, young knight, so many blocks. Though I can say..." Roxie's eyes glazed over as she tilted her head, listening. "The language has not been heard for many moons. From a land we never knew, and never will again."

Roxie turned to Ellie. "From a world of your ancestors. From a world of your magic. And yet not at all." Her gaze drifted to the sea. "Not at all."

Lorelei's brow furrowed. "From a world of fairy magic? Where are their ancestors from?"

"Well, everywhere, aren't they?" Omari said. "The fairies brought humans into their cities when Camelot fell and people needed a place to go. I'm not sure where they were before that."

Lorelei blew on her freshly painted nails. "Do they have elf magic?"

But Caedmon didn't listen to Omari's answer. His gaze was homed in on Ellie, whose eyes had gone wide, lips pressed

(246)

together, like she was doing everything she could to keep from screaming her thoughts aloud.

Roxie wasn't referring to Ellie's fairy magic. She meant her witch magic.

A bell rang across the mountaintop, sending birds scattering to the sky.

Roxie gasped, hand to chest. "Oh, little knights, I apologize."

Omari paled, and even Lorelei set her nail polish down. "Uh oh."

"What is it?" Ellie asked.

Omari grimaced. "A trial."

Sure enough, knights in full armor swept through the castle grounds, rallying draftees.

"A trial?" Ellie squeaked. "We're not ready for a trial." She looked to Caedmon, panic-stricken. "Are we?"

Sir Masten strode to a castle tower balcony, blowing from an ear-splitting horn, and hollered, "Draftees! Meet at the edge of the orchards in ten minutes' time. Your trial is about to begin."

"I'm not sure we have a choice," Caedmon mumbled. He rubbed his bleary eyes. Curse or no, Merlin still told him his family would be safe if Caedmon became a knight, meaning he couldn't fail them now. He was going to compete.

He doubted he'd succeed, though. Everything felt...hopeless. Lifeless.

His energy had been so consumed by saving Ellie, and then finding answers, that now, at the prospect of working harder, pushing further, all he wanted was to disappear. If not for the fear of his family turning lifeless and still, he would have laid down on the stone table and slept for a year.

"Caedmon?" Ellie nudged his shoulder.

"I'm tired," he whispered. How could his mind work like this? How could he feel completely fine and then completely drained?

Roxie gasped, eyes wide in horror. "Little knight, little fairy, you must beware. Be very ware, or wary be, of the curses blooming beneath thee."

Lorelei placed her hands on her hips. "What about me? Should I 'be ware or wary be?' I'm competing, too, you know."

Roxie removed her hand and chucked it at her, sending Lorelei squealing.

"The curse caster might be here, on this day. I feel her magic. I smell her ruin. Her evil magic hovers like a cloud above the mountain, ready to unleash a storm."

Sir Masten's horn blared again.

Caedmon's head was swimming, partially because the way Roxie spoke was so confusing. How was he supposed to watch out for some nameless witch harnessing evil magic *and* win the trial?

Ellie gripped Caedmon's hand. "Listen to me. You can do this. Saint Guinevere is with you."

"I don't believe in saints."

"Then *I'm* with you. Do you trust me?" She smiled, revealing that gap in her teeth, emphasizing her smattering of freckles.

The band around his chest loosened. "Yeah. I do."

She squeezed his hand again. "Good. Remember, you can do this."

"Be careful, children," Roxie called. "Tread lightly, friends, and wary be!"

TWENTY-EIGHT
CAEDMON

CAEDMON CLENCHED AND UNCLENCHED HIS FISTS, gathering courage, as he joined the other draftees and stepped from the cliffside onto a glass platform. With a jerk, it lowered to the treacherous sea.

Sir Masten had given them no indication as to what their trial would be, though he did give Caedmon an encouraging clap on the shoulder before mounting his skyvor to circle above them.

Maybe they'd have a swimming contest. That wouldn't be so bad.

If not for Roxie's warning.

The witch was here, brewing magic, and she could be anyone. Caedmon sniffed, trying to detect a curse like Dame Ethyl Botts taught him, but all he smelled was salt.

He turned to ask Ellie—but she wasn't there.

Caedmon spun around, scanning the draftees for her dark curls. He caught Lorelei's eye and joined her side. "Where's Ellie?" he whispered.

"I have no idea." Her surprise sounded genuine. "She was with us when we got to the platform."

Caedmon had to force himself to breathe. Think. Maybe she'd decided to skip the trial.

But he could only hear Roxie's ominous warning. It choked him, made him dizzy, leaving him with a single, horrifying thought: *What if the witch had Ellie?*

"Sir Masten is here," Lorelei murmured, as if reading his thoughts. "Roxie is here. Ellie's fine. There's no reason to think she's not fine."

What she said was logical, but it didn't ease the twinge in his chest.

He opened his mouth to challenge her—when the glass platform vanished, unleashing utter chaos.

Screams.

Flapping capes.

They plummeted to the sea—a free fall of flailing limbs. Killian Rye's foot smacked Caedmon's nose. Wind roared in his ears, his heart shooting to his throat, blood streaming from his nose into his eyes.

A strangled yelp escaped his lips—then icy water stung his bare arms. A wave flipped him over, sending water up his nose. He opened his eyes despite the sting just in time—a glint of purple scales slithered near his leg. His stomach dropped.

Serpentelles.

Nadia Farhi shrieked as Killian Rye jabbed one in the eye.

(251)

They were *everywhere*. Four of the draftees hadn't come up for air. A talon yanked his ankle and dragged him into her quiet, watery world. He kicked and wriggled out her grasp, pushing to the surface.

"They hate fire!" he shouted over everyone's shrieks. "Someone make a fire!"

Lorelei screamed as two sets of talons grabbed fistfuls of her hair and dunked her head underwater. Caedmon lurched to help but she popped up on his other side, seething and kicking the snarling creature.

"Never—attack—a—DeJoie!"

Nadia hurled a pouch of Evermore dust at Lorelei. "Lorelei! Here!"

Lorelei gathered the magic in her palms, cried a spell—and released a ring fire over the sea.

Soaring on Aurelius above them, Sir Masten beamed, clapping his hands—and disappeared.

The entire sea disappeared.

Caedmon stumbled backward in shock.

More students popped up beside him, swaying from side to side, spitting out saltwater.

For a wild moment, Caedmon thought Sir Masten had drained the sea, but he was standing in a windowless, cavernous hall, candelabras swinging from the arched, rocky ceiling. Somewhere above, the ocean churned.

Frogmen and women who looked like Sir Blainsey's

cousins marched around the underwater city, inspecting wounds and offering bandages. One of the frogmen nodded, tapping his clipboard. "Now that you've passed the teamwork test, welcome, draftees, to your next trial: the treasure hunt."

Caedmon gasped for air, numb to the claps on his back, the murmured thanks. Gingerly, he touched his sore nose. Teamwork test. Had he just helped save them? Had Lorelei saved everyone? He rapidly counted. There were only thirty-nine of them.

His heart seized. So, not quite everyone.

Sir Blainsey marched forward, clapping his webbed hands. "Ooh, I do love this trial. Only get to do it every few years. Such a delight. Such a treasure! Bah!" He croaked at his own pun, tears leaking from his eyes. "Treasure!"

The first frogman narrowed his gaze, mustache twitching. "As I was saying. The treasure hunt. You will all receive a scroll." With a click of his fingers, a bunch of scrolls appeared in thin air, dropping to their hands, one fluttering to the ground bearing Ellie's name. Caedmon picked it up, nerves returning in full force.

He had to get this trial over with and find her. Make sure she was okay. Maybe she ran off to the bathroom. Or maybe she saw they were going onto the platform and freaked out after the last time she fell and nearly died, so she decided to forfeit.

His heart eased a little.

(253)

That made sense.

"There will be no cheating and no leaving until you finish," the frogman declared. "Any questions?"

Nadia raised her hand. "Where are we?"

"Far beneath the depths of the sea." A horn blasted. "Begin!"

Squiggly lines swirled along Caedmon's scroll, forming a map marked with clues. No, not clues, he realized. Instructions.

GO THE WAY OF THE CURSE, AND ALL WILL BE WORSE.

GO THE WAY OF THE SPELL, AND ALL WILL BE WELL.

Caedmon's heart pounded, Dame Ethyl's lessons filling his mind. This was about detecting magic.

I AM EASILY FOUND IF YOU KNOW HOW TO FIND.

YOU WILL EASILY DIE IF YOU LEAVE YOUR WITS BEHIND.

Okay. Okay, simple enough. To find the treasure, he had to follow the trail of spells and ignore the trail of curses. Ridiculously difficult and could likely kill him if he walked into a curse—but simple.

Lorelei pranced to his side, golden curls glistening on her shoulders, immaculate despite being drenched.

"Lorelei, that was amazing. Your spell—"

(254)

"Yes, peasant, I am perfection embodied and you should be grateful you get to stand before me."

Caedmon suppressed a retort. Just when he was beginning to like her...

"Have you found the first spell?" she asked.

The frogman rammed his scepter into the tile floor, the boom reverberating off the walls. "Teamwork is over! I said no cheating!"

Lorelei blinked innocently at him. "Sir, I am a DeJoie." As if that explained everything, she turned back to Caedmon, Sir Blainsey shrugging to his indignant comrade.

"Anyways, peasant, I think I figured it out. Likely because I am exceptional."

"Is this how you usually make friends?" Caedmon grumbled.

"Of course not." Her deep blue eyes widened. "Grandmother hires them for me."

Caedmon didn't have time for this. "What was your idea, Lorelei? Can you tell where the curses and spells are?"

"Yes." She smiled and walked away, miniature high heels clicking on stone. After a beat she turned around, her smile dipping, and just for a second, she looked less like a confident princess and more like a girl playing dress up, wondering why she was alone. "Aren't you coming? Peasant?"

Caedmon sighed. He didn't believe in Ellie's saints, but if they were listening, he prayed they would help him as he set off after the princess.

(255)

When they reached a fork in the hallway, Lorelei strode left without stopping.

Caedmon scrunched his nose. "Wait, shouldn't we check for curses first?" He inhaled deeply, trying, for the life of him, to detect even the smallest trace of magic.

"Relax, I know a shortcut."

"Is this like your shortcut into the Urokshi forest?"

"That wasn't a shortcut, that was a glorious staircase carved by the great knights of the past that you should be grateful you had the chance to see, Caedmon Tuggle. *Grateful.*"

"We nearly died! Ellie fell off!"

Lorelei whirled toward him, scowling. "Do you like her or something?"

"I—do I—what?" he spluttered, cheeks heating. Where had *that* come from? He didn't. At least, he didn't think so. He'd never thought about it. But a *girl* had never asked him who he liked. He decided he didn't like it. Hanging out with Bert sounded like a far preferable alternative. "No! Ellie's a friend."

Lorelei squinted, examining him. "Hmm…if you say so. It's just that you spend a lot of time together."

"Because she's my friend. She's helping me grant a wish as a last chance to get into the Fairy Godmother Academy."

"Ellie didn't get into the Fairy Godmother Academy? That doesn't make any sense." This seemed to truly surprise Lorelei, which at least got her off the subject of crushes.

(256)

"Why wouldn't it make sense?"

"Because my aunt Tillie is part fairy and handled her application. I remember it. Her mother's really important in different social circles around Aurelia, so her name came up. She should have gotten in."

Unless they'd somehow found out Ellie was a witch. If they did, did that mean Ellie was in danger? He still didn't think clamping powers made sense, but if Ellie was in trouble, maybe she should Register. The punishment for being late would be better than the punishment for not Registering at all, right?

Lorelei slipped into an alcove off the main hall. "We're here."

"How do you know?"

"I told you. Pure brilliance. Plus, I asked some knights from year six and they told me the route changes every time, but this is a good spot for eavesdropping and figuring out what everyone else is doing." It was true. The alcove seemed to swallow light. If they weren't too loud, they could sit here all day.

Except that'd be cheating. And not very knightly. Caedmon crossed his arms. "We need to follow the rules."

Lorelei sighed dramatically. "Please, you started cheating the moment you followed me. I mean, why don't you think for yourself for once?"

"You asked me to follow you!"

"Your point? One of these days, you'll have to do something on your own."

"What's that supposed to mean?"

Lorelei fully faced him, eyes narrowed, like she was assessing him. It made him squirm. "That you're letting some girl with a weird toad fixation do all the hard work, while you mope around."

He gaped at her. Was she delusional? "I'm training to become a knight! I'm at the trial!"

Lorelei scoffed. "Sure. Okay." She held up a hand. "I don't care why you're moping. But if it's for a reason, and not just because you're annoying, maybe do something about it." Her tone softened, just a fraction. "It might help."

Heat flashed in his skull, making him feel like his brain would burst. He wanted to yell, to prove her wrong.

Except she had a point.

And it made him sick.

"Why are *you* here if you find me so annoying? Go do your trial." He made to shove past her. "I'll finish on my own."

A redheaded student burst out of an adjacent room and sprinted down the hall, face white, eyes bulging. Lorelei held her finger to her lips. "See?" she whispered when he disappeared. "Now we know not to go that way. I'm helping you because you need me, Caedmon Tuggle. You'd be remiss without your princess."

"You're not my princess."

She smiled. "Yes. I am."

(258)

He fumed, glaring down at her, while she looked innocently up at him, bright eyes sparkling.

They stood there a moment longer than necessary, staring, glaring, and, in Lorelei's case, smiling. Caedmon broke eye contact first. "Whatever. I'm going to figure this out myself."

"I thought you wanted to win."

"Not by cheating."

Though that wasn't really the problem. He let Jimmy cheat off him countless times. If he was being honest, Lorelei's comment cut deeper than Caedmon liked to admit.

He would detect the curses himself, find the treasure himself, and if Lorelei wanted to tag along, fine. But he wouldn't follow her.

They returned to the fork in the labyrinth and veered right, down a hallway lit by mossy candelabras made of frogspawn and leaves.

He glanced at his instructions again—but they'd changed:

TO PASS THROUGH MY ARMS, EAT MY GARDEN BELLY.
LISTEN TO THE VOICE OF THE LOST, TO THE SONG OF SORROW.

Eat my garden belly…Pass through my arms…What could that mean? It didn't sound like a curse or spell, but he was so new at magic; he probably just didn't get it. The hallway forked again. With nothing else to go on, Caedmon followed his nose toward a fresh scent that reminded him of his mom's cooking.

"Here." He stopped before an emerald door carved with markings he didn't recognize. "We're meant to pass through the door by eating our way through it!"

Lorelei stared dubiously at him. "You're going to eat the door?"

Even her attitude couldn't spoil the feeling of accomplishment rising in his chest. It'd been a while since he engaged his mind this way—solving puzzles and organizing problems so they made sense. He liked it. It felt like his mind was clicking again. He picked at some of the leaves on the doorway, shoving them in his mouth.

Lorelei clapped her hands to her cheeks. "Don't tell me you just ate a random poisonous plant."

Caedmon waved one under Lorelei's nose. "It's just mint. See?"

"What's mint?"

"What...*mint*. Like, mmm, minty..." *Like, mmm, minty?* Caedmon's cheeks heated. When did he lose the ability to speak normally? Probably since the *crushes* conversation. "Just eat some."

"Absolutely not. You shall not lure a princess to poison!"

"You're seriously telling me you've never heard of mint?!"

"Well, *you* had never heard of twenty-four and a half realms, so don't even start with me."

Caedmon placed the mint leaf in her hand. "Eat the mint. I promise, it won't kill you. And if it does, your ghost can haunt my ghost."

Lorelei sighed, rolling her eyes. *"Fine."* As soon as the mint touched her lips, the door swung open, sending moss and flowers cascading to their feet.

But Lorelei's eyes bulged. She grasped her throat and gasped. Did not being exposed to mint make her allergic or something? What had he done?

He grabbed her arm, yanking her back toward the entryway. "Quick! Sir Blainsey! Someone! She's dying!"

Lorelei wrenched free and collapsed in a fit of giggles.

"Wh—" Reality dawned as she breathed normally, beaming at him. "You were *joking?*" Caedmon could punch a wall. *Where* was Ellie? This would be so much more bearable with her.

With a whoop of laughter more carefree than Caedmon had ever heard her, Lorelei dashed past him, through the forest door. "Come, peasant! It's not polite to keep a princess waiting."

Yeah, he could definitely do with punching a wall.

Voices filtered down the hall, a bell ringing in the distance. Thirty minutes gone. Groaning, he followed Lorelei, the leafy door slamming behind him.

It was an explosion of flowers.

In pots and pans and snaking through cracks in stone—

(261)

bright and spikey, and demure and soft, petals were everywhere, making it nearly impossible to wade through the thick foliage.

Caedmon glanced back at his scroll. How was he supposed to find the voice that was lost in here?

Lorelei cooed. "I love petal fugues."

"Petal fugues?"

Lorelei plucked a bright fuchsia flower and tapped its stem. The faintest melody quivered on its petals.

"Perfect! It sings! It must be the lost voice!" He scanned the map. The treasure hunt was meant to culminate in a place called the Chamber of Rubies. If they could get this flower to the Chamber before the final bell rang, he'd win the trial, and be well on his way to becoming a knight and saving his family. If only Excalibur lay at the end of the hunt, too.

Lorelei tilted her head. "Is that what we're looking for? Because if so, you're in trouble." She gestured around her. "Most of these flowers can sing."

"*How?* Can they...hear us?"

Lorelei looked at him like he'd just announced the earth was flat. "Obviously...?"

Caedmon had to ignore that unsettling discovery for a moment. "Then we need one that sings about sorrow."

Lorelei tilted her ear to a blue spiky flower, which spit pollen on her cheek. She grimaced. "Not that one." She stopped at another cascade of white blooms curling around deep green vines. "Oh, I just love Guinevere's flower!" She kissed a petal and bowed her head. "May you find peace; may you have vengeance."

Caedmon stepped away from a snapping orange flower that looked like it wanted to eat his hand. "Vengeance?"

"For her murder."

"Guinevere was murdered? As in King Arthur's wife, Guinevere?"

Lorelei held the hem of her dress away from a blue flower spouting juice. "Has no one told you about the murder of Guinevere?"

"No...Who murdered her?" Caedmon crawled to the center of the garden to listen to more flowers.

"No one knows. King Arthur found her in his bed with a dagger in her heart. Everyone there said her hair began to glow, and a blind girl found her sight. King Arthur declared Guinevere a saint, made a temple in her honor, and we've wished for her peace and vengeance ever since."

"Was she a witch?"

"I don't think so."

"What about Lancelot? Where was he in all this?"

"Who's Lancelot?"

Caedmon turned toward her. "Don't tell me you haven't heard of Lancelot."

"Stop acting like I'm the clueless one! You're the one who didn't know about Guinevere." She pulled a bag of glitter from her pocket and dusted it over the flowers. "Much better," she

(263)

murmured, before returning to Caedmon. "Really though, who's Lancelot?"

Caedmon picked his way through the garden, hunting for a hint of sorrow. "Lancelot was King Arthur's most trusted knight who had an affair with Queen Guinevere. It's just weird he's such a big part of our stories and not mentioned in yours."

Lorelei sighed. "Yes, well, that's how stories go, isn't it?"

"I guess so." Caedmon continued checking the flowers in contemplative silence. Some songs were happier than others, some nonsensical, most didn't have lyrics, and none were particularly sorrowful.

After ten minutes, Caedmon's stomach churned in anxiety, as uneasy as if he was still falling through the sky. What was the witch doing now? Was Ellie safe? Had Roxie told Sir Masten they were in danger?

Caedmon kept one ear trained on the door, listening for a sign of the witch. Not that he knew what to listen for. But it didn't matter either way—there was nothing. Not even the other draftees.

Which was strange. Shouldn't they be here? Or had Caedmon misunderstood the instructions?

He was so sure of it though, and it made sense. All the clues added up. Unless…they weren't the correct clues. "Lorelei, can I see your treasure map?"

Lorelei held up a finger, her ear bent to a wriggling daffodil. "And then what happened?" Lorelei gasped at whatever

(264)

the flower said. "I hope you told her that was the last time you'd accept such behavior. Remember, darling, you're a queen. Always be a queen. Don't let anyone steal your sunshine. And the next time Natalie pushes you into the storm, you yank her right out with you. See what *she* thinks of being left alone in the rain." Lorelei set the flower down and fluffed her hair. "Can I help you?"

"Were you just giving the flower advice?"

"What else did it look like?"

"I...never mind. Can I see your map?"

She handed him her unused scroll. The squiggle marks and instructions were entirely different from Caedmon's—she, too, was meant to follow the trail of spells, but it said nothing about a doorway. Quickly, he compared it to the one he'd snatched for Ellie. Hers was identical to his. So either every other map was different...or someone had tried to place Ellie and Caedmon on a specific path.

Fear had fingers of ice and knives. It latched onto his mind and tried to drag him down. He breathed.

Forced his mind to function.

To keep going.

What if Lorelei was wrong? What if Sir Masten wasn't enough to stop the witch? *What if she had Ellie?*

Roxie said evil magic hovered like a cloud above the mountain, ready to unleash a storm. Maybe this was the storm, and he was in it. Shivers rippled down his arms. If that were true, it meant they weren't any closer to finishing the trial.

If he turned back now and followed Lorelei's instructions, he'd likely finish last anyway, or maybe even be disqualified for cheating off someone else's scroll. It would be safer, but spineless.

But if he followed his own instructions, it could lead him straight to the witch.

Going after her without Excalibur was the exact opposite of what he'd want his friends to do. But if there was the smallest chance she'd kidnapped Ellie, Caedmon would never live with himself if he turned back now.

Even if it was a trap.

His head pounded, drowning out Lorelei's voice. *You're a knight, Caedmon Tuggle*, Ellie had said. She was wrong. He wasn't a knight.

But he could try to be.

He glanced around the flowers again. If he were a witch trying to lure Caedmon down a particular path, what would the clue mean? What would be sorrowful?

What did he know? Whoever cast the spell was from the same place that gave Ellie her magic. That it was potent magic. And…there was something lost about it. The magic was from a lost place. That's what Roxie had said in her riddling way, wasn't it?

"Lorelei, are any of these flowers here from someplace that's lost?"

"Lost?"

He quickly explained everything he'd just realized, including his belief of who waited for them at the end of their hunt. Lorelei should be able to decide what kind of danger she was willing to put herself in.

When he finished, her brow was puckered. "*Well*, it couldn't be these, as they grow in Grandmother's backyard." She continued pointing out flowers she recognized, draining Caedmon's hopes, until finally, she stopped at a tropical plant with multicolored petals. "This one. I thought I recognized it because we have ones just like it at home." She gagged. "But the smell is awful. And instead of leaves, it has thorns." Together, Caedmon and Lorelei bent and listened to the flower's song.

"At night I bloom beneath the moon, and an evermore-shattered sky. Here, I weep, at the end of the Deep, as you lay down your swords and die."

Caedmon sat back on his heels. It sounded sorrowful, but it didn't bring them any closer to understanding who they were up against. "What kind of clue is that?"

"A strange one." Lorelei said breathlessly. "The Deep. It's a myth. Well, supposed to be. It was a hole in the earth that opened when Iselkia fell during the Fall of Camelot."

"Iselkia?" Where had he heard that before?

(267)

"One of the three Arthurian islands. They were really powerful, and the contamination of magic hit them the worst, as they were closest to Camelot. If this flower was around to watch the Deep, it must be from Iselkia." She frowned. "But no one has been able to visit Iselkia since the Fall. Grandmother always complains the cloud of magic around it is too thick."

Caedmon tapped the petals. "Um, hi, flower. Could you please tell us what you know about magic from Iselkia?"

Lorelei stared incredulously at him. "What are you doing talking to that flower?"

"You said they could hear us! And you were talking to the daffodil earlier!"

"That's because *daffodils* are cursed fairies meant to live as flowers for disobeying the Fairy Godmother. Everybody knows that. Most flowers hear us and come up with songs to help them understand the world." She looked back at the now silent Iselkian flower. "But once their song has been sung, they begin to die." Sure enough, some of the flowers they'd listened to were already wilting.

Caedmon leaned against the mossy wall, raking his hands through his hair. "Okay. Think. Why would the witch want us to know about a flower from an island that's been gone for centuries?"

Lorelei walked around the flower, frowning. "I'm not sure, but I think I was wrong."

"I didn't think that was possible."

(268)

Lorelei scoffed. "It rarely is. But look. It wants to sing again."

They bent their ears to its petals. This time, the flower's voice was so soft, Caedmon might have imagined it if not for Lorelei's similarly shocked face. *"The Deep has come. The Deep has taken. Drowning, I am. Dying, are we. Rise, my love, and let me bloom. Rise, my love, and cast our world in your light. I give you my ashes. I give you my all. Rise."*

The flower wheezed her last word and crumbled to burning ash in Caedmon's palm. He snatched his hand away, rubbing it against his tunic. "What was *that* about?"

And that's when he felt it.

Magic.

It tingled up and down his arms like a beast's talons hunting for the right place to puncture. Bile rose in his throat. Ellie was right: He had to *feel* it. And he didn't ever want to feel this again. "There's a curse in here," he muttered, voice low. Lorelei's eyes widened, but she nodded. And she didn't run away.

She sprinkled Evermore dust on a bright blue flower and muttered an incantation. "Evermore magic isn't strong enough to fully protect people from a witch's curse, but it could buy us an extra minute in case..." She trailed off, biting her lip.

"Thanks, Lorelei."

She smiled—not her usual smirk, but something softer, kinder.

(269)

He turned toward a statue of a weeping angel in the back of the garden. The source of the magic. And stepped forward.

The curse thrashed and lunged for his lungs, like it wanted to squeeze and torture.

Lorelei's magic held fast.

The statue spread her wings and the door behind her creaked open as she stepped to the side, tucking her wings in tight. Bowing her head, she became still once more.

Cold darkness flooded the garden, hollowing Caedmon's stomach.

Lorelei gripped his arm.

"Hello, Caedmon Tuggle," rang a regal, bell-like voice that inexplicably made Caedmon want to scream. "How very long I have awaited this moment. Now *bow*."

TWENTY-NINE
ELLIE

"PLEASE BE HERE," ELLIE MUTTERED, CURSING HER-self for not looking earlier. "Please, magic, saints, fairies, and all things good in this world. Let me find the spellbook."

The resolve had gripped her as soon as she'd stepped foot on the glass platform—making her step right back off.

Caedmon was a knight, whether he realized it or not, and belonged in the trials.

But not Ellie.

She was a witch.

And it was time the world knew.

The book wasn't in her wardrobe. Nor atop it. Not her bookshelf or windowsill.

Growing desperate, she dropped to her knees and fished for it beneath her bed. She could picture it—curling blue let-ters; musty brown leather; thick, aging pages.

Roxie's words sang through her memory, the revelation she'd unleashed threatening to spill from her and consume her bedroom in magic. The one who cast the curse was here, likely preparing to intervene in the trials, meaning Caedmon was in terrible danger.

What's more, *the witch hailed from the same land as Ellie's magic.*

If Ellie could find out where her *own* magic was from, she could figure out which old tongue the witch cast her curse in and finally track the witch!

Hopefully before anyone else got hurt.

Fortunately, there was a spell to discover one's own origins. But she needed her book.

She nearly screamed. It wasn't under the bed, though she did find a dead mouse Bianca had likely been hiding.

Groaning, she sat back in bed. "Where are you?" she whispered. "Where would you be?"

She could still picture the first time she read it. The book had been tucked beneath her mother's bed for as long as she could remember, and Ellie had spent her life practicing self-control by not peeking to see what was inside. But year after year, it called to her.

Ellie's cheeks heated at the memory of stealing it. Not because she stole it—but because she *liked* stealing it.

She enjoyed yanking it out from beneath the bed skirt and shuttering away in her closet to read by fairy light. Yes, her mother might yell at her if she found out. Yes, she loathed getting in trouble.

(272)

But oh, the thrill of sneaking into her own corner, disobeying the one woman she tried so very hard to please. For in a small part of her heart, she knew: She could never please Mother. Never in a trillion years. The dragons could rise, the sky could fall, and still, Mother would look upon her with scorn.

So that day—fed up, with that temper Mother so deplored building in her chest, making her want to shatter glasses and scream—she stole it, and she had kept it tucked in her closet in Roses and Needles Finishing School ever since.

Of all topics, it detailed the history of witches' magic. Where it came from. What happened during the Fall of Camelot. How it could become contaminated. And—likely why Mother kept it hidden—how that particular writer believed the theory of magic contamination had been a myth. And that clamping witches' power was a mere ruse—a distraction to keep people from looking too closely at the real cause of the Fall of Camelot.

All her life, Ellie had been told witches would turn evil if they accepted the might of their magic.

Yet there were voices, however small, who believed otherwise. The author of this mysterious book.

And Caedmon's. *Accepting who you truly are is one of the bravest things a person can do. So maybe, casting that spell won't make you evil. Maybe it will make you brave.*

In the hours since calling Galahad to her aid—which she

(273)

was certain happened, despite his mysterious disappearance—magic had been knocking against her mind, hunting for a way in.

It didn't feel evil. It felt…like home.

Like her truest self.

At long last, it was time Ellie accepted who she was. Ellie steeled herself. She would be brave, not evil.

It was time she became a full-fledged witch.

A knocking interrupted her thoughts. She peeked through her door hole, but no one was there.

The knocking resumed.

From below.

The floorboards. Her fingers grazed the floorboards, testing, pulling, until—one came loose. She wrenched it up, revealing what she sought. The book seemed to glow, waiting for her.

Calling to her.

To that slumbering magic in her bones.

She flipped through it, pages as stiff and unyielding as she remembered, as if made from something tougher than parchment or paper—something to last a thousand years.

Her fingers paused, heart racing, as she arrived at the contents she needed.

Witches' magic originates from three
known locations in this world. There is a way

(274)

to discover one's origins, but it requires a gift. Only those with magic in their veins can see the answers they seek. Prove you are worthy with the incantation below, and I shall reveal my secrets to you.

She held her breath. Never once, in all the years she'd pored over Mother's book, had she dared to prove she was worthy.

That she was a witch.

Her gaze darted back toward the orchards where other students had gathered at the cliff's edge despite the early morn, eager to judge who'd succeed.

And who would perish.

"Ellie."

Ellie jumped at the crisp accent, the concerned tone. Omari Evelant stood in her doorway, sweating. "She's here isn't she?" he gasped. "The woman who cast the curse?"

Ellie nodded. Omari Evelant was in her bedroom. She could scream.

But this was not the time for screaming. This was the time for magic. "I'm a witch," she blurted.

He backed into the door. "You're—*what*?"

"I'm sorry I kept it secret, but I can't let the DeJoies clamp my powers. And now I have to cast the spell to accept my witchcraft. It's the only way to find the person who cast the curse. Please don't hate me. Don't be afraid of me. I—"

"Hey." Omari shook his head and knelt beside her. "I'm… surprised but I'm not *afraid* of you." He took her hand and squeezed it. "And how could I hate the girl who reminds me of my little sister? I think you're really brave."

He gently withdrew his hand and smiled, oblivious to how his words speared her, reminding her: Omari Evelant had a girlfriend and only saw Ellie as a little sister. As a replacement little sister, no less. Even if he didn't have a girlfriend, Ellie wasn't ready for things like boyfriends. It felt too adult, and she was still trying to figure out what having friends felt like. Omari was older than her—and not an option.

"I'm here for you. Whatever you need to do."

Ellie swallowed. That was more than she had ever hoped for. And today, now, she could be grateful that as she accepted her true self, there was someone standing by her side.

She clenched her shaking hands. "If I turn into an evil monster, don't let me kill anyone."

He laughed. "Never."

There'd be no going back after this. No reversing the magic. The moon tattoo would appear on her hand, marking her forever. Not only that—everyone would know she'd lied. Registered witches and sorcerers never developed the birthmarks. The magic wasn't strong enough. But when an unclamped witch or sorcerer accepted the entirety of their magic, the mark was there for all to see.

And people knew to run in fear.

(276)

Heart pattering, she took a deep breath, the spell she'd known and ignored all her life rising to the surface, breaking free—she was breaking free—

"A witch of yore, I claim my magic now; from dusk to dawn my power rightly reigns!"

The windowpanes shattered, sending Bianca hissing and diving beneath her blanket. Her toads hopped to and fro, and a whoosh of silver sparks swirled around her hair, lifting her curls to the sky.

Warm energy shot from her heart to her limbs, then out to the world, spearing toward the sky in crimson and silver ribbons.

A storm cloud gathered in her room, starlight and lightning raining down upon her, as a great flapping echoed in the distance.

It was done. She beamed at Omari.

Ellie was a full-fledged witch.

THIRTY
ELLIE

HOLY SAINTS, WHAT HAD SHE DONE? SURELY SHE'D gone mad.

Then why did it feel so right?

Those emotions Mother always hated boiled in Ellie's heart, flooding her body, bursting everywhere. She felt like a caged animal who'd been set free, and now the world would know her secret.

They would know she was a witch.

No more hiding.

Her mother's book swam in and out of focus.

"Ellie?" called Omari's faraway voice. "Are you all right?"

A glass of water touched her lips.

"Here, drink."

She obeyed, guzzling greedily, forcing herself to focus on her bedroom, to remain in her body and mind. She hadn't become a witch to burn across skies and declare herself free. She was still a fairy godmother. She still had a friend to help.

A sword to find, a curse to break, lives to save.

The book, once partially blank to her, unfurled with curling script, describing curses and spells, and all she could do with this marvelous magic of hers.

"My origins!"

Ellie read the passage aloud:

Witches' magic is known to originate from three locations. While all witches draw upon the night, and many spoke in Old Arthurian, for their most powerful spells, they used the tongues and properties of their ancestors.

The first, from the Gardens of Nighever, deep in fairy groves. Before the Fall, their magic was strongest in Old Arrendia and drew upon the magic of midnight-blooming latticewords.

The second, in a wind-soaked land, sheltering lakes of unfulfilled wishes. Avalon— where the tongue of Old Avalonian strengthened their curses and spells.

The third, people seldom speak of. The third is a faraway land people say is no more. It fell alongside Camelot and has never been seen again. But once, when starlit witches led armies atop valiant chevolants, a land called Iselkia reigned.

Rome had yet to fall to the Pendragon rule.

Egypt had not yet known Arthur's conquest.

And the dragon was still free.

Beneath each description was a list of ingredients used to strengthen each language's spells—and find those who cast them.

Omari blew out a puff of air. "Wow. So, which one are you from?"

"There's a spell...." Beneath, in swirling black ink, beckoned the spell to find her origins—which would bring her one step closer to tracking the witch.

Ellie shivered. It wasn't a pretty, tame spell from the Renaissance, but brutal, unyielding. Old Arthurian.

It could be dangerous, she reminded herself. Magic spells created before the Fall were said to cause undo harm and could bring the skies crashing down once more.

But Ellie was feeling dangerous.

And wild.

Throwing caution to the wind, she leaned out her window, heedless of the shattered glass.

"Wait, Ellie—"

But she was through with waiting. *"Vengor Issai!"* she yelled. The spell's translation was scrawled below it: SHOW ME MY BLOOD. Brutal and direct, like the witches of yore were said to be.

For a moment, all was still. Even the magic in her heart seemed to quiet.

(280)

Until shadows spilled and a great rumbling rose from the depths of the sea.

The waves undulated, creating a whirlpool, as a winged mass loomed on the horizon. What had she awoken? What was coming for her? If she could only see...

Ellie leaned farther out the window, as if she could dive into the water and grab the answers she sought.

Omari's hands caught her blouse, catching her before she fell. Even so, her vision blurred, head dizzy.

Was she crying?

She blinked, but every time she opened her eyes, the shapes grew fuzzier, sounds more distant, so she kept her eyes wide lest she lose her sight entirely.

Fear gripped her heart for the first time. "I can't see," she whimpered, panic rising. "I can't see!"

"It's okay! Ellie, stay with me. You're all right. I've got you."

But he didn't have her.

For she was far away. Sight and hearing returned, placing her in an unfamiliar world. Wherever she was, happiness and prosperity thrived, with golden pillars supporting a glorious city rising out of a cerulean ocean, marketplaces selling fabulous silks and pearls.

And magic.

So much of it. Everything floated or sang, witches practicing freely on the streets, dancing through walls of fire, while black-winged chevolants soared through cloudless skies.

(281)

Chevolants. That couldn't be. Or if it were…this was…she was…

She gasped, the shadow of a dragon wing passing over the glittering sea. She whirled on the spot for a better look, but it disappeared behind golden turrets.

This was before the Fall of Camelot.

Everywhere she turned, people in brightly colored robes swished past, though their faces were drawn, worry lines creasing their foreheads.

They all marched in one direction.

The people closest to a sky-high set of golden gates climbed, screaming for their princess.

Ellie followed the commotion, drawn by some tug on her heart, like a string had wrapped around it and yanked.

Whose princess? Where was she? And when, exactly? How long until Camelot fell? Centuries? Or minutes? Was this even the Pendragon Empire, or a time far more ancient?

A great rumbling shook the earth, knocking Ellie to her knees. She didn't feel the plush rug of her bedroom. Only the golden city stone, far away and long ago. Someone shoved her, the torrent of people intensifying.

Those still practicing magic stopped, while vendors rushed out of the marketplace, screaming.

Though the wind was still and the sky clean, the ocean whisked its waves into a frenzy, until an enormous tidal wave

(282)

frothed at the mouth, threatening to drown the world. Sun glinted off its curves, turning it a deep red.

More clamored for the castle. "My princess! Princess, you must come! Please!"

It wasn't a trick of the light, Ellie realized with dawning horror.

The ocean had turned as red as blood. Ellie's breath stopped. No, it couldn't be. This couldn't be happening.

This couldn't *have* happened.

The chevolants neighed and whinnied, and from somewhere beyond the sky, a magnificent screech tore apart the wind.

A screech quite like what she imagined a dragon would sound like.

Again, the earth shook, and the looks people gave one another...It was as if they understood.

They knew what befell them.

Collectively, they stopped, sorcerers and witches sending flares of magic to the sky, others bringing ever-colored flowers to their lips and bowing. As the ground rumbled once more, golden pillars and towers split from the earth, sending chunks of stone hurtling for the city, and the tidal wave of blood poured from the sky, a bolt of lightning flashing in the east. The world ripped open and swallowed people whole. Ellie shrieked, shielding her eyes, for she couldn't look, wouldn't look.

The screams quieted.

The world settled.

Through half-closed lids, Ellie glimpsed a world of ash, its people gone, the chevolants spiriting to the earth. She widened her gaze—

Dappled sunlight streamed through her glassless window, shining on her mussed bed, her mother's book on her floor, Omari kneeling before her, checking her temperature.

She was back in the Château des Chevaliers.

Shaking. From head to toe, her body quaked, like it was trying to expunge whatever it just saw.

Ellie collapsed to the ground and cried. All those people, gone. All that life. Their torment, their hopelessness. Their realization that the end had come, and they were powerless to stop it.

Omari gently patted her back, nudging the glass of water toward her. "Where did you go?" he whispered.

She wiped tears from her eyes, banishing the horrible images she would remember for the rest of her life. "Somewhere I never want to see again," she croaked.

She'd asked magic to show her where her magic came from.

Magic had done so—and more.

There were only three places witchcraft was meant to come from, one being the Isle of Iselkia.

If she was right...Ellie had seen the great kingdom's downfall.

She had witnessed the Deep.

Ellie stood, forcing her hands to steady, Omari scrambling to his feet after her. Ellie glanced at Mother's book again, barely daring to breathe. Ellie had Iselkian magic in her blood.

"The curse caster is from the lost Isle of Iselkia."

Omari's eyes widened.

"I don't know how, but it's true."

A flap of wind snagged her attention. She reeled back at the enormous creature flying outside her window.

Was she somehow in the past once more? Trapped between times?

Omari's gasp answered for her. "A chevolant...?"

She ran to Galahad, his inky wings absorbing light. He whinnied, nuzzling her. She'd never heard of the chevolants being immortal—but surely if some had survived the Fall of Camelot long enough for Galahad to have been born, someone would have noticed in the past few centuries. Right?

"He came to me when I fell. I thought I imagined it but... he's real."

"I think he wants you to ride him."

Another bell rang. The trial was almost complete, the curse caster nowhere to be found. What if the witch was waiting for the trial's conclusion for a grand entrance? What if she'd already cursed half the people here? Ellie was running out of time. She had to do something, now. Scanning the list of ingredients used to find Iselkian magic, Ellie took a deep

(285)

breath. It was time to make her tracking potion. Unlike her failed fire magic under the mountain, this had to work.

"I won't be long."

The chevolant reared back on its hind legs in midair. Without waiting for reason, fear, or Omari to persuade her otherwise, Ellie climbed onto the creature's back and soared for the sea.

THIRTY-ONE
CAEDMON

DESPITE HIS SHAKING LEGS, CAEDMON STEPPED through the doorway the commanding voice had opened, Lorelei close beside him, leaving the peaceful garden of singing flowers behind.

No sign of Ellie. Though that didn't mean the witch wasn't holding her captive somewhere else.

The room was dark and cold, candles snuffed, windows shuttered, bare but for a throne carved of tropical, thorned flowers, atop which sat a long-limbed, lithe woman masked in gold, sheets of white silk draped around her elegant frame. Her flowing silver hair was tied in a regal knot. "I thought you were a knight. Yet you are afraid."

"I am not afraid."

A slash of red-painted lips. "Then you are foolish, too." She clicked her fingers and candles sprang to life, flames dancing on a phantom wind, illuminating the orange and fuchsia petals of the throne.

The Iselkian flowers.

Flowers that told tales of despair and annihilation, that even now, hummed their discordant melody, curling around the woman's frame. Supporting her.

Like she was their ruler.

"Where's my friend?" Caedmon's voice was low, steady, belying his rapid heartbeat.

The woman cocked her head, candlelight flickering across her gilded mask. "Caedmon Tuggle. A pleasure to finally make your acquaintance." She waved a careless hand. "I do not have your friend." She gave a slow, sharpened smile. "Ellie Bettlebump, I presume?"

Caedmon broke out in a cold sweat. How did she know Ellie's name?

"Oh yes, I know of whom you speak."

"Why did you bring us here?" Lorelei challenged. "Why did you want us to know about the Deep?"

"It is a lost memory. With lost magic. And lost things should not remain so."

"What do you mean?" Caedmon asked.

Her smile grew. "Come now. You can do better."

Caedmon glowered. He didn't have time for games. "You're the witch who cast a curse on this mountain." The blood was pumping so loudly in his ears, he could barely concentrate. For weeks, all he'd done was picture this person—who could it be? Who could make the Knights of the Round

(288)

Table scared? What would he do if he confronted her, this horrible woman responsible for Jimmy's death?

And what did she want with *him*?

Now that he was here, he was painfully aware he had no magic, no sword. Nothing but searing anger that blotted his vision. Suddenly, he was half there, half in the moonlit park near the Boulder Falls graveyard as Jimmy barreled into him, sprinting from some horror in the forest. *There's something in there. My—my chest hurts. Something's wrong.*

And a white-coated doctor with permanent frown lines. *There's nothing more we can do. He's gone.*

Jimmy's lifeless face became Carly, then his mom, his dad, his grandpa.

Ellie.

"Yes," the witch said, interrupting his thoughts, voice biting. "I cast a curse. So when the mountains fall and the seas rise…look to the skies."

Caedmon's stomach hollowed. There was no warmth in those gray eyes. No heart, no passion. Nothing. Cruelty was a calculation, a means to an end, and if she did not feel, what was she capable of?

"Remove your mask, peasant," Lorelei commanded, though her voice wobbled.

"Ahh. The DeJoie girl. I thought it was you. For a while."

"You thought what was me?"

The woman flicked her fingers. "The point is you're

unimportant. Your life is small. And meaningless. I'd planned to remove you from my tangled little web, if only to make my life easier," she said, as casually as if speaking of the weather.

Caedmon grabbed Lorelei's hand, prepared to yank her away and run.

The witch's eyes narrowed. "Perhaps I shall still. Curious that you, Boy of Nothing, would be drafted to serve as an *esteemed* Knight of the Round Table. But when I looked at the seven and followed the three, it was your face I saw in the water. I admit, you're less interesting than I would have expected." She sighed. "But I suppose that's how it goes."

Caedmon flushed. Did everyone think he was incapable of being a knight? Or that it was a ridiculous idea? And why did she see his face in water? "I will be a knight. And I won't let your curse hurt anybody else." Not here, and not back in Boulder Falls.

"You will be fortunate if you survive long enough to turn thirteen, let alone become an anointed knight." Her gaze intensified, slits of gray behind the gold mask. "Some fates were written long before your time. There are lives I claimed long ago, and there is nothing to be done. Though I admire you for trying. Truly, I do. It is a noble effort. And that is, after all, why this place exists." She gestured above, a purple ring glinting on her thumb.

"Whose lives?" Lorelei asked. "What do you want? For I won't let you have it. The DeJoies—"

"Quiet, witch." She glanced above, a smile blossoming on her lips. "Interesting. Very interesting."

"What's interesting?" Caedmon asked as Lorelei scoffed.

"I'm not a witch. DeJoies aren't born witches."

The woman cocked her head, the gesture purely animalistic. Predatory. "And yet."

Lorelei's brow puckered, but before she could respond, the ground rumbled beneath them, screams sounding from somewhere in the distance.

Debris drifted to Caedmon's shoulders. "Stop this! Don't hurt anyone else. Just tell me what you want with me."

"You think this is me?" The witch leaned forward. "You will not die by my hands today. Your friend, however...*Ellie* is becoming who she's meant to be." She swept to her full height, silks billowing around her. "Which means I must go. Thank you, Caedmon Tuggle, Boy of Nothing."

"For what?"

She paused, candles spluttering to darkness once more. "Allowing me to know you. It helps me understand, see. It helps me understand how we've gotten here, at the end of this road, and the beginning of the new. And what role you must play. Until we meet again."

Before Caedmon could stop her, she vanished in a cloud of white smoke, sending chills up his arms.

The screams grew louder as Sir Blainsey's voice echoed

(291)

down the corridor. "Draftees to the entrance! This is not part of the trial! Report to the entrance immediately!"

Lorelei and Caedmon looked at each other. The world shook, the chill lingered, and Caedmon's pulse wouldn't slow. What had just happened?

THIRTY-TWO
CAEDMON

IT TOOK EVERY OUNCE OF CAEDMON'S WILLPOWER not to collapse and sleep for a hundred years.

But he couldn't. Not yet.

First, he had to make sure Ellie was okay.

Omari had filled him in on everything that had happened—no wonder Ellie hadn't attended the trial.

The curse caster's voice lingered in his thoughts, haunting him. Somehow, she'd known what Ellie meant to do. Whoever they were up against was even more dangerous than he'd realized.

But since disappearing on some flying horse Omari called a chevolant, Ellie was nowhere to be found.

She wasn't in her room at the top of the long spiral staircase, nor in the library, orchards, or Sword Garden. "Maybe Lorelei can look for her in the girls' bathroom," Caedmon suggested when they met in the Great Hall an hour later.

"Lorelei's passed out in the east-wing drawing room,"

Omari said. "Snoring. Cora and Rosalind are taking care of her. They've stopped Roxie from trying to put bones in her nose twice now."

"Then I need to talk to Sir Masten." It was time to persuade the head knight to intervene. Before anyone else got hurt.

Omari continued searching for Ellie as Caedmon climbed the spiral staircase to Sir Masten's heavy oak doors. The head knight bent over a textbook, brow furrowed. Caedmon could have sworn he read the word *Excalibur* in fine gold print before Sir Masten shoved the book aside, strode toward Caedmon, and clapped him on the back, nearly knocking him over. "Caedmon." He beamed, dark eyes twinkling. "Well done, boy. Well done."

"Well—?" Caedmon stopped short as Sir Masten retrieved a gold medal hanging from his wall and placed it around Caedmon's neck.

"You won the trial, Caedmon. I'm very proud."

Ellie burst into the room, sweat dripping down her forehead, and spread her arms wide as a starfish. "Hello!"

Caedmon slumped in relief. "There you are! We were looking everywhere for you!"

Sir Masten blinked, mouth twitching in amusement beneath his beard. "Ellie. I'm glad you are here, as I'd like to discuss your absence from the last trial and your high risk of failure as a knight. I'd ask you to wait outside...." He muttered a prayer to the saints. "But I don't believe you'll listen."

She slammed the door and strutted inside, hands on hips.

(294)

"That is correct. I'm about to make a massive declaration and you—" She stopped, arms dropping to her sides, gasping at the medal around Caedmon's neck. "Wait, stop everything immediately! You won the trial?!"

"No, I didn't even follow the right instructions." Though that's what Sir Masten said, wasn't it?

The head knight grinned, relaxing into his leather chair. "You chose to do what was brave. You acted like a true knight. Not to mention helping your peers fight the serpentelles."

Caedmon leaned against the wall, stunned. He won. He actually won a trial.

Ellie bounced on her toes. "Oh, oh, oh, I'm so thrilled!"

"Is that all, you two?"

Still beaming, Ellie slammed a compass on Sir Masten's desk. "No. Sir, I have a way to track the witch who cursed this mountain."

Sir Masten looked from her to the compass. "Only an Unregistered witch can find an Unregistered witch."

Her smile dipped a fraction, but she stood her ground, hazel eyes turning molten. "I am an Unregistered witch. A full witch. I can cast spells and curses and I don't care if I go to prison because I've accepted myself and nothing can stop me now."

Caedmon clapped his hand over her mouth. She somehow kept speaking—something about her identity and brilliance— it was a blur. He had to get her out of there immediately. When

(295)

he'd told her to be herself, he didn't think she'd go and tell the knights her biggest secret!

Sir Masten, however, surprised him, and chuckled. "You have gumption." He pocketed the compass. "Now it's time to return to your studies."

Ellie shoved Caedmon's hand aside. "But—I—"

Sir Masten shook his head, pointing to the door. "Out. Now. Both of you. I told you once before that I don't want to hear another word about it. Don't make me repeat it. You'll never sleep at night again if you get wrapped up in the likes of the curse caster."

"Why won't you help?" Caedmon blurted. "This curse affects you, too! You'll train me to fight but not find the witch whose curse could hurt my family?" *And hurt me?* he added silently, realizing with a jolt how much it bothered him. He'd begun to think of Sir Masten as a mentor. But he didn't seem to care.

Sir Masten rubbed his eyes, heaving a sigh of the weary. "How do you plan to take on someone dangerous enough to cast deathly curses? If I catch you contacting her in any way, I'll chain you to the library." Sir Masten paused, looking at Ellie, eyes burning gold, gaze drifting to a new mark on her hand in the shape of a crescent moon. "You really are an Unregistered witch...."

Ellie rubbed the silver mark with her thumb. "With magic from the lost Isle of Iselkia." Her voice was breathless, eyes

(296)

wild with excitement, despite her declaration being incredibly dangerous.

Hadn't she just said this could land her in prison?

Caedmon's hunch was right. A part of Ellie really did enjoy dangerous situations. A bit like Jimmy had.

And he was not going to lose another friend to their recklessness.

"We'll let it go," Caedmon said abruptly. "We'll go back to our studies. Sorry, Sir Masten."

Without waiting for Sir Masten's reaction, he grabbed Ellie's hand and pulled her out of the head knight's office, all the way back to the Sword Garden.

Once alone, he took her shoulders, heart beating erratically. "Your magic is from Iselkia?"

"Yes, but why—"

"I met her," he interrupted, his thoughts barely able to stay organized enough to speak. "I met the woman who cast the curse." He explained the colorful flower's mournful tune and desire for its queen, crumbling to ash before the masked woman appeared. "So not only is the witch from Iselkia; she wants us to know. It's like…she's challenging us, trying to see how much we can figure out. She seemed to know about you."

Ellie frowned. "What do you mean?"

"When you accepted your magic, it's like she was waiting for it."

"But…nobody told me to do it. It was all my decision.

(297)

My own." A hint of defensiveness crept into her voice, like it couldn't have been anyone else's plan, for it would take something away from her.

"Okay…just…be careful."

Ellie bit her lip and shoved her curls out of her face. "Well, we'll just have to be prepared when we find her. Which we're doing now, no matter what Sir Masten says. I made the potion I need using Iselkian ingredients, so when I listen for her again, I should be able to track the ripple her curse caused."

"That's amazing! What—" Caedmon groaned. "I didn't think—your compass. Sir Masten still has it."

An embarrassed smile spread across Ellie's face. "We don't need the compass. I just wanted something to slam on Sir Masten's table for dramatic effect. We just need me." She faltered. "That is, if you still want my help. I'm sorry I wasn't there for the trial."

"Are you kidding me? You're the best, Ellie. Let's find the others. We should leave tonight, once we've planned."

Ellie stifled a yawned, reminding Caedmon they hadn't slept since the previous night.

"And maybe after we take a nap," he amended. "After you." He smirked, nudging her. "Witch."

THIRTY-THREE
ELLIE

LORELEI FLIPPED HER HAIR. "THE FIRST QUESTION isn't when, it's how."

"It's who," Roxie corrected.

"And when."

"You just said it's not when."

Lorelei rolled her eyes. "That's because it wasn't the *first* question. Then…where was I?"

Ellie blocked out their chatter as she scanned her spellbook for inspiration, time ticking away the seconds, anxious sweat pooling beneath her arms. The longer they waited, the farther the witch could travel, and Ellie had no idea how far her limited magic would reach.

Omari ducked beneath tendrils of low-hanging ivy, meeting them in the amphitheater, where they prepared for their adventure. He grinned, momentarily stopping her heart. He knew. He knew she was a witch, and he accepted her.

He passed out jeweled daggers, keeping an elegant sword

for himself. "I'm not a sorcerer, so I thought it'd be helpful to at least have a weapon to…" He glanced at Ellie. "What are we planning to do once we find this woman, exactly?"

"Erm, working on it," she squeaked. She might have devised a way to *find* the witch but hadn't had the foresight to figure out what they'd *do* once they saw her. A fool's mistake, and one difficult to remedy with so little sleep. She was wired with adrenaline, but her thoughts were jumpy and erratic, having trouble forming logic or sense.

"At the moment, we're going with, 'Can you please take back your mysterious but obviously deathly curse and explain how you're from an island that fell to ruin centuries ago?'" Caedmon said.

Omari raised an eyebrow. "Doesn't really roll off the tongue, does it."

Caedmon joined Ellie's side away from the group, whispering, "Is there anything in that spellbook that will freeze her somehow?"

"I'm looking," Ellie snapped, then closed her eyes, tears leaking from the corners. "Sorry, I'm just so tired. And I haven't trained enough to do almost anything in here, so I'm trying to find the simplest spells. There was one I found to make her eyelashes grow, so I thought we could, you know, temporarily blind her…."

She trailed off as he gave her a dubious look. "Well, I don't know!"

Lorelei flounced to the center of the group. "You needn't

(300)

worry, peasants. I've come to save the day. I brought Evermore dust for everyone and my tiaras."

Roxie's smile was feral. "To…?"

"Oh, they're quite sharp! Never underestimate the power of jewels." She nodded sagely. "And I thought we could bargain with one."

"Not everyone cares as much about worldly jewels as you," Roxie hissed.

Lorelei's gaze was cool. "No. But she clearly cares about Iselkia, right?" Lorelei held up a crown unlike the others. It was neither pretty nor dainty, but fierce and demanding, jagged waves of silver cresting into glimmering stones.

"This belonged to the royal Iselkian family, long, long ago. I found it in my collection after my *much*-needed beauty sleep. A fabulous idea, no? Perhaps she'd be willing to lift the curse for a priceless relic of Iselkia."

Everyone was silent, assessing her.

"That's…a really good idea," Ellie admitted.

Lorelei tossed her hair. "I know. By the way, I see that moon mark on your hand you keep trying to hide from me."

Ellie's breath caught. Saints above, this was so not the time for a highly uncomfortable but admittedly inevitable confrontation! Didn't Lorelei know Ellie had a witch to catch?

"I know you're a witch. I've known for weeks. So stop lying to me and letting everyone else know what's going on because it's *rude*."

(301)

Caedmon grabbed Ellie's arm, like he could pull her away and keep her safe.

But Ellie knew better. She knew the second she cast the spell that she would never be safe again. The moon mark from accepting her heritage shone silver on her hand, curling around her knuckles. There would be no hiding now.

She stepped out of his grasp and faced Lorelei, and for a heart-stopping moment, all she saw was the witch screaming at the border all those months ago, tortured by DeJoie soldiers.

Blood rushed in her ears, and suddenly, she wished she was what Mother feared. Wished her temper really could make flames spit from her tongue like a dragon's. "You're right. I am an Unregistered witch," she declared, letting some inner flame fuel her. "And I don't think I'm wrong. I think the world is wrong. You can tell your family, and they can try to punish me, but I won't let them. I will find Loreena Royenale and learn how to make the world better and safer with witchcraft, so by the time your family finds me, I will be too powerful for them to do anything about it. They can try. And they can fail."

Ellie's heart beat so loudly, she had no idea if her friends gasped or spoke or stood in silence. She saw only Lorelei, those azure eyes revealing nothing.

Slowly, Lorelei walked toward Ellie, velvet cloak trailing in fallen flower petals, and extended her hand. "You're a good person, Ellie Bettlebump. I will never tell my family the truth. I swear it."

Ellie blinked repeatedly, opening and closing her mouth in shock, then flung her arms around Lorelei. "Oh, I knew you were nicer than you seemed! What great friends we shall be! What wondrous stories we shall share!"

Roxie visibly relaxed, reattaching her foot, which she'd apparently been holding in case she had to throw it at one of them.

Omari cleared his throat. "Um, not to interrupt, but I think I found a spell that could work."

Ellie disentangled herself and scanned the page. "An immobilizing spell! I'll stop the curse caster from doing anything, and then we can discuss the bargain." She slammed the book shut. "Perfection!"

Now that they had a plan, they needed a way to travel. Galahad swooped toward them on Ellie's request—earning much deserved praise and accolades—but he wasn't large enough to hold them all. "I'll just go," Ellie insisted. "Flying Galahad will be faster than sitting around here thinking of other ideas."

This earned her a definitive, exclamatory "No!" from everyone, so Ellie dropped it. But she *vehemently* disagreed.

"What about the pirate?" Caedmon asked.

Ellie shot him a glare. "No time for piracy. The longer we wait, the farther she goes and the harder this will be, and if you think now is the time to wear an eye patch and profess your undying love to the sea, be my guest! But I have—" She paused, a certain sandy-haired, freckle-faced boy coming to mind. "Oh, that was an actual suggestion, wasn't it?"

"It was."

"Ahh. The pirate…"

"You know a pirate?" Lorelei asked.

"Mickey Murphy," Caedmon explained.

Roxie's head swiveled around so it was completely backward, her eyes above her back. Lorelei shrieked. "I know Mickey Murphy," Roxie said. "He visits the Urokshi from time to time, bringing us enchanted seeds from which knowledge blooms, and jewels to tell us who is good." Her gaze lingered on Lorelei. "And who is not."

Lorelei stuck her tongue out at Roxie, her cheeks rosier than usual.

"He said to let him know if we ever need his help," Caedmon reminded her. "I think now, we do."

Ellie bit her lip. "I don't know….Trusting more people seems risky. But how else can we travel?" Before anyone had a chance to answer, she clapped her hands. "It is decided."

Lorelei glanced up from her collection of tiaras. "It is?"

"We will engage the pirate."

"Wait." Caedmon jumped to his feet and looked at each of them in turn. "This will be dangerous. None of you have to be involved."

"But—" Ellie interrupted.

"I'm serious. Whatever this witch wants, it has nothing to

(304)

do with any of you. There's no reason you should put yourselves at risk for me."

"No offense but I'm not doing it for you." Lorelei gathered her tiaras and stalked toward him. "I'm here for me. That woman called me a witch and I want to know why. She's obviously mistaken, but what could lead her to that mistake? It's strange. And I'm going to figure it out."

"So the pretty princess cares about more than tiaras and jewels?" Roxie said.

Lorelei smiled. "You think I'm pretty? That's so sweet. I'm here because I'm a DeJoie. DeJoies do not cower. Now. You said something about a pirate?"

THIRTY-FOUR
ELLIE

MICKEY'S SHIP CRESTED OVER THE HORIZON, BLACK sails flapping in the wind.

Galahad flew them down to the ship one at a time so as to avoid Sir Masten's notice. Preoccupied though he seemed, they doubted he'd miss an enormous pirate ship anchored beneath the floating mountain. So, they flew.

And now, they would sail.

"Are you all sure?" Caedmon asked for the fifth time as Galahad landed with Ellie.

Mickey propped his feet up on the steering wheel, grinning. "I told you to call me when you had an adventure. *This* is an adventure. Don't you agree, Bones?"

Roxie's glowing eyes turned black. "We have discussed that nickname, Mickey Meryl Murphy."

"Your middle name's Meryl?" Lorelei asked. "Isn't that a girl's name?"

"There's nothing you can say that would embarrass me, Bones. Where to, Ellie?"

This was it, her moment. Standing at the bow, Ellie clutched the vial of Iselkian ingredients she'd gathered— thistle, seaspray, and yew tree roots. She closed her eyes, the slipping sun beaming hot against her eyelids, and gulped the contents.

As before, she *listened*.

Her breaths were loud in her ears, the sea turbulent and demanding. For a panicked moment, she couldn't hear anything at all, but then—

Open, wild waters. A tug on her heart. A whisper. A scream. The potion flowed through her bones, creating a tether between herself and the Iselkian curse. Like a heartbeat.

"We go east."

Soon, so soon, they would find the woman from the lost Isle of Iselkia. Soon, they would finally have answers.

Caedmon joined her at the bow of the boat and rested his elbows on cracked wood. "Ellie...didn't you say some numbers are magical?"

"Hmm?"

"Just something the witch said. That..." He squinted in recollection. "She looked at the seven and followed the three, and it was my face she saw in the water."

Ellie nodded slowly. "Well...there were different magical

(307)

numbers according to the fae." She turned to her friends. "Right?"

Omari nodded. "I can never remember them all. Only the main ones." He ticked his fingers. "Three is the magic of unity."

"And seven is the magic of fates," Ellie added.

Caedmon smiled. "Like your statue!"

"Ellie has a statue?" Lorelei pouted. "I want a statue. Also, don't forget twelve."

"I don't think twelve is a magical number," Ellie said.

"I turned twelve on June 12, and that makes it a magic number." They all stared at her. "It was my golden birthday!"

"What do you think she meant?" Caedmon asked.

Ellie had no idea.

Water frothed in their wake, the ocean's tongues reaching for the rotted wood. A boat like this really shouldn't have been afloat. Ellie jerked upright as white sunlight danced in the corner of her eye. She spun around.

Mickey.

It shouldn't have been afloat—because magic was at the helm.

Holy saints almighty—*was Mickey a sorcerer?*! She bolted for the pirate and grabbed his arm, pulling him below deck.

"Oi, easy on the stolen jacket!" He smoothed the leather. "It's Italian. Someone make sure we don't crash!" he called. "I'm being kidnapped!"

The rooms of the ship were just what Ellie would expect

(308)

from a boy left to his own devices: messy and filled with an odd stench Ellie didn't want to investigate. She plopped down on a stained chair, pointing at a moldy couch. "Sit."

He obeyed, hands in the air. "Whatever it is, it's not my fault. Blame the flying horse. He has a mad look about him. Think he wants to eat me."

"Chevolants don't eat people. Now where did you…"

She stopped, his words taking effect. "You don't know what a chevolant is."

He leaned back, the picture of grace. "Course I do."

"It's funny. As a pirate, I would have taken you for someone brave enough to visit the Horse Realm to see the chevolant races."

"I *am* brave enough to visit the Horse Realm. Went last month."

Ellie laughed. "Liar. There is no Horse Realm. Where are you from? And how are you a sorcerer?"

His easy smile faded. "How do you know I'm a sorcerer?"

She revealed the mark on her hand. "I'm good at sensing magic."

He whistled. "Never heard of that before. Hey, has anyone ever told you that you're a bit intense?"

Now it was her smile that faded. "Yes. They have. But I am who I am and you're stuck with it."

"Good. I like it. You're weird but in a watch-me-march-through-life-like-I'm-the-Queen-of-the-Jungle kinda way. It's refreshing. No wonder Princess Isadora liked you."

(309)

"I—the mermaid princess liked me?"

"Yeah, wanted to see why you weren't invited to your sister's wedding. How's that going by the way?"

"Ever so poorly, but—hey! No distracting me!"

That disarming smile returned, green eyes crinkling. "Worked though, didn't it?"

"How did you learn magic if you're from the New World?"

"Whoa, I never said I was from the New World."

"You're as ignorant as Caedmon! Don't lie to me. Please, just don't. I haven't slept. I just declared I'm a witch, which might get me imprisoned or permanently banned from the Fairy Godmother Academy. And I saw Iselkia fall, and chevolants are back, and the curse caster is weird and confusing, and I'm really, really, really hungry! So don't mess with me, Mickey Meryl Murphy!"

Mickey leaned as far back as he could go without becoming one with the couch. Slowly, as though afraid of disturbing a wild animal, he opened the second drawer of his nightstand and pulled out a box of cookies. Just as slowly, he handed it to her.

Which obviously meant they'd just become friends.

She scarfed down the chocolatey goodness for five whole minutes, glaring at Mickey whenever he tried to speak, before the hunger—which she hadn't felt growing until it wanted to tear her stomach in two—was satiated.

"Those were good."

"You ate all of them."

Ellie raised an eyebrow in what she hoped was a threatening gesture, though she accidentally waggled both instead, probably making her look terrifyingly weird.

"They're called Oreos. From the New World. Where I'm from. But hey, don't tell anyone? Kinda ruins the street cred. Or *sea* cred." He grinned at his joke.

"Where in the New World are you from?"

Mickey looked at the ground. "I don't want to talk about it."

Ellie opened her mouth to protest—but that was none of her business. At least he had stopped lying. "How are you a sorcerer? No one in the New World is meant to have magic."

Mickey shrugged. "No idea. All I know is one day, I started being able to do things I couldn't explain."

Ellie rested her chin in her hands, his words from all those weeks ago creeping into the room. "Do you think…do you truly think dragons are waking? Do you think *Camelot* is waking?"

He scoffed. "You mean that dragon rumor I told you about? Nah. It was just a story. I may not be from your world, but I've seen enough of it to know everyone's moved on. There's no Camelot anymore."

"But you were born with magic," she persisted, the idea taking shape. She couldn't say why it mattered so much exactly, only that she knew, deep in her bones, that it did, and was worth seeing through.

Camelot waking up, Mickey's magic, the curse caster, stories of Iselkia—it all seemed connected, yet disconnected. Stars in the sky before silver ribbons drew them together, forming a

(311)

constellation telling stories as ancient as the sea, foretelling futures as terrible as the Fall. "Where did you learn to use your magic? I can tell that this boat is powered by it. Just like I can tell we've gone farther east, and I doubt anyone here is steering that boat."

Mickey shifted in his seat. "I made a deal with someone I shouldn't have. But he taught me. Still teaches me, actually."

"Who is he?"

His cheeks turned red. "I shouldn't say. You'll judge me."

"No. I won't."

"...Malgwyn."

Ellie frowned. Malgwyn the Fire Starter. As powerful as Loreena Royenale, they were two sides of the same coin. Both Unregistered. Both well-known, Loreena for her goodness, Malgwyn for his wickedness. "What are you doing learning magic from someone like him?"

"I told you you'd judge me."

"I'm not judging *you*, Mickey. That doesn't mean I understand what you're doing."

Mickey gripped his head. "He was the only one willing to help me control this magic. And he's not as bad as everyone says. He's not *good*, but he's not evil, either."

"But how can you be sure?"

He considered the question, the ocean's waves the only sound in the silence. "Guess you can't. But he's what I've got." He teetered on the edge of his seat, hesitating, then grabbed a jar of green flames from his bedside table. "Here."

(312)

Ellie palmed the jar. She didn't need Mickey to tell her the fire was magicked, a spell hovering over them like a haze. The flames hissed her name, like they knew her face and had waited a long time for this reunion. Ellie dropped it on the bed. "I don't want it."

Mickey placed it back in her hands. "Malgwyn created them. They're powerful. Really powerful. They'll take you where you need to go in an instant. He gave me a couple when I did well in my last lesson. But I don't need them. I have my ship. You needed my ship—so you may need this someday, too. Just...be careful. Only use it if you have to. It comes at a cost."

"What kind of cost?"

"He didn't say. Just that he'd know when they were used. And he'd name his price then."

Ellie shuddered. "I don't want such a gift."

"You might. Someday."

Ellie held it out for Mickey. "It sounds like wicked magic."

"Malgwyn doesn't believe in wicked magic. Only wicked people."

"Then he sounds like a wicked person."

Mickey refused to take it back. "It's a gift."

"But I don't—"

The boat shuddered beneath them.

"What was that?" Ellie asked.

Mickey shook his head, running back upstairs, Ellie at his heels.

(313)

There was nothing. The sky had blackened, no sun, no moon, not even stars to light their way. The world had turned to nothing.

Only the gentle waves rocking the boat reminded Ellie an ocean churned beneath. Otherwise, she could have been in a great void, lost in space, with nothing until the ends of time.

A shoulder bumped hers. "Ellie?"

"Cad—what happened?"

"I don't know. We passed this old pillar in the water and then the world went dark."

Something slid beneath their boat, nearly knocking them over.

Ellie jumped. "Sea serpents?"

"The sea serpents have been dead for centuries," Lorelei whispered.

"Not all of them," Mickey murmured. "Not lately. Pirates call them the igani."

Ellie felt a strange ripple of cold go through her, and suddenly, the darkness lifted, and what she saw nearly made her heart crack in two.

"What is this place?" Omari asked.

It was impossible. This island had been lost for centuries, unreachable, its relics destroyed. And yet…she knew those pillars of golden dusk, those sandy shores and fallen stones. Ellie took a shuddering breath, holding onto the boat for stability. "It's the lost Isle of Iselkia."

THIRTY-FIVE
CAEDMON

CAEDMON EXPECTED WILDFLOWERS. AN OVERGROWN ruin, like the castles in Ireland his grandma once took him to. Maybe an ice-blue sea, or bright turquoise waters with colorful birds swooping through trees, the city's buildings long since fallen.

Gone, but filled with nature.

There was no life here.

Caedmon forced one foot to follow the other, out of the boat and onto an expanse of rocky, ash-covered land, most of which appeared as though it crumbled into the sea long ago, algae clinging to stone peeking out through still, murky waters. Even the clouds seemed darker, like no wind could shove them away no matter how fiercely it blew.

Omari raised his sword, dreary light casting shadows across his face. He looked about as nervous as Caedmon felt. "You're *sure* this is Iselkia? It just…it can't be. The magic around the island is meant to be too thick. No one has been here in centuries."

A howling wind rustled their capes, as if in challenge.

Ellie nodded, trembling. "I know but...this is the same place I saw in my vision. I'm sure of it."

Mickey picked up a stray coin and examined it. Serpent heads spilled off the side, making it jagged and sharp. He pocketed it. "This place looks like a bomb went off."

Caedmon whirled toward him. "A bomb?"

Omari frowned. "What's a bomb?"

Mickey smirked, avoiding Caedmon's gaze. "You hear a lot being a pirate."

Lorelei rolled her eyes. "So disgusting."

Mickey flashed a toothy grin, as if it were the best compliment he'd ever received.

Ellie held up her hands. "Everyone, shh! I think the potion wants me to go that way." Caedmon followed her gaze through blackened roots and brittle bone, into a sickly gray fog.

"The tide doesn't look like it'll stay out for long," Mickey warned. "Look at that shoreline. I don't think we have a lot of time."

As he spoke, the waves inched forward.

Ellie peered into the emptiness for a moment longer, then nodded to herself. "It's this way. Stay close." She glanced at a lake with water still as stone. "And don't touch the water."

Mickey wrinkled his nose. "Smells poisonous."

"Rotten filth, poisonous curses, I shall find you, yes, I shall punish," Roxie murmured beneath her breath.

(316)

"We're not punishing anyone," Caedmon ordered. "Not yet. We're only using Ellie's immobilizing curse."

Roxie scowled, but didn't protest.

They crept through the ash, avoiding poisonous lakes. At every step, Caedmon wanted to close his eyes and find himself back in bed, comfortable and warm. But every time he closed his eyes, his mind found the witch's cold, hateful smile. Carly and his parents, dead in the hospital. Jimmy collapsing into him outside the graveyard. It was enough to make him sprint. Enough to make him fight. Even when his fear felt so alive, it could feast on him.

The city had once been great, legends said. It didn't seem possible. All was too far lost, only the occasional broken building and shattered statue remaining.

"This is it," Ellie whispered, making Caedmon jump.

It was more of the same—ash and the occasional murky lake, too still for the sour breeze.

Caedmon gripped Omari's dagger. Lorelei raised her tiaras, diamonds glittering despite the clouds.

But no one was here.

It wasn't more of the same though, as he first thought. Though barely recognizable, it seemed like they were standing in the remnants of a great hall, gold marking the fallen stone, the etching of an enormous, crumbled ceiling above. Some of it was tinted blue, as if it had once been patterned and brilliant. But not here. Not anymore.

(317)

Caedmon stumbled, heart jumping to his throat—he was wrong. They weren't alone. At the end of the hall stood a dais and a single, elaborate throne of carved silver waves, atop which sat a young woman. Her brown skin was smooth and clean despite the ruin, a crown of stars atop her cascading curly hair. Yet for all her youth, it was as though she was gone to the world, eyes unfocused and glassy. The strangest was her dress, white and flowing other than a dark red stain over her stomach.

Critters lived in her dress, nibbling on the hems of her sleeve and burrowing into the folds of her skirt. Cobwebs and leaves laced the chiffon, like she'd been sitting for a thousand years, as much a part of the stone as wind is part of the sky.

She was a queen of ruin, reigning over ash, and didn't even seem to know.

Shivers rippled down Caedmon's arms.

Ellie was staring at her, aghast. "I lost the witch," she whispered, though the queen did not stir at her voice. "I was following her and the magic just…disappeared."

Beyond the mists, ocean waves crashed against the shore.

Mickey cocked his head, green eyes dimming. "I told you. The tide is coming in. And when the tide comes in…"

Omari inhaled sharply. "The igani can come pay us a visit."

"And we don't want to be here for that," Mickey finished. "I mean, maybe this lady does." He jerked his thumb at the queen. "But I'll be far away on my own island by then."

(318)

"We can't just leave her here," Caedmon said. "She needs help. Ma'am?"

The queen remained lifeless.

Caedmon crouched in front of her. He expected her to smell, what with the rats. But oddly, a cloud of rosewater and fresh mint lingered around her. He cleared his throat. "Um, can you hear me?"

The woman crowned in dust and filth stared into the endless sea, chapped lips moving soundlessly.

"Your Majesty." Ellie curtsied, her frilly dress sweeping across scattered thorns and dried roses. "I am a witch and a fairy godmother-in-training. I can assist you. The Fairy Godmother herself will grant you your greatest desire, freeing you from the tombs of your sorrow."

Still, the queen did not stir.

The others joined in: Lorelei promised part of the DeJoie inheritance; Omari swore to serve as her knight; Mickey offered up Roxie to go hunt for her, to which Roxie grinned viciously; none of it wiped the blank expression from the queen's face.

In the distance, the igani growled, and the crashing waves grew louder. They didn't have time for this.

"We need to go," Mickey insisted. "This place isn't safe."

"Not until we find my prey!" Roxie screeched.

The queen's glassy eyes blinked, fingers twitching, like maybe she could hear them and was trying desperately to break free of her haze.

(319)

Omari nodded. "Let's just take her and see if one of the Château's healers can help sort her out."

Ellie and Omari each propped up an elbow, sending spiders and mice skittering into the stone. As soon as she left the throne, streaks of violet lightning shattered the sky.

The queen gasped. She toppled into Ellie, dropping to her knees, hands clutching the red stain in her dress. The glassiness in her eyes disappeared, a sheen of fear growing. "Arthur," she whispered, her voice wobbly. "Where is King Arthur?"

How old was this woman?

"He's...he's at peace," Ellie stammered, looking helplessly at Caedmon.

The woman shuddered in their arms. She took a last breath, wincing through the pain. "Please...find...my..."

Her eyes trembled closed, but rather than die, her body vanished, turning to light—wispy, red-stained gown fluttering into their hands and silver crown thumping in the sand.

Shaking, Lorelei placed one of her tiaras on the dress, tears streaming down her face. "For the beautiful queen."

From where her blood had pooled, a single flower bloomed, singing a mournful tune. As if at last, centuries later, the Isle of Iselkia could breathe life into its shores once more.

Mickey was sickly pale. He shook his head, like he could shake away the horrible scene. "We have to go." His voice wobbled. "The tide is almost in. And the Knights of the Round Table can't come here to protect us if something goes wrong."

(320)

Caedmon obeyed, rushing back to the boat in a shocked haze, though Mickey's words clanged through his bones, reminding him of something forgotten. *We've looked for Excalibur everywhere we can. We've never looked where we can't.*

Where can't you go?

Beyond the realms of knights.

Caedmon skidded to a halt, sending sand flying, Sir Masten's words reverberating in his ears. Iselkia was lost...beyond the realms.

They say it was kept, it was given, and it was frozen.

What if...what if the first Excalibur shard wasn't frozen in ice? What if it was frozen in *time*?

His feet made up their mind before he could think it through.

"Caedmon, where are you going?" Lorelei yelled.

The encroaching sea crashed. His feet slammed the earth—he was faster than he used to be, he realized. Not as fast as a true knight—but getting there.

The thought made him run faster.

"Caedmon!" Omari grabbed at his tunic. Wow, so he was *really* fast.

"It's Excalibur," he panted. "It has to be here. It's..." The sea serpents' screeching intensified. "*Agh*, where are you?" he shouted at the sword without thinking.

He stumbled to a stop, silver glimmering out of the corner of his eye.

(321)

There—a flash of metal hidden in a scabbard.

He dropped to his knees, reaching beneath the dead queen's throne.

Maybe I'm wrong, the logical part of his mind claimed. *Maybe it's nothing.*

His fingers wrapped around the ruby leather scabbard—and all doubt whooshed out.

Warmth cascaded from his hands to his feet, like a live fire engulfing his bones. It didn't burn—but it *wanted* to.

Because it was pure magic.

"Excalibur?" he whispered, hardly daring to believe it.

It seemed to hiss in response, sending more warmth through his limbs.

His heart skipped. It really was a piece of the lost sword.

Dormant for centuries. Found, reclaimed.

He'd done it. His whole chest filled with golden light. He'd found a fragment of Excalibur.

"Caedmon!" Omari tugged again.

Caedmon jerked. A creature with a thousand teeth slithered toward them, maw open, hunting.

Ready to kill.

THIRTY-SIX
ELLIE

THE DISTINCT SOUND OF A SNARLING ANIMAL FILLED Ellie's heart with dread. Where *were* they? Omari had sprinted after Caedmon. Saints, what if they'd fallen into the marshes? Mickey grabbed her hand, jolting her out of her frozen panic. "We have to get on the boat!"

"We're not leaving them."

The growling was louder, closer.

"There's no time! Come on!"

"Not until—"

Omari and Caedmon hurtled into view. "Go!" they shouted. "Run!"

Lorelei whimpered and bolted for the boat.

Ellie's heart seized. An enormous obsidian snake the length of fifty large men trailed them. She let Mickey half drag her away, Galahad cantering alongside them, bursting into flight the same moment they leapt onto the boat.

The waves rippled and the creature splashed into the

water's depths before bursting forth, wrenching a scream from Ellie's throat. It swatted its tail at the sails, jagged teeth snapping for Ellie's vulnerable skin as it screeched so loudly, it could beckon long-forgotten monsters from the grave.

"Everyone, hold on!" Mickey yelled. With an incantation Ellie didn't recognize, the boat veered left, narrowly escaping the thrashing snake.

Hard right—another narrow miss.

The third time, the igani struck.

Everyone screamed, clinging to scraps of wood, sliding about the tipping boat.

Galahad kicked his sparkling black hooves against the creature's slimy body as Mickey crawled toward the steering wheel, muttering a spell over and over.

The blasts of his magic speared the beast, and it screamed. Furious. But it didn't abate.

Omari lunged for it, planting a dagger in its side. Blood spurted over the boat, and it growled, chomping and thrashing for a kill.

Something sparkling and bright flew through the air, landing in the creature's eyes. "Got you!" Lorelei cried.

With a final screech, the igani released its hold on the boat, and slunk back into the water, a diamond tiara sticking out of its bloodied eye.

Mickey murmured another incantation, sorcery brimming around him in golden light, as water leaking into the

(324)

boat leaked back out, the splintered wood knocking itself back together.

For a moment, all was still, a violet dusk yawning into the horizon.

Omari pulled himself upright, his leg bleeding. "Is everyone all right?"

Roxie hissed. "No, young knight not quite as little as the other young knight."

Caedmon lifted a scabbard. "I found—" he started.

"I am not all right," Roxie interrupted. "The curse caster has vanished with nary a trace. Treacherous woman!"

Ellie swept her hair from her face with trembling hands, breaths coming out in panicked gasps. Mickey still murmured spells, spiriting the boat away from the island as quickly as possible, but it wouldn't calm Ellie's beating heart.

They had almost died.

More sea serpents could attack at any moment.

She gripped the boat, squeezing her eyes shut. This terror wouldn't help. Ellie had led them here to find the curse caster, and they'd failed, meaning Ellie still had a job to do.

She was the fairy godmother. She was the *witch*. They needed *her* to pull herself together and lead them. No one else.

Flashes of blood and serpent scales battered her mind as she tried to organize her thoughts. Why had the curse caster brought them here? Was it just to watch that woman die? That poor, lost queen of this poor, lost place. Who was she? How

(325)

long had she been alone? What had she wanted Ellie to find? What did she want with King Arthur?

If she truly was once a queen of Iselkia, had she been alive for far too long and was simply released from a wicked curse?

Cursed...

Was she, too, a victim of the curse caster's magic?

A red tidal wave collapsed over the island in her mind, people bringing flowers to their lips and screaming for their princess.

Was the woman not a queen, but a princess? Was she the princess the Iselkians hoped would save them? And if so, where was she that fateful day? Bleeding to death in their final moments? How had she gotten hurt?

And how, in the name of every saint under the sun, had they traveled to Iselkia—by *accident*—when no one had touched its sands in 715 years? There were too many questions without their answers. Too many spinning thoughts with nowhere to go.

"She outsmarted us," Ellie murmured, looking to the horizon, the potion's swirling magic yanking her away from the island. The effects of the potion were fading, but she could feel their opponent was west, where the sun set and the birds dipped beneath a rising moon.

West.

To the Château des Chevaliers.

Roxie joined her side, the sparkles of her dress catching in the fading light. "You feel her, too, girl?"

(326)

Ellie rested her forearms on the boat, the remains of the sun slipping into darkness. "Yes. How do you feel her?"

Roxie's smoky eyes glimmered. "I know when evil magic defiles the great home of the Urokshi."

Ellie's hands curled. "She outsmarted us," she repeated. "She won't again."

Above, Galahad neighed.

Ellie had complied by coming to the island together. And it had cost them. They took too long. If she'd flown Galahad on her own, she might have gotten here fast enough to stop the witch. He was quicker than the boat, even with Mickey's magic.

Caedmon and Omari joined them. "It was a good idea, Ellie," Omari said.

Except it wasn't. It hadn't worked. The witch wouldn't get away with anything else, though. Not on Ellie's watch.

Galahad neighed again, swooping lower in the sky. Just low enough...

With a cry, she leapt off the boat.

Her friends screamed for her, but no one was louder than Caedmon, who flailed, jumping off as well. Ellie caught his hand, and with a swoop, he clambered onto Galahad's back as the chevolant rose to the clouds.

"Wait!" Lorelei's voice made them turn just in time to see her hurtle the Iselkian tiara toward them. Their one and only bargaining chip. Caedmon caught it on the tip of his fingers, and they were off, into the dying sun.

(327)

"What were you thinking?" he yelled, but she barely heard him over the rush of wind in her ears. Already they were spiriting toward the castle at a speed far faster than the boat could match.

"Ellie!" Caedmon shouted over the roaring winds and flapping wings.

When she didn't turn around, he grabbed her shoulder, nearly sending them plummeting to the sea.

"What, Caedmon? What is it?"

He glowered, the whites of his eyes lined with red, the exhaustion and fear she felt reflected in his gaze. "We do this together!"

Tears blurred her vision.

She really had made a true friend in all this madness.

And that mattered to her more than anything in the world.

Wordlessly, she nodded.

"Promise?"

"I promise."

THIRTY-SEVEN

ELLIE

HAD THE CHÂTEAU DES CHEVALIERS ALWAYS BEEN SO quiet?

The water barely stirred beneath the floating mountain, and the glass turrets reflected the night sky, stars winking at the moon.

It would be peaceful if not for the pounding in Ellie's head, the words *she's here, she's here, she's here* repeating in a torturous loop.

From above the world, Ellie spotted Bert clinging to the mountainside, munching on flaming fig pies. A couple of six-year knights were on a midnight walk through the orchards, holding hands, while shattered swords dangling from steel branches clinked in the Sword Garden, swaying outside Caedmon's bedroom window.

"Where do you think she is?" Caedmon whispered.

"Roxie said she could feel evil magic in her mountain."

"Galahad, can you bring us to the Urokshi secret stairs?"

He answered with a flap of his wings, carrying them to the Star Speaking tower. Fortunately, Sir Remy had ended his last class, leaving the terracotta balcony empty.

Lightning flashed in the east. The skyvor Aurelius circled the château, as if protecting it.

Alone.

"Where is Sir Masten?" Caedmon whispered.

The Urokshi entrance was already open, the ancient staircase spiraling to the pit of the mountain.

The curse caster had beaten them.

They climbed. Galahad couldn't fit down the staircase to quicken their journey, leaving Ellie and Caedmon stuck walking the normal way. They tried to move as quickly as possible but couldn't risk full-on sprinting and accidentally falling into a trap. They had to be quiet—thoughtful.

It was torture.

What the witch would be able to do in the time it took for Ellie and Caedmon to find her, Ellie both didn't want to know and felt desperate to stop.

What if she cursed someone else? What if she stole more enchanted leaves from the Urokshi to…what? Bring someone back to life? Hadn't Roxie said she needed horrible, dangerous magic for that? Magic greater than even the most powerful witch could possibly possess? Where could she find such magic?

She followed the dregs of the potion's tracking magic past the fork leading to the Urokshi city, down into the cavernous labyrinth Galahad had taken her to all those nights ago, where wicked winds had whispered of drowning cities, and solemn statues guarded empty crowns.

It was darker than Ellie remembered. Still and silent. This time, she couldn't risk conjuring a light.

"Do you think we were wrong?" Caedmon whispered.

Ellie frowned. It was possible. But Roxie said the woman would be here. What had they missed? Just as Ellie was about to suggest retracing their footsteps, a man's anguished yell echoed through the corridors.

Ellie gripped Caedmon's wrist. Together, they crept toward the noise, Ellie repeating the immobilizing curse again and again in her mind. She had to be ready. They couldn't afford to get this wrong.

All had gone still once more, though Ellie's eyes were beginning to adjust to the darkness. They passed a temple she recognized, its statue's palms open and inviting.

But no, her eyes weren't adjusting....The hallway was brightening, a light emanating from an open doorway—the very same Ellie swore she saw aglow her last time here.

She took a deep breath. This was it. What they had been

waiting for. The answers they sought might be just a few feet away. She stepped forward. Caedmon shot out his arm, stopping her. "Wh—" she started, following his gaze, and choked on the rest of her question.

A stream of blood flowed through the open door. Ellie's stomach twisted. They were too late. The witch had come to hurt, and hurt she had.

"Hello."

Caedmon and Ellie whirled around.

The woman, masked in gold, perfectly immaculate in white, cocked her head, examining them. "You took longer than expected."

Her words rang in Ellie's ears. She was waiting for them. Bringing them to Iselkia to watch that woman die, goading them to come back to the château…How could she have known they would come? Galahad flew so quickly, Ellie felt they defied time. And still, they were too late.

Someone was inside that room, bleeding. Possibly dead.

"Go on. See. I don't have time to linger."

Caedmon shot Ellie a look, but she didn't need his encouragement. She didn't care about the bargain. About playing nice. Whatever softness in her heart for this woman hardened, replaced by something bitter beating against her rib cage. *"Lo moore ri!"*

The woman's fingers, placed demurely in front of her, twitched. She smiled. "You should have practiced your witch-

(332)

craft more. Do not try to curse me, for you will lose." She swept forth, eyes haunting. "You will *always* lose."

She caught Caedmon's gaze darting to the pool of blood. "Look. Now." Invisible daggers poked Ellie's back, pressing her forward. She winced, Caedmon grunting beside her, as they reluctantly walked toward the door and peered inside.

Nothing could have prepared her for what she saw: Sir Masten, Leader of Knights, Protector of the Realms, lay sprawled on his back in a pool of blood, eyes open and vacant.

He was dead.

THIRTY-EIGHT

CAEDMON

"IT'S SYMBOLIC, ISN'T IT?" THE WOMAN SIGHED. "PRO-tector of the Realms cannot even protect himself. He's an emblem for all that went wrong with the Knights of the Round Table."

Caedmon looked and looked, but all he could see was Aurelius, circling the château above, a lightning storm flashing in his wake. *No warrior falls under the skyvor's watch*, Sir Masten once told him.

But Sir Masten wasn't under his watch tonight. He'd let himself go unprotected so Aurelius could watch over everyone else.

And now he was gone.

Caedmon took a strangled breath. He was back at Jimmy's funeral. Back in the nothing place. Listening to Jimmy's mom sob.

Ellie's shoulders trembled beside him. From what felt like far away, she took his hand and squeezed. Whether for him or herself, he had no idea, but it brought him away from the funeral, away from the past, to the woman before him.

Three murders. This woman was responsible for *three murders*. Something inside him caught fire.

"Why?" Ellie's voice was thick with tears.

The smallest sneer twisted the witch's lips. "He is not in my future." Those same invisible daggers pushed them back toward her. "I wanted to thank you for allowing the last Iselkian queen to die. It was time."

"How many years was she like that?" Ellie asked.

She simply smiled. "A long, long time."

"*Lo moore*—" Ellie tried the immobilizing spell again.

The woman's eyes flashed. Ellie coughed, clutching her throat. She stared at Caedmon, eyes wide.

He tried to lunge for her—but he was completely immobile. And was blazing hot. His blood seemed to boil. He yelled, writhing in pain. His head seared—it would split open if the magic didn't stop. Through his blurry vision, Ellie clawed at water gurgling in her mouth. She was *drowning*. The realization cleared his vision, even as the heat turned unbearable. He wouldn't let anyone else he knew be murdered. He couldn't. Never. Ever. Again.

Something deep within him pushed against the magic, furious. Somehow, he stepped toward her.

Ellie gasped, spitting the remaining water onto the floor. It took Caedmon a moment to realize the heat had disappeared. With newfound control over his limbs, he pulled Ellie closer. She trembled from head to toe.

(335)

"Do heed what I say, Ellie." The woman spoke with bored elegance. "How I despise repeating myself."

"Why did you do it?" Ellie gasped, water still tricking down her chin. "Why kill him? What do you want?"

Caedmon grimaced, the pain from the curse lingering. "And who are you?"

The masked woman considered Ellie for a moment, bending closer so she was eye level, gaze clear and emotionless. She brushed a lock of unruly hair behind Ellie's ear. "I wanted to see you. To be sure..." She scanned Ellie's face. "I did think I would want you dead eventually. Not out of spite; you're simply a nuisance. But now that I'm here, I find myself curious." She glanced above, the distant clanging of bells echoing through the mountain. "It seems they know their knight has fallen." A gleam of triumph shone in her eyes. "It seems they know their reign of magic is ending."

She strode into the darkness, silky dress billowing behind her. "Oh, and children." She turned, red lips curving in a smile. "No one has yet to recognize me, so I see no harm in answering your question, Caedmon, Boy of Nothing." She peeled back the golden mask to reveal a cold, cruel, beautiful face. "My name is Croven."

Once alone, Caedmon and Ellie shivered, too shocked to move, too horrified to speak. He couldn't say how long they stood

(336)

there, water dripping onto his left ear from a crack in the stone above. The world felt as though it would never right itself again.

He squeezed his eyes shut, tears warm on his cheeks. Just that afternoon, Sir Masten had said he was proud of him. Had given him a golden medal, its weight suddenly heavy around his neck.

Fury pulsed through him. *No one else can die. No one.*

When they were sure Croven was long gone, Ellie dropped to the ground, her head to her hands and squeaked, "I failed."

"Stop."

"I did. I promised I'd help you protect your family, and the Knights of the Round Table, and everyone, and I failed. I can't defeat her, Caedmon. And without Excalibur, we don't have strong enough magic to fight her."

Caedmon blinked. In the chaos, he'd almost forgotten. "Well...actually..." He pulled the shard of Excalibur out of its encasing. "I found one of the missing shards."

Ellie scrambled to her feet, eyes wide. "You *what*?!"

"We're one step closer, Ellie. Become a knight, find the sword. And we just might stand a chance at beating Croven. I still think the kept piece is with the knights somewhere," he added. "But we have to find where."

Ellie gasped, hand flying to her mouth, staring around her in shock. "Oh...Oh saints. Caedmon! When we visited the Urokshi, I remember seeing jewels down here and hearing

(337)

something banging. I was so certain someone was down here. *Do you think Sir Masten was trying to reforge Excalibur?*"

Caedmon nodded slowly, the realization a spine-crunching weight. "So I wouldn't have to. Because all who try die." Caedmon raked his hands through his hair, wishing they could talk just one more time. "He knew," he said bleakly, not bothering to hide his tears. "He told me once he was heading toward the same fate, no matter what happened. He knew he'd die. He knew Croven would come for him."

As he spoke, gold dust glittered in the doorway. A second later, the blood vanished. Every limb of Caedmon's locked into place, warning of Croven's return. But the wind didn't stir. He forced himself to walk over to the door and look.

Sir Masten's body had disappeared.

THIRTY-NINE

CAEDMON

THE FOLLOWING WEEKS PASSED IN A DAZE.

A tall, broad knight named Dame Gwendolyn was declared the new leader, though the ceremony was lackluster, most of her colleagues and the students donning black, too stunned to celebrate.

It hadn't been Croven's magic that claimed Sir Masten's dead body but Merlin's, for in death, all knights returned to the château to be honored in a funeral.

Caedmon barely paid attention to the ceremony, letting grief overtake him and drag him underwater until the world grew muffled and distant. He couldn't imagine training without Sir Masten. Couldn't picture the Château without his enormous presence.

The strongest knight of the realms was dead; how long before Croven murdered another? How many more caves had the Urokshi evacuated as vile creatures broke through their gates? Where was Caedmon's family now? Was everyone safe?

And the ever-lingering question: *What did Croven want?* She'd been near him twice now without hurting him—and yet Ellie remained convinced her curse involved him somehow. Why?

He couldn't help but feel they were hurtling toward impending disaster. Croven had disappeared. For now. But they knew she would return. And when she did, would they be ready?

As the days passed, he repeated Sir Masten's clues on a continuous loop. *It was kept, it was given, and it was frozen.* He kept feeling like he was missing something, like remembering a dream, but he couldn't figure out what.

Ellie wasn't able to find Croven through her tracking potion again, claiming she sensed the witch blocking her and wasn't powerful enough to break through the wall.

They spent hours poring over every text they could find in the library, but none of the books described a woman named Croven in Iselkia. Too much of their culture and history was lost to time.

If anything, it only made Ellie more relentless.

She was crazed by it, spending more hours in the library than Caedmon, her hair perpetually frizzier than normal, clothes unwashed, often on backward. One day, she showed up for their swordsmanship class wearing two different shoes. Dame Gwendolyn, who had taken over swordsmanship training, gave Ellie a week's worth of detention, along with a notice

(340)

that froze Caedmon's heart: Ellie was at the bottom of the list of draftees and would be sent home without her memories if she didn't improve.

The following two trials were so stressful, they barely scraped through, so when Dame Gwendolyn called Caedmon and Ellie to her office, nerves twisted his stomach.

Sweat trickled down his neck, every footstep toward Dame Gwendolyn's office echoing in his ears. He would beg, he realized. He would bargain. He would refuse to give up his shard of Excalibur if they tried to send either of them home. He didn't care how low it brought him.

Anything for his family.

Ellie's bushy hair bounced beside him as she walked, nose stuck in a book. He grabbed her elbow to stop her from crashing into a pillar. And anything for Ellie, he realized. He wouldn't let the knights send her away without her memories.

Rather than move to Sir Masten's tower, Dame Gwendolyn kept her rooms in the south-facing part of the château, overlooking the orchards. It was a surprisingly cozy yet elegant space, with a fire warming the hearth and a gleaming, polished desk topped with enormous books.

Dame Gwendolyn removed a pair of glasses from her cropped, blond hair as she welcomed them inside. "Ahh yes, Caedmon. Ellie." She pushed the glasses up her nose. "I wanted to speak with you about a few new lessons."

"You're not sending us home?" Caedmon blurted.

(341)

"I—Ellie, are you listening?"

Ellie jumped, dropping the book on Excalibur she'd been absorbing at an inhuman speed. "Erm…yes?"

The head knight let out an exasperated sigh. "Sit. Both of you."

Caedmon and Ellie exchanged glances before sliding into high-backed leather chairs.

Dame Gwendolyn peered at them with hawklike eyes. "Let the ordained knights handle this."

Ellie shifted. "We don't know what you—"

Dame Gwendolyn held up a hand. "Do not insult my intelligence. I know what you've been up to. The Knights of the Round Table are traditionally not meant to associate much with the rest of society—rules decreed by Merlin's magic when Camelot fell. But these are extenuating circumstances. All the magical realms have been alerted to Sir Masten's murder, and all who have knowledge of this Croven have been asked to come forward."

Caedmon frowned. "We didn't tell you her name."

Dame Gwendolyn's eyes twinkled. "No, but you have spent many nights whispering about it in the library. Bert told me."

Caedmon swallowed. He'd definitely take the books to his room from now on. "Croven is Unregistered. What if the knights can't stop her? My sister was already attacked by a malevotum—what if something else comes after her?" He tugged his hands through his hair, his parents' reactions as real

(342)

as Dame Gwendolyn's face before him. He'd already seen Jimmy's parents break when their son died; he couldn't live through that with his own family. How would any of them survive?

"Fairies and the DeJoies' most trusted Registered witches and sorcerers have all created complex protection spells to shield them from harm—the very same we've used upon our island to prevent this Croven from entering again. Our longstanding agreement with the Urokshi meant we would not use magic to interfere with theirs, but again, extenuating circumstances. You are safe. Your family is safe. We have also sent out more inquiries into the legendary Loreena Royenale's location."

Ellie perked up. "I've heard about her! She's Unregistered and so powerful and wonderful and magnanimous and—"

"Have you been acquainted?" Dame Gwendolyn asked.

"No, but I know these things."

The knight adjusted her glasses. "Be that as it may, she has yet to respond to our pleas. I wouldn't wait for her assistance with bated breath. Regardless, Caedmon, your family is safe."

Caedmon seethed. "So you want us to go back to our rooms and pretend nothing's wrong while the adults keep secrets from us?"

"I want you to be able to sleep at night. And I want you to be prepared. Properly this time. I've spoken with the Fairy Godmother, and she has agreed to work with me on assigning you a fairy tutor so you may practice your fairy magic for as long as you remain a draftee, Ellie."

(343)

Ellie gulped, shrinking.

"Caedmon, I will be giving you private lessons on Evermore dust so you are equipped with some more spells, as well as increasing your swordsmanship classes. I understand that you tutored with Sir Masten."

Hollowness swept through him. "Yes."

Her tone softened. "I will never replace him. But I will train with you in the meantime."

Caedmon nodded his thanks, throat suddenly scratchy and tight.

"Rest assured, we care just as much about finding Croven as you do. And when we do, she will answer for her crimes."

Her gaze drifted to the orchards, where enormous pink birds swooped through the vines, toward the sea. "Sometimes, isolated here, somewhere in the middle of the world, it's easy to think we're alone. That the world has forgotten us. And that what the Knights of the Round Table do is of no consequence to the realms." A fire lit in her eyes. "But it matters. It matters very much. We protect, we serve, and we set the example of chivalry and honor, so that when we are in need, the realms... they answer. They hear our call, and they respond, as Merlin intended all those centuries ago. Some traditions become archaic with time. I like to think that is not true here. That the world will always need a place for young knights to train and learn what it means to make the world a better place. This is why the fairies and witches and royalty have come to our aid, and will do all they can to stop this threat from hurting anyone else."

Dame Gwendolyn returned to grading essays. "Now. Go. Get some rest. We increase your training in the morning."

FORTY

ELLIE

ELLIE AGREED TO SLEEP, IF ONLY BECAUSE HER BODY refused to be awake any longer. As soon as she entered her bedroom to a resounding chorus of croaks and meows, she collapsed in bed, Bianca curling onto her chest.

But she wouldn't rely on her extra training.

It wouldn't be enough.

Perhaps for another knight-in-training, but not Ellie. Not for a witch.

No, Ellie needed to harness her witch's magic. There was no one to teach her, but Ellie had herself. And that, she was beginning to understand, sometimes had to be enough.

As soon as dawn broke, her glass turret rosy and warm, she shrugged on her emerald velvet tunic and cloak, fed Bianca, tucked her mother's book on witchcraft into her bag, and crept down the spiral stairs into the brisk morning. Bert, with his hundreds of horrible legs, scuttled into the library, a bag of cupcakes in his mouth. Ellie sped in the opposite direction, toward the Witches' Wood. She couldn't have any company for this—for her safety and others.

As this could go horribly wrong.

She didn't stop until surrounded by the towering trees, pine needles reminding her of lonely Christmases with Bianca and her toads, banished from supper. (It was certainly not her fault that the toads had a weakness for Christmas pudding.*)

Galahad had been living in the woods, away from prying eyes, and swooped to the ground with a jubilant whinny. "I'm sorry I haven't been able to see you much. But I brought you apples."

Galahad stretched and dove into his bag of treats as Ellie reached into her pouch of Evermore dust and sprinkled it on the earth, praying that the Fairy Godmother didn't have her eyes on her today. At once, a small campfire roared to life.

Despite the heat, she shivered.

This broke *so* many rules and definitely qualified as a mishandling of Evermore magic. Ellie flipped through the book's contents, landing on a witch's spell that caught her eye the other day. *To see your enemies through the Flames of Eyri requires an ironclad will. An unconquerable desire.*

Ellie tensed. She had to walk through the flames if she

---

* I must disagree. Ellie murmured in her sleep about Christmas pudding every night from July 23 until December 24. By Christmas day, the toads simply couldn't take the anticipation anymore. 'Tis why they've also secretly taken to hopping around Omari, much to the boy's confusion, to see why Ellie enjoys his company so much. Mr. Petalbloom, in particular, has been unimpressed and demands Omari sit an evaluation to test his worthiness for his darling Ellie. They plan to revolt.

wanted a chance of seeing Croven—of figuring out where she might be hiding. The book promised the enchanted flames couldn't kill....

But they would hurt. And if anyone found out, the punishment would be worse than detention. This was reckless. Exactly what Caedmon wanted to prevent. Exactly where her heart yearned to go.

Into the unknown wild, into the heart of her magic.

Her limbs alight with nerves, Ellie squeezed her eyes shut and whispered the Old Iselkian incantation.

Shadows and snippets of moon cascaded across the clearing. Ellie reached for Galahad's mane, ready to flee should someone see.

But she was alone.

After a few more tries, the Evermore flames turned black, writhing with white, glowing eyes.

She took a deep breath, teetering on the edge of the flames—and dashed through them.

Flames spun around her cloak, burning her feet. She collapsed on the earth, and rubbed homemade fairy salve over her wounds, which immediately cooled to mere memories of burns. Sweat trickled down her forehead as each breath grew steadier and calmer. Her will wasn't great enough yet, her magic not strong enough. But she would not tire. She would not abate.

Galahad whinnied, pawing the ground.

"It's okay, Galahad." She wrapped her fingers around her glimmer of starlight, allowing its hope-giving magic to sweep through her. "I am not afraid."

Again, the fire burned her. Again, she quickly soothed the burns.

Again and again, she failed. Again and again, she tried.

The bells for breakfast came and went. Ellie ignored the gnawing in her stomach. She wiped sweat and ash from her face, panting, picturing Croven. How she hurt Caedmon. Her bell-like voice flooded through Ellie's mind, the scent of mint on her breath burning Ellie's senses. "I will be stronger than you," Ellie vowed.

And ran.

The flames didn't hurt, didn't burn, but they became solid, unmovable things, rendering Ellie still, Croven's face washing through Ellie's consciousness.

As if she were real.

Right before Ellie's eyes.

Ellie gasped, reality catching up to her mind.

The forest surrounding her wasn't one she knew.

It was a snippet of graveyard and moss-covered trees, where shards of glass dangled from spindly branches.

She couldn't place the forest, but it nudged the back of her mind. She *should* know it. Maybe, once, she did know it. Perhaps she had read about trees of glass leaves in a book somewhere.

Croven was distracted, bent over something, silver hair tumbling from its bun. She felt so real, the forest so true, a whooshing brook nearby meeting Ellie's ears, winds cooling her healing burns. Croven whirled toward her, gray eyes narrowing.

Immediately, she gathered her composure, slipping away from whatever held her attention, and glided to where Ellie stood motionless, as if roots had grown from her toes, deep into the earth.

Ellie couldn't breathe as Croven neared, closer, closer—

She reached to tuck a lock of hair behind Ellie's ear—and swished right through Ellie's head.

Croven smiled. "As I suspected. You needn't look so terrified, dear. I cannot harm you from here. And you cannot harm me." She sat on a throne of thorned flowers and clasped her hands. "Not today, at least. Now, would you like to tell me how you find using the Flames of Eyri? It's a personal favorite spell of mine."

Ellie's mouth was too dry and ashy to speak.

Croven's eyes brightened. A slow-creeping storm over still waters. "How strange your magic becomes as it grows. I admit, I am, at last, mildly impressed. You must have found me when my guard was down. It will not happen again," she added lightly. "But you are here now. You must have had me in your mind's eye. What troubles you?"

"What troubles me?" Ellie spat, the pounding terror in her

heart receding to rage. "You killed Sir Masten. He knew how to defeat you. And you *killed* him."

Croven smiled, which somehow made her look colder than when she scowled. "Your loyalty to the Knights of the Round Table is truly quaint." She peered back at whatever had distracted her. "Do not try to come see me again. Goodbye, Ellie."

She turned away, and the connection disappeared, leaving nothing behind but the scent of fresh mint hovering in the air.

FORTY-ONE

CAEDMON

ELLIE BURST THROUGH THE CLASSROOM DOORS JUST as the last bell rang, taking her place beside Caedmon in their Curses and Spells class.

"The Flames of Eyri," she gushed, her face red from the cold, eyes bright.

Caedmon concentrated on Dame Ethyl's notes on toxic pixie feet fumes. "What?"

"I found Croven!"

Ellie proceeded to tell Caedmon a story that had his ears burning.

"But the magic that let me see Croven wasn't because of the Evermore dust," she explained in a rushed whisper. "It was me. I wasn't actually there—she couldn't hurt me. It's why I tried to find her a few more times—"

"You did *what*?"

"But it didn't work. I've been reading about how to strengthen it though, so I'll try it tonight. Sometimes it can get strong enough where you can move through space and go where you imagine."

"Could you take people with you?"

"I've never heard of it."

Caedmon shook his head so hard, it seemed likely to rattle off like Roxie's. "No. This all sounds way too dangerous. Walking through fire is literally the example people give of dangerous things, right after transporting yourself to where a known murderer is hanging out. No, no, and no."

"Don't you want to protect your family? To know what she wants with you?"

Caedmon stiffened. "Of course I do! But you can't go there by yourself, without any way of defeating her. That plan doesn't work. You're not dying for my curse."

"But Caedmon—"

"Remember, children—" Dame Ethyl cut in as she passed out cursed hats. "They must be spoken to politely, or they *will* attack you."

Ellie scowled. "We'll talk about this later."

"No. We won't."

By the time Caedmon met Dame Gwendolyn for his nightly swordsmanship in the abandoned training arena, he still hadn't spoken to Ellie—was still fuming over how impulsive she'd been. Again.

(353)

Dame Gwendolyn joined him in the center of one of their training circles, but when Caedmon parried, she met his wooden sword with steel.

Smiling, she reached into her scabbard and handed him a real sword. Caedmon gaped, his anger momentarily subsiding.

"Sir Masten wrote out lesson plans for you. He thought you were ready."

A lump formed in his throat. Wordlessly, he took the sword, testing the weight in his hand.

Dame Gwendolyn's pale eyes gleamed. "Well, Caedmon. Show me what you can do."

Day after day, night after night, Caedmon trained until his muscles ached, his hands were covered in blisters, and his feet were sore enough to never want to move again.

But he kept going.

And slowly, imperceptibly, he became the fastest.

He became the strongest.

He couldn't master real magic like Ellie. He was no match for Croven. But this, he could do.

He would be the best no matter the cost.

As he worked, he ruminated over all they'd learned of Excalibur. All the clues, all the pieces. All the missing gaps.

It was kept, it was given, and it was frozen.

(354)

When I looked at the seven and followed the three, it was your face I saw in the water.

Seven is the magic of fates.

Merlin believed in woven, united threads of fate, but his plans were never as clear as they seemed.

And through the clues, Sir Masten, dying so Caedmon wouldn't need to. Telling him to understand.

But it was Ellie's reminder, once again, to be polite to his Evermore homework, that shifted the earth beneath Caedmon's feet.

They were the last awake, huddled next to the dying fire of the southern sitting room, bottles of Evermore dust and Dame Ethyl's bizarre ingredients spread out around them, as Caedmon's head spun.

Ellie poked Caedmon's arm. "What are you thinking?"

He swallowed twice, breathing difficult. "It *wanted* to be kept," he rasped.

Ellie sat up. "Excalibur?"

He jumped to his feet, blood thrumming. Swords made with magic had feelings because *magic* had feelings. Dislikes. Wishes. "It wanted to be kept, given and frozen! It *wanted* to stay with the lost queen of Iselkia, frozen in time. If I'm right, and the knights kept a piece, we have to think of where Excalibur would *want* to be kept, not where Sir Masten would want to keep it!"

Ellie's eyes widened. "Do you think it felt guilty?"

(355)

"Guilty?" Could magic feel something so complex?

"Well…" She spoke slowly, as if testing her words, weighing their measure. "The sword was made by Merlin, used by King Arthur. And Camelot was their creation. They were the ones who were meant to protect everyone. And they did. Until they couldn't. Maybe it wanted to be kept, given, and frozen by those it failed to help…"

"Like Iselkia," Caedmon finished. "Is there anything in the academy that has anything to do with Iselkians?"

Ellie's mouth dropped open. "Oh…oh my goodness. Caedmon! That's it!" She beamed, the giddiest she'd been since she found Croven in the forest. "Beneath the castle, near the Urokshi city, Sir Masten was killed right next *to an ancient fae temple dedicated to the lost Iselkian Princess Dianna*! I saw it when I met Galahad. I was wondering what it was doing there, but it's the perfect place! Although…" Her smile dipped. "I never saw a sword."

Caedmon pressed his palms to his forehead, mentally putting himself back in the ashen land of Iselkia, where he found the first shard. "When we were in Iselkia," he said slowly, "I *asked* the sword where it was. I didn't mean to, I was just so frustrated. Maybe we didn't see it in the mountain before…because we didn't ask." They hadn't earned it, hadn't yet understood.

"Magic needs you to be polite," Ellie whispered.

Caedmon grinned. So close. They were *so close*. "We have to go back under the mountain."

(356)

FORTY-TWO

ELLIE

THE UROKSHI WOULD NOT LET THEM PASS. DAME Gwendolyn stationed guards around their city entrances, citing "meddlesome kids," and no amount of bribery swayed them.

That was—no amount of bribery with the trained guards.

Roxie, on the other hand, eagerly accepted Lorelei's diamond necklace in exchange for a magic screen that let them slip around the Urokshi undetected. But it was so rule-breaking and potentially knight-academy-disqualifying, they decided to wait to use it until the last possible moment.

Ellie wished she could revel in their victory, but thoughts of Croven gnawed, keeping Ellie awake, keeping her wishing she could be a better fairy or a better witch or a better *something* and magic this all away.

Ellie found Croven in the fire three more times. Every time, she was in the forest. And every time, Ellie felt certain she'd seen it before, if she could only remember.

She leaned against her bedroom window early one morning,

head throbbing from racking her brains for the memory. Owls swooped around glass turrets, and the sea glittered beneath fading stars.

Somewhere out there, their witch wandered among leaves of glass and whispering rivers. Who else would she kill?

Too restless to stay in bed, Ellie showered and dressed, and finally raced downstairs before breakfast to practice her witchcraft. Thunder rattled, rain hissed, pines creaked.

A sniffling caught her attention. She stopped.

The sniffling turned into sobbing.

Her feet turned right instead of left, following the noise into one of the castle's drawing rooms, filled with musical instruments, enormous stained-glass windows, powder-blue curtains, abandoned daggers, and a tiara-clad blond head peeking out from a couch.

"Lorelei?"

The princess looked up, eyes rimmed with red. "Oh. Hello." After an awkward moment she added, "I'm not crying."

"...Okay."

"I had a bad allergic reaction."

"Oh."

"To makeup."

"I see."

"My friends will be here in a moment to help. You're not one of them. Go away."

Ellie joined Lorelei on the edge of the couch despite the

insult. "That's funny. You've spent an awful lot of time with me for not being my friend."

Lorelei shifted away from her. "Well. I've changed my mind. I'd rather be alone."

"Is that why you've been visiting us in the library less?"

"No," she snapped. "I've been spending less time in the library because I find you all revolting."

Ellie didn't move, for she finally understood why the princess looked familiar; she was lonely. It was the same look Ellie used to give herself in the mirror at night, wishing she had friends to laugh with, when no one was there.

Lorelei's lower lip quivered. She dumped her head into her pillow and shook, silent sobs racking her body.

Ellie scooted closer, running a comforting hand down her back. "Perhaps if you stopped calling everyone peasants…"

"But you *are* all peasants," she wailed.

Ellie swallowed her response. "What happened? Did you have a fight with someone?"

Lorelei sighed and dabbed her tears with a silk handkerchief. "Not exactly. It's really nothing. I had a silly argument with my grandmother, and when I felt like I had no one to tell, I just…"

Ellie nodded. "I understand. You just felt lonely."

"Princesses don't get lonely," she mumbled.

Ellie coughed. "Well, even for times you're not lonely, I'm here for you."

(359)

Lorelei pursed her lips, more tears leaking from her eyes. "It's just…you, Omari, Caedmon, and Roxie all like someone else more than any of you like me. I'm nobody's favorite. Nobody likes me the most. I don't have a best friend."

Ellie wanted to lie. To tell her this wasn't true. But lying was against the Fairy Code of Ethics. Besides, she had a feeling it would only help today. And that wasn't good enough. "Maybe that's true. But I think you could be someone's favorite someday! You're really clever and brave. You were the one who saved us from the igani! But you *have* to stop calling people peasants."

Lorelei smiled weakly. "I suppose I can give it a try." She rubbed her face, groaning. "Ugh, you're too nice to people. You shouldn't be nice to me. It's what I told Grandmother—you're too nice and I refuse to spy on you anymore, but she threatened to have my favorite unicorn killed if I didn't, and it all just got so muddled, and…"

She trailed off, gaze meeting Ellie's.

Ellie could hardly breathe, hardly think. She snatched her hand away and clenched her jaw, refusing to allow the welling tears to spill. "You…Have you been spying on me? Is that why you've been helping us this whole time?"

Lorelei's cheeks turned a deeper shade of red, but she jutted her chin in defiance. "There's no need to make a fuss. Yes, Grandmother did ask it of me, but only because she knew *your* mother went to Omari's father to ask *Omari* to watch over you.

(360)

And of course, Grandmother always has to know what's happening. Plus, my cousin Olivia told her she thought you were an Unregistered witch, so she thought it best I intervene."

Ellie gaped at her. Omari...

That moment in Ellie's room, the day she claimed her magic, Omari had sat by her side.

But not as a friend.

Not as someone accepting her true nature.

As a spy.

Her heart was breaking, cracking into shards. "Did Caedmon—"

"No!" Lorelei adjusted her tiara. "Caedmon has no idea. Roxie thought it best to leave him out of it. She's been trying to get me to stop, but of course, she swore a vow not to tell when I first found her and told her Caedmon was looking for her."

Another twist, another punch. Ellie's lungs would collapse.

She couldn't trust anyone but Caedmon. Lorelei, Omari, Roxie...All these friends she thought she made, all this life she shared with them—it was a lie.

This time, she couldn't stop the tears from streaming down her face. She launched from the drawing room, into the storm, freezing rain mixing with her tears as she ran for the Great Hall, all plans to practice magic forgotten.

She had to find Caedmon. For they had lied to him, too. Her body shook, tears drying, fire building in her heart, magic exploding off her skin. How dare they? How could they?

(361)

"Caedmon!" She burst into the Great Hall. All eyes found her—she was a spectacle, sparks flaring in her wake, sopping wet and surrounded by toads who'd found her in the storm. "Caed—"

"Ellie?"

She whirled toward the sweet, crisp, accented voice. Omari Evelant sat happily beside Grace Otania. Did Grace know her boyfriend had been spying on Ellie? Had they all been making fun of her behind her back? After a lifetime of teasing, of being ignored, she thought she would be strong enough to handle it. She thought she would be able to swallow the hurt.

But she couldn't anymore. "You lied!" she screamed. She didn't care who heard her. She didn't care that some of the students snickered or that Omari's eyebrows shot toward his hairline.

"What do you—?"

Lorelei slipped out from behind Ellie and grabbed Omari, pulling them out of the Great Hall, and slamming the door as other students craned their necks to watch. "I'm sorry, Omari, I got tongue-tied...." She whispered something in his ear. Ellie fumed. Even now, they had the audacity to talk about her as if she didn't matter, as if she were worthless.

Omari shook his head, frown deepening. "Oh, that? Ellie, your mother just asked someone to keep an eye on you and make sure you don't get hurt. I wasn't *spying*. I was just trying to be a good older brother."

(362)

"*I* was spying," Lorelei clarified. "But Omari, you were asked to spy, too." She rolled her eyes. "You were just too distracted by Grace to realize it. Also, Ellie isn't your sister, and definitely doesn't think of you as a brother, you oblivious toad."

"She…" Omari shook his head. "My father wouldn't ask me to spy."

Lorelei huffed and turned back to Ellie. "Listen to me. I never told my family you're a witch."

"I don't believe you." Ellie's voice was raspy, harsh, unrecognizable. She turned and sprinted back through the corridors, over the looping bridges, toward the pine trees—and straight into Dame Gwendolyn, sending a stack of books the professor was holding flying everywhere.

"Goodness! Ellie! Do watch where you're going."

"I'm sorry, Dame Gwendolyn." She trembled, hands barely able to grasp the tomes as she restacked them.

Dame Gwendolyn caught her shaking hands. "Ellie? What is it?"

"I'm fine. I…"

She squeezed her eyes shut. Her emotions were distracting, awful things sometimes. She wished she could whisk them off to the Forgetting Place.

She gasped, the thought ringing in her mind, like someone had just shaken her awake. Oh, dear saints—*the Forgetting Place*! That was why she only barely remembered Croven's forest! She must have banished the memory!

(363)

"*No*," she moaned, dropping her head in her hands. The Forgetting Place spell wasn't permanent, but if she wanted to find Croven, she'd need to sift through countless horrible memories of Mother. Of being alone. Of being afraid.

"Sweet saints, Ellie. Are you all right?"

Taking a deep breath, Ellie smoothed her hair and met the head knight's concerned gaze. "Dame Gwendolyn, I've been trying to find Croven and I—"

"Have you been pursuing her on your own after I specifically told you not to?"

Ellie's throat closed. "I…It was just to…"

"I have been tolerant because you witnessed a terrible tragedy, but I will not be tolerant again. Return to your room at once, Ms. Bettlebump."

Ellie could scream. Why wouldn't people *listen* to her? "But I can find Croven! And if we use Excalibur—"

Dame Gwendolyn pinched the bridge of her nose. "Don't you understand? Sir Masten *died* trying to reforge it for Caedmon. For us all, as our magic fades. He had no more luck than any of the dead ones before him. That sword has been lost for hundreds of years. It has seen the end of too many knights and you will not be another. The best fairies in the realms don't know where Croven is. I do not know what you think you found, but it is false. Go to your room at once." She shook her head, brow furrowed. "You might as well pack your bags as well."

(364)

"But—"

"I'm sorry, Ellie. This has gone on too long. You will be sent home without your memories in the morning."

Ellie sucked in a breath. Her chest would cave in from all the disappointment. Still, she nodded, tears leaking from her eyes as she made a show of trudging toward her tower. She chanced a glance over her shoulder—the headmistress was gone. Clouds growled, and once more, icy rains poured from the sky. For a moment, Ellie stood there, in the misty, silvery sheen, breathing heavily, Dame Gwendolyn's latest edict sticky as syrup, momentarily immobilizing her.

But she would not let herself forget this place. Her mission. Caedmon.

Trembling, she raised her chipped scepter. "Fly, memories," she whimpered, whole body convulsing now. "Fly back to me from the Forgetting Place."

She winced through the onslaught of jagged thoughts and spiteful words.

Instinctively, she grabbed her speckle of starlight for luck. Courage. Hope. It warmed her heart, even as the memories snagged and scraped.

Less elephant and more ballerina in your curtseying, Ellie.

It is your existence that insults, Ellie.

I wish you were different.

I wish you were not born a witch.

And...*there*! Ellie blinked in and out of time—between

(365)

twelve and six years old—wandering a forest of glass leaves alone, because Mother left her by the side of the road.

The Rubissia Forest. She laughed through the pain. Croven was in the Rubissia Forest!

Ellie knew where Croven was, and this time, she wouldn't let her get away. If Dame Gwendolyn wouldn't help her, she would go to the one person in the world who would.

FORTY-THREE
ELLIE

ROXIE'S MAGIC SCREEN AGAINST THE UROKSHI GUARDS worked, and soon, Caedmon and Ellie were rushing from Sir Remy's Star Speaking tower into the heart of the mountain.

Please, saints, be with me this day.

Ellie deplored returning to those slick, stone steps, venturing down, down, to the site of Sir Masten's death. She still half expected blood to coat the corridor or Croven to emerge from the shadows, but it was empty.

At least Caedmon was at her side.

He was furious with Lorelei and Omari when she explained what had happened, and they had agreed to ban the traitors forevermore.

She couldn't have their treachery distracting her.

Ellie brought Caedmon to the fae temple dedicated to Princess Dianna. If she was wrong, fine, they would find another lead. But if she was right...

She stopped before the solemn fae goddess bowing to

Dianna's crown and turned to Caedmon, who took a deep breath.

Placing the first shard in the stone hands, he whispered, "I'm ready to find you. I understand Sir Masten's sacrifice."

Ellie's heart leapt. White smoke burst around the statue, and as it dissipated, a shard of steel glimmered in her stone hands, along with a jeweled hilt.

Ellie inched closer, whispers beckoning her forward. A dragon slithered around the sword's hilt, staring at her with glinting ruby eyes. In that moment, she knew. Nothing else in the world could be Excalibur. Nothing else could pulse with this emerald and crimson magic. "This is it."

Caedmon became transfixed by the dragon. It almost seemed alive. "I think..." His breath caught. "I think you're right."

"That's two shards," Ellie whispered, like the truth might beckon them away. "Caedmon, I think we go find Croven now, third shard or no. Excalibur will still be powerful even without the third piece. We can face her."

Caedmon blinked slowly, staring at her.

"Erm...Cad?"

"This statue says it's a temple of unity," he marveled. "It... *no*." He stumbled into the rocky wall, eyes wide, as though someone else had just died.

Ellie wrapped her arms around herself. "What? What is it? Why are you looking at me like that?"

(368)

Caedmon met her gaze, face bleak. "Ellie...we don't need to go without the third piece. I...I know where it is. One was kept. One was frozen. And one...was *given*."

"So?"

His breath hitched. "Ellie...how old were you when you were given your fairy scepter?"

"I was seven. Why?"

"Dame Ethyl said my name has been on the list for five years. So...when I was also seven."

Ellie hated math problems and numbers and...all her breath whooshed out at once. "Seven is the magic of fates."

"That's what the fae believed, right? And didn't you tell me Iselkians worshiped the fae? And Croven said—"

"When she looked at the seven and followed the three, it was your face she saw in the water."

"Exactly. What's three again?"

Ellie's head was spinning. "Unity. Just like..." She met Caedmon's gaze and knew their thoughts were shared. *Woven, united threads of fates.* They were the threads. Standing before the temple of unity, where the second shard of Excalibur chose to hide.

Her brain pounded against her skull, too full to absorb what was happening.

Maybe...

Maybe Caedmon was never meant to find Excalibur on his own, just like Ellie was never meant to accept her witchcraft on her own. Maybe they were meant to be linked. Woven.

(369)

"Ellie, there's a *reason* you found your fairy scepter in a fate temple. There's a *reason* your fairy scepter can't perform the secret charm. It's not because of your secret."

They both looked down at her scepter. "It's because it has a secret of its own."

"I thought you didn't believe in the goddess of fate," Ellie whispered, unable to accept the truth of what he was saying.

"I don't think she's the one who sent it. I think...the same magic that sent me my message is the one that sent you your scepter. Ellie...*you were given the third shard of Excalibur.*"

Ellie stared down at her trusty scepter. Her lifeline to the fairy world. Tears streamed down her cheeks. "Scepters are only ever given." Her voice was soft, breaking. "If I break it open...I may never get another."

Caedmon nodded gravely. "I know."

She swallowed a sob, suddenly seven years old again, wishing on stone. But perhaps...she'd wished for the wrong thing. She wished for a fairy scepter because she was tired of being alone. But she was not alone anymore.

Ellie let her fingers brush over her glimmer of starlight for courage and took a deep breath. She let every fairy charm she had ever learned pour through her heart. Every night she spent studying for the Fairy Godmother exam. Every hope, every doubt, every ounce of frustration.

Every thorn of shame for her secret witchcraft. For truly,

(370)

deep in her heart, she had always known the life of a fairy didn't fit her.

She was a woven thread of fate.

A witch.

A friend.

Tears catching on her lashes, Ellie gathered all her strength and smashed the fairy scepter against the cave wall.

Crystal cascaded around them, but Ellie hardly noticed.

Caedmon was right. The third Excalibur shard glittered, silver and sharp, hovering in midair, drifting slowly to the fractured blade. As soon as the three pieces touched, they gleamed hot with fire, melting and cooling, a blade remade. Excalibur, reforged.

Ellie wiped the tears from her face and looked to Caedmon. Together, she'd promised. They'd do this together.

So, together, they grabbed the hilt and pulled the sword from the statue's hands, metal scraping against stone, jewels glinting in the sparse candlelight.

It was glorious, perfectly sharp, with a magical energy buzzing around it.

"With this, Croven won't be able to use her magic against us. We'll make her take back her curse, and I'll be ready to use my own magic in case..."

She swallowed. In case someone got hurt. In case Croven was in the mood to kill.

"And you have what we talked about?"

Caedmon patted his cape. "Right here."

Good. Ellie sucked in a breath. It was now or never. She turned away from her shattered scepter, boots crunching on broken crystal.

"Are you sure about this?" Ellie pulled the jar of Malgwyn's flames from her cloak. She tried not to scowl at it. Lorelei had been the one to return Mickey's gift after their chaotic journey home from Iselkia.

She had left it beneath her bed ever since, Mickey's warning haunting her. Using these flames would come at an unknown cost. One she didn't know if she was willing to pay.

But Roxie, Omari, and Lorelei had betrayed her.

Dame Gwendolyn wanted to send her away.

Sir Masten was dead.

They had nowhere left to turn, no time to risk flying Galahad, as it could take days, and Croven might leave the forest.

The time was now.

Caedmon's eyes blazed. "Do it."

FORTY-FOUR

ELLIE

THEY TRAVELED THROUGH FIRE.

Ellie allowed herself to be swept up with the flames. Her magic leaned in to it, lapping up the roaring heat.

Color and sound distorted, time disappeared, and all Ellie knew was fire—until the world righted, and she stumbled into a mossy clearing in a thick, overgrown forest, where glass leaves clinked in the wind, and wildflowers sprang up between old, forgotten graves. Her heart stopped. There, a brush of white, a shift of chiffon. Croven stared at her from behind a draping veil of ivy. Ellie clutched the sword, Caedmon close beside her.

"I see you've found me."

"In the forest," Ellie said more confidently than she felt. "Where you always are." Better to scare her into thinking Ellie knew more than she did.

Croven stepped out from behind the ivy, her pale eyes bright, elegant, demure gown trailing in the grass. "I do like it here, yes." Her gaze drifted to the sword. "Excellent work. Thank you."

Ellie's grip tightened. She wouldn't let the witch have Excalibur. She'd guard it with her life. That kind of power in the witch's hands couldn't be good for the world. She raised the sword high in the air, glancing at her friend, who nodded, reaching for the hidden item in his cape. Her secret weapon was ready.

"Release your curse!" Caedmon bellowed. "If you do, maybe we'll let you go freely."

Croven's eyebrows lifted. "You're more spirited than I realized. Interesting. I must say, Ellie. I'm quite pleased you worked out the clues."

Ellie's heart raced. Caedmon stopped.

"Did you truly think I would let you reforge Excalibur without my influence? That Sir Masten could recreate the sacred hilt on his own?"

Ellie's mind worked furiously, her gaze caught on memories. Croven had *let* Ellie find her. She'd *led* them to Iselkia. *Wanted* them to find Sir Masten's body. And in the flames, using mind magic...

Croven wasn't letting her guard down by accident. She'd wanted Ellie to find her. Wanted Ellie to see. Everything they'd done had been because Croven wanted them to. Including bringing her Excalibur. She hadn't hurt them again and again because she *needed* something from them. "Because... you want it," Ellie breathed. "You placed the curse on the

(374)

knights' magic so they would seek Excalibur. So *we* would seek it. That was you, in the mountain. You led Sir Masten to the jewels he needed for the hilt."

Croven smiled, though her face held no warmth. "Very good."

"And the leaves you stole from the Urokshi…" Caedmon inched in front of Ellie, like his fragile body could protect her fragile body. It was a noble effort—but she couldn't let him die for her. "You're trying to bring someone back to life."

Sure enough, a glass coffin Ellie hadn't noticed glinted behind the wall of ivy.

Croven sighed. "Yes, my husband."

"From Iselkia?" Ellie asked.

She laughed. "Gods, no. Not clever enough."

"You miss him." Surprisingly, Caedmon's voice was filled with compassion, reminding Ellie he had lost people he cared about, too. "I get it. I get wanting to bring someone back."

She laughed. "Not all wives love their husbands." An elongated sigh. "But I need him alive."

Caedmon shook his head fiercely. "But the Urokshi say it requires malevolent magic."

Ellie gasped. "Malevolent enough to poison an age. Malevolent enough to shatter a city." Her mind raced after her thoughts, trying to catch them before they slipped away, for the story almost made sense. "In Iselkia, the queen, she was cursed, wasn't she? To stay frozen in time since the Deep? But

(375)

you needed that to lift. I thought maybe it was to bring life to your homeland, but that's not it, is it? You want to find the evil magic from the Fall. It converged there," she explained to Caedmon. "And died with the island. But if the good in the island is brought back to life…so too…is the bad."

"Well done, child. Yes, malevolent magic, Iselkia, all correct."

"But…but you can't!" Caedmon spluttered. "The last time that magic was used, it caused…"

She waved a hand. "I do not wish to wipe out nations or entire civilizations. But if magic hurts, then it hurts. If it kills, it kills. I require it more than needless people require life. So yes, Caedmon Tuggle, I can, and I shall."

"Why?" Ellie cut through her absurd explanation, for there was a more burning question that mattered. "You wanted us to go to Iselkia. You wanted us to bring you Excalibur, when I'm sure you could have done it yourself."

"The last piece you've woefully yet to understand. This is where your intelligence falls short. I did not need all of you." Her gaze found Ellie, and there was no mirth there, no joy. Only a restless vindication. "I have been looking for you for a long, *long* time. I knew it would be harder until you claimed your witchcraft, but I didn't expect it to be so difficult." Her jaw muscle twitched, like the effort still pained her. "You did a good job burying that magic of yours. I couldn't see you." Her eyes gleamed. "So I followed the three. Your magic of unity.

(376)

And it led me to him." She inclined her head toward Caedmon. "Bring Excalibur to me, Ellie."

Ellie's eyes watered as she glanced at Caedmon, at the hilt of the true Excalibur peeking out from his cape—the swords they'd switched in their travel, a secret all their own.

Caedmon had no business being here because Croven had never wanted him.

The curse was about Ellie.

This knight of new for realms of old, is one. My curse is cast beneath this midnight sun. Bring me to the crescent moon. Let this magic unspool the knightly doom. Let it call upon the lost. The magic is mine. Ellie's heart raced. She curled her hand into a fist, her witch mark gleaming. She was the crescent moon. She was the one with magic.

All of this had been to test her, break her.

Maybe Roxie had mistranslated Merlin's message to Caedmon. Maybe kin wasn't about his family…it was about her. Maybe he had to become a knight and find Excalibur to keep her safe from the witch hunting her blood.

A small smile played on Croven's lips as she watched comprehension dawn on Ellie's face. "My magic has been at work for many moons, unraveling the magic we lost in the Fall. But I need Excalibur to channel its full might." Her gaze cut to Caedmon. "You see, you never had any chance at fighting me. You were cursed to bring me Ellie from the day your name appeared on the knights' draft, and your fate became entangled with hers."

(377)

Ellie gripped a tiny orange pebble concealed in her pocket, the last trick she revealed to not even Caedmon, in case all went wrong and she needed a quick escape.

It was a banishing stone. Incredibly rare and valuable, they could send someone far away from you. They only worked once, and only on others. Most fairies were gifted them at birth. Ellie found hers in a slippery river beneath the shade of a prickly tree.

Croven wouldn't take her best friend.

Not this day.

If she used it on Croven, the witch would just find a way to return. This was the only way to protect Caedmon.

"Caedmon Tuggle, I banish thee to thy family home!" The stone glowed hot in her palm.

Caedmon's eyes widened. "Ellie, no! You promised! We're in this together!"

"Not anymore," she whispered. "Croven's right. This was never about you. Just me. You can go live in peace."

His horrified expression rippled into thin air as he vanished, taking Excalibur with him.

"He's safe from you," Ellie rasped. "You will never find him."

Croven merely raised an eyebrow, Ellie's act of defiance seemingly nothing to her. "I don't need to. He is no knight."

FORTY-FIVE
CAEDMON

CAEDMON WHIRLED ON THE SPOT, THE FAMILIAR white shutters of his house staring back at him. Excalibur still hung at his waistband, concealed by his blue cape. What had Ellie been thinking? She needed him! Croven would kill her! She didn't even have Excalibur to protect herself!

He had to find her.

He'd do anything it took—she would be okay. She'd helped him learn to live again, and he would help her keep living.

Maybe Excalibur could help. He started to unsheathe it when his mom trudged outside carrying a trash bag, her hair limper than he remembered, her frame thin and bony, like she'd lost too much weight too quickly. She kept her head down, gaze on the dirt.

The pang in Caedmon's heart intensified, the words he'd said in anger flooding back.

She must hate him.

But he couldn't run forever. Not if he needed their help finding Ellie. He cleared his throat. "Mom?"

His mother's head snapped up. For a moment she simply stared at him, blinking, as if she thought he was a hallucination. Slowly, she turned away, head bowed again.

"Um, Mom?" he tried again. "It's me. Caedmon."

This time, she screamed, her hands flying to her mouth, the bag of trash spilling onto the ground. She let it lie there, which was never something his mom would normally do, and sprinted toward him. Before he could apologize, she'd crushed him in a hug. The door swung open behind them. "Kara, are you all—"

His dad's voice caught.

"Mom, I'm sorry," Caedmon murmured into his mom's arm. She smelled like lemon and sage, exactly as he remembered. Before he could stop them, tears leaked from his eyes.

His mom's own tears splashed onto Caedmon's head as his dad's arms wrapped around them both.

"I'm sorry. I didn't mean to say I wish you'd died instead of Jimmy. I shouldn't have. I'm sorry that hurt you so much."

"Caedmon." Her mom wrenched herself free, wiped her eyes, and held him at arm's length. "That is not why I'm crying! I was so..." Her voice trembled. "Where have you *been*? I thought you'd been killed! Or kidnapped! I was so scared. I didn't know if I'd see you again."

"Really? I didn't think...after what I said..." Caedmon trailed off, focusing on his shoes scuffing the cold, frozen dirt.

(380)

His mom squashed his cheeks between her palms, angling his head toward her. "Caedmon Tuggle, you listen to me. No matter what you do or what you say, I will love you. Don't cringe. Don't be embarrassed. Look me in the eye and tell me you understand. I would rather die a thousand deaths than have anything happen to you. *Tell me* you understand."

Caedmon swallowed, words difficult. "I understand," he managed to mutter.

"We are your parents," his dad added. "No matter how badly you think you've messed up, you can always come back. Wherever we are, you have a home."

The door slammed again, this time revealing Carly, clutching her stuffed bear. She squealed at the sight of Caedmon and burrowed into their hug. "Caedmon's back!"

Caedmon squeezed his little sister until she coughed. Until seeing her, he hadn't let it sink in that she really was okay—not that pale, limp girl carried into the ambulance. "You have no idea what I've done for you guys, thinking you were going to die."

"Caedmon, buddy, what do you mean?" his mom asked.

"It's a long story, but Mom, Dad, I have to find a way to get out of here as soon as possible. My best friend's life depends on it."

FORTY-SIX
ELLIE

TIME NO LONGER EXISTED FOR ELLIE.

Seconds were minutes, hours were days.

She had water but little else. A slice of bread to ward off starvation.

Croven hadn't explained why she kept her alive, though she mentioned a full moon during an incantation. From her cage in the grass, Ellie slept beneath the sun and kept vigil over the moon, whispering the few spells she knew, praying one would stop its course.

It was not to be.

Perhaps not even witches could alter time.

Once, long after speaking became a forgotten thing, Croven approached her cell, crouching so they were eye level. "You saw it, didn't you?"

Ellie groaned. She didn't know what she was or was not supposed to see. Only that she was delirious.

More water and a gorgeous platter of roasted vegetables appeared in her cell. "Eat. Then speak."

She considered resisting—but she was too hungry. Ellie gulped down the water and devoured the dinner. The days of her caring about getting food on her clothes were long gone.

"Did you see it?" Croven repeated.

"See what?" Ellie croaked.

Stars glistened in Croven's eyes. "The Deep. The magic that brought down Iselkia. What did you think of it?"

Ellie cringed, the tidal wave of blood splashing the edges of her mind. "It was terrible."

"Yes, it was." Croven gripped Ellie's chin. "You heard the dragons. You watched their shadows rippling in the poisoned waters. You listened as children screamed." Croven's gaze roved her face. "I can see it."

Ellie wrenched free. "Get out of my head!"

"My family line was one of the handful to survive, along with yours, it would seem. Bless those ancient relatives who had the wherewithal to protect themselves before Iselkia fell. For the people knew, didn't they? They knew their deaths were coming."

"Yes," Ellie whispered. "They knew."

"I was born in Iselkia, against all odds, and have devoted my life to salvaging the island's decay. The day I claimed my magic, I heard people scream for their princess. But she wasn't

(383)

there to help, was she? No, she wasn't helpful at all. All those people died, bringing the depths of my magic with them. And yours, too, if you ever wish to claim it. It is true what they say, you know. That witches brought down Camelot. Not all witches, though. Only one witch. Binding all Iselkian magic to the curse. So, you see, by ending the curse laid upon the last queen of Iselkia, which kept her frozen in time, I've set our magic free, as well."

"Who cast the curse?" Ellie rasped. "On the lost queen?"

Croven's eyes glinted. "I've always wondered the same thing, Ellie dear."

"And why did you curse me? Why do you want to kill me?" Ellie whispered. "Why do you need me dead for your husband to live?"

Croven tilted her head. "It's complicated. Prophesies... curses..."

"Tell me."

She picked up one of Ellie's curls and dropped it. "You need to wash."

"I'm in a cage."

A challenge lit in Croven's eyes. "The youth are poor problem solvers." She sighed. "Only an Unregistered witch who's recently claimed her magic..." Her eyes narrowed, "And whose magic has grown up alongside the sword of Excalibur can *wield* Excalibur for the spell required to wake my husband. You must wield it, and then your blood must spill. And only that witch—*you*—could awaken the magic of Iselkia." Her nostrils flared. Almost like she was jealous.

Ellie forced herself upright. "You knew Merlin gave me a shard."

A hollow laugh. "Oh, I knew. I have always known. Even before it was given, I knew. Why do you think you were able to go to Iselkia? An island whose very soul was tied to Camelot?"

Ellie inhaled sharply. *Excalibur...*her *scepter* had let them in. "But...you were there, too. I was following you. How did *you* get in? And how were you born there?"

"My birth...was unusual. And I have lived a long time. I know more about magic than *Loreena Royenale* ever will. I know how to conceal my tracks. How to make it seem like I am here when I am there. I know how to be invisible. Even to the gods." Her voice rang with pride, but something in her eyes was...haunted. Alone.

She took Ellie's hand, examining the witch's mark it bore. "I do admit, I regret the witch has to be you. Your magic is something I wish I could have seen grow. And watch how it changed you."

"Being a witch won't change me."

"You are disobeying your mother. You defied the Fairy Godmother laws. It already has changed you."

Croven's words unspooled into poison in Ellie's gut. Her jaw clenched. She couldn't let this woman distract her. She had too much to lose. Wrapping her fingers around the bars,

(385)

she glared. "If you bring malevolence down upon people, the realms of—"

The haunted look in Croven's eyes winked out, leaving nothing but endless cold. "The realms will not care, for those in power will be in the DeJoies' pockets. They'll have extra magic to protect themselves. Not all are as peaceful as they pretend. See how they froth at the mouths for the return of the might of all magic. See how they yearn for a land without rules." She shrugged. "In truth, I care not. I find most people ghastly. But do not, for one second, believe the world will do more than share a brief obituary for those who are lost, only to forget about it the next morning."

"And if you're wrong? If people fight back?"

Croven wrapped her hands around Ellie's, squeezing, and said in an utterly cool manner, "Then I will listen to them scream."

FORTY-SEVEN

CAEDMON

CAEDMON SPENT THREE WHOLE DAYS WITH HIS FAMily, his mom force-feeding him casserole as he explained over and over that Ellie was in danger and needed his help.

But even if his parents believed him, which was still up for debate, how was he supposed to help her? He couldn't return to the forest without more of Malgwyn's flames, and he had no idea where in the world the château was, so he couldn't even ask Dame Gwendolyn for advice.

He tried speaking to Excalibur, hoping to trigger magical properties, but it only made him feel ridiculous.

All Caedmon knew was he refused to let Ellie suffer. He would not sit quietly in his bedroom while Ellie screamed from Croven's torment. He hadn't completed his knight's training and wasn't a sorcerer.

But he had Evermore dust.

He had the gift of magic.

"You just have to feel it," he muttered to himself as he

foraged in the forest for potential magical ingredients. His parents still didn't believe his story, but they'd indulged him, driving him into the woods.

Ellie always said most magical creatures didn't need to abide by the DeJoie human laws, which meant borker bats and phoenixes could be hiding in plain sight, now that he knew what to look for, like how gremlins enjoyed disguising themselves as mossy branches so they could slip into your shoes, steal your secrets, and spread them in the wind.

His parents stood back, whispering and frowning as Caedmon examined every piece of bark on the ground. They definitely thought he'd lost it, but at least they weren't stopping him. "We're going to wait in the car, buddy," his mom called after an hour of fruitless searching. "The parking lot is just behind those trees. Please don't get lost. Don't go too far. Don't talk to strangers."

"Mom…" Caedmon bit back a groan. His parents would never let him be more than a few feet away from them ever again. "I'll be fine. I promise. I told you: I wasn't kidnapped before. I *chose* to be a Knight of the Round Table."

His dad gave him a big, false smile. "Sure, bud. Totally."

"We'll check back in ten minutes," his mom promised, before disappearing behind the trees.

Caedmon plopped in the dirt. His parents' concern about his sanity was the least of his worries. He ran his hands over the ground, closing his eyes. *You have to feel the magic*, Ellie had

(388)

urged him. This wasn't Dame Ethyl's trial or another botched lesson. This mattered. Somehow, he had to figure out a way to make the magic listen.

The fallen leaves didn't work.

There was nothing in the dirt.

A high-pitched squeal jumpstarted his heart.

"What the—"

"Aha, caught your secret!" a gremlin squeaked, making a mad dash for a foxhole.

Caedmon seized it by the waist and wrestled its cloak off it. "Aha, caught your cloak!" Caedmon waved the jeweled, velvet fabric at the seething gremlin.

One magical ingredient down…

He gasped, staring around the forest. With his parents gone, all the magic he'd been searching for had come out of hiding. More gremlins stalked the earth, a crimson phoenix soared through the sky, and pixies danced in circles around trees.

Caedmon spent another hour hunting for ingredients, waving his parents off whenever they came too close, for all the magic slunk back into trees and clouds and burrows in the earth when they approached.

He couldn't describe what he was looking for, exactly, or what the ingredients would do. He had a faint idea about some of them from his lessons, but not enough.

Intention, Dame Ethyl's voice rang in his mind. *Your spell must be well-intentioned.*

(389)

I have to find Ellie. I have to find Ellie. I have to find Ellie.

Caedmon uttered the same five words in his mind, over and over, searching for items he knew had magical properties.

I have to find Ellie. I have to find Ellie. I have—

And then—he felt it.

Magic.

There was no other word for it.

A rush of golden sparks swept through him, euphoric and brilliant. It was like the ingredients *knew* where they wanted to be, and this time, Caedmon was listening.

It almost felt like chemistry, but more spectacular, special.

Magical.

Three hours later, there was one last ingredient he needed. One he couldn't find in the forest. Moonlit ice. That strange, same magical compulsion that guided Caedmon paused him when he went to ask his parents for help.

They couldn't be there. He had to be alone.

The following few hours were excruciating.

Once home, he waited by his door until his dad snored and the hallway light flicked off.

Sneaking out wasn't the best way to earn back his parents' trust, but time was slipping through Caedmon's fingers, and he couldn't risk delaying another second.

He crept out of the house, to the shores of Lake Michigan. The sun had long since set, nighttime casting the world in a silvery sheen.

He nearly sprinted to the water's edge—how long had it been since Ellie sent him back? What had she endured?

He gritted his teeth, banishing the images of her screaming, Croven laughing mercilessly above.

That wouldn't help him now. He needed to concentrate.

Using a pot he'd snuck from the kitchen, he carefully pulled each ingredient out of his backpack and examined them.

The last time he'd created a spell, he hadn't had any control over it. This time, he had to find a way to manipulate magic to do what he needed. There was no time to mess this up.

The acorn wanted the entire gremlin cloak, and the Lake Michigan moonlit ice wanted nothing to do with either.

But whatever the ingredients wanted to concoct, it didn't feel right.

It didn't feel like Ellie.

Magic glimmered and bent in his palms, becoming malleable, guiding him toward his friend, until at last, the concoction whirred, murky and mossy. He plunked the final ingredient into the pot and sat back in the frosted sand, rubbing his freezing hands together. *This has to work. Please work.*

The mixture exploded.

Stars and moons shot out of his parents' cooking pot, nearly singeing his ears.

He fell back in the sand, Excalibur slipping into the water. He grabbed it.

(391)

"Ahh!" Caedmon nearly dropped it back into the freezing waves. The sword was glowing—and the concoction had disappeared.

The pot was clean and gray. Just a simple kitchen item. Nothing magical in or around it, as if all Caedmon's efforts had been imagined.

But Excalibur's glow brightened, stars dancing around the blade.

He didn't know what, exactly, he'd done, only that the magic had somehow glommed on to the sword.

"Bring me to Ellie Bettlebump!" He slashed it through the air...

And tore open the world.

Where he'd brandished Excalibur, a tear in the air appeared, as though everything around him was merely knit together with thread.

On either side of the seams, Lake Michigan glistened in the night.

But through the widening hole...

A pirate ship loomed.

Swift as if magicked there, black sails swallowing light careened on a frothing wave, sailing straight for him, a majestic flying horse flapping overhead.

"Galahad!"

"Oi! Is that Caedmon?" called Mickey Murphy. "I think that's Caedmon!"

"Tell him his princess awaits!" yelled a familiar voice.

"I'm not doing that."

"Did he miss his Roxie? Will you ask him?"

"I'm not doing that, either. Why'd we invite them along again?"

"Roxie threatened to steal your femur," replied Omari. "And Lorelei…"

"Gets what she wants."

Caedmon could nearly see Lorelei's smug expression. He yelled in relief and sprinted to the hole in the world. The pirate ship grew closer, Galahad in the lead. Caedmon took a deep breath.

"Sorry, Mom and Dad," he muttered. "I'll be back." He stepped through the hole, onto Galahad's back, and soared free.

In a swirl of feathers, Galahad landed on the pirate ship, neighing proudly.

Omari reached him first. "Caedmon! We've been trying to leave the château for days! The knights around your home told Dame Gwendolyn you were back, and she forbid us from seeing you—something about how you couldn't stop meddling, and you might as well stay here where you're safe. But anyways, we're here now and we're…"

He glanced at Lorelei for support, shifting from foot to foot.

But Caedmon didn't need an apology. They were here,

looking for him, trying to help Ellie, and that was all he needed. "It's okay—"

"Omari didn't spy on you," Lorelei interrupted. "He was only told to. I, however, can be a terrible person, and did." She shrugged. "Ellie Bettlebump was an interesting subject. But... I'm sorry. I am. I swear it on my best tiara. It's the three hundredth and eleventh I received for my birthday last year. It's simply *dripping* with diamonds."

Omari coughed. "Lorelei."

"Right. I'm meant to be apologizing."

"I'm not the one you need to apologize to. You'll have to see if Ellie can forgive you."

Lorelei's eyes gleamed in what Caedmon could only describe as pure challenge.

"Quickly," Roxie hissed. "Your kin doesn't have much time!"

"No, my family was fine all along. It was Ellie. Ellie was the one who was cursed."

Roxie rolled her eyes, which had the effect of rolling her entire head, so it rattled off her shoulders. "Yes, yes, little knight, you say tedious things, things I have known for days! I study language. I worship magic. I found the truth within the lies. Kin is not just blood. Friendship, too. Brotherhood. Sisterhood. Knights of the Round Table have bonded you."

"We're going to find Ellie," Lorelei declared.

(394)

Omari unsheathed his sword. "We are Knights of the Round Table. Protectors of the Realms. And Ellie's friends. Let us go with you. Let us fight. Do you know where she is?"

Caedmon didn't—but he knew something that might. Caedmon pointed Excalibur north, east, south, and west. When he turned westward, Excalibur glowed so brightly, it nearly burned his hand. "She's west, Mickey. Hurry!"

He glanced behind him just once and could have sworn the shadow of a man flickered on the shores of Lake Michigan, smoke swirling around a long, sweeping purple cape.

When he blinked, the world knit back together, and the image was gone.

FORTY-EIGHT

CAEDMON

MAGIC SAVED THEM THAT NIGHT. IT GUIDED THEM, splitting the world at the seams, lakes undulating into oceans, rippling into rivers, cascading through ponds and lochs and even one neighborhood pool surrounded by palm trees and a stunned elderly couple. If there was water, Excalibur and the boat found their way, leaping across the world.

At last, Caedmon's stomach turning from the journey, the boat stilled to a halt in a bubbling brook surrounded by whispering flowers and twittering birds. Moss furled up ancient trees as gossiping winds whirled through the forest, hunting for lips to chap and secrets to steal.

"This is it," Caedmon whispered.

Glass glimmered through the trees. Caedmon gestured for everyone to stay behind him as he crept into the forest, keeping his footsteps as light as possible, careful not to crunch any twigs, Galahad swooping above.

"The moon will be full tonight, Ellie." Croven's voice made the hairs on Caedmon's neck rise. "Rest. It'll be over soon."

Caedmon sucked in a breath. She planned to kill Ellie tonight. Still hiding, he reached Croven, a wisp in the night, long hair twisted into braids atop her head. She held up a single finger, though with her face turned, Caedmon couldn't read her expression. He crouched lower, into the ferns and overgrown bushes. Omari grabbed his family sword, and Lorelei clutched vials of Evermore dust.

A bolt of green fire speared toward Caedmon as Croven turned, smiling.

On instinct, Caedmon raised Excalibur. It was light, like wielding liquid. Sir Masten's training had served him well. The sword glowed green, shielding Croven's curse, then turned silver once more.

Croven's eyes narrowed.

Another bolt of magic burst toward him, hissing like a snake. Again, he swung Excalibur, narrowly saving his thigh, and the sword glowed.

His heart skipped a beat. It was absorbing Croven's magic.

Every swordsmanship lesson flew through his mind. He readjusted his stance and corrected his grip. This was just another class.

More flashes of magic came—he blocked them all.

His arms and feet knew where to pivot, how to move, his mind going quiet as his body took over.

(397)

They could really win this. They could exhaust her long enough to restrain her and free Ellie.

His friends, still hidden in the forest, could sneak up from behind, and—

"You're better than expected."

A bolt of magic aimed for a spot in the sky. "But there's only one sword, and six of you."

Galahad whinnied. The majestic, ancient creature plummeted to the earth, wings bent and broken beneath his bloodied body.

Caedmon lunged for the chevolant, but a second bolt of magic to the left sent Lorelei screaming, flung from her hiding spot, arms pinned against a tree by thorned vines thick as cobras.

"No!" Caedmon ran toward her, ready to slice through them, when a wind knocked him off his feet, Excalibur clattering out of reach, leg landing bent in a horrible position beneath him. He gritted his teeth, the crack of bone sounding at the same time a flash of mind-numbing pain tore through him.

He struggled to move, but it was pointless. His leg was broken. He winced, reaching for the sword, yelling as his limbs strained at the effort.

Omari, Mickey, and Roxie all hurled different weapons at Croven, to no avail. Galahad cried, pawing his way toward Croven, blood smearing the dirt, but he could barely lift his head.

Expression unnervingly calm, Croven raised her arms.

Trees creaked. Flowers recoiled.

The faintest smile contorted Croven's face.

And she brought down the forest: Bark stripped and vines shredded; winds slapped their faces; blood pooled around Omari as he slumped to the earth; Roxie screamed as her bones splintered, one by one; Lorelei cried a prayer to the saints; Mickey struggled with a snapping snake Croven set upon him.

Caedmon dug his fingernails into the earth and dragged his body closer to Excalibur. If only he could reach it…

Croven strode through his friends' bodies, white dress floating above the blood and branches, keeping her pure and clean. "Do not fight me, children. For you will lose."

With some of the foliage gone, Caedmon glimpsed the clearing—and the cage it held. The dark curls spilling out the prison bars.

Ellie.

Lying utterly still.

Croven was winning. Despite the power of Excalibur, despite their surprise attack, she was stronger than them.

Caedmon's hands curled to fists.

No. Maybe in magic, she was stronger. Maybe she could kill them with a flick of her fingers.

But they were stronger in what counted. He would not lose hope—not for Ellie or their friends who'd risked their lives to do what was right.

(399)

They were Protectors of the Realms, Knights of the Round Table, and they would not give up.

Excalibur, lying innocently a few feet away, glowed a soft orange. Suddenly, Caedmon's leg untwisted, a soothing warmth spreading through his limbs. He breathed in the dirt and moss, not daring to move and reveal what had just happened. Somehow, miraculously, the sword had healed him. Excalibur wanted him to win.

And he would not let it down.

The moon, bright and full, rose higher in the sky.

Croven strode toward Ellie, snapping her fingers so the cage disappeared, and jerking her awake. "This way, dear. The time has come."

Caedmon inched closer to the sword, so carefully, so slowly. Croven would come retrieve it any moment.

"You know my name. You know my song. Let me go," Lorelei whispered. Caedmon paused. What he'd thought was a prayer was something else entirely. Lorelei was speaking to the plants. His heart jolted. That was right! The DeJoies could communicate with plants!

Slithering and silent, the cobra-like vines unfurled, freeing Lorelei, though blood leaked from the thorn marks.

Croven whipped her head toward them.

Caedmon leapt to his feet as Croven smirked, and with a swish of her hand, translucent smoke swirled from her fingers.

Caedmon gasped.

(400)

No.

Not smoke.

Malemento vapor.

The poison's magic eddied around them, invading their lungs and minds.

Caedmon couldn't breathe, his darkest memories pulling him down, down, to the worst part of himself. The part that reveled in shame, that bathed in remorse. Jimmy's death, the awful way he'd treated his family since. He couldn't scrape himself out of it.

All thoughts of Excalibur fled his mind.

All was dark.

All was lost.

In the distance, beyond the fog, Ellie screamed.

FORTY-NINE

ELLIE

ELLIE'S BREATHING WAS LOUD IN HER EARS, VOICE ragged in her throat. Winds scraped her face. Trees keeled over. Through the chaos, Croven's lips twisted in a hateful smile.

The malemento vapor burned away the forest, leaving nothing but memories sharp enough to draw blood. Mother telling her she was unworthy. Nights alone at finishing school, wishing for a friend. Mother tearing her veil of starlight.

Starlight.

Ellie fumbled for her pocket. She could never best Croven in normal witchcraft. In spells or curses or triumphs of magic.

Her fingers closed around her speckle of light.

But not all witchcraft resided in complex spellwork. Starlight was a witch's hope. The magic of pure light. And wasn't that what Dame Ethyl taught them? That the antidote to malemento vapor was hope?

What was stronger than the purest magic of hope in this world? Suddenly, she was back in her glass turret, accepting her magic, reading about starlit witches riding into battle. Perhaps it hadn't been a metaphor. Perhaps…it'd been their secret weapon.

Witchcraft swirled through her bones, eager to be used, needed…wanted.

In that split second, Ellie didn't simply accept she was a witch. She did more than know, more than begrudge.

She *loved* it.

Croven wanted to capture a witch? Fine. Ellie would be a witch. She raised her star to the sky.

FIFTY

CAEDMON

LORELEI SHUDDERED ACROSS FROM CAEDMON, TEARS streaming down her face. Even Omari, though unconscious, twitched, sweat beading down his forehead as malicious dreams took him.

Through the vapor, Ellie pulled her curls back from her face and rose to her feet, shrouded in starlight. Shakily, she took a step toward Croven.

Another.

"You. Will. Not. Curse. Me. Again."

Her voice rang through the clearing, and Caedmon could have sworn that the very trees bowed. "You will not hurt my friends. You will go quietly to prison."

Croven set her gleaming pale eyes upon Ellie.

Caedmon had never seen such hatred.

Such evil.

Her magic burned away a layer of Ellie's beaming starlight. Another. Still, Ellie faced her.

If ever there was a time to find a spot of hope in his darkness, it was now. And, he realized, it wasn't so hard anymore.

He couldn't say why Jimmy died. All Caedmon knew was he was alive, and he had something to fight for.

With more strength than he'd ever used, Caedmon broke through the fog and grabbed the sword of Excalibur, sprinting to Ellie's side just as a bolt of lightning shot for her heart.

Ellie poured her starlight into Excalibur, and together, they clutched the glowing weapon and pointed it at Croven.

The stroke of lightning rebounded and hit Croven in the chest.

Vines wrapped around her wrists.

Snakes and flames and every other curse she'd cast burst from the sword's blade, enveloping Croven in her own magic.

Her screams were vicious as she battled against it, but it was useless, the combined magic of Ellie's starlight and Excalibur too strong. In a swirl of smoke, her dress whipped around her, and Croven vanished.

The sword stilled, becoming dull steel once more.

All was quiet.

Trembling, Lorelei stumbled toward them, tiara askew. "Is…is everyone okay?" she squeaked.

Slowly, Roxie rose to a seat, clutching her broken bones, glassy eyes brimming with slime tears.

(405)

Ellie glanced at Caedmon. "Croven's curse. I...I can't hear it anymore. I think it's broken." They crept toward the veil of ivy. But when they pulled back the vines, the clearing was empty.

The coffin, and whoever it contained, were gone.

FIFTY-ONE

ELLIE

ELLIE COULDN'T RECALL ALL THAT FOLLOWED IN THE hours after Croven's disappearance. There were blurs and smudged memories: saying goodbye to Lorelei and Omari as they brought Roxie to the Urokshi for healing, sailing to Boulder Falls on Mickey's pirate ship.

She awoke in the Tuggles' spare bedroom three days later. Sunshine streamed through the windows, springtime daffodils peeked through the late frost, and Galahad, blood cleaned and wings fluffed, nuzzled her face.

"I'm okay." She laughed, wiping chevolant slobber from her cheeks. Though Galahad had needed healing, he insisted on staying by Ellie's side, causing Caedmon's parents to faint when they arrived. She ran a hand down his soft back. Fortunately, the magical creature had mostly healed himself, though his wing was still slightly bent.

A letter that looked as though it had burned at the edges

lay on the bedside table. Rubbing her eyes, she read it, then dropped it on the flowery quilt.

Malgwyn.

Coming to claim his price.

You did well. I will find you when you're ready. You will repay me in blood. —Malgwyn

Ellie instinctively reached for her starlight for comfort, only to remember she lost it in the forest. With both her scepter and starlight gone, she felt unanchored.

Later, when she showed the letter to Caedmon while sitting on the shores of Lake Michigan, her friend crumpled it, as if he could wrinkle Malgwyn's words to make them go away. Though if they'd learned anything from that year, it was that words, whether in hushed curses or stolen secrets given to people never meant to hear them, couldn't be banished so easily.

They sat in silence, huddled in their jackets and scarves as the waves lapped against the shore.

"Your sister's wedding is this summer. Do you still think you won't go?"

"I can't, can I? I'm not invited." This bothered her less than it used to, though. She didn't need to please Mother. Still, it would have been nice to witness her stepsister's wedding. Besides, she had bigger problems now. An icy wind curled around her shoulders, sending chills down her spine. "Croven's

(408)

still out there," she said quietly, almost hoping the wind would swallow her words. "Isn't she?"

Caedmon squinted at the endless silvered blue. He opened his mouth to speak, but his voice caught. Glancing at her, he nodded.

"She said something strange about her husband....Do you remember?"

"That not all wives love their husbands?"

"I don't think she was trying to bring him back because she missed him. She must want something else. But what? And she needs me for it because my witchcraft grew up along-side Excalibur," she said, remembering Croven's words. "But I still don't understand how she knew I had it at all."

"Maybe...maybe she'll leave you alone after what happened. Maybe she'll give up."

Ellie shook her head, remembering those pale eyes—haunted, yearning. "No...I don't think so. She wants the magic of Iselkia. It's awake now, but she said she needed Excalibur to channel most of it. She won't stop."

"But maybe her curses won't work anymore." Caedmon's voice was strained. Desperate. "Maybe with Excalibur reforged, the Knights of the Round Table will be so powerful that they'll stop her." He squirmed. Like the very thought that they weren't finished—that the threat to his friend's life wasn't over—was too hard to sit with. Like he wanted it gone.

Ellie could only nod. "Maybe." This time, the wind did

(409)

swallow her voice, leaving them alone with thoughts of witches and uncertain futures sprawling before them as the pale dawn darkened across the sky.

"This looks like a rather glum holiday." Dame Gwendolyn's clear, sharp voice rang through the empty beach. "And I do admit, I'd prefer to see you practicing magic or swordsmanship."

Caedmon and Ellie spun around and saw their headmistress adorned in her signature silver armor, two swords hanging at her hips.

And beside her...Ellie scrambled to her feet, heart rattling in its rib cage.

Short and stout, with faded, wrinkled blue sparkly wings, and a face stretched from too much plastic surgery, floated the Fairy Godmother, her puffy white hair powdered with glitter.

A tall, lithe woman stood with them, emerald cape billowing in the breeze.

Though they hadn't met, Ellie recognized her from textbooks immediately: Loreena Royenale, the greatest witch of the century, possibly of all time. Her extraordinary powers would have scared the DeJoies of today, but decades ago, when Cateline DeJoie ruled the family, she saw something special in Loreena and allowed the girl to keep her magic, citing unusual circumstances.

Feared yet revered, she was kinder looking than Ellie had

(410)

expected, with a soft smile and warm pale eyes, like a happy, glittering sea.

The Fairy Godmother pointed at Caedmon, who couldn't seem to stop staring at her. "You." Her voice crackled. "Stop giving me funny looks, boy!"

Caedmon held up his hands. "I'm sorry! I just didn't realize fairies had...wings."

"Loreena, what is wrong with this child? He knows nothing. I don't understand."

"He's from the New World, Francis."

"Others have been trying to persuade her to retire for a century," Dame Gwendolyn whispered.

Caedmon stifled a snicker by snorting into his sleeve.

Ellie would still pray to the fairies and behave well, for the Fairy Godmother was always watching, but she wasn't so intimidating anymore.

"You, Ellie and Caedmon, have had quite the journey," Loreena Royenale said. "May I request you tell the tale?"

Dame Gwendolyn nodded encouragingly, and seeing as the Fairy Godmother knew all anyway, Ellie obliged, spilling her story, beginning with her rejection letter to the Fairy Godmother Academy, ending with her revival at the Tuggle house. She hadn't been injured or in need of a healer. Only rest and comfort, which the Tuggles provided in full.

Caedmon chimed in with his own version, and when they

finished, they sat in silence, awaiting their punishment. Would they be put in prison? Dame Gwendolyn had already been prepared to banish Ellie. Would she be sent back to finishing school?

A horrible thought occurred to her: Would she lose all memory of this year? All memory of the only friends she'd ever had? She wouldn't allow it. She refused to lose any piece of this year, as difficult and terrifying as it was at times.

The Fairy Godmother was the first to speak. "Your dear friend Lorelei brought your application to my attention. It seems someone got rid of it!" she croaked, her voice hoarse, as though she'd spent a century smoking. "But of course, Ellie, dear, you can join the academy! Where all"—she wheezed—"esteemed fairies go!"

"That's...that's great, Fairy Godmother. Thank you." It was all Ellie had ever wanted. So then why did her stomach twist into itself? She pictured herself in the flowering turrets, dressed in the signature blue robes—but it didn't feel like her.

"And there's this." The Fairy Godmother handed Ellie a package wrapped in velvet. "From Lorelei. She had it specially made for you, and told me to say that if you don't forgive her after such a gift, it is you, not she, who is in the wrong." The Fairy Godmother shook her head. "And I thought I was wacky.* Be gentle: Girls in school were always too intimidated to be

---

* Oh, my dear, make no mistake: You are as wacky as they come.

(412)

friends with Lorelei, so she's still learning. The academy keeps an eye on her."

Ellie gasped as the velvet slipped over the most glorious, glittering ring she had ever seen. Pearls and diamonds swirled around...

Around her starlight. Lorelei must have found it in the forest for her.

Don't lose this. It was very expensive. Now you have to forgive me. —Lorelei

Ellie slipped it over her finger. It fit perfectly. Instantly, the star's magic cascaded through her, soothing and energizing all at once.

It was like a friendship bracelet.

A really expensive, valuable, Lorelei-would-likely-murder-her-if-she-lost-it friendship bracelet. Ellie held it close and beamed.

Loreena Royenale cleared her throat. "May we speak for a minute, Ellie?"

Ellie nodded, following her a healthy distance away from the group. The Fairy Godmother launched into a detailed account of her latest wedding planning woes for Ellie's sister, making Ellie's heart twinge. Apparently, the flowers Bella wanted were only in season once every hundred years and they had eighty-seven years left to go, making Bella collapse in a fit of tears.

Ellie couldn't quite understand the dramatics, but still, she wished she had heard of it from her own sister.

"How are you faring?" the legendary witch asked Ellie once they were out of earshot.

It wasn't the question she'd been expecting. Exhausted? Confused? Sad? Thrilled? Proud? Everything was hitting her at once.

"I'm a witch and a fairy and a knight," she found herself saying. "Yet not really any of them at all. I'm only part fairy, I've barely trained as a witch, and I didn't become an anointed knight. I...I don't know where I belong."

Mother reviled Ellie's utter honesty at times.

But she was sad—and she didn't want to hold anything back. It felt good to say it aloud, like a brick had been resting on her heart, and pixies had come to usher it away.

"Do you know why you could face Croven and not perish? Not every witch can work in harmony with the magic of starlight—because not every witch has a heart like yours. It was the power of your witch's hope that shattered the foundation of Croven's curse. Your heart saved you. Your ability to face your darkest memories and conjure hope and courage, to find light in this world. And no matter if you decide to be a witch, fairy, or knight, you will carry that heart with you. You belong here, in this world, giving light, for it is a wondrous thing."

Tears filled Ellie's eyes. Never would she forget that horrible moment when she didn't believe she'd be able to stand and

(414)

face Croven, when Mother's voice telling her she was nothing had filled her mind, leaking into her heart. She'd been so close to failing.

But perhaps Ms. Royenale was right....Perhaps she *was* someone who wouldn't give up. And that, in and of itself, was encouraging.

"As for a physical home," Ms. Royenale continued, "I believe Dame Gwendolyn and I can bend the rules on knighthood for yourself and Caedmon, just this once. If you wish, you may join us at the Château des Chevaliers to begin your training in earnest."

Ellie's heart leapt. "Truly?"

"Ever so truly."

"You'll be there as well?"

"Oh, yes. Dame Gwendolyn has asked me to return to the Château des Chevaliers to help train the new generation of knights."

"You're a knight, too?"

"I was once. Long ago. That time has passed. But I do still hope to pass on some kernels of wisdom, no matter how small."

Ellie wiped her tears on her sleeve. "Can we start now?"

Her eyes widened in surprise. "If you'd like?"

Ellie took a deep breath, clearing her mind. "I know Excalibur amplified my starlight. But I don't really understand why it shattered the foundation of Croven's curse," Ellie admitted.

The woman's eyes twinkled. "You are asking about very

(415)

complex spellwork. We will study it in more depth when you're ready, but simply put, every spell and curse is layered with strands of magic. If you break the foundation, the rest of the layers have nothing to cling to and flake away. The pure hope of your starlight was the direct antidote to the fearful foundation upon which Croven built her curse. Does that make sense?"

"I think so..." Ellie chewed her lip.

"Was there something else?"

"It's just...Croven could have kidnapped me—but she didn't. She waited for me to come to her."

Loreena smoothed her auburn bun, gaze distant. "Yes... Yes, I imagine she couldn't. Some spells, particularly using magic as ancient as that which is required for raising the dead, call for...autonomy. No party may act unwillfully. For her spell to work, she needed you to bring Excalibur to her. She could manipulate—but never force."

Loreena's words were threads of light. Croven would need Ellie to come to her.

And Ellie never would again.

Loreena smiled kindly. "Try to put thoughts of Croven aside for now. In the meantime..." She placed a letter with Ellie's family crest in her hand. "I suspect I'll see you at a certain wedding this summer."

Ellie tore open the paper.

For a moment, her heart dipped, for her mother's handwriting didn't stare back at hers.

(416)

It was her stepsister's.

Dearest Ellie,

I'm terribly sorry for not writing you this year! How are your lessons at Roses and Needles? I do miss it there sometimes.

So Mother hadn't told her Ellie was drafted. Interesting.

Her Majesty Isadora, princess of the mermaids, informed me you're not attending the wedding?! She threatened to attack me with fish if I didn't let you come. Quite feisty for a thirteen-year-old. Firstly, I'm so very sorry you thought you couldn't come to the wedding! I know we've never been overly close, but you're still family, and it would mean worlds and moons for you to come. Secondly, I must know how you met the princess. She spoke ever so fondly of you. Oh, Ellie. I'm so very glad you're finally making friends. You deserve it, and I'll have none of this "not attending the wedding" nonsense. I suspect Mother is behind it, and trust me, I will speak with her, though I doubt it will help. Please don't take Mother's words to heart. She loves you, as do we all. I will see you in July. Bring your friends! I'll be the one in the gown getting married. (Ahh!)

Kisses,
Bella

Loreena Royenale had the courtesy to stare stoically at the water as Ellie dried her tears. Caedmon, however, did not share such tact, and kept standing on his tiptoes and mouthing, "What is it!?" over the Fairy Godmother, who bemoaned something about blueberry cakes being unseemly for royal weddings.

"I'm to attend my sister's wedding!" Ellie bounded over to Caedmon, her heart more full and solid than it had ever been. For she knew what she wanted.

And it was hers for the taking.

"And I know where I want to be next year. Fairy Godmother, I appreciate the acceptance into your academy. Truly, I do. But it is not where I belong."

She looked to Caedmon, whose eyes brimmed with the same electric excitement she felt. "I'm a knight. And I'm going to train as a witch under Loreena Royenale at the Château des Chevaliers. That is where I belong."

Caedmon beamed. "Can I go back, too?"

Dame Gwendolyn's eyes twinkled. "We can make an exception. The Knights of the Round Table owe you our gratitude. Since you reforged Excalibur, our strength has returned, and we have refortified the gates shielding the realms from monsters. With our renewed magic, we've been able to round up the escaped malevotums. Boulder Falls should, at last, be safe."

Caedmon grinned.

(418)

"The Urokshi thank you as well; they have returned to the evacuated caves of their city." She smiled. "And Roxie tells me your swordsmanship is what saved you from Croven's wrath. I'm deeply proud. Though I'd advise you properly inform your parents of your whereabouts this time. Perhaps provide an address. Set up quarterly visitations so your parents don't have heart attacks."

"I thought the Knights of the Round Table was meant to be secretive."

Dame Gwendolyn looked to Loreena Royenale, who said, "Our world is changing. And so, too, should some archaic rules." Loreena Royenale's gaze returned to the horizon, a small smile playing on her face. "Though some archaic magic, should, at last, come to light, to prepare us for the changing world. For while Croven has been beaten, she is not gone, and will try to bring malevolent magic to life once more. She simply cannot help herself. On that day, we shall be ready. For the first time in centuries, fairies, sorcerers, knights, and witches will work alongside one another once more. We will greet the New Age together."

"For the realms," Dame Gwendolyn said.

"And beyond."

Ellie and Caedmon followed Loreena Royenale's gaze. For a moment, it simply appeared as though a cloud drifted across the indigo waters, though as it grew closer, a man came into view, his sweeping purple cape and silver-buckled boots skimming the water, long silver beard blowing in the wind.

(419)

The Fairy Godmother sighed. "Must Martin always make an entrance?"

"Who's Martin?" Ellie asked. Perhaps he was another knight.

"I just call him Martin. He calls me Pix. Helps us blend in when we want to stop at the pub."

Caedmon eyed her up and down. "You sure?"

"Well, sometimes they think we're playing this Hall-oo-ween game. Don't tend to ask unless they've had a few drinks. Ahh, children."

Dame Gwendolyn crossed her arms. "Why are there children drinking at the pub?"

The Fairy Godmother's gaze narrowed, glasses slipping down her nose, and, being half Dame Gwendolyn's size, she fluttered high in the air to look down at her. "You are all children in my eyes."

"Who is he, actually?" Caedmon asked.

The man was almost before them—close enough to see him blow a puff of smoke from a long, carved pipe, bright blue eyes twinkling mischievously.

Loreena Royenale smiled. "His name, young knights, is Merlin."

MADAME MYSTÉRIEUSE

There's more to say, though not this day. For now, I leave you with this.

Loreena spoke true: Croven has come, and the malevolence she brings could drown the world.

The Fall of Camelot did its worst. Another could leave us forever-cursed.

The fight has begun, the fight of the age.

But I shall not abate.

Not this day.

'Tis why I've told the tale, clandestine yet true.

Yes, dear reader, the secret is out, the secret is yours,

To share the story and tell the tale of the Knights of the Round Table beyond the veil.

In castles they gather, in them we trust, to do what is right, and what is just.

Until we meet again, dear reader, until that fateful day.

Between your nows and thens, your whens and wheres, I shall travel the world and pray,

That if magic darkens into blackened skies, and cities crumble before my eyes, the dragons, at last, will rise.

ACKNOWLEDGMENTS

WHAT A GIFT TO BE ABLE TO PROPERLY THANK THE many people who have helped me along this long and winding yellow brick road.

First, I have the best professional team.

Katelyn Uplinger, thank you for your endless support and encouragement. Thank you for believing in my writing and standing by me through the years. You are a rock. I feel so supported and solid having you in my corner. Bob and the D4EO team, thank you for all that you do.

Ruqayyah Daud, I couldn't have asked for a better editor. You saw straight into the heart and soul of this story, and every edit and plot redirection helped make the tale I wanted to tell shine all the brighter. Your nuanced observations have made me a better, more thoughtful writer, so I will forever be grateful for your guidance. From the bottom of my heart, thank you.

Jake Regier, thank you for your meticulous copyedits.

It takes a village for a book to come together, so thank you to the entire Little, Brown Books for Young Readers team, including Alvina Ling, Olivia Davis, Jenny Kimura, Karina Granda, Mara Brashem, Stefanie Hoffman, Shanese Mullins, Sydney

Tillman, Christie Michel, Megan Tingley, Jackie Engel, Emilie Polster, Marisa Russell, Victoria Stapleton, Shawn Foster, and Danielle Cantarella.

The cover art for this book made me cry. Manuel Šumberac, thank you for your gorgeous illustration.

Ginger Knowlton, thank you for your invaluable feedback, and Kelly McCall, thank you for being so supportive of my writing career.

My critique partners and writer friends are stellar individuals. Lindsay Landgraf Hess, it's impossible to overstate my gratitude for sharing this writing journey with you. Thank you for being such a phenomenal cheerleader, caring friend, and insightful critique partner—and for loving Ellie and Caedmon through the years!

Elora Cook, thank you for being so sweet and so supportive, and for your shrewd editing eye. I love our brainstorming sessions, life chats, and hilarious movie nights. I'm so thankful to have you as a friend!

Judi Lauren, you changed my writing career forever. You helped me improve my writing through Pitch Wars, and I will never be able to thank you enough for it. You're also such a kind and thoughtful friend. Merci for all of it—and for loving Paris as much as I do.

To my non-writer friends who have cheered me on over the years: I love you all. Julia, thank you for reading every single one of my books since we were twelve. I'm infinitely

(424)

grateful we were paired up to write bad poetry together in seventh grade. You are one of my core roots in life, and I love and value our friendship so much.

My whole extended family: I've always known I have a supportive, beautiful net beneath me. Thank you for being wonderfully kind. To my new extended family: Thank you for welcoming me with open arms and making me feel at home far away from home.

Nana, thank you for playing make-believe on rainy summer days, and for teaching me that living a life of writing and music was the only path that would ever feel like home.

To the fur babies who have sat by my feet or in my lap as I wrote over the years: Cody, Murphy, Piper, Louie, Brooke, Duke, Boulder, Maverick, and Macallan, you are all ridiculous and I love you.

My brother, Mitch: Thank you for being your hilarious, steady self, and for being my first audience as I read stories to you in endless games of make-believe in our backyard. And thank you for your help researching how Caedmon would need to train! The speed with which you provided the *Count of Monte Cristo* swordsmanship lesson, as though you'd been secretly waiting for years for someone to ask you about it, was very impressive.

My new family, Chris: I still get giddy calling you my husband. Thank you for being my go-to listener as I unravel plot snags, for supporting our household as I've pursued this lifelong dream, and for inspiring me to celebrate the small wins every day these past six years. For reminding me that, with every tiny step, I've jumped forward a new lily pad. Since our first date, your belief in my writing has never wavered, and how lucky am I to have this ceaseless voice of reassurance in my ear, so loud that it drowns out my deepest fears.

And my parents, who first allowed me to believe this dream could belong to me: What sometimes felt uncertain and unreachable to me was obvious to you. You not only supported me in my wish to be a fantasy writer; you actively encouraged it and rewatched Lord of the Rings and Harry Potter hundreds of times right alongside me. Mom, thank you for being my first editor, and for sharing your love of Camelot and the mystical world of medieval Arthurian literature. This book stems from that deep place of magic and wonder. Thank you for reminding me that I never needed a great and powerful wizard, and that I had my ruby slippers on the whole time. Dad, thank you for your boundless enthusiasm and steady, loving reminders to get out of my own way. (U2 definitely stole your mantra.) You've always noticed when I'm being too hard on myself and never stopped reminding me to pursue what I want, fearlessly and unapologetically. I love you both and never would have made it to this point without you.

And to you, sweet reader, for loving stories and believing in magic: Thank you for letting Caedmon and Ellie into your heart.